THE BLACK TIDE: THE COMPLETE ADVENTURES OF BELLOW BILL WILLIAMS, VOLUME 1

Ralph R Perry

THE BLACK TIDE

THE COMPLETE ADVENTURES OF
BELLOW BILL WILLIAMS, VOLUME 1

RALPH R. PERRY

ILLUSTRATED BY

ROGER B. MORRISON
& JOHN R. NEILL

STEEGER BOOKS • 2019

PUBLISHING HISTORY

THANKS TO

Gerd Pircher

ALL RIGHTS RESERVED

Visit steegerbooks.com for more books like this.

TABLE OF CONTENTS

THE BIG KICK

*Strangest of all the war's mad vagaries was the feud
between Bellow Bill Williams, late of the South
Seas, and a U-boat commander in Irish waters*

CHAPTER I

BELLOW BILL WILLIAMS

"NAW, WHAT'S THE fun in pearling down in the South Seas compared to the war being fought right here? Why wouldn't I come? I'm looking for excitement—for the big kick, see?" rumbled Bellow Bill Williams.

A brown stream of tobacco juice arched from his lips, cleared the taff-rail of the cargo steamer Bombay by a nicely calculated inch, and splashed into the calm North Atlantic. Bill tongued the quid of fine-cut to the opposite side of his upper lip and settled his gigantic shoulders more comfortably against the side of the steam steering engine house.

Though he was speaking conversationally to a fresh-faced young English apprentice seaman of seventeen who was curled on the deck at his feet, in the hush of twilight Bill's voice boomed from stem to stern over the quiet ship. Shouting orders from the quarter-deck to the bow above the roaring of South Seas hurricanes had developed the deep chest tones that had given Bellow Bill his nickname. His physique matched the power of his lungs.

Six feet three inches in height, fifty inches around the chest, tipping the scales at two hundred and twenty-five, he could have established his right to the chief mate's uniform he wore by the weight of his fist alone.

Though his size made statements that would have sounded like braggadocio on the lips of a smaller man seem less than the literal truth, Bill's prowess did not rest on physical strength alone. When Bill went on a drunk the effect on the water front

1

resembled a tidal wave. Wrecked saloons and black eyes among the police followed in the wake of his celebrations. Yet his sprees were never less than six months apart, and in the intervals fine-cut chewing tobacco was his only vice. He possessed the strongest body, the quickest brain, and the greatest daring in the Marquesas Islands, where men succeed by their wits and their two fists.

A mass of curly hair the color of coppery gold pushed his hat far off his forehead. His eyes were a dark, almost violet blue with the whites clear white as china. He wore a blue flannel shirt, open at the throat, which revealed the coil of a dragon tattooed on his chest by a Chinese master of colored inks and needles. Around both wrists ropes were tattooed in pale blue; and stars, butterflies and serpents in purple, green, and crimson covered his arms from wrist to shoulder, merging into the more ambitious pictures on his body. A dragon on his chest, a full-rigged ship on his back, a snake coiled around his hips.

White, yellow, and brown tattooers had worked on Bill. His skin was an epitome of wanderings that had covered the Seven Seas; in his twenty-five years of life he had ranged from sealing in Bering Strait to labor recruiting in the Fijis. Yokohama, Shanghai, and Capetown knew him as well as Seattle, New York, and London.

WHEN A coppery blond head rose above the crowd on a water front, and a spurt of tobacco juice shot accurately into the gutter from a clean-shaved, blue-eyed face, wise seamen knew there was excitement somewhere in the vicinity.

"But you're a Yankee, and the States are blooming neutrals," argued the apprentice. "The way this war's fought ain't fun, anyhow. While pearling—" The apprentice's eyes glowed with longing. Pearling and the South Seas. There was romance and excitement for you.

"I don't need a silk-hatted politician to tell me when to fight, nor an admiral with a fathom of gold lace on his uniform to learn me how!" roared Bill. "I've been fighting since I was younger

"Can you swim a half mile, Kory?"
The Fijian grinned widely

than you, lad. Ten years of the sea and fighting—fist, gun, and dynamite. I heard the Boche were sinking unarmed cargo boats right and left, and I says, 'Kory, you soot-faced cannibal, we'll get a berth and see if they're men enough to sink us.' Sooner or later all kinds of fighting come to be between man and man. Bayonet to bayonet ashore, and at sea, one fellow's skill and nerve matched against some other man's, on the enemy ship."

"Is Kory really a cannibal?" asked the apprentice, who had been itching to put this question ever since the Bombay left Buenos Aires with a cargo of frozen beef. The ship was now within three hours' sail of Queenstown, in Ireland, but the eighteen days of the passage had detracted nothing from the fascination Bellow Bill's savage Fiji Island servant had for the English boy.

Kory looked like a cannibal. His teeth were filed to sharp points. Across his coal-black face was tattooed a mass of wavy lines which spread from the ear to ear. Half the nose and half the chin were covered in a blue mask which, in contrast to the black skin and the whites of the rolling eyeballs, was demoniac.

Whenever the apprentice encountered Kory suddenly, he

could not repress a shudder. The tribal tattooing hid all expression on the black's face. He did not seem to be a man at all, but some savage dog in man's shape—a dog who acknowledged only Bellow Bill as master.

"You likum long pig, Kory?" demanded Bill lazily.

The Fijian's lips closed over the pointed teeth; the mop of kinky black hair, three inches long, that sprouted from his head in every direction, shook slightly; his bony and heavily muscled figure tensed obstinately. He did not intend to answer the question, which is *tabu* in the South Seas.

"Not regularly, he ain't. Though he admitted once that no meat was as good as a man's hands, roasted; and he didn't speak from hearsay, either," grinned Bellow Bill. "I know, because—well, we were pearling, and a diver got drowned. Kory found the body, but he didn't take it quite far enough into the bush. I wondered what was up, and went ashore for a look-see. So did quite a bunch of blacks from the same tribe as the drowned diver.

"You've noticed that long scar on my chest? A splitting knife did that. It hit me under the heart, but the point glanced on a rib. I bled a lot, but I could shoot. Dropped two black fellows, and the rest ran. They saw me still on my feet, though the knife hilt stuck out of my shirt as though the point were inside me. They thought I had a charm that kept knives from killing me.

"Since then Kory won't leave me. Figures I couldn't get him into any trouble that would be worse than what I got him out of that day—I like pearling. Not so tame yet that a man can't have some fun. When this war's over you and me and Kory might go give it a whirl, hey?"

"THAT WOULD be top-hole!" cried the apprentice excitedly. "Would you really take me, Bill? Of course, this is duty; but dodging submarines isn't any fun. I haven't seen a U-boat yet. Why, we're sailing right through the worst place now, and look!"

Indignantly the apprentice flung an arm in a sweeping gesture that embraced the horizon astern, dark gray in the twilight. "It's the time and place for an attack, and there's nothing there! This job's as dull as delivering coal."

But Kory, glancing in the direction the apprentice indicated, bounded swiftly to his feet. With his tattooed nose wrinkled like a scenting hound, he peered astern.

"Whale there," he grunted. "No—little ship; black, small like whale. *Hieeyah!*"

A gun flashed from the murk astern. The rumble of a six-inch shell speeding toward the Bombay with a thunder like coal tumbling faster and faster down a gigantic chute, drowned Kory's scream. It exploded with a benumbing crash. A smoking chasm gaped ten feet wide where the projectile struck on the after well deck.

The young Englishman clapped his hand to his chest. His blue eyes widened with amazement, and he slowly reseated himself. He was trying to smile, but from his pink and white face the blood was draining, leaving the skin like chalk.

"I'm glad you liked me, Bill. Have—fun—" he whispered. His head drooped on his breast. A tiny fragment of the U-boat's shell had nicked the great vein of his heart.

He died while Bill stared, before the big mate realized the lad had been wounded at all.

Bill had seen men die before. Many of them. Friends. He had thought he was calloused against violence, but this shocked him. This kid, flushed and bright-eyed with dreams of adventure, killed like an ant that is crushed under a careless heel. The Boche that killed him hadn't even seen him, hadn't even known he was there. He hadn't joined the Bombay for excitement, but duty. The duty of stopping a flying chunk of steel with his heart!

"Close in and give us a chance at you, you murderer!" Bill snarled at the murk astern.

A gun flash winked back at him; the rumbling thunder of a second shell filled the air; the crash of an explosion which tumbled the port wing of the bridge into twisted, jagged wreck brought Bill to his senses.

Kory, groveling on the deck, clasped him around the ankles. He did not blame the black for feeling terror. The flesh of his own back crawled. He was experiencing the appalling difference that exists between being shot at and being under fire. After every shell there was too much steel whining around him. To kick the black to his feet relieved Bill's nerves.

"GIT FOR'ARD," he snarled, wrenched a chew off his plug, and set the example himself. A shell plunged into the poop deck he quitted. Steel droned through the air around him. The Bombay, her steering gear shattered, yawed and came to a stop, offering her entire broadside now as a target for the German gun.

Bill walked on. Six feet three inches of height, a two-foot spread of shoulder, offer a broad target, but he neither flinched nor hastened. If his name were on one of those flying shreds of steel, he was done for. If not, no need to hurry. The ship would be sunk, of course, but some way, somehow, he might square accounts with the German that had murdered a pink-cheeked, innocent kid.

Amidships the skipper and second mate were lowering a lifeboat. The crew lay along the rail or crouched in the flimsy shelter of ventilators. Whenever a shell sounded every man seemed to shrink into himself, like a frightened rabbit.

"What's your hurry? We ain't fired a shot yet!" bellowed Bill in a voice that made the terrified men jump.

The thoroughly panic-stricken skipper yelled, "Our six-pounder's smashed to 'ell!"

The lifeboat swung out, and the men dived into it head-long, ludicrous in their haste. They knocked one another down, slipped, and swore. An oar used to fend off from the side snapped. A shell hit the ship, and exploded. The men at the falls dropped the ropes, and the boat fell almost to the water, bow first, before Bill and Kory could check it. By the narrowest of margins the crew avoided drowning then and there. The skipper and mate, seeing other hands on the boat falls, instantly jumped into the boat; the men they jumped upon howled curses.

"Jump, Bill!" howled the frantic skipper. "For Gawd's sake, ferget about Carter and jump before we're hall blowed to 'ell!"

Instead Bill took a firm grip on Kory's collar and stepped to the side. The tobacco that spurted from the mate's lips splashed the skipper's upturned face It was no accident. Bill could not cope with panic, but the sight of it disgusted him.

"Forget nothing!" he boomed. "Wipe yer face and listen! Them Boche will come alongside. Me and Kory will wait and treat 'em like we've treated pearl poachers. Man to man, see?"

"You'll be shot!"

"Oh, maybe not, if you ain't yellow," growled Bill sarcastically. "Row half a mile away from the ship, and stand by for us. Show a lantern now and then. Have you got nerve enough for that, you drooling London swine?"

"Yuss," said the skipper sullenly.

"Then 'urry!" boomed the coppery-haired mate, who looked larger than ever in the twilight.

With ragged strokes the boat pulled away from the ship's side. Bill looked around him, selected the forecastle as the safest place, and pushed Kory ahead of him until the two were protected by the mass of the anchor winch and the heavy plating of the bow. From the waistband of his trousers Bill produced a single action, .45 caliber six-shooter. The blued steel was worn to a silvery polish by much use. He whirled the cylinder, and spat grimly on the deck.

"**CAN YOU** swim a half mile, Kory?"

The black grinned. He could swim ten miles.

"Little black boat like whale will come alongside. Men on deck. I shoot—then we dive. Swim to our boat. These pale-faced, white sailors can't swim, and them U-boat killers won't be wise. Maybe they'll send men aboard to blow the bottom out of this old hooker with a bomb, now that the crew's rowed off. Wait till they're on board. Then I shoot, and you use a club. When all men are dead, we swim like seven bells. Savvy you?"

"Me savvy." A vessel apparently deserted was an old trick to trap pearl poachers, but nevertheless the savage's voice faltered, and he crept close to the huge white man, quivering like a dog in a thunderstorm whenever a shell struck. Bill sat frowning. Though he had faith that the Germans would come within his reach eventually, the Bombay might sink first.

Yet as the minutes dragged along, the way the old vessel endured her punishment began to amaze him.

Oh, she was sinking, of course. A small fire had broken out, and eight direct hits had ripped the decks to iron junk and peppered the superstructure with flying bits of steel. But the old wagon didn't seem in any hurry to sink. The fire wasn't making much headway, and best of all, the winch offered complete protection from shell fragments.

On the other hand, the U-boat had apparently not observed the departure of the lifeboat. The Germans approached very slowly, just keeping the ship in sight as the night grew dark. Nearly a half hour passed before Bill saw his enemy, but at last the light of the fire revealed a small submarine circling the Bombay at a distance of two hundred yards. Though the gun crew was still on deck, the range was too great for Bill's revolver.

"If I just had a cannon, now," he muttered. "What a target!"

The flickering light from the burning ship revealed every detail of the submarine. Her bow plates were dented on the starboard side, as by a collision. Her conning tower had been patched, and the paint on the new plates was fresher than that which covered the remainder of the hull.

Of the men around the gun, one was taller than the rest, and wore a monocle. The firelight glinted on the glass, and Bill, recognizing the commander, half raised his revolver. Still too far, though for a cannon the range was point-blank, a miss impossible.

"Kory, a ship could hide a gun, in a place like this, where only a direct hit could put it out of action!" Bill muttered. Excitement and the far-reaching possibilities of the idea kept his voice to a whisper. He scarcely noticed that the U-boat was about to shoot; but as the six-inch gun blazed, the lurch of the Bombay told Bill she had been struck mortally at last.

The thud of exploding boilers mingled with the sharper crash of the exploding shell. With a huge gap torn between wind and water the ship began to settle rapidly by the stern, and the crew of the submarine filed toward the hatch to go below.

"Dive, Kory!" Bill shouted. Poor as his opportunity was he would not be robbed of it altogether. He rested his revolver on the rail and emptied it at the distant mark. His bullets fell close, for the German nearest the hatch jumped below. The commander, however, turned and stared; then stooped. A flood of light from a searchlight on the submarine bathed the bow of the Bombay. Across the water sounded an order in German, and the crew started back toward their gun.

As the long barrel swung toward them, Bill and Kory leaped into the sea. Gayly enough they began to swim toward the lantern which marked the position of the lifeboat.

Their pleasure was short-lived. They swam in semi-darkness for fifty yards. They were beyond the circle of firelight and counted themselves safe when the U-boat moved around the bow of the sinking ship. The beam of the searchlight settled on their bobbing heads, and behind them a Luger cracked spitefully.

CHAPTER II

QUEENSTOWN FRITZ

BILL DIVED AND swam a long distance under water, then came up for a breath and a glimpse of the lifeboat's lantern. He poked his head into the pitiless glare of the searchlight. Again the Luger cracked, and this time the bullet cut the water within five feet of Bill's ear. The U-boat was much closer.

Like a porpoise Bill ducked under and swam until his lungs were bursting, but when he rose the searchlight beam pounced on his head, and a bullet that splashed his face drove him under. The U-boat was within fifty yards, and Bill no longer had breath for a long swim.

He could not see Kory, but knew that the black must be some distance ahead, since the Fijian was a faster swimmer and trained by diving to hold his breath for minutes. Neither of the two, however, could hope to outdistance or avoid the U-boat by pitting human muscles and lungs against steel and electricity. One of them might have a chance if the submarine could be slowed down.

Bill's lungs were smarting. He could taste blood in his throat, yet when he rose again he surged head and shoulders out of water, breathing in long gasps. The searchlight found him instantly. He turned to face it, eyes half shut against the glare, and waited for the shock of the bullet.

Instead the U-boat stopped her engine and drifted close. A man aboard her laughed—light, low-voiced, mocking laughter that rubbed Bill's nerves raw.

"You damned swine, shoot and get it over with!" he thundered.

"Ach, Gott! It is either Stentor or Neptune!" mocked the voice. "Why should I kill, and spoil my fun? It is fun to be a submarine, *nicht wahr?* Dive, big man, before I shoot! Just as your *verdammte* destroyers play with me!"

Bill ducked under water, for that mocking voice had no more mercy than a cat has for a mouse with which it amuses itself. This time, however, he turned in the water and swam back in the direction he had come. He hoped to throw the U-boat off the track, but when he came up, as quietly as he could, the searchlight playing over the sea quickly found him. He was tired, and for the first time in his life he felt the clammy fingers of

Fear along his spine. His life was in the hollow of this U-boat commander's hand—and the man laughed.

"Ach, an old U-boat trick!" the mocking voice applauded. "So I have done many times, and your stupid destroyers are fooled; but not me! Submerge again, big man with the yellow hair!"

"You go to hell, Glass Eye," Bill called. Without rest he would be unable to stay under the surface for ten seconds. If he did have to be shot, it was not necessary to furnish more sport, so he breathed deep, sucking new strength into his big lungs while the U-boat glided up to him and stopped. The conning tower was not ten feet away, and the light of the searchlight blinded him.

"Herr Leutnant Von Festburg, if you please," said the submarine commander sarcastically. "Big man, you swim like a porpoise. Now answer my questions—if you please." The cold irony of the voice made Bill grit his teeth, for he knew the Luger was leveled at his head.

"Turn out the light and let me see you," he growled.

"Herr Leutnant, there is a destroyer close by," suggested a sailor in German.

"So?" replied Von Festburg coolly enough, but he extinguished the light.

A FAINT glow from the interior of the submarine rose through the open hatch, and when Bill's eyes became accustomed to the darkness he could distinguish the features of his enemy. Again Fear laid a finger on his spine. Von Festburg's nose was like a hawk's beak, his face lean, cleanly shaved, and blandly cruel.

"Your ship—its cargo. The truth, now!" he snapped.

"The Bombay. Frozen meat from the Argentine. Eight thousand tons."

"Why did you hide aboard to murder me?"

"Murder you! You killed a kid that hardly knew what struck him when you were too far off for us to see!"

"So? An English swine," said Von Festburg coldly. "Besides, there are no individuals in this war, big man. A boy, a woman—

what are they? Pawns. We do not shoot to kill them, but if they die, what matter? The war is nation against nation, ship against ship, and shells have no eyes. Why is it I do not shoot you?"

"I don't know. You'd damn well better," Bill snarled.

"What would Germany gain? What is one Englishman more or less?" sneered the U-boat captain. "One less swine!" The light glinted on his monocle. "You threaten me—you, shivering in the water. Me, that all the Queenstown destroyers seek! Tell them I have sunk twenty thousand tons of shipping this week."

"It's the cold water that's making my teeth chatter, not you!" Bill roared. "If you think one man don't matter I'll learn you different, Glass Eye! I've—"

Bill snapped his chattering teeth shut. Goaded by the other's mockery, he had been about to bawl out his idea, his scheme that would make U-boat warfare a man-to-man test of wits and courage. He stopped, yet knew he had said too much—knew it by the soft intake of Von Festburg's breath.

"So?" the German whispered.

But Bill dived before the Luger flashed, avoiding the bullet by an inch. Down, down, down, he swam, turned at random and swam on far beneath the water till his chest was cracking and sparks seemed to flash across his eyes. He looked upward as he approached the surface, dreading to find the sheen of a search-light on the water.

The surface was dark. Catching a lungful of air, he dived again, swam and rose again into darkness. This time he dared to heave himself upright. The lantern from the lifeboat was swinging in wide circles, and he heard Kory's wild, high-pitched yell. The thud of a propeller was in his ears. By him, so close the bow wave smashed over him, a destroyer charged. She showed not a glimmer of light, but the crash of exploding depth bombs marked her course.

"Ahoy!" Bill shouted, satisfied that Von Festburg had been driven under the surface. Guided by his voice the lifeboat rowed toward him, and Kory pulled him over the gunwale.

"Gor'bli'me, wot was yer doink?" spluttered the Cockney skipper. "I seen him chasing yer, and I s'ys, 'Next the blighter come and sink us!'"

"Gimme a chaw of tobacco," Bill growled. "We were talking. Swing that lantern, Kory, and bring the destroyer back. I got a scheme to put up to her skipper."

"'E won't listen to the likes of you," said the Cockney dolefully.

In this respect, however, the captain's pessimism was deceived. When the survivors were taken aboard the destroyer, the news that Bill had stayed on a sinking ship to fight a U-boat with a revolver was quick to reach the commanding officer's ears. Word was brought for Bill to come to the cabin.

CHAPTER III

TO PAY BACK A LAUGH

LIEUTENANT RANDALL, CAPTAIN of H.M.S. *Dartmoor*, proved to be a much taller man than Bill himself. The ex-pearler had to stoop when he entered the tiny cabin of the destroyer, but Randall almost crouched when he rose to shake hands. He was six feet five—a slender, narrow-shouldered, narrow-hipped lath of a man with long, bony arms and legs and long slender hands that had the grip of a band of spring steel. His cheekbones were high, his nose long and straight, his eyes light blue, twinkling, and set beneath flaxen eyebrows that curved upward almost in a semi-circle.

He reseated himself, put his head on one side, and waited with an indescribable air of eagerness, like a greyhound poised for a spring.

"You—ah—wanted to see me, Mr.—"

"Williams. Bellow Bill Williams."

"Er—ah—Williams!" drawled Randall, accentuating the name triumphantly. "Have—er—ah—peg?"

"Don't care if I do."

The Englishman rang for a steward, who appeared with a bottle of Haig & Haig and a syphon of soda.

"Sorry we've no rye. Discomforts of war, eh, what?" said Randall more cheerfully. Bill filled his glass to the brim with straight Scotch, and tossed off the drink. As that enormous peg disappeared, Randall's head went slightly more on one side. He seemed to be waiting eagerly for Bill to collapse where he sat. The men who can drink a tumbler full of the best Scotch whisky without drawing breath, or showing the effects immediately, are rare.

"Captain, I've been laughed at by a Prussian named Von Festburg," said Bill. "He runs a little, patched-up sub with a dent on the starboard bow and a patch on the conning tower—"

"My word, that's Queenstown Fritz!" said Randall eagerly.

"You know him?"

Randall poured a modest two fingers of whisky into his glass and sloshed in soda. He nodded.

"He has—er—laughed at us, too," he replied. "We would jolly well like to send him to a detention camp, or the bottom. But—ah—preferably the former. He's a sporting blighter, rather. He operates around Queenstown right under our noses. Sank a ship yesterday and gave the survivors the stub of a ticket to the Queenstown theater dated the evening before. Must have come right ashore among us. Sporting, but annoying, what? The intelligence is fairly mad. His submarine has been sighted a dozen times, but he always gets away."

"I don't call it sporting to hunt me like a damn seal," growled Bill, his deep voice making the cabin ring. "Or to kill a young kid. From now on, captain, this war is between me and Queenstown Fritz. I won't mind if I get other submarines, but I want *him*. Captain, he—" Bill checked himself. In his mind was the moment when he had been taught what fear felt like. "He—

laughed," Bill continued. "I ain't taking that from any Dutchman."

"Er—ah—have another drink?"

"I AIN'T drunk or out of my head. Captain, I sailed half
around this world to get into a fight, and, damned if I don't find
there's none of what I call fighting to be had. A submarine blows
the keel off a ship, or slams shells into her from five miles away.
Down she goes, leaving a little oil or ashes on the water. That's
the German side of it. Then along comes a destroyer. *Boom* go
a couple of depth charges. Deck gets ripped off the submarine.
Up gushes some air and some oil, and that's war for the Allies.

"Heads I murder you, tails you murder me. What's the fun
or the sport in that, or the percentage, either? The Allies have
fifty ships afloat to every German submarine. Of course, the
Germans get the best of it! Why shouldn't Queenstown Fritz
laugh? He said the whole English navy was after him, and that
seemed to be the best of the joke for him. Well, now," added Bill,
slowly clenching a tattooed fist, *"I'm* after him. If the English
navy'll give me some help I'll bring you Queenstown Fritz's hide
inside three weeks."

"With—er—ah—your six-shooter?" asked Randall. He was
not sarcastic. His light, drawling tones were a gentle reproof of
Bill's boastfulness, but the Englishman still held his head sidewise like an eager greyhound.

"I lost my Colt when I dived overboard. Captain, all the tricks
and ambuscades in this war have been played by the Germans.
I say, give me an old ship and the worst damnedest coward-
liest crew you can scrape out of the saloons. The quicker the
crew takes to the boats, the better. But between decks, mount
an old gun. Some old gun with the rifling all worn out that the
army can't use any more. I don't want anything that's good for
anything else! Just a ship from the mud flats, a bum crew, and
a bum gun.

"The sides of the ship must be fixed so they'll fall away quick.
Put sand bags all around the gun, and let me and Kory hide

there. Just the two of us. Send the ship out alone. She'll be slow, unarmed. Queenstown Fritz will think she's his meat. After he's shelled her, and her crew has run away, he'll come alongside. Then I'll drop the ports and drill a hole clear through him. I hope," Bill boomed, "that he's on deck and looks down the muzzle of the gun before I fire! Do you savvy the scheme, captain?"

"My word! You hate Queenstown Fritz, what?" said Randall.

"No, I just hate to see anybody so damn cocksure of himself," boomed Bill. "That'll be fighting like I understand it, sir! An even break—Fritz's eyesight against my nerve. They'll shell hell out of a ship before they come close, and me and Kory will have to lie doggo till Fritz is damn sure no living men are left aboard.

"Captain," Bill went on earnestly, "I sailed and fought with Germans and English both in the South Seas. The Germans believe in organization, and they're always best at it. But the English way is to turn one man loose on his own, letting him take chances and win if he can. That's the Yankee way, too—and we'll have Fritz laughing out of the other side of his mouth!"

RANDALL SPRANG up. His restraint and his drawling mannerisms fell from him like a cloak. He was all greyhound, quivering, eager, striding from side to side of the narrow cabin with bent head.

"Can't have cowards," he declared. "Fritz uses torpedoes half the time. Ship will be sunk, and God help the men in the life-boats if Fritz learns what you had in pickle for him, eh, what?"

"That's war, isn't it?" Bill rumbled. Though he had liked Randall at first sight, he had dreaded lest the reserve of the English, their respect for tradition, and their dogged reliance on weapons and methods proved by time, should cause his scheme to be dismissed.

Randall's glee, however, reassured him, and had Bill known history better, he might have spared himself anxiety. By the reckless daring of gentlemen adventurers, the British Empire was spread from Great Britain to the Seven Seas. The English fear bad form, and laughter. They hesitate to adopt new enterprises only from their innate dread of appearing ridiculous.

"The Admiralty will be our problem," said Randall, thinking hard. "Winston Churchill's our man, if I can reach him. He enjoys new, daring ideas. I'm only a naval lieutenant, without influence. Er—ah—your idea'll take time!"

Bill's face fell.

"And—my word! You're not a British subject?"

"I could enlist!"

"And be transferred to the Mediterranean or the Grand Fleet like as not. I could take you aboard here—"

"There's Kory."

"My word! The recruiting office would never stand for your black savage," Randall frowned. "You see, Williams, your scheme would have to be kept very secret, and I'm sure the Admiralty would want the first—er—mystery ship manned by Englishmen of—er—proven loyalty and discretion. No offense, Williams, but you Yankees do draw the long bow."

"You mean you'll put over my idea, but I won't be aboard the first ship?" Bill stammered.

Randall put a hand on the huge pearler's shoulder. "That's war, old bean," he said softly. "I'll do everything I can, and see you get credit, and recommend you; but that's what'll happen."

"And it'll take the Admiralty a long time to fit out the ship?"

"Three months at least."

"I ain't waiting three months to settle with Queenstown Fritz," said Bill grimly. "Is there any naval outfit that is assigned to this port, and where I could get Kory in?"

"The trawlers—mine sweepers."

"Then look for us in the mine sweepers after to-morrow morning," said Bill. "And Mr. Randall—I've done some fighting,, and I've never waited for any brass-bound Admiralty to tell me when or give me guns!"

The expression on Randall's lean face became cryptic. The

traditions of the naval service, of obedience to orders, of discipline, and teamwork struggled with the personal freedom of action which Englishmen hold so dear. At last his eyebrows rose into half moons, and his eyes twinkled.

"Er—ah—I have no control over you, old bean," he said softly. "This conversation is—er—unofficial. You are exhausted and—er—probably have had too much to drink." The commander smiled slightly. "But if you should take any steps, remember Queenstown is full of spies, and—er—consult me." Again slender fingers with the strength of spring steel tightened in the muscles of Bellow Bill's shoulder. "Remember I'm a friend," said Randall softly. "Queenstown Fritz has laughed at us both, eh what?"

CHAPTER IV

BILL MIXES IN

THE DESTROYER RETURNED to Queenstown about ten o'clock the same night. The survivors of the Bombay were put ashore, and Lieutenant Randall accompanied Bellow Bill and Kory to a recruiting station. Bill gave his birthplace as Australia, and when the recruiting officer objected to Kory on the ground that no wild men were admitted to the British navy, Bill blasphemously insisted that the black was a British subject. Lieutenant Randall's influence turned the scale.

Bill was sworn in and ordered to the trawler Mary, commanded by Skipper Herbert Innis. Kory was to go along as mess attendant. The trawler, said the recruiting officer curtly, was in Queenstown. Bill could join her at once, if he wanted.

On the dimly lighted street outside the office Bill stood irresolutely. Before he boarded another ship he wanted a hot meal and a night's sleep in bed, and late as the hour was, he decided to seek the former.

Even in wartime a sailor man of six feet three who shouldered through the crowds like a barge, followed by a six-foot black whose face was a weird blue mask of tattooing, could not move without attracting an embarrassing amount of attention. Sailors, police, and civilians stared.

Truculently Bill stared back, almost as keenly interested in the crowd as they were in him.

He sensed an aura of latent hostility, of overstrained nerves, for which he was at a loss to account. Though Lieutenant Randall had warned him the city was a hotbed of suspicion, the Englishman had said nothing of the muttering of rebellion which was to culminate in the daring descent of Sir Roger Casement on the Irish coast and the Easter uprising.

The tension that Bill sensed was the consequence of a crowd divided into loyalists and nationalists. The staring annoyed him, and he hastened to enter the first restaurant he saw. It was dimly lighted, as though closed for the night, but its unusual sign piqued Bill's interest.

Some artist had painted a lead gray ocean into which two blood red cargo ships were sinking. The stern of one vessel and the bow of the other were projecting from the water. In the background was a red streak of the setting sun. The picture was a savage, gloomy representation of disaster and defeat which attracted Bill by its crude color and morbid interest. Under the picture was the title, "Inn of the Two Lost Ships."

Bill jerked the door open and paused abruptly. He had intruded upon a quarrel.

"—and why should an O'Rourke begrudge Ireland the use of a worthless hulk? Ruin and penury is what your loyalty, as ye call it, has brought on your gray hairs!"

The speaker was a swaggering, handsome, black-headed young Irishman whose clean-shaved face was flushed dark by fury. Borne on the flood of his anger and oratory, he stopped speaking with an effort; then turned menacingly upon Bill.

"**WHO MIGHT** you be, and what do you want, and your blue-faced nagyur?" he snarled.

"Supper!" Bill boomed in tones that made the other jump. Followed by Kory, the big pearler strode to the only other table in the tiny restaurant and seated himself—taking care, however, to sit far from the table with his legs gathered beneath him, for the dark Irishman's face had turned a deeper red, and the man's two companions rose purposefully.

The people into whose midst Bill had burst formed a strange group. First, the three young men, all dark-haired, all of military age, yet not in uniform. These glowered at Bill like three dogs from which a bone has been snatched. Opposite them were an old man wearing the white apron of a cook who kept his eyes grimly upon the three young men and an astonishingly pretty girl of eighteen dressed as a waitress. She glanced at Bill, making a sign to him to remain.

Though the sign of "The Two Lost Ships" might proclaim the place a restaurant, the colleen was no more the typical waitress than the old man was a typical chef.

A mass of blue-black hair was piled loosely on her head, her eyes were a deep summer blue, her ankles slender, and her teeth even and white. Her sleeves were rolled to the elbow, and on the left arm, as white and firm as ivory, was the red print of five thick fingers. After her glance at Bill she tossed up her chin defiantly and confronted the leader of the three young men.

Looking closer, Bill saw the print of her fingers on the dark, flushed countenance. The man had caught her arm, and she had slapped his face. Then and there Bill resolved to stay where he was.

The old man was too slight of physique to give the girl any protection. He was over sixty. His hair was thin and gray, but his eyebrows were jet black, bushy, and stretched in an unbroken dark bar across a face that was hollow-cheeked and seamed with wrinkles as deep and harsh as the slashes of a knife. It was a face that misfortune had tortured. The man was in revolt against his fate; fighting a battle against hopeless odds that had turned him sour and desperate.

"We do not serve at this hour, sir," he said harshly. "If you will go to the Parnell Arms you will be cared for."

The girl glanced at Bill. Almost imperceptibly her head shook in dissent.

"I'm a stranger here," the big pearler boomed. "Come, sir! It's a public house, and my ship was sunk to-day. Ham and eggs are quick to fry."

"Will you ask my daughter to wait on a blackamoor?"

"He's no negro, but a Melanesian," said Bill.

AT THIS the Irishman who had been slapped stepped forward.

"I asked what you were," he said ominously.

"Oh, a sailor in his majesty's navy," Bill began. He never finished. The Irishman struck him in the face so unexpectedly he was knocked sidewise out of his chair. As he sprawled, the two other men leaped to stamp him under their boots.

Kory overturned the table and flung himself at the leader's throat. A straight left took the black in the face. He tottered, and pitched headlong, but his body and the overturned table shielded Bill for half a second, and with a roar that made the ceiling shake the pearler leaped to his feet and hurled himself with his great arms outspread at the knees of his enemies.

He brought down all three in a kicking, swearing heap that rolled and thrashed across the floor, but in that tangle Bill was busy with fist and boot. A blow over the heart stretched one man helpless. He caught the leader by the throat, but the third man rolled sidewise and sprang erect. The girl screamed. The man was drawing a revolver, backing away from Bill to wait for a clean finishing shot.

The face of the Irish leader was turning black under the grip of Bill's fingers, but he was kicking and battering at the sailor's face—more and more feebly.

Bill pulled the man toward him for a shield, and struck at the exposed angle of the jaw. The leader went limp. Bill tried to hurl the unconscious body at the third enemy with the gun, but the weight was too great even for his strength.

The gunman side-stepped. A bullet would have done for Bill if the old man had not stepped forward and knocked the revolver upward as it exploded, There was no second shot. Bill crossed the room in one tigerish leap. His fist drove into the stomach, wrapping the gunman around Bill's arm like a wet rag. The man dropped.

"Thanks," Bill boomed. "And now, what the blue chain lightning is all this about?"

"Drag these men into the kitchen and hush that bull's bellowing," snarled the old man with savage vehemence. "Eileen, stand at the door! That shot'll bring Mike Lafferty! Quick!"

He caught the unconscious Irish leader by the collar and dragged him toward the kitchen. The girl sprang to the door, locked it, and set the table on its legs.

Wholly bewildered, Bill dragged the two men after the first. In the kitchen the old man was working with a wet rag to bring the Irish leader to. His face was drawn into a snarl, he swore fiercely when a heavy knock fell on the outer door. "Get your black—and the revolver!" he snapped.

Coming back with Kory in his arms, Bill saw the big Irishman was beginning to stir. He caught up a pail of water and sloshed it over the other two. They groaned, and sat erect. The old man picked up the gun, and cocked it.

"Out through the alley, O'Connor," he snarled. "I'll hold back the police till you're gone. I've that much love for Ireland, wrong and hot-headed as I think ye!"

"**OPEN IN** the king's name!" bellowed a voice from the street. The front door creaked on its hinges as a heavy man flung himself against it.

"It's all right—it's all right, Mr. Lafferty! Don't you be whistling for more police, now. I'll let ye in if ye'll take your shoulder off the door," called Eileen to the policeman in the street.

Her self-possessed voice was a superb bit of acting that Bill was forced to admire. He admired also the way the three injured men pulled themselves together.

Though he would have sworn that none of them would be able to stand for at least five minutes, they staggered to their feet and tiptoed out of the rear door of the kitchen without giving him as much as a look. O'Rourke thrust the revolver into a pail of garbage.

"Sit down," he snarled under his breath to Bill. "You raised a rumpus and my friends knocked you down. Do you understand?"

"No—but I'll back any story you tell," Bill whispered.

He seated himself, and O'Rourke instantly threw a glass of water in his face that there might be an explanation for the puddles on the floor and began to dab at the big pearler's bloody mouth, cut by the first blow of the fight.

A policeman pushed past Eileen into the kitchen. He was a big man with fiery red hair—the efficient and officious type who arouse hostility at sight.

" 'Tis the truth I'll have from ye, Dennis O'Rourke. Don't be saying my own ears didn't hear a shot, when there's plaster knocked off yer ceiling!" snapped the policeman. "Where's the O'Connor bhoys? They came in here. 'Tis little they do we don't know about."

"They're gone. Thinkin' belike you'd like an excuse to stick them in jail," snapped O'Rourke. "This stranger here came in with his blue-faced nigger, and the nigger caught Eileen's arm. The O'Connor boys broke their heads for them, and 'tis obliged I am to them."

"What do you say?" the red-headed bobbie demanded of Bill.

"My black meant no harm," the pearler answered with assumed sullenness. "We wanted a bit of a meal before we sailed on the mine sweeper Mary—"

"Sailors, hey?" said the policeman in a more friendly tone. "Will you be making a charge, O'Rourke?"

"Not if they can pay for the damage," answered the gray-headed man. Bill nodded, but still Michael Lafferty was not satisfied.

"The O'Connor boys are not good to have for friends," he went on warningly. "There's many thinking they're headed for a noose around their necks. Wild lads, they have always been, and not too friendly to England, nor hating the Germans too much. Your restaurant does not pay, O'Rourke, but ye'll do well to seek no help from the likes of them."

"Bad talk!" growled O'Rourke.

"In friendship—as far as my sworn duty allows!"

"Aye, but, Lafferty, you've no right yet to call the O'Connors traitors. Nor me," said O'Rourke sternly. "I do not love England myself, but Germany I hate." The deeply-lined face of the old man writhed like one in torture.

"I owned two ships when the war began," he went on as though he chanted a litany. "Both torpedoed within sight of this harbor. The insurance would have kept Eileen and me, but England needed shipping, and with my last farthing I equipped a third. Set on fire by a shell ten miles off this port, it was! It lies in the harbor now, in the mud. A hulk, blackened with fire—engines and a hull, no more. Two thousand pounds it would take to fit it to carry cargo at sea, and I wi'out a ha'penny! A ship owner, that has to cook bacon—and Eileen waiting on water front navvies. In times past the O'Connors would not have presumed to ring my front door bell—and now Terence O'Connor can invite Eileen to the theater, and never keep the engagement! Don't be telling me to have no truck with the O'Connors! No more than I can help—but they offer to buy the fire-blackened hulk that is all I own, and I would trade with the devil himself to get Eileen out of this den!"

"**BE QUIET**, father," pleaded the girl.

" 'Tis the devil you're trading with—or the Kaiser, which is the same thing, I doubt not," said Lafferty. "The O'Connors are

not sailors nor have they a dollar of their own—though Terence
went to the theater day before yesterday."

"With a girl?" asked Eileen sharply.

"With a tall, hooked-nosed man—a stranger, pale-faced, and
seeming to despise the ground he walked on."

Bill jumped. "By damn!" he ejaculated, for this description
tallied closely with Von Festburg's.

"Ye know the stranger?" demanded the policeman.

"No—my tooth caught in my cut lip," Bill lied.

"Then if there is no complaint I'll be going," said Lafferty.
He made no secret of his disappointment, and at the door he
turned. "No good comes of taking the devil's silver, or traffick-
ing with quare folk!" he warned. He gestured toward Kory and
Bill to show whom he thought "quare" and was gone.

"You have made a liar of me and something worse of Kory,
who knows better than to touch a white woman," Bill began
when the street door slammed behind the bobbie. "Yet your
daughter signaled me to stay here. Why?"

O'Rourke frowned. Crouched in his chair, he peered upward
through his thick eyebrows. "I didn't know that," he answered.

"I feared O'Connor would talk you into selling," said the girl.

"And why not?"

"Lafferty has told us," Eileen argued. "The O'Connor brothers
are hand and glove with the Germans, daddy. You may laugh, but
a woman knows those things, even without evidence."

"I know damn well the one called Terence is—with evidence,"
Bill rumbled. "I would tell you, but I think that the fewer who
know what I do, the better my chance of turning it to account.
Can you tell me, sir, what the Germans might want with your
ship? She will float, and steam, but a hull that has been gutted
by fire is hardly fit to carry cargo."

"She will hold coal." O'Rourke growled, but he was reluctant
to answer further. His words fell one by one. "England's rule is
Ireland's bane. Germany would be a worse master, I think, even
if I had not cause for hate, but there are some who see this war

as an opportunity to be free of England. There is—talk—of an uprising."

Bill's face showed surprise.

"Folly!" spat O'Rourke. "Waste of life—but will I hand hot-headed fools like the O'Connors over to Lafferty—which means, to an English hangman? No! But let that pass, even though I kicked that revolver aside more for O'Connor's sake than yours. If there is an uprising Germany must land arms. If a ship loaded with arms leaves from a neutral port, the British secret service will know, and the rising be nipped in the bud. But suppose my old hulk were refitted enough to put to sea. She is scarcely seaworthy. Who would be surprised if she were driven ashore at some lonely spot on the Irish coast? And why could she not be met at sea by a submarine like the Deutschland, which would load her with arms? The arms could be smuggled ashore and the English be none the wiser."

"But, father!" gasped Eileen. "Thinking that, you let Terry O'Connor talk of a sale?"

"Thinking that, I have not sold yet. You had no reason to slap Terry," said O'Rourke sternly. "If they do not get my ship they will get some other. This inn does not make profit enough to keep us alive and why should I refuse them because of a suspicion that may be unfounded? I am no Mike Lafferty, sworn to poke my nose into the business of others!"

"**WHAT DID** the O'Connors offer?" Bill asked thoughtfully.

"A thousand pounds—however they were to get it!" O'Rourke snapped.

Bellow Bill believed he had a hint as to the answer of that conundrum. Terry had taken Von Festburg to a theater. They were reckless, all right—and so would he be.

He reached into his pocket, and brought out a thick wad of Bank of England notes. The new hundred-pound bills repre-sented the price of his schooner and the profits of five years' pearling and adventuring. Slowly he counted out a thousand pounds—about half his money—and passed the sum to O'Rourke.

"Your ship's mine," he said. "And my word upon it, she'll be used to square your slate with the Boche. I hate one German myself."

Like a starving man O'Rourke snatched the money. "My sign comes down to-morrow!" he cried. "But who shall I say bought—"

"You shall not say!" boomed Bill. "One word that I bought a ship and my scheme is spoiled—particularly if the O'Connors hear. Go on dickering with them as though you meant to sell in the end."

O'Rourke shook his head doubtfully, and slowly pocketed the thousand pounds.

Bill rose beaming. To help this dark-headed, blue-eyed girl out of her troubles pleased him, but more than that he was secretly athrill with the thought that Queenstown Fritz had come ashore to see O'Connor once. He might come again, and if he planned to refit the hulk for sea that scheme dovetailed with one which had sprung, full-fledged in glorious detail, into Bellow Bill's mind.

CHAPTER V

MINES IN THE CHANNEL

HE SAID AN abrupt good-by to the O'Rourkes and went to the Parnell Arms, where he and Kory spent the night. Early the next morning he went to the water front, where he found the Mary about to start out for her daily routine of mine sweeping. The trawler was a stubby, broad-beamed vessel of about a hundred and twenty tons burden, capable of a speed of about nine knots. She was manned by a crew who had been fishermen from boyhood, and the disregard of rank and regulations

aboard her would have an officer from the regular navy tear out
his hair in double handfuls.

Bellow Bill liked the system. He presented his orders formally
enough to a broad-shouldered, fat-bellied individual of fifty-
five, who wore a black woolen jersey. A fringe of beard which
had once been carroty, but which age had dimmed to a nonde-
script rusty gray, circled his chin from ear to ear.

A man less martial or venturesome in appearance could
scarcely be imagined. He looked like a plump, kind-hearted
grandfather who loved his peace and comfort. As Bill
approached, he wiped the grease left from breakfast off his lip
with the back of a hairy hand.

"I'm looking for Captain Herbert Innis," rumbled Bill.

"Hi sye? I'm standin' right 'ere—Skipper 'Erbert Hinnis
'imself," the rusty bearded man answered reproachfully. "Hi
ain't deaf, I'll 'ave you know.'Ave you 'ad your bloater?"

"My which?"

"Your bloater. For breakfast. Nothink like a bloater at six bells
to stick to yer ribs all day. Hit's a fish—wot did yeh think?"

"Thought you were talking of a corpse, at first. No, thanks—
I'm ready to turn to if you tell me what to do," said Bill.

" 'Andle the cables," said Innis.

Another trawler had left the shore at the same time as the
Mary, and now came alongside. A heavy wire rope was tossed
aboard, and Innis showed Bill how to make this fast to the
stern bits. Though the pearler knew nothing of mine sweeping,
he caught the idea. The two trawlers would steam on parallel
courses, dragging the heavy wire through the water between
them. He was surprised, however, that they should begin to
sweep within a hundred yards of shore—particularly since
Queenstown harbor consists of a large bay, almost completely
landlocked.

"The Boche don't lay mines in here, do they?" he asked.

"Ho, yuss!" said Innis mildly. "Nervy blighters come into the
channel. Follow when yer sweeping, 'n' drop heggs right in the

water you've s'yled over. We 'ave mine fields laid, too, but that Queenstown Fritz 'e knows bloody well where they are."

"You know him?"

" 'O don't?" said Innis sweetly. "Now, Yank, when yer picks hup an hegg, don't be getting hexcited if it fouls in the cable. My larst myte, 'e tried to poke a mine clear wiv an oar. 'E must have knocked off the 'orn, 'cos 'e blew the stern hout of the boat."

"What happened to him?" Bill asked.

" 'E went up with the smoke, 'n' never come back to sye," Innis remarked. "Three trawlers I've 'ad sink beneath me 'cos green 'ands lost their 'eads."

BILL STARED at the plump little man with respect. Any one who had been blown up by a mine three times and mentioned the fact as coolly as Innis did could cover Queenstown Harbor with dropped h's, as far as Bill was concerned.

"Ever sink a sub?"

"We don't carry nothink but a one-pounder, to hexplode the mines," remarked the skipper regretfully. "There—we've fouled one—yer'll see 'ow it's done."

The trawler's speed was checked momentarily as the cable caught in an obstruction. To the surface bobbed a round mine the size of a bushel basket, with four projecting horns which contained the firing mechanism. The Mary's one-pounder cracked spitefully. Struck by the shell, the mine exploded. The concussion made Bill jump. A seventy-foot column of black smoke and water leaped into the air so close that the descending spray wet his face.

"That's nothink," remarked the plump skipper mildly. "When they start rolling along the cable toward the boat they may startle yeh. We'll 'ave an 'ard day. Fog's shuttink down."

From seaward a gray mist was rolling in toward the trawler, blotting out the headlands. As Bill looked around he noticed the hulls of three ships beached near the dockyard on Haulbowline Island on the opposite side of the bay, and asked Innis which of these had belonged to O'Rourke.

The hull Bill was interested in proved to be the center and largest of the three, and he followed the skipper to the trawler's bridge, took a bearing on the hull, and located it upon the chart of the bay, while Innis busied himself with checking his course. Astern another mine was picked up and exploded, and then the fog settled down as thick as cold, drifting steam.

Nothing was to be seen now save the cable, which curved out from the Mary's stern into the grayness of fog and sea like a bar of dark iron. Occasionally, the bar seemed to quiver, and after an interval that seemed long, the mine would drift slowly into sight. Bill wearied of the crash and roar of the explosions. Though his new duties were perilous in the event of a mishap, Innis and the gunner were so expert he had nothing to do except stand by with hands in his pockets.

The knowledge that some submarine—perhaps the patched vessel navigated by Queenstown Fritz—had crept into the channel the night before and placed these mines irked him. The German had the devil's own nerve—but why not? A submarine was invisible, and could go where it pleased.

In the narrow channel between the headlands the mines were sown more thickly. Three were picked up at once, and the triple explosion parted the cable. Innis stopped his engines and blew the Mary's steam whistle. The other trawler loomed out of the mist and drifted alongside.

Both ships drifted backward with the tide while a new cable was brought up from below decks. The crews worked swiftly, anxious lest position be lost in the fog, for both sides of the channel were lined with mines, and an error in navigation would put one or both of the mine sweepers over the English mine field.

INDEED, WHEN sweeping was resumed, the cable brought up a mine almost instantly, though the ships were traversing water that had already been swept. As the roar of the explosion died away Innis whistled frantically, and shouted to let go the anchor. He came running aft, his plump face dead white, his eyes popping.

"Wot kind of mine was that? Did yeh see, Bill?" he gasped. "It cawn't be no Boche mine—we've swept these waters!"

"It was, though," Bill reported positively. "It had horns exactly like those we've been picking up since the start."

"It cawn't be!" Innis wiped his forehead anxiously. He was at a loss. Phlegmatic and without nerves when confronted by dangers which he expected and to which he was accustomed, a novel situation took him beyond his mental depth.

"I ain't making a mistake," Bill rumbled. "Have a chew, skipper? Go on below and have a bloater! What's the fuss when we've been picking mines up all the morning?"

"Cawn't yeh see that if that was a Boche mine, a sub must have dropped it since we passed," snarled the plump little man. " 'E must be followink us hout—"

Excitedly Bill spat over the rail and mouthed a fresh handful of fine-cut.

"And why should he wait to follow us?" he roared.

"Sheer deviltry."

"With all the mines we've been picking up in front of him? Like hell! Think faster than that, skipper!" Bill snapped. "That sub's afraid of those mines and is letting us clear them out of his road! That U-boat was in the harbor all night, and he's been bottled in by mines laid by his own friends! And then the nervy devil has the crust to lay mines behind himself! I know one German commander with that much gall!"

" 'Ow do you know so much when this is your first day in the navy?"

"A sub came into the harbor last night expecting to be out before dawn. He couldn't go. Something held him up," said Bill tensely, thinking how urgent the O'Connors had been to finish their deal with O'Rourke quickly. "He knew—this German did—that the channel was to be mined by another U-boat. I'm guessing, but I'll lay a hundred pounds I'm guessing right," said

Bill earnestly. "Now that sub is bottled in the bay by his own mines, what are we going to do?"

Innis thought. The fog dripped to the rigging in great drops which pattered on the deck in the utter silence.

"S'trewth, I don't know." It was a whisper. "We hain't got no wireless 'n' our hown ships will be followink us through the channel."

"Sweep it back as we came!" Bill urged. "Lie across the inner-edge of the channel and stop outgoing ships. Give me a boat and Kory and I will row ashore and warn the destroyers!"

Still Innis hesitated. Bill gripped his shoulder. "Toss a coin— or here, this is quicker!" he urged. "I got a star tattooed on my right arm. Is it red, or blue? Guess wrong, and you'll let me follow my scheme, huh?"

"Blue," Innis chose. Turning his wrist upward, Bill jerked back his sleeve. The star was red.

"KORY!" HE called. Within seconds the trawler's boat was in the water, and Bill and Kory were bending the oars in their haste. Guided by Bill's pocket compass, they rowed straight across the fog-shrouded waters toward the destroyer base. The trip consumed a half hour, but as Bill leaped on the dock it was his good fortune to run into Randall. Swiftly he told his story, and when he finished, the lieutenant wrung his hand and turned on his heel.

"We'll try to get him, though we can't keep the channel closed long. Some ships are due," he called over his shoulder. "But what makes you think it's Queenstown Fritz?"

"The theater ticket he bragged about!" Bill bellowed back. "I know what held him in the bay last night, too!"

But the fog had swallowed Randall. Within five minutes a destroyer got under way, followed by a second and a third. Kory plucked at Bill's sleeve.

"Cold!" he suggested.

"Yeah, it's cold, and we're left out of things," grumbled the pearler. "Back in the boat with you, and swing an oar to keep yourself warm!"

By his memory of the chart and his compass Bill laid a course for the O'Rourke hulk and set out on the long pull across the bay. He had intended to inspect the vessel at the first opportunity, and this was the first that had presented itself. He wished that Randall had taken him along, but he was sailor enough to realize that a warship on emergency duty does not bother with observers.

From the direction of the channel he heard the *brrumph!* of exploding depth charges. The sound was astonishingly clear. Fog either blankets noise altogether or seems to magnify it, and in this fog even the faint plash and drip from Kory's oars sounded loud.

The thick white mists in front seemed to echo a similar plash and drip. Bill, with his attention fixed on the distant explosions, did not notice, but Kory's animal-keen ears caught the sound. With infinite care the black lifted one oar into the boat, laying it on the thwarts noiselessly, and passing the other to Bill, motioned him to scull.

Soundlessly Bill followed the boat ahead. By his calculations they were near the O'Rourke hulk. In a moment there was a faint whistle—a long note, and five short ones of the same pitch—the first bar, though Bellow Bill did not recognize it, of an Irish patriotic song.

"Oh, Ireland shall be free—"

"Yes, Ireland shall be free," answered another whistler out of the fog—faintly, more distant than the first; slightly to starboard. The boat Bill followed headed toward the sound, and Bill, sculling faster, followed. There was a faint thud, such as the bow of a skiff makes when it bumps the side of a ship.

"You're early," whispered a voice.

"Quiet, *Dummkopf!* Where were you last night? Did you buy?"

"No, but O'Rourke will sell. Give me another thousand pounds to fit this hulk for sea," answered the first man.

Bill knew both voices. Mentally he could see the faces of the speakers. Terence O'Connor's dark, swaggering good looks, and the pale, hawk-beaked features of Von Festburg. The German must have heard his own mine explode behind him, and warned by the fact that the trawlers stopped sweeping, turned back toward the bay, avoiding the mines he himself had laid. Leaving his submarine awash, with only the periscopes showing—safe enough in the fog—he had put off in a small boat to return to the rendezvous where the O'Connors should have met him the previous night.

Bill swore softly. It was his luck to encounter Von Festburg now, when he had nothing in his pocket but a jackknife. On the hulk were at least three men, possibly five, if Terence were still accompanied by his brothers. All would be armed.

"Be quiet and wait!" he whispered to Kory. He drew off his boots and lowered himself into the water. The concealment of the fog would serve him for a weapon.

CHAPTER VI

FOG PLAYS NO FAVORITES

WITHOUT A SPLASH or ripple he swam until he saw the dark stern of the O'Rourke hulk. Holding onto the rudder beneath the overhang of the stern was a German sailor who sat in a small rowboat made of canvas which could be folded and stowed away inside a submarine. The sailor looked up now and then, and Bill assumed that Von Festburg was sitting near the taffrail directly overhead, where he could drop into his boat at the slightest alarm.

To swim under the water and capsize the boat would have been simple. The temptation to cut off Von Festburg's retreat was strong, but the act would have alarmed the monocled German without effecting his capture. Once the boat was overturned Bill

"Jump!" Bellow Bill roared. "I'll toss him after you!"

would have been forced to conceal himself in the fog, and before he could summon help the boat could be bailed out and all the conspirators would have disappeared. Instead Bill swam to the shore, and drew himself up a rope hung over the bow of the hulk.

While he was climbing, some one on shore coughed. The sound was muffled, as though the cougher had held his hand over his mouth, and would have been inaudible thirty feet away. Nevertheless, Bill felt a premonition of disaster. For sixty long seconds he crouched motionless behind the rail waiting to learn if his own movements had been heard and to size up the effect of this new factor upon the situation. If the O'Connors had taken the precaution to leave a sentry on shore his task was far more difficult.

The fog swirled mostly against his face and gathered in drops of moisture on the fire-blackened rail of the hulk. No second sound came from the shore, and at last Bill shrugged, shifted his quid to the other side of his cheek, and walked aft, noiseless in his bare feet.

Until he crossed the after well deck he relied upon the concealment of the fog, but after he climbed the ladder onto the poop he dropped to hands and knees and crawled inch by inch along the side of the steering engine house until he could look around onto the stern.

On the deck less than eight feet away four men were seated. Von Festburg faced Bill; the three O'Connors had their backs toward him. The German was counting money into Terence's hand.

Fiercely Bill chewed his tobacco into liquid pulp. He could not expect to overpower four men as big as himself with his bare hands, and there were the sailor in the skiff and the man on shore to consider. If he hesitated, he was going to get cold feet. His only hope was that an armed man, suddenly startled, will think first of his weapon. Bill rose.

"Hands up!" he rasped, and leaped directly behind the youngest O'Connor. Over the Irishman's shoulder Bill spat a mouthful of tobacco juice straight in Von Festburg's face. His left hand twisted in O'Connor's collar and jerked the man upright.

For an instant Von Festburg was blinded. The O'Connors snatched out revolvers, but their brother's body shielded Bill. They hesitated. In that second the O'Connor whom Bill held reached for his gun. Bill's fist smashed him behind the ear. As he slumped, Bill seized him around the body and jerked the gun from his pocket. Von Festburg fired blindly, but Terence, with an oath, knocked up the German's pistol, and the bullet flattened against the deck overhead.

"Hands up!" Bill gritted, and now he spoke from behind a revolver leveled from beneath the youngest O'Connor's armpit. Terence dropped his gun, seized Von Festburg's wrist and twisted the Luger away.

"I'd rather hang than shoot my brother—drop yer gun, Danny!" he cried hoarsely. The third O'Connor—Danny—let his weapon slip through his fingers.

"HANDS UP, I said!" Bill snarled, but still none of the three obeyed. Von Festburg wiped the spittle from his face; Terence and Danny backed against the rail. They were tensed, breathing through their noses, ready to leap on Bill if his attention flickered.

"To the submarine, Hans!" called Von Festburg in German. "I am caught—do not wait! Rush the mines in the channel and put to sea!"

"Stop him, Kory!" Bill shouted. He understood the sense of the order, if not the words. He dared not try to shoot the sailor himself. The O'Connors would be on his neck. Terence was nerving himself for a rush. Bill could shoot him, but to drop all three men before they came to grips was impossible. In a flash he decided to bag the biggest fish and let the small fry go.

"Into the water with you, Terence O'Connor! Jump," Bill snarled.

"Ye'll not hang my brother?"

"I'm fighting the Boche, not the Irish! Jump—I'll toss him after you!" Bill's aim shifted to Von Festburg's stomach. "You'll stay," he snarled. "Spitting in your face squares for your laughin', but you've a murdered lad yet to pay for!"

Bill shoved the unconscious O'Connor toward Terence. The latter caught his brother, tossed him over the rail, and dived after him, Danny at his brother's heels. Splashing in the water under the stern told they were swimming away. Bill was conscious of relief. He had no quarrel with them. They were brave. Most men would have pulled trigger, whether they killed a brother or not. A bullet is a cleaner death than a rope.

The next sounds were less to the pearler's liking. From the fog to seaward came a single shot, followed by a wild scream of pain from Kory. The German sailor had won clear. Fierce, mocking triumph flashed across Von Festburg's face.

"You have bungled, English swine," he sneered.

"Don't try to talk me into throwing away the drop," said Bill. "It wasn't the English navy that got you. It was me, the man you laughed at."

"By stupid luck."

"Luck comes to a man willing to take chances," Bill said softly, but none the less his anger rose. "I've a mind to smash your glass eyes and bust you one in your hooked beak," he went on. "You played with me, damn you, and it would just be fair—"

Bill stopped. From the shore a police whistle shrieked, and from the bow sounded the footfalls of a man, coming at a run. The sentry!

Had it not been for the bewilderment and consternation on Von Festburg's face, Bill might have shot him then and there, but the German obviously knew nothing of this newcomer. He tensed, ready to leap for Bill in case of an interruption. Bill dared not turn his head. The running footsteps leaped up the poop ladder, stopped abruptly as the man caught sight of Bill and the German.

"Surrender—in the king's name!" came the crisp order.

"In the king's name, eh?" Bill thought swiftly. That meant the police. He let his gun fall—and instantly Von Festburg hurled himself backward over the rail into the water. Behind Bill a revolver blazed and a bullet went by his ear. Glancing backward, he saw the red-headed policeman who had examined the O'Rourkes.

"Damn you, he's a German and you've let him go!" Bill roared.

"Halt! Where's the O'Connors? You're under arrest!" Lafferty screamed.

BUT BILL, furious at the escape of his prisoner, dived over the rail. He dived deep, swimming under water, but when he rose the policeman blazed away at him from the taffrail of the hulk, shooting wildly, but forcing Bill under water until he had swum out of sight of the ship—a matter of ten yards or so in the fog. When the pearler rose for the second time he listened for the sounds of Von Festburg's escape—but heard nothing. Evidently the German was a skillful swimmer, and the fog which had served Bill so well was now shielding him.

Nevertheless he could not escape by swimming alone. If Bill could find his boat he could easily pick up his prisoner. The pearler cursed the fog. He had lost all sense of direction.

"Kory!" he called softly.

The answer was a groan of pain, and the sound of Bill's voice seemed to remind Von Festburg of his predicament.

"Hans! To me—quickly!" he called in German.

Bill raced grimly toward the sound: of the groan. Victory would reward the first of them to reach a boat. He was favored by fortune at first, for Kory was less than fifty yards away. Only when he had drawn himself over the stern did Bill comprehend how mockingly fate had tricked him. The bullet which struck Kory had pierced his right forearm and glanced on a rib. The Melanesian was bleeding profusely, and required immediate attention if his life were to be saved. Still worse, when Kory was shot he had dropped the sculling oar. One oar still remained, but by sculling Bill could not move as fast as Hans could row.

He did his best—tied Kory's wounds swiftly and sculled in the direction of Von Festburg's voice. In the thick fog it was impossible to keep a straight course. After sculling five minutes, without hearing a sound Bill knew he had lost the German. He swore, and because that did no good, stuffed his cheek with water-soaked tobacco and thought the situation over.

Bill was not going to return to the shore. Red-headed Lafferty would be as likely to put him under arrest as to give him assistance. The cop must have been trailing the O'Connors; it must have been he that had coughed. Once he learned Bill had permitted the three brothers to escape, what wouldn't he do?

Thoughtfully Bill took out his pocket compass and set a course that would take him to the mouth of the harbor. Presumably the channel was still blocked by mines. The whole fight on the hulk had not taken fifteen minutes. He could be aboard the trawler again in an hour. The search for Queenstown Fritz was still in progress; he could warn Innis and Randall that their quarry had not escaped.

Bill grinned sourly. Fritz had the devil's luck.

CHAPTER VII

QUEENSTOWN FRITZ
GETS PERSONAL

HERR WOLFGANG VON FESTBURG was lashed by a personal hatred which only blood could expiate. Gutturally he cursed because he had not pistoled Bill at their first encounter. The big *Dummkopf* had tossed a monkeywrench into the nicely adjusted plans of the Wilhelmstrasse. By one stupid stroke of luck the blundering *Schwein* had torn down the structure of prestige Von Festburg had risked his life a dozen times to build around the name of Queenstown Fritz.

Arrogant to the core, the German gritted his teeth over the insult to his pride, but his humiliation was also a blow at the legend of German invincibility; his personal defeat, a setback to the morale of the Irish revolutionists.

For the freedom of Ireland, Von Festburg cared nothing. For the fate of the Irish patriots, less. But trouble in Ireland would reduce the number of soldiers England could send to the Western Front, and the Wilhelmstrasse had ordered him to foment an armed uprising by every means within his power. In his overwhelming pride, his first step to this end had been to demonstrate the weakness and what he called the stupidity of the British.

First, he had sunk fifty thousand tons of shipping off Queenstown harbor, taking care that his submarine was seen by every torpedoed vessel, that every one might know that a single submarine was doing all this damage in mockery and defiance of the naval forces stationed near by.

Successful in this, he had become more daring. His venture ashore when he attended a theater with the O'Connors had been a master stroke. News of the exploit had spread all over

Ireland. The English had been too stupid to capture a German who paraded under their noses. Von Festburg had intended that similar publicity should be given to his daring feat in remaining overnight in Queenstown harbor.

But now—the news would pass from mouth to mouth among the revolutionists that a common sailor had spat in his face, had forced him to swim for his life and to yelp for help. Von Festburg had been afraid when he dived into the water, afraid afterward that his submarine had abandoned him, afraid that when the fog lifted he would be picked up still rowing frantically around the harbor.

Even when Hans rowed him to the U-boat he felt little better. His second in command stared at him.

WHILE THE U-boat drifted at a snail's pace toward the entrance to the harbor Bellow Bill sculled in the same direction and at almost the same speed. The fog grew thicker every hour and as darkness began to fall he could scarcely see ten feet. Even with his compass he might have missed the trawler if he had not been guided by the sound of exploding mines. That the trawler had begun to sweep the channel made him scull till his muscles cracked, yet when he overhauled the Mary he found the trawler had taken in the towing cable ready to return.

Bill came alongside without hailing, climbed over the rail, and pulled Kory after him.

"Wot the 'ell! Wot *'ave* you been doink?" gasped Innis, staring pop-eyed at the wounded black.

"Playing tag with Queenstown Fritz. He's still inside. Why the hell did you sweep the channel?"

"Becos' there's some bloomin' ships comink in," retorted Innis with dignity. "I 'ave you know no bloomin' Yank is captain 'ere! Do yeh think we can close the port forever while yer paddle haround—*gor'bli' me!*"

Innis screamed the expletive, leaped a foot from the deck, eyes starting from his head, his arm pointing over the side.

" 'It 'im! Fire, Charley!" he yelled.

Out on the greasy, fog-wreathed sea a dozen yards from the trawler a periscope slid into sight. The trawler's one-pounder chattered, throwing up foam around it. The black iron pipe slid out of sight, leaving a swirl on the water as Von Festburg dived and started full speed for the open sea.

"Where's Randall?" Bill bellowed. "Whistle for him!" At full speed the pearler ran for the bridge, jerking the whistle cord in a series of long blasts, ringing the engines to full speed, and throwing the helm over to go in pursuit. Innis panted after him, and seized the wheel.

"We hain't no bloody warship!" he shouted.

"Going to turn tail with ships coming in?" Bill roared.

" 'Tain't horders for a mine sweeper—"

"To hell with orders!" A push thrust the plump little skipper away from the wheel. "My left arm—blue star or red?" Bill snapped.

"Red! But yer'll 'ave to tyke the responsibility!" Innis yelped, glad in his own heart to have an excuse to follow the submarine, however mad the venture in view of the fog and their armament of the two ships. "Gor'bli'me! Queenstown Fritz follers yer like a dorg!"

Bill thrust out his left arm, palm down this time, and jerked back his sleeve. The star he exposed was blue, which put the trawler in his hands. He slapped the little skipper on the shoulder. "Damned if you ain't a poor guesser," he condoled, grinning from ear to ear. "Bear down on that whistle, skipper! Randall will come a running when he hears us toot, and we can't expect to keep in touch long now Fritz is submerged!"

To Bill's amazement, however, the submarine fled so close to the surface that a distinct trail was left on the surface of the water. The chase had not gone a quarter mile when Von Festburg poked out his periscope, producing two parallel lines of foam which could be followed even in the fog. These lines moved farther and farther apart, showing that he was making better speed than the trawler; soon the lines of foam were blotted out by the disturbed water of the submarine propeller. The submarine had risen to the surface.

" **TRY A** shot dead ahead," said Bill, unable to account for this maneuver except on the supposition that Von Festburg had exhausted his air tanks while lying on the harbor bottom. The one-pounder spat. From the fog ahead sounded a faint *foo-oot toot toot* of a destroyer's whistle. Randall had heard the uproar and was coming to investigate. A submarine on the surface would be easy prey.

The intoxication of triumph dulled Bill's wits. At full speed he steamed into Von Festburg's trap before he guessed its existence. Ahead the dark bulk of the submarine loomed suddenly through the fog. The gun crew was on deck, the gun trained. Bill set his teeth and held his course, hoping to ram.

The gun belched in his face. A six-inch shell ripped into the trawler's box at the water line, smashed aft and exploded in the engine room. The shock knocked Bill down. The hot, searing powder gases rolled over him in clouds. Aboard the shattered trawler men screamed as the hot steam from pierced boilers hissed through the engine room. A second shell ripped out the bow—and Von Festburg moved ahead into the obscurity of the fog. Bill heard him laugh.

"I'm 'it," said Innis. A flying splinter had gashed his cheek to the bone. He tied a handkerchief around the wound, as though he were tying up a sore tooth. Bill was untouched, but Charley the gunner lay like an empty sack on the broken deck beside his one-pounder. In the engine room not a man was left alive. The steam bad killed those who survived the explosion. Kory had escaped injury. He was unlashing the trawler's lifeboat.

"She's sinking," said Bill. The suddenness and completeness of the disaster numbed him. "I'm—sorry."

"Yuss. That gunner, Charley, 'e was my sister's honly son," said Innis dully. "I'll 'ave lots to hexplain. Disobeyink orders—"

Bill lifted the plump little man into the boat, picked up Bert's limp body, climbed in after Kory, and pushed away from the side as the trawler slid bow first beneath the sea.

"Here's Randall!"

The destroyer passed at full speed, dimly to be seen in the fog. Depth bombs exploded, one after another. By the noise of the engines Bill could hear the naval officer steaming in a wide circle, once and twice, swinging wider and wider to pick up the trail of the submarine.

At last the destroyer stopped to listen for the sound of the submarine with underwater listening devices. For ten minutes there was silence, but these tactics also failed. Von Festburg had not stayed on the surface, nor was he moving. The destroyer moved out of the fog and stopped alongside of the boat.

"It's Queenstown Fritz, and he must be close by!" Bill shouted.

How close they learned in the next half minute. The fog formed a narrow circle of which the wreckage left from the sunken trawler was the center. Through the calm sea at the edge of this circle the top of a periscope poked like a malignant eye. Two white streaks marked the path of torpedoes. Before a gun could be fired a double explosion lifted the destroyer upward. She lurched, a huge cavern blown in her side, rolled over, and sank.

THE CREW of the forward gun fired once as the water rose about their knees. They missed, and were reloading when the deck dropped from beneath their feet. Randall never moved. He was at his post when his ship went down, and for an instant Bill feared there would be no survivors. Though the destroyer was mortally hit and had sunk like a stone, not a man had leaped over the rail. Superbly disciplined, they would not run, though they could not fight.

The uprush of air from the hull threw half a dozen men to the surface. All of these had had battle stations on deck. Those below never had a chance. Bill thrust the trawler's boat into the swirl left by the sinking hull. The suction was slight, and by his promptness he was able to seize Randall and draw him aboard.

Two men caught the sides of the boat, three more snatched floating wreckage. These six were all that survived out of a crew of seventy-odd men.

Randall gasped, and opened his eyes.

"Shouldn't have rescued me. Tricked—be tried—Board of Inquiry—disgraced—" he muttered.

"Wasn't your fault, and you're my buddy," Bill gulped. "That Boche hid on the bottom right near us, knowing you wouldn't drop bombs where we'd git blown up, and that you'd come back."

"Old trick. Should have known. Not an excuse a court of inquiry will accept," said Randall, speaking more strongly as his strength returned. "Fritz has made a proper ass of us!"

Out of the smooth water poked the periscope, followed by the patched conning tower and the dented hull. With maddening slowness the hatch opened and Von Festburg stuck head and shoulders into view. He smiled as he recognized Bill, and wetting a hand on the conning tower, wiped the last brown smear from his pale face.

"Come aboard, big man," he invited sulkily.

Bill sat still. In the German's eyes was a cold and venomous hate.

"Come, *Dummkopf!*" said the German testily. "Shall I sink your skiff and drown you all?"

"Tell the blighter to go to 'ell," said Innis in a dignified whisper.

"Nix. Fritz means it. He'll drown you," the big pearler muttered, and with a grim face of one who knows his death will not be pleasant, let himself into the sea and swam to the submarine. He expected to be shot, but to his amazement as soon as he was on deck Von Festburg got the U-boat underway.

For fifteen or twenty minutes they steamed rapidly into the fog. All the while the German was smiling at Bill. Once he let the pearler see he held a Luger. When the fog hid the U-boat completely its speed was checked. Coolly and deliberately Von Festburg spat into Bill's face, and raised his gun, smiling in mocking amusement, when the big pearler gathered his muscles to spring toward the conning tower.

"It is pleasant, no?" the German whispered. "Wash it off in the sea! I was going to shoot you, but it will be better—for Germany and my Irish friend—if the stupid English save me the trouble. Ireland," he pointed, "lies there! Swim ashore, big man, explain to the English why you are alive—if you can!"

The conning tower hatch clapped shut. The U-boat dived, leaving Bill floundering in the water. He struck out for the coast. At the beginning of the swim he wondered if Von Festburg had pointed in the correct direction. To let him swim straight out to sea would be a grim revenge. In time, however, Bill heard the low splash of surf. His feet touched bottom, and he walked onto a sandy beach.

Bill thought, then, that he had tricked Von Festburg. He spent the night with a farmer, and walked into Queenstown the next day. He was barely inside the city limits when he was arrested by a naval patrol, but even then he did not appreciate the subtle cruelty of Von Festburg's vengeance. That he was arrested was ludicrous.

"Say, buddies, who wants me?" he grinned. "You ain't pinching a guy that gets shot out of three ships in two days, are you?"

The petty officer in charge of the patrol, however, did not respond to the pearler's attempt at levity.

"Everybody wants you," he answered solemnly. "The admiral, the Intelligence, and a bobby named Michael Lafferty. They want to investigate you, Terence, Daniel and Patrick O'Connor, and Sheumas and Eileen O'Rourke. The whole crowd's under arrest."

"On what charge?"

"Treasonable communication and commerce with the enemy," answered the petty officer. "You'd better stop grinning. Lafferty picked up the money the German was payin'. To which of you, and for what?"

CHAPTER VIII

MIKE LAFFERTY TESTIFIES

BILL'S GRIN DISAPPEARED. He slipped a pinch of fine-cut tobacco under his lip and spat thoughtfully.

"Then will you tell Lieutenant Randall I would like to see him at once?" he requested, and let the patrol lead him down the street toward the naval prison. Every dozen yards he spat reflectively. Though he did not see how a court-martial could convict him, a searching and public inquiry into the events of the last three days was the last thing in the world he desired, particularly if the O'Connors and their sympathizers were to be present.

His scheme for a decoy ship would be revealed. The information would get to Von Festburg—Bill did not doubt that for an instant—and once warned, the wily Boche would never be trapped. In order to keep Bill's plans secret the inquiry must be held in private, and must end in an acquittal even for the O'Connors, who were almost certainly guilty. Bill liked the three dark, handsome young Irishmen. They had nerve, and were true to each other.

He mouthed more tobacco, and walked so deep in thought that he was led to a cell like a man in a dream. Suspicion and red tape might be his undoing. If Randall failed to trust him implicitly, he was done.

But when the tall young naval officer entered Bill's cell half an hour later his first act was to shake the pearler's tattooed fist.

"Er—ah—top hole that you got away. Bally nonsense to put you here because you got us in a scrap, what?" Randall began awkwardly.

"What did the Admiralty say about my scheme?" Bill demanded.

Randall brightened.

"The admiral here was keen as mustard for it. He says it's not a new idea. There was something of the same sort tried way back in King Charles's time, and it seems the Admiralty was already workin' on a dodge of the kind. Their ship isn't ready, though. They approve, but they won't transfer me because I was doin' destroyer duty, and you—er—ah—" Randall colored with some embarrassment. "You aren't known, what?"

"You aren't doing destroyer duty now," said Bill. "Is the admiral here a sport?"

"Still rides to hounds at sixty. But—er—my word, Bill! You're grinning as though you'd been left a legacy!"

The pearler's eyes were dancing. The big head with its mop of curly blond hair nodded. "I never knew a sporting Englishman to refuse a wager," Bill hazarded. "We'll have to take some chances if we're going to be the men that put over our idea. So, you tell the admiral that I'll fit out a decoy ship at my own expense and bet him that the six of us he's going to try for treason will bring him Queenstown Fritz's scalp in two weeks. If we fail he can hang any of us that seem to need it. We can't escape off a ship that will be under your command and manned by a navy crew. Will that heat up his sporting blood?"

Randall's jaw dropped at this extraordinary proposition.

"I bought a ship yesterday from O'Rourke," said Bill. "Furthermore, Terence O'Connor will advance the money to arm and recondition her. You'll not be too particular where he got it?"

"**MY WORD**, I would, though, and so'll the admiral!" the lieutenant exploded. "What have you been doin' ashore?"

"Fixing things so that we fight Queenstown Fritz quick!" Bill roared. "Don't you want to command the first mystery ship? Won't the admiral want the first one to sail from his district?"

"Yes, but—ah—"

"Then go to him and tell him to examine us in his private office and we'll show how treasonable our communication with the enemy has been!" Bill thundered. "A private inquiry is all

I ask! Didn't you tell me Queenstown was full of spies? How much of our plans will stay secret after an open trial?"

Randall nodded as though to concede the truth of this point, but he was far from convinced. Though he consented at last to bring Bill's proposal to the admiral's attention, the pearler was surprised when a sentry brought him word, an hour later, that his request for a private review of the case had been granted. Either the admiral's sporting blood had been very keen, or he was curious to see the prisoner who had the effrontery to make such a proposition to the English government.

Bill wondered which had been the predominant motive, and how much evidence Lafferty had been able to collect against the O'Connors. If his wild scheme succeeded, he could soon take the sea against Queenstown Fritz. If it failed, three hot-headed young Irish lads would hang, the O'Rourkes would be condemned to the penury of running their unprofitable restaurant, and he himself would go back to some other mine sweeper as a deck hand; become a cog in a vast war machine, and be compelled to admit that Queenstown Fritz was both the abler fighter and the cleverer man.

The admiral called the inquiry for two o'clock. Five minutes before the hour Bill was conducted to a small, bare room furnished with a table and a dozen chairs. Toward the front the three O'Connor brothers, O'Rourke, and Eileen sat in line. In the rear were Innis and Lieutenant Randall. Beside them Michael Lafferty paced to and fro, as red and nervous as a fox.

Bill was given a seat beside Eileen, and had barely settled himself when Admiral Wilson entered. The flag officer carried his sixty years like a boy. His hair was snow white, but his face was a clean, tanned pink that told of abundant exercise.

"Which is Williams?" he asked crisply. When Bill rose, the admiral nodded and his brown eyes twinkled in a way that gave the pearler hope. "So you wish to equip a ship at your own expense. Very—ah—patriotic," said the admiral briskly. "However, we'll see. Lafferty—I'll hear your testimony first."

The red-headed policeman spoke with the eagerness of one who has uncovered a dangerous conspiracy single-handed and expects praise. He testified first how Terence O'Connor had attended the theater three evenings past with a hawk-nosed stranger, and later had been shadowed to the O'Rourke Inn, where a brawl had occurred in which Bill had taken part. All this was no news to the pearler.

"THE ACCUSED Williams is a big man," Lafferty went on, "but the O'Connors are handy lads with their fists, and armed to boot. I doubted he could best the three without help, or that O'Rourke would not lay a charge if his daughter had been slapped by a blue-painted blackmoor. So I stay but a minute to talk, and slipped out after the O'Connors. They are on their way to the water front, and are not pleased when I lay me hand on Terence's shoulder.

" 'Best go home,' I say, and big as they talk, they go. When they are inside, I called Officer Carty, and he and I watched the house. Three times Terence O'Connor tries to slip out. Each time we shadow him, but the night is clear. He sees us and turns back. Your honor, I am dead for sleep, but send Officer Carty away and hide in a doorway down the street all night.

"In the morning out come the O'Connors. They go to O'Rourke and talk for an hour, and then come out, smiling like men well pleased. There is a thick fog now, and I follow them unbeknownst, though 'tis hard they try to throw me off the trail—doubling and twisting through the street before they start walking around the bay.

"I am still behind when they come to the O'Rourke hulk, and when they climb aboard I hide on the bank. For a half hour I hear no sound, and the fog is chilling me to the bone. I am minded to follow on board, when there is whistlin' in the fog, and in a minute the accused Williams wades up the bank.

"Yer honor, I coughed. He dropped behind the rail, and, knowing he heard me, I waited before I followed for his suspicions to die down. I was still waiting, when on the hulk a revolver is fired. I board. There on the stern stands the accused Williams," cried Lafferty excitedly. "He is pointing a gun at a German officer—the same hook-beaked man that was in the theater with Terence. 'In the king's name!' I cry.

"*Whoost!* Over the rail goes the Boche, while Williams stares at me—and him with a gun in his hand that could have easy shot the German.

"*Whoost!* Over he dives after, and will not come back, though I fire at him. In the fog he is out of sight. There is money scattered on the deck. I pick it up. What has become of the O'Connors, I am thinking? Then I hear splashing in the fog. I run ashore—and collar the three as they wade up the bank. In Terence's pocket is one thousand pounds! Short only the notes I have picked up on the hulk. It is all new money in bills of one hundred pounds, and if your worship will compare the numbers of the notes ye will see they run in series."

Lafferty laid a bundle of notes on the table and wiped his forehead triumphantly.

"Mr. O'Rourke is also accused," reminded the admiral.

Lafferty now became less triumphant. "I have naught against the old man and the colleen. A hard time they have had," he began reluctantly. "Nevertheless, when the O'Connors are behind bars I remember their long talks with O'Rourke. I got a search warrant and went through the inn. I find another thousand pounds—in new notes of a hundred pounds each." Lafferty put the notes, Bill had given O'Rourke on the table. "It is known that neither O'Rourke nor the O'Connors had money three days ago," he concluded.

"Do any of the accused wish to cross-examine the witness?" demanded the admiral curtly.

TERENCE O'CONNOR'S ruddy face had become pale as a sheet. He was guilty. The threads of evidence Lafferty had picked up were twisting into a rope for his neck, yet the facts were irrefutable, and he declined to cross-examine. O'Rourke's black eyebrows drew downward stubbornly. He shook his head.

"Were the numbers on the O'Rourke's notes in sequence with the O'Connors'?" challenged Bill.

"No."

"What was I doing on the hulk when you shouted?"

"Pointing a revolver at the Boche, but ye were slow to fire if your intention had been to make him prisoner," Lafferty retorted nastily.

"If I had him prisoner, maybe I was a little slow in shooting him in cold blood," Bill retorted. "I wanted to point out that a man carrying a large sum of money is likely to take one-hundred-pound notes, and that though O'Rourke's bills are not the same as you found on the ship, they will match these." Onto the table Bill tossed the remainder of his savings. "At least I got the money all at the same time from the bank at Sydney," he went on with a frank stare at the admiral.

"I bought the O'Rourke hulk the night of the 'brawl,' as Lafferty called it. I'm a plain sailor, sir, a roughneck working on my own to hit back at the Boche hard and quick, and I seem to have snarled this affair into a hurrah's nest by workin' in the most direct way, but this is the how of it—"

"One minute," the admiral interrupted. "Twice you persuaded Skipper Innis to follow your plans by means of a guess at the color of a star tattooed on your forearm. Will you explain that?"

Bill's face became embarrassed, but he rolled up his right sleeve, displaying a forearm the size of a ham. Under the fur of blond hair were dozens of designs, among them a blue star. Bill turned his wrist upward. More designs, among them a red star.

"It's a trick of mine for getting my way, sir," he explained gravely. "On the left arm it's the same. I can show blue stars or red by a turn of the wrist."

Innis gave an indignant squawk.

The admiral smiled.

"Very ingenious, Williams," he remarked significantly. "Ingenious rather than plain, and—scarcely sporting, what? Now go on. You may be a roughneck, but not a fool."

Nervously Bill shifted his tobacco. His heart was in his throat, for Lafferty's testimony had been more damaging than he expected. Unless O'Rourke and the O'Connors were quick-witted he was going to make something more than a fool of himself. He would give them all the warning he could.

"That Terence knew the man he took to the theater was a German officer has not been proved," he began. "Nor has what he meant to do with the money he received been proved. The fact is, Terence met Queenstown Fritz the second time at *my* suggestion—and he meant to use the German's own dirty bribe money to outfit a ship against him. You look flabbergasted, sir, and that may sound extraordinary. Yet it's the truth—isn't it, Terence?"

The shadow of the noose was dangling before Terence O'Connor. Though his eyes almost started from his head, he managed to nod.

"That's the cream of the joke, sir," Bill addressed the admiral gravely. "Queenstown Fritz made one mistake. He had sport with me in the water, so I knew his ugly face. I stopped at the Inn of the Two Lost Ships, and heard Terence offering to buy O'Rourke's hulk. He said that he had met a gentleman at the theater who offered to put up the money, and who was to meet him at the hulk that night to look the ship over. The O'Rourkes needed the money, and they were saying that Terry's meeting the gentleman was the act of Providence. As he described the man, though, I cut in. 'That's a damn U-boat commander, and no gentleman,' I said. Terence called me a liar, but I convinced him."

"Physically?" the admiral demanded.

"Not then." Billy's countenance was impassive. Only the slight movement of the quid in his cheek revealed the mental tension under which he was speaking.

"TERENCE IS not of the party that loves England too much," Bill went on daringly. "But when he learned he had been on the point of taking German money, he was all for telling the police. 'You will not. You will keep the appointment,' I told him; and at that Eileen jumped up. 'You'll do no such thing, Terry!' she cried out, and sprang between us. Her father caught her by the arm. He hates the Germans as bad as me," Bill explained, "and he guessed I had a scheme in mind. He must have used more strength than he realized, for her arm was bruised.

" 'The three of you will meet him at the hulk and take him prisoner,' I went on. 'Who knows what spies the Germans have among the police. And if you do not,' I said, 'you'll have difficulty explaining how you took a German to the theater.' It was then that Terence took a swing at me," said Bill. "In the ruckus there was a shot fired, and when Lafferty came O'Rourke smuggled the O'Connors out and told Lafferty the first story that came to mind.

"Afterward, however, he and I talked. I told him the scheme I had explained to Lieutenant Randall, and which you know. I paid him a thousand pounds for his hulk, and he promised to explain my scheme to the O'Connors. They could not take Queenstown Fritz that night because Lafferty prevented them, but the next morning after they had seen O'Rourke and learned I did not mean to get them into trouble they were well pleased— as why shouldn't they be? They kept the appointment, and so did I. We had the Boche under our guns when Lafferty butted in, and, as he says, *whoost!* No German."

Bill sat down abruptly.

"Ingenious—very ingenious, if not entirely—ah—plain," murmured the admiral. "Frankly, now, Williams, why were you so anxious for a private hearing of this case?"

"Because while Queenstown Fritz was counting the money into Terence's hand I stepped up and got the drop!" the pearler roared. "That was chance, sir—but so far as he knows, the O'Connors are friendly to him. If you acquit us and let them outfit that hulk for sea, he will be more apt to approach it without suspicion—which is what we want."

For the first time Admiral Wilson became thoughtful.

"If I agree and your surprise failed, it would reveal the scheme to the Germans and handicap the better equipped ships the admiralty is fitting out," he remarked, as though thinking aloud.

"No, sir," said Bill. "I planned to mount the gun on the after well deck and hide it by a tarpaulin thrown over the cargo booms. Queenstown Fritz will have to go back to his base before we would have time to rig up any elaborate gadget; and in my way, the gun would seem to have been hidden by accident."

"Ingenious," the admiral murmured. In deep thought he gave orders that the O'Rourkes, Lafferty, and the O'Connors should leave the room. When they were gone he looked up with a grim smile on his pink face.

"**WILLIAMS, YOUR** story is the most amazing lie I have heard in forty years of seafaring," he remarked curtly. "Nevertheless, if your suggestion could be carried out successfully it would turn the tables on the U-boats and on certain—er—disaffected elements, in a way that I'm unable to resist. To use the enemy's funds and local disloyalty for weapons—by gad, sir, it's more than ingenious! If I were positive of your own loyalty—"

"Gor'bli'me, sir, hif you'd seen 'im a rammin' the U-boat, you'd 'ave no doubt 'e 'ates that Fritz sufficient!" shouted Innis.

Randall cleared his throat.

"Quite so, sir," he murmured. "I would be satisfied if—er—ah—Bill would be my second in command, and gunner, sir."

"But can you handle the O'Connors?" said the admiral bluntly. "In sight of a submarine one man can give away the whole show."

"I can keep them under my eye till we sail," said Bill. "Afterward—well, frankly, sir, they've proved damn loyal to each other, and I don't think they'd go back on me."

"O'Rourke will expect no compensation for his ship?"

"If we succeed, he ought to get her full value."

"Oh, of course," said the admiral testily. "Bonus to all hands, a D.S.O. to the commanding officer, and all that—*if* you succeed. But any decoy ship concedes the advantage to the U-boats. However, go on. By gad, sir," said the admiral bitterly, looking

at Bill, "I wish I weren't so old and high in rank that I could
have some fun in this war. All I do is to decide how you younger
men shall risk your lives. This afternoon's work is a refreshing
contrast. You all have—er—a kind of private grudge against
this—ah—Queenstown Fritz?"

"Yuss!" growled Innis emphatically.

CHAPTER IX

TRUE COLORS

WHILE THE HULK was being outfitted the O'Connors were
an enigma. Bill christened the ship the Eileen. Of this Terry
seemed to approve, though he said nothing. The three brothers
were unnaturally silent for South Irishmen. They barely main-
tained the pretense that they were owners of the ship. Day and
night they were never out of Bill's sight. He ate and slept with
them, and interviewed the dock workmen in their presence.

"Since I'm going to be first officer of this old wagon," Bill
would say when workmen came for orders, "I think we should
just give her a coat of paint and overhaul the engines, don't you,
Mr. O'Connor?"

"Yes, Mr. Williams," Terry would agree.

Just those three words, no more.

Bill did not believe that the Irishman communicated with
friends ashore, yet he could not be sure. He arranged, therefore,
that all the really secret refitting should be done by the ship's
own crew after the Eileen left the dockyard.

His preparations were of the simplest kind. He had the after
well deck strengthened enough to support a twelve-pounder.
Randall insisted that the ship must show her true colors before
she opened fire, and therefore Bill had a hole bored through the
deck at the foot of the mainmast and arranged that a weight
could be dropped into the hold which would hoist the red and

white cross of St. George—the English naval ensign—to the truck. Once hoisted, the flag could not be lowered. It was Bill's intention to fight his single three-inch gun until the ship sank.

Whenever he could spare time he and the O'Connors went aboard an armed merchant vessel being repaired on the opposite side of the pier. Here Bill learned to load, train, and sight the twelve-pounder. Kory was drilled to load, but the sighting of the gun fascinated the black. He fingered the two hand wheels until, as a favor, Bill let his servant operate the gun.

Then one evening at dark Randall and twenty reservists came aboard disguised as merchant sailors. The Eileen, in ballast, cleared for Cardiff and steamed very slowly for the harbor entrance.

Under cover of darkness the naval men uncrated the twelve-pounder, which had been brought aboard in a heavy wooden box labeled "spare engine parts," and bolted it to the after well deck at the foot of the mainmast beneath the cargo boom. A tarpaulin flung over the boom concealed the gun, and a telephone was strung between the gun and the bridge in order that Bill and Randall could communicate while waiting to go into action. The three O'Connor brothers were sent to the fire room.

Just before dawn the old ship poked her nose out of Queenstown Harbor. Sunrise found her in the waters where Von Festburg preferred to operate.

THE WEATHER was ideal for submarine attack. The sky was clear, and the sea barely rippled by a soft westerly breeze. The Eileen's engines gave her a speed of less than eight knots, so that a U-boat could almost overtake her while running submerged.

Bill sat with the telephone on his ears and his eye at a knife-slit cut in the tarpaulin.

Kory kept lookout on the other side.

"Periscope! Bobbed up astern!" whispered Randall from the bridge.

At the same instant Kory touched Bill's shoulder.

The black's eyes rolled excitedly in his blue-tattooed face. He pointed forward.

"Pipe! Stick up quick! Take down!" he said.

"Shut your blue face!" Bill ordered. He was so intent on keeping concealed that it seemed the submarine could hear.

"Kory reports something forward," he breathed.

"He's right, too! There—that's plain enough!" Randall snapped. "He must have seen a fish, I guess. Stand by, Bill! He's rising, but he's too far off to shoot!"

The pearler crowded Kory aside. A thousand yards away a periscope projected three feet or more from the sea. As the submarine moved parallel to the Eileen the periscope left a white streak of foam on the sea.

Already cognizant of the fact that the ship carried no visible gun and no wireless, the U-boat commander was taking his time and looking her over carefully, heedless of the fact that he could be seen himself.

"Let him rise clear out of the water!" Randall instructed. "To hit the periscope or the conning tower won't sink the sub or do a bit of good—"

"Hitting Fritz's glass eye with a twelve-pound shell won't do good? Be your age, buddy!" Bill chuckled.

"—We must put a hole in the pressure hull, the cigar-shaped body of the submarine," Randall went on like a professor. "Range nine hundred yards. Still too far."

"I was waiting till I see Fritz's monocle! Leave me be and preach to Innis and the panic party," retorted Bill in exasperation.

Satisfied that the Eileen was an unarmed merchant ship the submarine poked her conning tower above the surface. Bill's trigger finger itched, but his target was still awash, with tanks full, and could make a crash dive in five seconds. Therefore, he waited, even when the conning tower hatch opened and signals were hoisted.

"Abandon ship. Bring your papers."

This was the cue for Herbert Innis. The cockney put on a show that would have done credit to the stage. Leaping into sight on the bridge he shook both fists at the submarine and bellowed profanity that traced the pedigree of the sub commander for generations.

"Sink an 'onest Henglish marster goin' about his lawful business, will yeh, yer bloated, stinkin' fishbelly!" he raved.

While he waved his arms the supposed crew of the Eileen poured up from below.

Greasy firemen in dungarees and sweat rags, sailors from the forecastle, one carrying his sea bag, ran pell-mell for the lifeboat.

The launching had not been rehearsed, for in default of drill Bill had chosen to rely upon the confusion natural to haste. The result was splendid. The boat went down with a run, bow first, and nearly swamped.

The sailors yelled to Innis, still waving his arms. The cockney leaped from the bridge, dived into the chart-house and reappeared with his hands full of the ship's papers. He ran down the deck, stopped, and ran back to appear again with the ship's cat in his arms. He pinched the cat so that it yowled and spat, tossed it into the boat—whereat Kitty took revenge upon the nearest sailor, and the confusion in the boat was no longer assumed.

Grabbing at a frantic tabby that raced from bow to stern, the lifeboat pulled raggedly away from the Eileen—leaving the old ship apparently deserted. There remained Randall on the bridge, Bill at his gun, and a skeleton crew, including the O'Connors, in the engine room.

THE SUBMARINE approached the ship, yet it did not blow tanks. Still able to dive at a second's notice, it moved alongside the lifeboat. Its hatch opened, and a stout, thickset officer took the Eileen's papers from Innis. Bill could hear their conversation. The German asked the ship's name, destination, tonnage, cargo.

"Kory, how the hell can I shoot with Innis and the men right alongside?" Bill whispered in an agony of indecision. The conversation seemed to go on forever. The submarine seemed minded to take the cockney aboard as a prisoner of war. Randall left the bridge, crawled aft, concealed by the rail, and joined Bill.

"Don't shoot!" he whispered. "My word, Bill, with the ship's papers right in his hands what does he want to take the captain for, too?"

"Dutch thoroughness, damn his soul!" Bill growled. "I'm not going to plug 'Erbert—wonder if the damn squarehead guesses what we are?"

Before Randall could answer, the dilemma was solved in the last way either of the two expected. Out of the fidley hatch Terry O'Connor crawled on hands and knees.

"Go back!" Randall ordered aloud.

The Irishman heard, for he shook his head. He was wildly excited, with a face white as chalk, and at the order he tried to move faster—with disastrous results. His toe caught in a ring bolt. He fell flat, and as he fell the ring bolt clinked audibly. The U-boat commander heard, for he snatched up glasses and trained them at the supposedly deserted ship.

"The filthy traitor!" Randall whispered. He drew his revolver, resolved that Terry shouldn't go unpunished. Bill caught the lieutenant's wrist.

"Not yet! He's trying to tell us something" he whispered, for Terry was gesticulating, pointing aft.

"What is it?" Bill called, raising his voice the slightest bit.

"I've seen—another submarine—astern!" Terry gasped. "Do ye think I'd be betrayin' the man that saved the lives of the three of us! Ye'll be torpedoed out of water if ye shoot! Let the German go—and give me back to the British!"

Surrender never entered Bill's head.

"Terry!" he instructed in a tense whisper. "Pretend you are a stoker left behind by accident. If you don't fool that U-boat"—Bill's whisper was like a trickle of icy water down the spine—"so help me God I'll shoot you in the back and hang your brothers!"

"Is it afraid ye think I am?" Terry snarled. Lying flat on the deck he drew a long breath, and then leaped to his feet with a wild Irish yell!

"Ye domned murthering spalpeens!" he shrilled, jumping onto the rail and shaking both fists at the lifeboat. "Will ye be leaving me behind to be torpedoed, me that can't swim a stroke! Come back, ye murtherers! Come back for Terry!"

Innis jumped at the opportunity to leave the side of the U-boat.

"By Gawd, we forgot 'im! Give way!" he bellowed. At full speed the lifeboat rowed back to the ship. Terence jumped, and the lifeboat, pulling madly, drove astern out of Bill's line of fire. All the while Terry cursed his shipmates at the top of his lungs.

The U-boat commander was deceived. Slowly he blew tanks, and the rounded pressure hull of the submarine began to rise inch by inch above the sea. Bill waited at the gun breech. Each second seemed an eternity.

"NOW!" RANDALL whispered. The naval ensign flew up the mast. Kory flung the tarpaulin aside; Bill swung the gun into line and fired—so swiftly that the fat little U-boat commander had no time to move. His mouth was open, his eyes wide, when the twelve-pounder spat flame. A jagged round hole sprang into being at the base of the conning tower, and the German disappeared as the shell exploded in the interior of the vessel. Another shot, and another, fast as Kory could load. Out of the open hatch floated a thin smoke, and then a yellowish mist. The reek of chlorine spread into the air, and the U-boat slowly rolled on its side and sank.

"There, damn you!" Bill roared, yet he felt little thrill over the quick victory. His success had been as easy as the shooting of a duck that floats on the surface of a pond. He swore to keep from thinking of the horror his shell had wrought in the crowded, confined interior of the U-boat, of the men pinned in a sinking coffin who strangled on the greenish gas. Randall was also white to the lips, but he shook his head.

"Don't be sorry, old bean. Our turn is coming next," he said softly. He pointed astern, where the periscope of the second submarine was in plain sight. It moved rapidly away from the Eileen, rising higher and higher as the U-boat moved out of gun range.

With gun revealed and the white ensign flying, concealment was no longer possible. Randall picked up his binoculars and walked to the rail. Height made him conspicuous, but he coolly jumped onto the rail and studied the second U-boat, which was blowing tanks three thousand yards away.

"Quite out of our field of fire," he remarked. "A decoy ship ought to be able to fight a submarine as well as surprise one. Well, at our first go at the bally business we can't be blamed for one mistake, what? The sub we sank was a U-C Mine layin' craft. One that's been blockin' Queenstown channel."

"An' the other?" Bill questioned, knowing the answer.

"Yes, that's Queenstown Fritz off there," said Randall, smiling wryly. "He'll torpedo or shell us now, just as he pleases."

CHAPTER X

THE BIG KICK

FROM A POSITION astern where the Eileen's twelve-pounder would not bear and from a distance beyond its range the U-boat shelled the helpless vessel for ten minutes. Every shot was a hit. The German gunners were maddeningly deliberate. Randall could see the flash of the gun. Each time there would be an interval of a few seconds while the missile whistling toward him, and he wondered where it would explode. A crash, and another smoking, jagged gap in the Eileen. Far away the Germans would begin to load methodically.

Bill lay flat on the deck beside the twelve-pounder with one hand gripping Kory's kinky head to hold the black prone. Even with the tarpaulin gone they were concealed as long as they hugged the deck, and less exposed to the humming splinters of steel which followed every shell burst.

The disintegration of the ship was rapid. A fire broke out on the poop. The smokestack sagged and was pitted with holes. The cabins behind the bridge were wrecked and beginning, to burn, so that a pall of smoke commenced to rise over the ship, concealing her outlines from the German gunners. Yet the hull was intact, the leaks few. The effect of the shelling was a nerve-racking strain on men compelled to lie grimly silent at their posts.

Not one revealed himself. The firemen stayed below, though any shot might pierce the boilers and fill the between-decks with scalding steam. After a dozen shells Kory ceased to tremble.

"You stay? You shoot?" he muttered gutturally.

"We stay," Bill rumbled deep in his chest. "You'd like to shoot, huh? So'd I." He patted the black's head as though Kory were a good dog. With unexpected vehemence Randall began to swear.

"You hit? Come on and lie down!"

"Oh, I'm top hole," the Englishman answered viciously. "Only I've bitten my pipe in two, and the bally bowl dropped overboard. I'd like a smoke no end, too."

"Come here and I'll teach you to chew, "Bill chuckled. "Say, what about sendin' away another panic party?"

"Good idea if we had an excuse. A ship with the white ensign flyin' can't be abandoned too easily,"

A shell struck the bridge. Splinters flew as high as the masthead.

"Well, you're damn hard to please about excuses!" Bill boomed.

"Fritz is going to torpedo," said Randall.

Finding gunfire slow to sink the Eileen, Von Festburg submerged and moved toward the ship with only his periscope showing. That he meant to torpedo was obvious. Bill used the interval to good advantage.

"Stand by to abandon ship when the torpedo strikes!" he bellowed down the engine room hatch. "Muster on the gratings, go over the side on anything that will float!" At three hundred yards Von Festburg discharged his torpedo. The explosion heeled the Eileen over as though she had struck a rock at full speed. Every hatch was blown into the air, and a burst of steam shot upward from the shattered boilers.

THE SECOND panic party had no need to act. With white steam clouds rolling out of the hatchway at their heels they ran to the single remaining boat, tried to launch it, and discovered the bottom had been punctured by a shell. Nevertheless they cut it loose, and the two O'Connors leaped after it, holding onto the sides to keep their heads above water. On pieces of wood, casks, anything that would float the rest of the party joined them in the water, and the lifeboats rowed back to pick them up.

The chief engineer wore a gold-braided hat, and waved his arms and shouted in the water as though he was the naval commander.

Bill eyed the periscope, which circled slowly around the ship less than a hundred yards away. He could see the dim shape of the U-boat's hull under the surface. For ten minutes Von Festburg patrolled, scanning the Eileen from stem to stern. The ship was sinking by the stern, and heeling over to port in a fashion that made Bill hold his breath. If the list grew much greater, the U-boat would be able to look over the rail and discover him lying by the gun.

Randall crawled beside him.

"Is he fooled?" the Englishman whispered.

"I—don't think so!" Bill whispered. "You're so damn' tall he may have recognized you!"

The fire on the poop was burning fiercely, and the deck on which Bill lay was growing hot. The smoke made him cough; Kory wiggled as an ember fell on his back. Randall flicked the spark away.

"Good man, your black," he said. "Eh—ah—we'll be seen in five minutes if that list keeps increasin'. You and Kory might jump. You—er—aren't *pukka* navy. Your surrenderin' would be no disgrace, what? I can't leave the ship!"

That Queenstown Fritz did not intend to rise was evident. The periscope moved slowly between the lifeboats, scanning the faces of the men aboard in search of the real commander. When the Eileen sank—a matter of minutes now—Von Festburg could make his choice of prisoners in perfect safety. He could return and warn all the U-boat commanders of the decoy ship stratagem.

"He saw you, "Bill whispered, and added, almost to himself, "We'll have to make the biggest bluff of all—"

"What do you mean?"

Bill did not explain. What he proposed was trebly difficult. His fighting instinct was for man-to-man combat, his lifelong habit to trust himself only, yet now he must rely on another. To play the part of a pawn in this crisis was hard, yet the steadily increasing list of the Eileen demanded the sacrifice. He was anxious lest Randall, being imbued with navy tradition, might refuse to cooperate, and also lest the vanity of Von Festburg might be proof against the temptation he meant to offer.

"What is it? I'll not surrender!" snapped Randall.

Bill pushed himself along the hot deck until his lips were against Kory's ear. He whispered in the lingua franca of the South Seas, which Randall would flat understand.

"Stand by. When tin fish comes high up, shoot, savvy?" he ordered.

Kory grinned. He understood, but whether he could choose the proper moment to open fire only the event could determine.

BILL DREW a long breath—and sprang to his feet. Catching Randall by the coat collar and the slack of the pants he jerked the amazed lieutenant upright. Randall struggled and fought, but his strength was no match for Bill's. The pearler turkey-walked him across the deck, heaved him over the rail into the sea, and leaped after him—like a mutinous and cowardly second in command that compels his commanding officer to surrender!

The lens of the periscope turned toward the pair struggling in the water. Bill lifted Randall high, and threw back his own head. He wanted Von Festburg to recognize them both without fail. They were the prisoners the German wanted.

The submarine rose to the lure. Conning tower and pressure hull broke the surface—and still Kory did not fire. The submarine's lid was thrown back and a pale face emerged.

"You again, swine?" Von Festburg drawled. "Three encounters are too many, big man! I shall carry you to a German prison camp, and laugh at you pacing behind the wire. I shall—"

The German's expression froze. The monocle dropped from his eye into the sea. Kory had sprung up. The twelve-pounder crashed, and the shell ripped into the U-boat at Von Festburg's feet.

The explosion hurled him out of the hatch like a figure of straw. Another shell whizzed over Bill's head and punctured the hull. But careless of the fate of the U-boat, the pearler was racing through the water toward Queenstown Fritz. Randall, however, shouted triumphantly. German after German was crawling from the U-boat hatch.

"*Kamerad, kamerad!*" they cried.

"Cease firing!" Randall bawled. Kory threw another shell into the gun breech.

"Belay and jump!" Bill bellowed. He realized that the Melanesian would obey his mighty voice alone; but he paused only for those three words. Ten feet away Von Festburg was sinking. Bill dived and pulled the German to the surface. He was unwounded. He gasped and opened his eyes while Bill caught his head in the crook of an arm and started swimming toward the lifeboats.

The submarine was not sinking quickly, but she was doomed. Water poured into the hull through two shell holes, and the deadly greenish mist of chlorine released from the storage batteries was floating out of the hatchway.

Kory jumped from the Eileen and came swimming toward Bill like a porpoise, his blue tattooed face one broad grin.

"Perfect, Bill! No other ship has sunk two U-boats yet; what?" gloated Randall.

"IT AIN'T perfect yet!" Bill roared back. As the lifeboat rowed alongside he thrust Von Festburg into Innis's arms and heaved himself over the side after his prisoner. The German settled himself sullenly in the bottom of the boat. Bill seated himself in the stern where he could grin down into the hawk-nosed face. His blue eyes danced with unalloyed glee, and he waited, tasting his triumph to the full, until Randall had been taken aboard and the Germans rescued.

"Isn't perfect yet? My word, what more do you want?" the lieutenant protested. "You'll get a D.S.O. or a V.C. for winning a victory when I was waiting to sink with colors flying! Eileen and her father will get the full value of the ship from the Admiralty. Enough to buy a new vessel if they want one. And the O'Connors! My word," Randall babbled, "they'll be mentioned in dispatches and rewarded for conspicuous service to the English crown! The testimony of ten thousand Mike Laffertys won't amount to a whisper against them! Isn't all that enough?"

"Nope," said Bill softly. "Getting a medal or doing my buddies a good turn ain't quite the cat's meow." Grinning, he bent and tapped Queenstown Fritz on the shoulder. "Who sank you— swine?" he drawled with sarcasm. "Was it the English navy, or was it me and a blue-tattooed nigger?"

"You," growled the German.

"Correct!" Bill rumbled deep in his broad chest. "You and Innis can have the medals, Randall! The big kick for me is to out-game a nervy guy—and if he's a Boche, to make him admit it!"

The pearler stuffed a handful of fine-cut into his cheek and settled back, completely satisfied. "When I get ashore," he murmured happily, "I want to take the news to Eileen. Then I'm goin' on a toot, and when Lafferty tries to arrest me I'll bust the teeth out of his gums. Medals? Hell, Randall, what are medals to a roughneck?"

VIRGIN DIAMONDS

Most seekers of "adventure" are ignorant of what the word means—but Bellow Bill Williams, of the South Seas, knew and loved its cruel and stern excitement

CHAPTER I

A JUNGLE KIMBERLEY

THE COLUMN OF smoke which had lured the schooner inshore floated above the tall trees which fringed the coast of Papua. The signal of distress, made of the last rags of a shirt, fluttered in the southeast breeze. The castaway himself, a white man whose black and uncombed beard hung halfway down a hairy chest, carried a log down the beach as the schooner hove to, and began to paddle toward her with his hands—as though he feared to stay for an additional second in the jungle.

The castaway was alone, and obviously unarmed, but nevertheless Bellow Bill kept the schooner's wheel hard down, refusing to reduce the gap between his ship and the coast.

"Here's your excitement, George." The pearling skipper's voice rumbled like the deep, vibrant bass tones of a vast organ. It carried clearly to the castaway in the water. "I've promised to shoot that man at sight, and he knows it."

"But you can't! He's shipwrecked, helpless. Look at him race to get here—"

Bellow Bill Williams shifted the quid of fine-cut chewing tobacco that bulged his cheek and stared quizzically at the "new-chum"—this newcomer to the South Seas, who had chartered his schooner ostensibly to investigate the sources of copra for a great American soap corporation, and who had talked of nothing but adventure ever since.

Bellow Bill had his own opinion—and a highly favorable one—of George Carstairs, but he wished at this moment that he

71

were alone and able to deal with this bearded castaway without impediments or witnesses.

"Don't see me going for a gun, do you, George?" The booming voice dropped to a whisper. "Just the same, that 'helpless' man there is Jacques Fortier. Six months ago he and his gang boarded the schooner Hattie and cut the throats of the skipper and *kanaka* crew. Fortier was a mite careless. One of the *kanakas* was not quite dead when he was tossed overboard. He swam till he was picked up, and whispered Fortier's name before he died. So we pearlers learned who the pirate was.

"The skipper of the Hattie was no friend of mine, but like a lot of pearlers who weren't afraid to take the law into our own hands, I swore to get Fortier. A number of other schooners had disappeared, you see. It might be my turn next, and anyway Fortier was already known as a pearl poacher and blackbirder. Too tough even for these seas.

"It happened that a British gunboat met Fortier first. His

He thought they were nothing but a feverish vision—until they threw their spears

schooner was shelled and driven ashore right here at the mouth of the Aikora River. It was thought none of her crew reached the bush. The country round here is uninhabited, anyway, and a man can't live in the bush unless he packs his own grub. So Fortier is officially dead, Looks it, don't he?"

"YOU'LL LET him aboard, at least?" Carstairs asked eagerly, and grinned from ear to ear when Bellow Bill nodded. The "business venture" to the South Seas was taking the turn George had hoped for, but never really expected.

He was a ginger-haired youngster of twenty-two with the broad jaw, and wide-spaced, tawny-yellow eyes of a lion cub. That he was heir to the largest soap business in the United States was not his fault. He had not come to the South Seas through his own choice, either. A month previous George had been planning a transatlantic flight.

"Understand, I've got nothing against the soap business, in

spite of the smell," he had informed Carstairs Senior. "I'll skim
kettles or run a branch office in Podunk, whichever you say;
but first I want the world to know I'm no stuffed shirt step-
ping into shoes you've filled with silk socks for me." George's
metaphors were mixed, but he was both earnest and excited. "A
non-stop flight from New York to Rome will show everybody
I've got some excuse for living beside being the son of George
V. Carstairs."

"If you'll start bucking the Foamy-Clean crowd you'll realize business has got more kick than sport," Carstairs Senior
began. Young George shook his head like one who recognizes
the beginning of an old argument.

"Maybe business was he-man stuff when you were my age,"
he contradicted. "Back in the '90s there weren't any trade asso-
ciations to restrain competition. Biting and gouging were usual
and necessary. But now our business is too big to fail, and you
know it, Dad. The banks would step in and reorganize if necessary, and that's why kids like me can't get much kick out of business. Too many people to help us and make it easy for us. So
we break speed records and make nonstop flights. It isn't our
bank accounts or our father's pull that licks Old Man Time and
Distance. It's us!"

Carstairs Senior hadn't made himself a multi-millionaire
without an understanding of men. At that moment he did not
argue. In his office the next morning he had his secretary get
the statistics on trans-ocean flights. Even when he found out
exactly what the risks were, he did not get excited. He stared at
the ceiling a second, and then called up his son.

"George, I need you in the business right away," he declared
with a very passable imitation of anxiety. "That Foamy-Clean
crowd are trying to corral our raw materials. Pack a bag and catch
a steamer for Australia. Charter a schooner, and go through the
islands tying up all the planters you can for a three-year contract
for their entire output of copra— The flight?— It's too bad, son.
Maybe nobody will have got to Rome until you're able to get

back and take a whack— Yes, you can fly to 'Frisco if you want— Fine! I knew you'd go. Business first, eh?"

Carstairs Senior was grinning when he hung up the receiver. The price of copra was unusually low. He didn't expect George to sign any contracts, but the kid was removed, as far as was geographically possible, from ocean flights. The father decided he had put over a fast one.

The son discovered it, too, when he reached Sydney and learned that most of the world's copra is grown by natives who don't understand the meaning of the word contract. For a day George was angry. Then he grinned, took a drink, and decided to make the best of it. After all, vast areas of the South Seas haven't even been adequately mapped. A young man ready to take chances might readily make himself famous for a long time, whereas these days the fame of an aviator lasts about a month, until some other pilot breaks the record.

GEORGE INQUIRED discreetly who was the most daring skipper south of the equator. From officials, exporters, and waterfront bartenders, the answer was the same: Bellow Bill Williams. According to the gossip, Bellow Bill's coppery yellow hair and swaggering six feet and three inches of bone and muscle had a habit of turning up in the places other schooner captains funked. Places where there was an excellent prospect of stopping a bullet or a native spear, and no profit openly in sight.

For profit Bill seemed to care very little. Sometimes he had made money by his adventures. More often, according to the gossip, he had been well satisfied to get away with a whole skin. But every one to whom George talked agreed that Bellow Bill could not endure the thought that there was any island which he did not dare to tramp from end to end, or any gang or individual operating with whom he hesitated to match strength and wits.

George hunted Bill up. He found a man whose shoulders would have blocked a door, lounging on the taffrail of a sixty-foot, two-masted schooner which reeked to high heaven with the rotten stench of pearl shell.

Bill was about thirty-five. A cotton singlet which was the only garment on the upper part of his body, revealed a dragon tattooed which seemed to crawl in coils of crimson, green and blue over the iron-hard chest muscles. Both Bill's arms were crowded from wrist to shoulder with stars and serpents and strange beasts; the artistry of tattooers, Chinese, negro, Malay, Polynesian, and white.

Haltingly, conscious of his new store clothes, George explained what he wanted: to see large copra planters; to poke the schooner's bowsprit into strange harbors.

Bill's eyes were dark blue and quiet as the sea at twilight. George found their stare disconcerting. He thought the pearler was about to refuse to charter his schooner, but at last Bill nodded.

"I been doing what you're thinking about for twenty years, and it's still fun. I'll go you," he rumbled in his great voice.

The two men understood and liked each other almost at once. A thousand miles sailing from Sydney to Papua had by now cemented their friendship, but though their ambitions were the same neither had ever really anticipated anything like the present opportunity. Here was Jacques Fortier paddling on a log at the threshold of one of the wildest and most unknown regions left in the world; very much alive though he should have been twice dead—once through the shells of a British gunboat; again through the hardships of six months in a savage country

Fortier abandoned his log and swam.

He swung himself over the rail and walked toward the two white men sitting by the wheel with a defiant hardihood which George could not help admiring. The black beard hid the pirate's features except for a pair of unwinking black eyes and a high bridged, bony nose. Physically he was shorter, but fully as heavy, as Bellow Bill himself. The hairy body was muscled like a gorilla.

"Coming back to be hanged, Fortier?" Bill boomed.

"That's for you to say," the pirate retorted.

He flung up his right hand, on which only the thumb and

first finger were left. The stumps of the three missing fingers had been horribly seared by fire.

"A shell did that." The clawlike hand touched scars that welted the hairy ribs. "Papuan spears made those. Bill, I've lived longer among the natives far in the interior than any white man has done yet."

"Yeah? That don't excuse a few other things you've done."

"Doesn't it?" sneered the pirate. He clawed in the rags of his trousers and sent a glassy-looking pebble half the size of a pea rolling across the deck toward Bill's feet. "Look at it! Feel it! That's the first diamond out of a virgin field! There's a pocketful like it already above ground, and the devil knows how many more still in the blue clay."

Fortier's jet black eyes glittered like a hawk's.

"Well?" he challenged. "Do you take me back to Sydney to be hanged—and never hear another word—or do I guide you two up there?" The maimed hand jerked toward the Papuan hills, misty green in the heat haze.

"It's another Kimberley, Bill. You and the new-chum can have the field. All I want is a pocket full of diamonds, and a chance to disappear while the damned English still think I'm dead."

CHAPTER II

THE TOWN ON THE BLUE CLAY

SWIFTLY BELLOW BILL reached for the diamond. The soapy feeling of the gem removed his first suspicion, and he passed the pebble to Carstairs.

"The diamond's genuine, but I wouldn't trust *him* if I held a knife to his throat," he grunted.

"Who asks you to? This is the Aikora, ain't it?" snarled the bearded man.

"About twenty-five years ago, the Aikora River was prospected for gold, George," Bill explained. "The prospectors found blue diamond clay and a geological formation like that of the Kimberley fields. Nevertheless they only stayed long enough to exhaust the placer gold. The country is worse than hell. The natives are bad, there's fever, and no food except what you bring in. A large party can't bring supplies up the rapids, and a small one the natives would *ki-ki*."

"What does that mean?" George demanded.

"Eat," said Bellow Bill succinctly, "For twenty-five years there's been talk of testing the Aikora, but you can't pan the gravel and run the way the gold prospectors did. You have to dig up blue clay that is nearly as hard as rock, wait for the rain and weather to crumble it, and then screen tons of dirt. Meanwhile—"The pearler's great shoulders shrugged.

"Are you trying to talk me out of this? "George demanded excitedly.

"I want you to be sure you really want to go. Fortier here is just about as reliable as a cobra. I haven't blackened his reputation. Nor he hasn't reformed, kid."

Fortier jumped to his feet.

"What kind of white-livered, stinking cur-dog d'ye think I am, to reform? To hell with that, and you too, Bill!" he snarled. "It's money I want—money enough to have a villa at Nice and an apartment in Paris. I want to walk the boulevards in a silk hat and have chic women stare after me and envy the blonde on my arm. I've done everything I know to get rich, and now—now, when it's too late, I got a chance to make a big stake."

A fleck of foam appeared on the grizzled beard. "I knew who you were when I saw your schooner's topsails, but I'd strike a bargain with the devil," Fortier gasped. "The diamonds are above ground, not under it. It's a virgin field and rich—rich! *Mon Dieu!* There's millions—millions that I hold the key to and can't get because I'm wanted for murder. An honest man that finds me naked on this damn coast turns me over to the British! So would any of my old gang, damn them! They'd know the price on my head is sure money, and they haven't the heart to face the Aikora. I've earned those diamonds by slavery and torture."

Fortier waved his maimed hand. "That wound festered while we were in the bush. I heated a stone red hot and pressed the stubs of my fingers against it until I was sure the infection was charred away. I've made *taro* and dug potatoes for naked savages and ate the scraps they tossed me. I'm tossing a Kimberley into your hands without even asking for an equal share, just because I need a schooner to take me away from this God-forsaken coast—and you, you tattooed ape, talk of reform! D'ye think I swam out here for love?"

"**WHO ARE** the natives?" demanded Bill imperturbably.

"Hill Papuans that ain't seen a white man since the gold prospectors was through. When the gunboat drove me ashore and sunk my schooner I started up the Aikora because it was travel or hang. I got to the hills—I don't yet know how. I kept walking when I was light-headed with fever and starvation. I was seeing things that weren't there, and my hand was swelled half the size of my head. Finally I came to a big rapid. I was lying in the water to cool my hand when I saw six or eight natives with their bushy heads of hair. I figured they were nothing but a feverish vision until they threw their spears. That's where I got the scars." Fortier tapped his chest.

"The devil knows why they didn't eat me. Probably I was too sick and too thin," the bearded man went on grimly. "They gave me yams and a bitter drink that helped the fever. They were fattening me like a calf to be the main dish at a big feast they gave once a year. Meanwhile I was a slave. I worked in the fields under guard, but pretty soon they let me wander around the village as I pleased. You know those Papuans' villages, Bill?"

"Grass houses built on piles," the pearler nodded. "I've been in the bush more than a little. Even know a few words of the Papuan lingo."

"The piles in this town are driven into the blue diamond clay," said Fortier hoarsely. "It's a big town. The community house is two hundred feet long, and the place has been settled a long time. The clay around the house has been tramped bare, and the rains keep washing it away. I picked this diamond out of the dirt after a big storm. It was one of six found while I was there."

"You mean the Papuans hunt for them?" rumbled Bill sarcastically. "What's a pebble to a savage?"

"Somehow they've found out how hard a diamond is," Fortier answered with a frankness which was hard to distrust. "They've got a kind of religion. I don't know much about it, except that there are three spirits they're afraid of. Manoin is the boss devil, and he lives in the woods. Another lives in the ground; a third sends the thunder and lightning. They are mighty scared of that devil, too, and if you had ever been through a few thunderstorms in that country you wouldn't blame them. Anyhow, diamonds being so hard, the Papuans believe them something the devils have made special, and that the stones are valuable to the spirits. The village I was in thinks that Manoin won't send the lightning to destroy any place where a lot of diamonds are. They have a wooden idol called a *karwar*—ugly looking thing about a foot high carved to resemble a man with a big head. The figure holds a shield and a spear, and is turned to face the mountain where the thunderstorms gather. Every diamond found in the village for generations is in the belly of that *karwar*. I'd estimate there was a double handful, and none of them are small."

"Why didn't you grab them before you escaped?" growled Bill.

"Because I only got a chance to escape by knocking my guard on the head with his own stone club, and if I'd copped the diamonds they'd have chased me a lot harder than they did," snarled Fortier. "Remember I didn't have a gun. Three armed white men would have an easy time stealing the *karwar*. Maybe we'll have to fight our way down-river, but what of it? I'll give you enough diamonds to prove the existence of a rich field, and take the rest. Once I'm safe in Paris, you can get capital, organize a big party, and go in to mine."

"The field would be named after the discoverers—The Carstairs Workings!" said George eagerly.

BILL SPAT reflectively over the schooner's side. "Well, there is diamond clay up the Aikora. That much I know ain't a lie," he rumbled. "Seems to me though, Fortier, that if you could get out with a double handful of diamonds you could organize your own company, even being what you are."

"You'll be right here in New Guinea and can get a permit from the government first," Fortier argued.

"In other words, we protect yourself by keeping you from getting the best of us?" Bill chuckled. "Well, that's no lie, either. I like that arrangement. Be frank if you can't be square, hey?"

"You'll go?" cried Fortier.

"The story of the Aikora clays has been plaguing me for years, and you offer an excuse to look into it," said Bill gravely. "We've got plenty of arms, food and medicine aboard, and we can moor the schooner in the mouth of the river and leave my two *kanakas* to look after it. The only drawback is—"

"Don't try to keep me from going with you just because I'm a new-chum!" George exclaimed. "I want to roll a handful of diamonds across my father's desk and say, 'Dad, from now on, the name of Carstairs means diamonds as well as soap!' The trip can't be any more dangerous than flying the Atlantic, and I'll make an entry in the log saying that you do this at my orders, and that I take full responsibility!"

"I'm not trying to pass the buck," rumbled Bellow Bill. "I'm responsible, but a man's got a right to run risks for anything he wants—money or notoriety or fun." The pearler spat thoughtfully over the rail, then continued as though Fortier were not waiting for his decision.

"What worries me is that Fortier lived among those savages six months, kid. They're simple blacks, George. They haven't even got chiefs, or priests. A man rates among them according to his strength and his savvy. I never knew of their keeping slaves.

What's more, Fortier is a dead man unless he gets off this coast, and that schooner of mine would provide an easy getaway."

"Can I sail her to Paris?"

"Oh, some of your gang are still in the South Pacific," Bill retorted. "Don't think you're fooling me. Part of your yarn may be true, but part of it must be a lie. You love money too well to give away a Kimberley to a stranger and a man you hate."

"You'll go? "Fortier snarled.

"I'll go—and be damned to you," said Bill coolly.

CHAPTER III

NYANG

THE PREPARATIONS FOR the expedition were quickly made. Bill sailed the schooner up the river far enough to be out of sight of passing vessels and anchored her a hundred yards from shore. Though Fortier assured him there were no natives near the coast, the pearler ran barbed wire around the rail to discourage a boarding party, and then turned the ship over to his Fiji mate, Kory.

The three white men loaded the skiff with provisions for two weeks, a few essential medicines, and the simplest camping equipment. They took a rifle and revolver apiece and started upstream.

The tropical forest came to the river bank like a high green wall. Here and there a tree was wrapped from base to crown in the flaming red foliage of a D'Alberti creeper, but the flowers that George had expected to see were absent. There were only the green leaves quivering in the heat, the thin hum of insects, and the moist stench of vegetation rotting in the jungle.

Nothing could have seemed more peaceful than the Aikora. On the surface, likewise, the relations between the three men seemed to be friendly. Bellow Bill was alert for treachery, yet having declared himself aboard the schooner, nothing in his speech or manner proclaimed the fact that his suspicions persisted. He yarned with Fortier about wild nights ashore in towns the names of which George had never heard.

The two big men had been in many lively places at the same time. They compared notes, and only by inference could George perceive that in each case Fortier had been outside and Bellow Bill inside the law.

Nevertheless, just before sunset, when Fortier suggested they pull to the bank and make camp, the big pearler shook his head.

"But it will be dark in half an hour!" Fortier exclaimed.

Bill spat out his quid and refilled his cheek with fine-cut.

"All day long something's been startling the birds," he remarked. The great voice was almost a purr. "They keep flying up from both banks—sometimes a little ahead, sometimes a bit behind, but on the whole keeping close to this ship of ours as a shark following a schooner."

"Might be the noise of the oarlocks," Fortier scowled.

"No, it's men. Look yonder!" Bill pointed toward a bend of the river ahead, where a low bar of sand jutted forty feet from the bank. From the tall trees shading the spot a flock of parakeets rose screaming into them, circled, and flew upstream. "Those birds would be going to roost now if something hadn't scared them. Question is, are the natives waiting to fight or palaver? They must have learned something about guns when the gold prospectors came through."

"They didn't palaver with me," said Fortier calmly. "Still I've learned enough of their lingo to tell them anything I want."

He stood up in the bow of the skiff and shouted a word that seemed to be all consonant sounds. From the tall trees at the river's edge the echoes rolled back. There was no other answer.

"That sand bar gives us a little room to shoot," said Bill placidly. "Row in, George."

Fortier drew his revolver. He was the reverse of excited; yet in the crisis his awkwardness robbed the three of the advantage of

their firearms. The Papuans did not palaver. As the bow of the
skiff touched the gravel half a dozen brown men sprang from
the undergrowth and sprinted for the boat. They charged in a
compact mass—an ideal target; but as the bow struck the gravel
Fortier was thrown off balance and fell straight backward. The
impact of his body doubled George up on the rower's thwart.
Over the new-chum's back Fortier rolled into Bill's lap, utterly
spoiling the pearler's shot.

THE SAVAGES howled with triumph. George yanked at his
revolver, knowing he would be too late. The stone-headed club
brandished by the savage in the lead seemed poised in the air
over his head when Bellow Bill shoved Fortier upon him, and
then, to George's consternation, leaped over the stern into the
river. Not to escape. The pearler's tattooed paw never let go of
the boat. Waist-deep in the water Bill gave a mighty pull that
yanked the skiff away from the shore. The Papuans dashed into
the stream. Bill dived to meet them as the craft drifted out, away
from them.

The two leaders Bill seized and dragged down. A third he
tripped. Rolling and wrestling in three feet of water, the excited
savages still tried to use their clubs. Bill fought grimly with his
hands.

He caught a windpipe and squeezed with all the strength
of his fingers. Releasing that man paralyzed, he seized another
by the body, and, rolling under water, broke the savage's back
against his knee. A hand was gouging at his eyes. Bill caught
the wrist, jerked the man close and twisted his left hand in the
savage's long bushy hair. Thrusting the squirming antagonist
out of water first as a shield against the clubs of the others, Bill
got to his feet. At his back a rifle cracked. The bullet missed him
narrowly. There was no second shot.

By pulling the skiff away from the bank Bill had placed
George and For-tier where they would be safe, whatever the
outcome of his own struggle, but also where they could take

no effective part in the battle. George was on his feet first with revolver clear at last.

Thirty feet across the water three savages were yelling and dancing around a churning, splashing commotion. From the midst rose a brown body which floated limply downstream. Momentarily there was a glimpse of Bill's yellow hair. The savages on their feet dared not use their clubs; nor did George—not too good a shot—dare to use his revolver. He caught up a rifle and fired at the howling, dodging men just as Bill rose. With an oath Fortier pulled the Winchester away.

"You'll hit him, you fool!" he snarled.

George snatched at the oars to row back. Erect and lightly poised, despite the rocking of the skiff, Fortier watched the battle.

Bill sidestepped the swing of a club, caught the man who had struck at him by the hair, and cracked the two heads together. The sound of the impact was like the rotten scrunch of a ripe pumpkin dashed against a stone. Bill flung the bodies at the last pair, spoiling their concerted rush, leaped for them and knocked the nearest senseless.

The last Papuan uttered a howl of terror, turned, and ran for the jungle. He had made less than three strides when Fortier's rifle cracked. The savage pitched on his face, his spine severed by the bullet.

"Leave be! They're licked!" Bill shouted.

Fortier ruthlessly sent another bullet through the man Bill had throttled, who had recovered strength enough to sit up in the shallow water.

"Don't leave any to carry the news," he retorted, and took aim at the man Bill had knocked unconscious.

Instantly the pearler leaped in front of the body.

"You damn murderer, if you can shoot like that, why didn't you start sooner?" Bill gritted. "I want to ask this fellow what tribe he's from and what he's got against the whites!"

"They're from my tribe. I'm paying debts!" Fortier snarled.

"You're piling up blood feuds!" Bill retorted. "Whack him with an oar if he lifts that gun, George."

Fortier shrugged and laid the rifle down. George brought the boat to the bank.

THE UNCONSCIOUS savage was a heavily muscled man, nearly six feet in height; he wore no clothing but a narrow loin cloth made of hibiscus bark. Legs and chest were covered with hair, but the face was beardless. Like all Papuans, his hair was trained to grow in a thick, woolly mass which sprouted fully six inches from the skull in every direction. On his chest was an elaborate design of raised scars made by slitting the skin with a knife and rubbing in dirt, so that the wounds had healed in raised cicatrices.

"Those tattoo marks stand for the men he's killed," Fortier grunted. "Better let me finish him off. His name is Nyang, or something like that. He comes as close to being the chief as the Papuans get."

"Kill the chief?"

"You've just killed three men of his tribe and he might not like it," retorted Fortier evenly.

Bill's answer was to dash water in the Papuan's face. In a moment Nyang groaned and sat up.

"Ask him how many men he came down river with," Bill directed. "Birds were flying on both banks of the river, remember."

As the savage recovered consciousness fully, however, he became too frightened to respond to the questions Fortier grunted at him. His eyes roved to the man shot in the back, and he shivered. He looked down stream, where other bodies still floated in sight, and suddenly, with a howl of sheer terror, he flung himself face down in the sand at Fortier's feet. Again and again he struck the ground with his forehead, gasping out; a long speech in which a word that sounded like *"barong"* was repeated over and over.

In the end he squirmed forward on his belly and clasped Fortier's ankles.

"What did he say?" Bill demanded. "He's talking too fast for me to understand more than a word or two."

"He's begging for his life."

"So I see. Why do the begging of you, that used to be a slave, instead of me?" rumbled the pearler. "What does *'barong'* mean?"

Fortier hesitated. "Why—uh—kill or death."

"Does it? Took you long enough to think."

Bill kicked the prostrate savage gently to attract his attention.

Nyang rolled his eyes upward. Bill's singlet had been ripped to tatters during the struggle, and at the sight of his huge torso, covered with brilliant tattooing, the Papuan pounded his forehead in the dirt, muttering, *"Barong! Barong!"*

"Death, huh?" Bill grunted.

Slowly he drew his revolver, cocked it, and aimed straight between Nyang's eyes. The savage grew paler and shivered, but did not utter a word.

"Like hell he was begging for his life!" Bill muttered.

He pointed at the dead man. *"Barong?"* he inquired.

The savage shook his head.

Bill pointed at Fortier, then at himself. *"Barong?"*

A nod.

The pearler indicated George, and asked the same question.

Nyang's head shook.

"**YOU LEARNED** this language badly, Fortier," Bill remarked coolly, "That word you thought meant 'death' is some kind of title. Probably Big Warrior, since the Papuans don't have chiefs. Certainly is funny you should be called that, when you were nothing but a slave." Bill smiled grimly. "That slave part was one of your lies. You said you'd been working hard five months and escaped down river. Yet you are fat, when if your story were true you'd be worn to skin and bone. I'm beginning to think you made yourself boss of this village on the blue clay you were telling about."

Fortier shrugged.

"Anyway, I'll do my own interpreting," the pearler continued. He pointed at himself, and raised one finger, at George, and raised two, at Fortier, and raised three. Nyang seemed to understand, for he raised three fingers in his turn. Then Bill pointed at him and at every savage whose body was in sight.

When he had reached the count of six he paused, eyebrows raised, and pointed to the other side of the river.

Nyang raised five fingers and then three.

Bill pointed at the skiff. For a second Nyang looked puzzled; then his face cleared and he raised one finger.

"Eight men and one dugout," Bill interpreted. "They attacked without a word, and they were posted on both sides of the river, which is pretty intelligent tactics for a dumb bunch of savages. Fortier, you're a sailor and know enough to balance yourself when a boat touches shore. You lost your balance at a mighty critical time."

"What of it?"

"Why, I think you meant us to be attacked and captured," said Bill coolly. "Pass over your belt gun!"

Fortier's beady eyes glittered dangerously, but Bill was within arm's length of him with clenched fists, and George had reached excitedly for a revolver.

Forced to obey, the pirate unbuckled his belt with a sneer.

"And now, George," Bill rumbled, "which way do we head? Up stream or down? Fortier controls the natives and wants our scalps."

The younger man never hesitated.

"Up stream!" George grinned. "Maybe that was Fortier's only lie."

CHAPTER IV

THE RAPIDS

WITH SIGNS AND the half dozen words of the Papuan language which were all he knew, Bill explained to Nyang that George and himself were traveling up stream for a friendly purpose. To bring the idea home he presented the savage with a steel bush knife present, and let him go. During the night George and the pearler stood watch, as much to prevent Fortier from arming himself as from fear of the natives. The darkness passed without an attack, but as the row up river recommenced with the dawn, Bill saw signs that the Papuans were continuing their surveillance.

The natives no longer skirted the river banks parallel to or ahead of the skiff, but on the left bank there was a continuous disturbance in the jungle half a mile or more to the rear. Bill made no comment, and George, though he frowned at the frightened birds and smoked incessantly, showed no disposition to change his decision to continue the expedition.

The sullen silence of Fortier in the bow of the boat weighed on the nerves of both men. George was finding adventure a thing of hard work, heat and discomfort. Despite the fight on the river bank, it did not occur to the new-chum that his life was in any danger. The whole affair was like a story in which he unexpectedly found himself an actor.

It was Bill, with his clear insight into the difficulties ahead, who worried. Not for himself. The struggle with Fortier was wholly to the pearler's liking. But to drag the son of a millionaire into a struggle where the outcome was more than dubious and the profit wholly problematical, seemed scarcely sporting.

At the head of the first rapid in the Aikora, therefore, Bill put his pride in his pocket. The three men were resting after the labor of portaging their skiff and supplies around a quarter mile of rushing white water where the Aikora roared down a deep slope studded with bowlders that spouted foam and spray for yards into the air. The water was deep and the banks precipitous.

It was the speed of the current which made a portage necessary, for above the rapids was a flat plateau which seemed to extend for ten miles or more before the voyagers reached the base of the foothills proper, where their boat must be abandoned.

The skiff had been set into the water just above the rapids, where the current quickened for the final plunge. The outfit had been restowed, and George had already taken his place in the stern.

"Fortier, we can't go on fighting each other and the natives, too," said Bill, breaking a silence which had lasted nearly thirty-six hours. "Let's settle the thing here. Roughnecks like you and me don't matter to anybody. If we want to take a chance and don't come back, that's our business. George hasn't got the right to do that. He's got a family, money, and all that kind of stuff. He ought to get a break."

"Getting cold feet, Bill?"

The pearler unbuckled his gun belt and tossed his revolver into the skiff. "If you were sultan of every bushy-haired human ape in New Guinea, you wouldn't faze me, working alone," he rumbled. "I'm just trying to work this expedition out the easiest way, instead of the hardest. If you'll convince me you're on the level with us, I'll give you your gun back. The three of us can get those diamonds for you—and you said there were plenty enough to make three men rich."

"I don't need a gun."

THE SNEER made Bill flush. "If there are just a few diamonds and you want to hog them all, say so. I'll divide the outfit and arms with you, and George and I will go back."

The bearded lips parted in a cold smile.

"Don't need an outfit," Fortier said grimly. "You were so damn clever that you found out all about me and the natives. Find out the rest."

"If you're scared that I'll turn you over to the English after we get outside, I'll give my word that I won't," growled the pearler. "I never would have done that anyway. I'd have killed you if you'd been in with the same gang, but the British have broken up piracy for awhile, and hanging you ain't going to bring the captain of the Hattie back to life. And if you want to lead this expedition," said Bill hopefully, "here we are on the firm sand. You're as big as me, Fortier, and neither of us are armed. Give me a licking and I'll obey your orders like a *kanaka.* That's every-thing I can offer you, sailor. Pick what you want."

"I'm satisfied," said Fortier.

Scowling, the pearler looked his bearded antagonist from head to foot, as though it were impossible to believe what he had heard.

"Well, that's that," Bill said at last, and followed George into the skiff, seating himself on the rowing thwart. "Shove off, Fort-ier."

"Bill!" Fortier's whisper was barely audible above the roar of the rapids. The pearler turned to look over his shoulder. "I'm satisfied because I knew you'd make a mistake, and you've done it." The bearded pirate was grinning from ear to ear. His beady eyes sparkled maliciously. "Ta-ta—and *bon voyage!*"

With a vigorous shove Fortier sent the boat away from the bank down stream into the grip of the river current, and dived for the shelter of the jungle underbrush. George fired, and missed.

"Damn!" roared Bill. He caught up the oars and rowed till the tough ash bent, trying to check the rush of the skiff down river, but was not able to counteract the force of the current. On shore Fortier lounged around. Foot by foot the skiff was moving to the brink of the rapids.

Seeing the inevitable, Bill swung the prow of the skiff down stream with two mighty strokes. The current caught the light

boat with a smooth rush that caught the breath. Ten yards ahead
the first great bowlder spouted foam.

"I'm sorry, kid. I was a fool," Bill muttered.

He turned on the thwart to face down stream, snapped the
oars into the bow oarlocks, and pulled.

The first bowlder flashed by.

"Eee-yow!" Bill yelled at the top of his voice.

"Ya-ay! Row, Yale!" shouted George, carried away by excitement.

Pulling frantically to keep the skiff's bow pointed up stream,
now and then missing a stroke with right or left oar to twist
the skiff aside enough to avoid some rock, Bill ran half the
rapid successfully. Had the stream been passable, he would have
reached the still water below dryshod, but a canoe in the most
expert hands could not have found a gap in the barrier of bowlders at the rapid's foot.

The boat was hurled into a wall of foam. Neither man felt
the crash that splintered the skiff into matchwood. They were
tossed into the air, smothered by a rush of water in which a
swimmer was helpless, slammed against stones—and thrown
to the surface at last in the great, still pool which circles round
and round at the foot of the rapids.

BILL'S HEAD came up first. He looked about, caught sight
of George floating limply, and grabbed him around the chin.
There was a bloody scar along the temple where George had
been rasped against a stone, but as he felt the pearler's hands he
opened his eyes and nodded to show he felt able to swim.

"Bones broken?" growled the pearler.

"Don't think so."

"Same here." Bill shook his wet head like a dog. "I'll say Fortier didn't want an outfit," he muttered. "Ours has certainly gone
to hell. Damned fool that I was, I never dreamed he'd wreck us.
Got your gun? Mine was in the bottom of the boat."

George fumbled at his hip and nodded.

"Don't try to use it. Powder's probably wet," Bill whispered. The advice seemed crazy to George until Bill swung his head sidewise. On the bank of the pool was the dugout which had followed them up river. To George's dazed senses the shore seemed lined with gigantic, bushy-headed apparitions.

"Eight of them, including our buddy Nyang," Bill muttered. " 'Sail right, kid. When you get your strength back, strike out for the other shore."

"We can't—get away?"

"Ain't going to try," said Bill calmly. "Pull my shirt off me, kid. Don't move or speak until you see me rush them, but then follow and get yourself killed. A spear point is pleasanter than starving in the jungle, but if they don't knock us on the head right away we've got a chance yet."

Bill swam to the very edge of the pool and then leaped to his feet in water that was scarcely knee-deep. He was stripped to the waist. The brilliantly colored dragon tattooed on his chest writhed as he filled his lungs, and from the mob of savages on the opposite bank arose a murmur. Nevertheless, they fingered spears.

"Nyang!" roared Bill peremptorily. "Come here, you damn hairy coal scuttle! Bring that boat! Think I'm going to swim across to you?"

Bill beckoned commandingly; pointed to the dugout, and the shore at his own feet. "Here! Here!" he repeated in the dialect.

The savages bunched together and began to jabber.

"Don't like that," muttered Bill under his breath. "Strut like an actor. George. They're like dogs. If they think we aren't afraid of them they'll be scared of us. Nyang!" he bellowed. The roar of the great voice made even George start. The savage addressed broke away from his fellows and started to shove the dugout from the shore. The remainder of the party followed more slowly. A few took paddles, but in the bow four men gripped spears and stone-headed clubs.

Nevertheless Bill continued to beckon as though displeased

by the delay. As the dugout approached he walked into the water. A spear was pointed at his breast, but he pushed the point aside with a careless sweep of his hand, caught the dugout's bow, and drew the boat far up the beach. He stepped back just as a war club was lifted, glared at the boatload of puzzled savages, and thumped his chest.

"Me—*barong—barong!*" he thundered.

The Papuans stared, uncertain whether to use their spears or not.

"NYANG!" BILL shouted.

Less frightened, and more convinced of Bill's friendliness than the rest, Nyang jumped over the side and waded ashore. The bush-knife Bill had given him the night before was in his loin cloth. The pearler reached out and took it, as a king might borrow a henchman's sword. Turning his back on the dugout, Bill strode up the beach to a sapling that grew at the water's edge, looked at the sun, and swung the heavy bush-knife impressively.

"You'll never cut through that!" George cried out. The sapling was nearly three inches at the butt, and appeared to be hard wood.

"Start shooting if I don't," Bill granted.

He rose on tiptoe. The flash of the sunlight on the descending blade was swift as the wink of a heliograph, yet Bill swung with such perfect coördination of shoulder and thigh that the blow did not seem to be the greatest possible to his vast strength. The sapling quivered and fell across the beach, cut through save for a shred of bark and fiber.

"Me—*barong,*" said Bill confidently. He pointed to himself, the other bank, and then far upstream. Giving the savages no time to recover from their astonishment he tucked the bush-knife under his arm and stepped into the dugout. The men who had wanted to spear him he thrust aside. The others made room as he clambered the length of the boat and seated himself in the stern.

George had wit enough to follow, and the inspiration to sit in the bottom of the dugout at Bill's feet. Nyang shoved the dugout into the stream. As he jumped aboard Bill took the bush-knife by the tip and handed it back.

"Though I hate to let it go," he muttered in George's ear. "Still, I guess we couldn't fight our way out. If I just hadn't killed a few of these muff heads yesterday! The men in these bush tribes are all related. That bird who was for spearing me was probably a brother."

"He can't be sure you killed any one. Fortier shot at all the bodies," George whispered.

Bill nodded absent-mindedly. For-tier, hurrying down by the trail around the rapids, had come into sight on the other side of the pool. He stopped short as he saw Bill in the stern of the dugout.

"Looking for a ship?" Bill hailed. "Come on aboard! This has got better engines and draft for river travel than the one I lost, but don't forget I'm skipper here. You'll sit in the bow, with the other treacherous, double-crossing riff-raff!"

In a whisper, as the dugout touched the bank, Bill added: "George has still got his gun, Fortier; and four bullets are plenty for you personally. And now, while these mop-headed niggers sweat this boat up the rapids, maybe you'll give me a civil answer to some of those propositions I asked awhile ago. It's too bad that every one makes mistakes—even ugly-looking pirates with whiskers."

"All right, damn you, I will!" snarled Fortier viciously. "The diamonds are where I said, but I didn't dare touch the idol without giving these blacks a better one, and I needed a white man's head for the ceremony!"

CHAPTER V

THE KARWAR

AN ABNORMAL HUSH hung over the Papuan village. The day was the third since the arrival of the expedition from down-river; the time, mid afternoon—an hour when the long community house with its high-peaked grass roof should have been murmurous with the activity of the savages.

To-day the women's chatter was stilled. Babies who cried were hushed instantly as by a hand across their lips, and even the men, who ordinarily lounged on the hard-packed clay which stretched bare and blue in front of the shoulder-high veranda of the great house, had withdrawn—whether inside, or into the jungle which crowded the village on all sides, neither George nor Bellow Bill could determine. The silence was portentous, and seemingly uncaused.

Far-away thunder muttered, yet the white edge of the storm cloud was barely visible above the high green hills that rose steeply behind the town. Other difference there was none. From their seat on the corner of the high veranda the place lay before the eyes of the two white men exactly as it had been for the last two days; exactly as Fortier had described it.

In the center of the stretch of blue clay before the house grew an enormous tree. Beneath this, facing the mountains with shield and spear raised, was the *karwar*—an idol of wood with a misshapen head about a foot high. Allowing for the rude carving the thing seemed to be a portrait of some dead Papuan rather than a devil conceived in the imagination of the artist. The mouth of the figure was open. In the gullet, presumably, were the diamonds. The savages had allowed neither white man to touch the figure, or even to examine it closely. They held it in a veneration akin to fear.

"Bill! Let's make a run for the river," said George tensely. "No one's watching! We can grab a dugout—"

"And get smashed up in the rapids again. Nothing to it, kid," rumbled the big pearler.

"But this damn quiet! Maybe they're getting ready for that—that ceremony Fortier threatened."

"Like enough."

"Then damn it, do something!" George exploded. He jumped to his feet, chin thrust out and tawny eyes glaring. "We're as good as prisoners! Even Nyang is avoiding us, and I'm not going to be killed and eaten by a bunch of stinking blacks! No one will even know what happened to me. 'Disappeared'—that's all the newspapers will say. And how!" George added with a snarl. "Damn it, Bill, I've seen you fight. Fortier knows the language. He's working these damn blacks up to take your head, and you just sit still and chew and spit, chew and spit." George glared around him for an enemy, and half drew his revolver, only to shove it angrily back in the holster.

"Can't you find anything to shoot at? Neither can I," Bill rumbled. "You're nervous, kid. Don't let the excitement get your goat."

"Excitement? We work like hell, we damn near get killed twice by treachery before we have time to think, and we wait in a lousy village eating sweet potatoes without salt while we wait for the official butcher to cut our throats!" complained George.

"That's what adventure is, kid—when it's real. Flying the Atlantic and climbing Mt. Everest and things like that are sporting, because they're arranged," said Bill coolly. "When you tell the world what you're going to do, why, you're a hero if you win, and if you lose you get a hell of a lot of sympathy. Maybe that helps some men to die. It wouldn't me. In real adventuring, if you win they say you did the trick for the money, and if you lose, you disappear. Sit down, kid, and try a chew of tobacco. The point is, our throats are still whole and our hands loose."

"You don't think I'm afraid?"

"Worse. You're excited. Fortier ain't scared of nothing, but he can't walk past that *karwar* without chewin' off half his beard. There's diamonds there all right, kid—I kind of admire Fortier."

"I'd like to break his neck!"

"YOU MAY have to, though it won't do us no good unless we checkmate his game, too. We can't *escape* down-river, George. The Papuans can travel faster than we. They've got to be willing to let us go. That's why I admire Fortier. Leaving aside the fact that he's a blackguard and a dirty murderer that don't care for nothing but money, he's a right able man. He was taken prisoner, and made himself a kind of boss-man among these blacks. That ain't much of a trick. I done the same.

"But he must have sat here like we're doing. He figured they were saving him to kill, and he seen them poking diamonds into that idol. He couldn't steal it and get away, so he persuaded them that he could get them a better one if they'd help him. His plan was to start up-river with a couple of adventurous fools, knock them on the head, with suitable ceremonies, and make another idol. Savages figure all white men are magicians. Stands to reason the spirit of a white-man could protect them better against devils than a Papuan could; but they think a lot of that idol they got. I wonder why they want a better one?"

"Who cares?" George growled.

"You do, unless you want to provide the steak and rib roast for the next feast."

"Fortier said the thunderstorms were bad," George suggested.

"That's my idea. Too bad we didn't carry a lightning rod, because there's a storm coming now that will be a buster." Bellow Bill listened to the muttering thunder, and to another sound, almost the same in pitch, but of human origin, that was audible at the other end of the long community house.

"Here comes Fortier and his playmates," Bill added briskly. "Keep cool, now, and watch that no one spears me in the back."

Along the front of the house came a line of more than twenty warriors in single file. Their tattoo markings had been daubed with whitish clay until they resembled skeletons, but, though each man was armed with a shield and a spear pointed with a long sliver of bamboo in preparation for war, they did not even glance at the two white men on the veranda. They moved at a shuffling walk which was almost a dance step. In rhythm to this they stabbed with their spears at the air. Three times around the long community house they marched in utter silence.

The thunder rumbled in the hills. Birds called in the jungle. There was no other sound.

"Where's Fortier?" George whispered. "That's Nyang leading that bunch."

Bill shrugged his shoulders and laid a finger on his lips.

After the third circuit of the house Nyang danced toward the idol. The men behind changed their formation and formed a long rank three paces in the rear, facing the storm. Nyang uttered a piercing howl.

Up came the shields. The spear points darted like one toward the oncoming clouds.

As though in answer a jagged sheet of lightning ripped from horizon to horizon across the blackness. The leaves of the great tree stirred in the great wind; from the hitherto silent savages huddled in the great house arose a groan.

"Tried to turn the storm aside, and failed. Now what?" George whispered.

FOR A moment Nyang stood with head bowed and shield and spear lowered. Then he began to speak to the *karwar*. The guttural accents began deep in his chest, rose higher and higher until he was screaming and dancing. The invocation was scarcely half completed before a native girl walked timidly from the house and advanced, step by step, toward the idol.

She was not beautiful, but she was slender and young and moved with a terror so manifest that George gripped his revolver to prevent a human sacrifice. His fears proved groundless. At the rank of warriors the girl fell flat on her face and wriggled forward over the ground until she was at the idol. Loudly Nyang shouted. She reached out, and the pale green light cast by the oncoming storm seemed to gather in the center of the diamond which she dropped into the mouth of the *karwar*.

The shields of the warriors were flung up. Their spears stabbed at the ragged cloud edge—but the only answer was a greater darkness, a more nearly continuous flash and boom of thunder and lightning, and the splash of the first drops of rain. The girl sprang up and ran for the house. More slowly the warriors slunk after her, trailing their spears. Invocation and sacrifice alike had failed.

There was a second groan from the savages, but a white man's shout drowned it. Pell-mell through the rank of the retreating warriors burst a mob of the younger men of the village, also clay-smeared and armed with shield and spear, but moving without ceremony. In a compact mass they ran to the veranda where Bellow Bill sat. The yellow bamboo spear points bristled at the edge of the planks.

"Watch my back, George," rumbled the pearler. He rose, ready to dodge a thrown spear, but did not retreat.

Fortier waited until the last of Nyang's party had got into the house before he stepped into the open. The bearded pirate had removed shirt and trousers. He wore a bark loin-cloth; his body was smeared with clay over the thick black hair on his chest. In his arms he bore two freshly carved wooden figures which he set down where all could see.

The carving was crude, but nevertheless the larger of the two *karwars* bore a grotesque resemblance to Bill's great head, with its thick, curly hair, and the chin of the smaller man was a caricature of Carstair's heavy jaw.

"Better step down and die decent, Bill," called Fortier hoarsely. "There'll be a dozen spears through you if you move, and I posted a party in the room behind you."

"Steady, George," Bill warned under his breath. "Killing won't suit you quite, Fortier," he answered aloud. "You've tried to hard to capture me alive. Call off your men and I'll step down and fight you—with my bare hands. If you lick me you can tie me up and execute me proper."

"To hell with you! I'm taking no chances!" Fortier screamed, beside himself with excitement. "Step down or I'll give the word!"

"It's *my* head the Papuans want. Turn George over to Nyang's crowd and send him down-river. I'll stand where I am until they're clear of the bank."

"No! No! No!" Fortier howled. "I need the schooner to get away—"

Behind Bill a revolver hammer clicked on a moisture-spoiled shell. With a curse George pulled trigger again. The heavy gun boomed. Fortier flung himself on his face, but George fired again and again. Twice the bullets ripped the clay near the prostrate figure: then the hammer clicked again and Fortier sprang up with a triumphant howl. He was unhurt.

"Kill! Kill!" he screamed.

THE SPEAR-POINTS hedging the veranda flicked backward for the throw—but there was no target.

A sweep of Bill's arm flung George to the rear where he was out of the savages' sight because of the height of the veranda floor. Bill himself dived headlong at the grass wall, crashing through the thin bamboos which supported it. Through the gaping hole he reached back, caught George by the collar, and pulled him headlong through. A few spears, hastily flung, skewered through the walls, but for the moment the two were shielded. They were in the room assigned to their own use.

"Follow me—straight through the walls. Fortier's got the doors guarded," Bill snapped and flung himself at the next barrier. He tumbled headlong into the central passage that ran the length of the community house. To the right the passage was blocked by the backs of a crowd who menaced a doorway with their spears. Bill leaped among them before the long weapons could be reversed.

At Bill's heels George went down under the weight of

numbers, but took a clay-greased young Papuan with him by the throat. Grimly he throttled the youngster, while bare and booted feet trampled him. Bill roared. A body collapsed upon George and was flung aside; a hand jerked him to his feet. From some warrior Bill had snatched a stone-headed club and laid about him in a circle. Four men were down, the rest had leaped back, howling and struggling to handle their spears in the narrow, crowded space.

"For God's sake, keep your feet, kid," Bill panted, and went charging into the mob. Fist and club cleared a passage through the savages. A chance jab of a spear gashed his ribs, but behind the broad, tattooed back George followed in safety, as a halfback trots through a football line in the wake of a plunging tackle.

Bill turned through the nearest door, knocked a warrior sprawling with a backhanded sweep of his left arm, and broke through the outer wall of grass.

Lightning blazed as the two leaped down onto the hard blue clay. A crash of thunder was followed by a drumming roar of rain which fell in vertical white sheets. At the corner of the house three of Fortier's young warriors were peering right and left. They raised a feeble yell at the sight of the white men—a sound lost in the roar of thunder and rain—raised spears, but advanced only half-heartedly to the attack. By brandishing his club Bill brought them to a halt.

"To the jungle, kid!" he panted and led the way across the slippery ground at a stumbling run. He had almost reached the thick wall of foliage when he heard George cry out. The shout was more of sheer surprise than pain.

Bill turned. George was on hands and knees. A thin bamboo spear transfixed the calf of his left leg, but he was trying to get up—still unconscious in his excitement, that he had been wounded.

Bill hurled his club at the warriors who had flung the spear. All three fled. The main body was still yelling inside the house, following Bill's path. The pearler was able to kneel by George, snap the haft of the spear between his hands, and draw the shaft through the wound. He was about to pick his partner up in his arms when George got on his feet—white with pain, but grinning gamely. Arm in arm they plunged into the jungle.

CHAPTER VI

THE STORM

FORTIER VAULTED THROUGH the hole torn in the outer house wall and ran across the open space, only to stop at the point where the disarranged leaves and vines marked the beginning of Bill's trail. The rain sluiced off the pirate's naked body, washing the clay with which he had smeared himself into long streaks. In the guttural language of the tribe he howled orders, curses; but with the dreaded thunder cannonading overhead and the glare of lightning brilliant, no man could have led the Papuans into the brush.

The gods were angry. Manoin himself waited in the woods for the daring savage. The women and old men who formed Nyang's faction were flat on their faces, shivering, terrified with the vast and unreasoning fear which makes a dog tremble and whine during a storm.

Even the younger men who had follow Fortier now slunk away from the bearded white man as though he, too, were a devil whose counsel had brought upon their village the greatest storm in their memory. Spears were cast down. The young warriors huddled body against body under the high veranda, arms raised to shield their eyes from the glare of lightning; fingers in ears to still the voice of angry gods. Fortier stood alone—and he had no stomach to plunge into the thicket single-handed and unarmed.

His coup had failed, yet the panic which had seized the village was his opportunity. With a last snarl at his abject followers he strode through the sluicing rain and snatched up the *karwar*.

He expected resistance. Nyang, indeed, did start to his feet and reach for a spear, but no other Papuan followed the example.

They groaned as they watched their protecting spirit being carried away. To their superstitious senses the thunder and lightning seemed to redouble in volume, yet the bolts left the impious white man untouched. The lightning flares gleamed on Fortier's wet skin as he tramped to the river, tossed the *karwar* into a dugout, and pushed off downstream.

At the end of the river trail was Bill's schooner. Fortier did not doubt that he could overpower the *kanakas* left aboard and disappear out to sea. Once a few diamonds were converted into cash he would defy Bellow Bill or the English police to find him again. Though the voyage down-river would be slow, the pirate believed he could keep ahead of Bill and George.

Meanwhile Bellow Bill pushed his way through the jungle by main strength. Vines tripped him and blocked his path. Under the canopy of leaves the lightning glare became a flickering greenish light. The rain drenched the two white men like a warm shower bath. They left a plain path behind, and for a time they expected at any moment to see the green tunnel filled with fuzzy heads and brown bodies. When they realized no pursuit was being made, however, Bill suddenly knelt, stripping off the rags of his shirt.

"Lemme see that leg," he commanded. George sat down. The pearler wiped off the blood and dirt and began to put a bandage in place. He worked slowly, and little by little he began to frown.

"DOESN'T HURT much," said George cheerfully. "Let it go, Bill. We'll circle and grab a dugout. To hell with the diamonds! I've had all the excitement I want."

"Kid, do you remember the seared stumps of Fortier's fingers?" Bill answered. "That wound will get infected unless it's treated properly."

"Blood poisoning?"

"Unless I can boil the bandages and carry you every foot of the way—and I haven't even got a match." Bill rose and tightened his belt. "Lie here until the rain stops, George," he ordered calmly. "Then if I don't come back for you, sing out. Remember all Fortier really wants is the diamonds."

"You're not going back to that village alone," George snapped.

"It's nothing but cool sense, partner. If I'm speared you won't be any worse off than you are now, really. If I work it, you'll be jake."

"But you could get me to a doctor—"

"I've seen what happens to a wound in the tropic brush. Yeah, I could get you to a doctor all right—in about a week. When I got to Port Moresby, the people and the newspapers would call me a hero." With grim mockery the pearler began to quote an imaginary conversation. " 'Did you hear what Bellow Bill did? Quite a guy, ain't he, to pack his partner down from the interior on his back? Too bad, wasn't it, the partner was so far gone he died in the hospital!' Like hell it wouldn't be my fault!" the pearler snorted. "I don't care what the papers or the outsiders say about me. They're always trying to make a hero out of somebody, and they never know the facts. What counts with me is what *I* think about what I did; and taking you to a dugout would be just plain cowardice, because it would be perfectly damn safe for me."

"I'd rather you'd do it."

"You're game," Bill conceded. "Shooting at Fortier was game, and I don't blame you for missing. You just didn't see that even if you killed him the blacks was sure to attack us—which was all they could do anyhow. You're game enough now to risk blood poisoning. But I'm going back because I know absolutely that you'll get it if you aren't taken care of."

Bill turned on his heel. Without a pause he walked down the path he had torn through the jungle and stepped out into the driving rain. He expected that Fortier would attack him with the best weapons the village boasted, and though a glance at the huddled mass of savages under the veranda revealed that danger from them was a thing of the past, Bill approached warily. He picked up the stone-hafted club he had thrown at the three young warriors and waited for Fortier to show himself.

Instead Nyang rose and crawled over the slippery blue clay. The brown face was strained with horror and dismay. His gestures were clear enough.

The *karwar,* gone; the bearded man, gone in a boat; the skies, angry. Tentatively Nyang pulled at Bill's arm and pointed down-river.

"You want your idol back, huh? "Bill rumbled. "No worse than I want the man carrying it. Well, we'll see. Got fire, got hot water?"

Nyang did not understand, so Bill walked into the great house. Despite the drenching rain, a few fires smoldered in the clay fireplaces. He added fuel to the embers, placed a clay water pot on to boil, and went out to get George.

BILL REALIZED that every minute he delayed was of ines-timable value to Fortier, but he did not hasten as they sat in the house. Nyang pulled at his shoulder and pointed to the river; ran out and returned with six older men, all carrying paddles as well as spears, and by a dozen signs urged Bill to take the trail. The pearler nodded, but his eyes never left the water in the pot. He sat chewing tobacco and tossing on small sticks until even George cried out the water must be hot enough.

"Boiling means boiling, kid," Bill grunted. He found Forti-er's shirt, prepared lint and bandages, and boiled everything for five long minutes while George tossed with impatience. Then he treated the wound. A surgeon could not have done a cleaner and a neater job with the materials at hand.

"And now what's going to help you is speed. Watch us make knots," Bill remarked cheerfully, signing to Nyang to lead the way. The savage had also made preparations. George was bundled onto a litter. Through rain which had commenced to descend with lessened force now that the storm was passing toward the coast, he was borne at a run to the river edge. Bill and the savages leaped into the boat and plied paddles like men in a frenzy.

They overtook Fortier at the rapids.

The bearded pirate had not dared to run the rocky gorge in his unwieldy boat, and had been too wise to abandon the craft. With a short length of bark rope he was working the dugout downstream by snubbing from tree to tree. He had made phenomenal progress. When discovered he was in the rocky cleft almost at the foot of the rapids where the great rocks in the stream were most abundant. The cliff shielded him from attack from the bank. He could be reached only by the narrow, slippery trail which wound along the water's edge.

Fortier had no weapon except a stone-headed club. He saw that escape was impossible. Nyang and three natives sprinted down the bank to guard the foot of the portage. Bellow Bill marched down the slippery river trail to block retreat upstream. A club was tucked under one tattooed arm.

From the dugout the bearded pirate plucked the *karwar* and up-ended the idol so that a few diamonds trickled from the gaping mouth into his sound hand. Near the bank was a flat stone, scarcely five feet square, and a long jump from the bank. Fortier leaped upon it, balanced the *karwar* on the extreme edge, and turned to face Bill, the club poised in his maimed right hand, the diamonds clenched in his left fist.

On the bank Bellow Bill hesitated, weighing the chances of making a leap for the stone and taking a blow while he was off balance, against the alternative of wading into the stream and fighting thigh-deep in rushing water while Fortier stood dry-shod.

"Don't like the look of it, hey, Bill?" the bearded pirate mocked. "You can have me speared from the cliff, but I'll push the idol into the water. The diamonds there will roll out and I'll throw these sparklers away." Fortier opened his left hand and let the smooth stones roll back and forth in his palm. "Half of them yours, Bill," he tempted. "Thousands of pounds and the proof of the mine, against a passage to the coast. Just to the coast, Bill. I don't ask to set foot on your schooner. I know you ain't a hotheaded fool to hold a grudge because I fought you. Every man for himself, eh, Bill?"

"**WILL YOU** wade ashore and let me tie you hand and foot?" rumbled the pearler.

"Like hell! I got to be able to protect what's mine."

"With a wounded partner I can't trust you no other way," said Bill coolly. "Protect your damned diamonds, then!"

He flung his club and leaped.

The heavy weapon struck Fortier in the chest and spoiled the blow aimed at Bill's head. Chest to chest the two big men came together. They staggered from the impact. A lunging foot knocked the *karwar* into the water, and diamonds pattered on the wet stone as Fortier gripped Bill's throat with his left hand and clubbed viciously at the back of the pearler's blond head. Both Bill's arms were wrapped around Fortier's naked body.

Inch by inch the bearded head went back. Fortier dropped the club. His left hand pounded at Bill's face. Blood spouted from Bill's nose. He grunted and shifted his grip to the deadly double Nelson—arms under and around Fortier's shoulders, both hands pressing upward against the bearded chin.

Fortier kicked for the groin. The sickening pain of the blow straightened Bill up in a conclusive jerk. All the strength of shoulders, back and arms was flung against the point of Fortier's chin. Before that spasmodic pressure a vertebra snapped. Fortier dropped, with a broken neck. Bill collapsed upon the limp body, quivering and retching from the foul.

Minutes passed before Bill was able to sit up, and when he saw George being carried toward him down the difficult river trail he refrained from making the effort necessary to wade ashore. From a hollow in the stone he picked a diamond which had not been brushed off in the struggle. There was only one. Bill coolly moved Former's body to make sure. The diamond, however, was large enough to make a jewel of two carats even after cutting and looked to be unflawed and blue white. Bill grinned to himself sardonically and filled his cheek with fine-cut. A virgin diamond—which would stay virgin. It would never have a companion. All the rest were in the river.

CHAPTER VII

THE NEW IDOL

THE THREE PAPUANS from upstream placed George's litter on the river bank. After learning that Bill was not badly hurt, the tawny-headed young man said nothing, nor did Bill. From downstream Nyang and his companions toiled up the difficult path and joined the group. The savage face was a picture of dejection. In his arms he bore the *karwar,* sadly damaged by the rocks of the river. The spear was broken off, the shield split, and the face battered. In mute dismay Nyang pointed out the injuries.

"Can't think that's a god no more, can you, buddy?" Bill rumbled. George took the image and held it upside down. No diamonds rolled out. With a grin Bill tossed the big jewel across the rushing water into the younger man's hands.

"Here's one to roll across your dad's desk—or have cut into a solitaire for your fiancée some day. A girl that loves you enough will believe the story of how you got it," the pearler chuckled. "Unless—well, first we've got to go to Port Moresby to get your wound healed. Afterward we can come back. Big party. Miners. Commercial development of the country."

"I don't need the money, or a business," George refused. "But hold on, Bill. You've taught me something of what is due a partner means. I'll finance a company for you if you want."

"And keep me here for life watching the works? You will not!" Bill snorted with emphasis. "But I'll tell you what: after the doctors are done with you, I know a place—'way down

New Zealand way—where a dying diver told me there was an untouched bank of pearl shell. Want to have a go at that with me, George? It'll be excitement!"

"Well—no, Bill, I don't," said the younger man, though he hesitated somewhat. "Once is enough. I don't mind the danger. It's the hardship, the strain. I've been in hell the last three days!"

"Why, I've had a good time this whole cruise!" cried Bill almost indignantly. "You'll get used to waiting and to drawing a blank. Suppose we haven't the diamonds? We've been to the field and we've trumped Fortier's ace. I didn't mean to kill him, George—though that's just as well, because he wouldn't be satisfied till he was dead or had hogged the field. I don't see any fun digging into blue clay when you know there's diamonds there, but if we don't, the Aikora'll just be what it always was—a question mark. And as for the pearls—the native yarn is that something kills every diver who goes over the side after them. Let's go and find out what that 'something' is. Sounds like a devil fish or one of those big clams."

"Men differ. That doesn't sound like fun to me any more," said George firmly. "No, Bill—after Port Moresby, home!"

"Shucks, kid, I never kept a partner yet," rumbled the pearler. "You'd make a damned fine one now that you're seasoned, but—" The tattooed shoulders shrugged, and the quid of fine-cut splashed in the water. In Bill's mind the matter was settled. He waded ashore and touched Nyang's shoulder, then pointed from the broken idol to Fortier's body.

"Boss devil," he mouthed slowly, making signs to clarify his meaning. "Worse devil than thunderstorm—or woods—or river. A man who never thinks of anything but money is the worst devil there can be. Carve *karwar* like him."

The Papuan nodded eagerly.

"So that's fixed," Bill grunted. "I wish the mop-head could really understand what I told him. It'll be hell for him and his tribe when whites come in to dig the diamonds; and we both come near owing him our lives."

"I understand, though," said George. "If I'm asked how I got that diamond I'm going to say it's the gift of a man who thought more of a partner—even a black one—than he did of a thousand diamonds like it."

"Aw, say it's from a roughneck who likes his fun. That'll be nearer the truth," rumbled Bellow Bill.

DEVIL PEARLS

*Bellow Bill Williams knew it wasn't kindliness
that led his worst enemy to give him the key
to a South Seas treasure—but he didn't know
what a strange menace guarded that hoard*

CHAPTER I

A DANGEROUS LEGACY

NEVER HAD SUCH pearls been seen, even in Fakarava, the chief harbor of the Paumotu Archipelago and the center of the pearling industry throughout the South Seas.

Each of the three gems which "One Eye" Kerrigan brought back from his last cruise was over half an inch in diameter. Each was perfectly spherical, and the weight of each was within a few grains of the same amount.

Such exact matching was as incredible as the size. Indeed, buyers believed at first that they must be examining a masterpiece of the art of the pearl imitator or pearl culturer.

Experts set that suspicion at rest. The nacre which coated the gems was the work of a pearl oyster, not of human skill; and though the Japanese have succeeded in making oysters coat small objects placed inside the shell with mother of pearl, such cultured gems are seldom spherical. The matrix is placed against one of the muscles with which the bivalve opens its shell, whereas the true pearl is found inside the oyster's flesh.

These gems of Kerrigan's were true pearls. Like wildfire rumors spread through Fakarava. The dirty, vicious, old pearling skipper had discovered a bed of pearls untouched for centuries, and he murdered every man aboard his ship to keep the secret to himself. No, contradicted another rumor. From some native who had preserved the ancient lore of the Paumotus he had learned the mystery which still baffles scientists: what causes pearls to grow in the flesh of an oyster, and how to initiate and expedite

that growth for his own gain. Once the secret was learned, One Eye had killed the native and his own crew.

For certain it was that One Eye Kerrigan had gone to sea with two native divers and a cook, but had sailed his schooner back alone—worn to a skeleton, racked with a cough, and with an insane and vicious glare in his single eye.

When he left the pearl buyers, all Fakarava was crowded around the door of the shop to induce or force him to reveal his secret, yet that greed-maddened mob quailed before the look on his face and drew apart to give him passage.

The wrinkled skin was drawn tight across his cheek bones and sagged in pouches upon his skinny neck. The face was mottled red and white in patches distinct as daubs of paint. He coughed and spat blood, glaring at the men that hailed him as friend, his dirty white mustache bristling above lips that lifted from his teeth in the snarl of a mad dog.

"Yes, there are more pearls, damn you all!" he snarled. "Now get out of my way and let me die in a bed. I'll tell the latitude

"Gimme that paper!" Twist commanded.
"And move slow, Bill"

and longitude before I croak, and you can fight for the pearls with the devils that guard them!"

Straight across the street he walked through a silent mob, registered at the hotel, and fell into bed, where he lay and coughed. A doctor, hastily summoned, reported that One Eye was at the last gasp of pneumonia. Only the venomous strength of his will had enabled him to reach Fakarava. By no possibility could he live out the night.

UPSTAIRS KERRIGAN lay and coughed. When he was delirious he babbled of devils and pools of ink. When he was sane he glared out of one eye at the ceiling and smiled at some secret of his own, in a way that made the doctor shudder.

Afternoon became twilight. After the quick sunset of the tropics, night settled down, dark and starlit; and still One Eye held his tongue.

"Devil or not, you'll dive, or I'll put a bullet through your black hide!" he screamed once—but never a word of latitude or longitude, and the disappointed listeners were only able to guess more accurately at the fate which had overtaken Kerrigan's crew.

As the shops closed and the day's work ended, all the white

men of Fakarava drifted one by one into the sick room, into the passages outside, into the hotel lobby.

All, that is, save "Bellow Bill" Williams. Kerrigan, who hated every one, hated Bill worst; and Bill refused to fawn on an enemy he despised, even for the sake of such pearls as have not been seen since Cleopatra tossed her earrings into vinegar and drained the mixture to prove to Mark Antony that she could spend more on a single draught than his vaunted extravagance had lavished on his banquet, when he feasted a hundred guests.

Bellow Bill sat in an *estaminet* which even the proprietor had deserted. A glass of beer was gripped in one huge, tattooed fist. His chin was bowed on his chest, for in his heart he envied One Eye Kerrigan the adventure which must have preceded the possession of the pearls. For money Bill cared less than the majority of men. He owned a pearling schooner and a bank account of several hundred pounds.

He needed no more, as he lived for the fun, and not the profit. That it had been One Eye Kerrigan, and not he, who had found a lagoon or a secret which had baffled the efforts of pearlers and men of science for decades, made Bill feel worse than the loss of an opportunity to be rich. He drained his beer and thrust a quid of fine cut chewing tobacco into his cheek.

The big head with its thatch of curly coppery-gold hair lifted. The shoulders, wide enough to block a door, shrugged. Bill wore only duck trousers and a thin cotton singlet. In the lamplight the serpents and dragons which covered his torso from throat to waist seemed to writhe as though tattooers, Chinese, Malay, European and Polynesian, had endowed the art of their needle with life.

After all, Bill implied by the shrug, he had had his fun. Let One Eye keep his money. Much good it would do the dirty old reprobate!

A sudden murmur of excited voices from the direction of the hotel came to his ears, but he did not move. He would go on collecting pearl shell, he supposed, and wait with what patience he could for the next unusual event.

Pearl shell—shimmering stuff brought by grinning brown men who could stay three minutes under water; romantic, exciting stuff that gave Bill an excuse for poking his schooner into the most out-of-the-way corners of the South Pacific.

For him pearl shell was a means, a door that might lead to an opportunity for the excitement he loved; and yet, in the eyes of the traders to whom he sold it, it was just so much merchandise that could be sold for a thousand a ton in Philadelphia, and which eventually became buttons and knife handles. Pearling was a prosaic business, after all.

THE DOOR of the *estaminet* burst open. The doctor who had been attending Kerrigan ran excitedly into the room. "Bill, One Eye wants to see you," he panted.

"Yeah, I'll bet he does!" boomed the pearler robustly. Bill's voice was as big as all the rest of him. The deep tones reverberated through the empty *estaminet* like the grumble of a brass drum tapped gently with the fingers. "He was afraid of me while he had his health. Now that he's passing out, he wants to spit in my face."

"It's the wish of a dying man," reproved the physician.

"Oh, I'm coming all right," Bill rumbled. "Let the mean old devil have his fun! I can stand it, but just don't think I expect anything from One Eye but dirt."

He rose, stretching. The doctor, however, on fire with suspense and impatience, snatched eagerly at his arm. Outside the *estaminet* Bill was dragged along at a trot. As they entered the hotel the crowd closed in behind him, and poured on his heels into the sick room.

The shuffle of many feet on the bare wooden floor brought Kerrigan out of a stupor. The one eye opened and fixed itself on Bill.

"Pencil—paper," Kerrigan whispered.

They were thrust into his hands. With his last strength he

scrawled half a dozen figures, folded the paper, and handed it
to Bill.

"In a deep pool by a lava cliff all pitted with blow holes,"
Kerrigan whispered. Every word was audible, for the crowd
held its breath. "The oysters are all in one spot. Big shells lying
on the clean black sand in six fathoms of water. You're the one I
want to go after them, Bill. A child could get them up, and you
claim to be a man."

The whisper ended in a fit of coughing, and Kerrigan sank
down against the pillow. The skin of the skull-like face had a
purple tint. He was so weak that a grimace meant as a sneer
became a horrible and meaningless twist of the lips.

"Look at it," whispered Kerrigan. "I know you, Bill. You'll—
go!"

Bill glanced at the scrawl:

20-16-18   136-37-42

Though latitude south and longitude west were omitted, the
position given was most exact. From his detailed knowledge of
the South Seas, Bill could locate the approximate locality. It was
some small island just beyond the limits of the trade winds, and
therefore remote from the usual track of pearling skippers and
island traders. He refolded the paper and stuck it into his pocket.

"You're right, I'll go! But why pick on me, One Eye?" he
asked joyously, and bent to the lips of the dying man to catch
the answer. Kerrigan was failing fast.

"Because I—hate you!" came the whisper. "The devils—that
got my crew—will get you. For you'll go, you fool! Bellow Bill,
he ain't afraid of nothing—"

The sardonic whisper ended in a choking gurgle. Kerrigan
shuddered, and was still. An expression of vicious satisfaction
was fixed on the purplish features immovable in death. The
doctor thrust Bill back.

"He's gone," said the physician; but with his professional duty
finished, curiosity could no longer be restrained. "Did he know

what he was saying, do you think? Does the position he wrote for you seem to be that of a real island?"

The doctor had not heard One Eye's last words. Like the crowd, he could not understand why Bill's face should be grim as well as eager.

"One Eye knew exactly what he was doing, and sized me up dead right," Bill rumbled. "Out of my way, now, lads. I'm saying less about these pearls than One Eye himself—for much better reasons."

CHAPTER II

SECRETS ARE HARD TO KEEP

BILL SPOKE CONFIDENTLY enough, but he knew the crowd would never permit him to walk out with the paper in his pocket. Had he been armed—had he not been jammed in a crowd with men touching both elbows—he might have tried to burn One Eye's scrawl. Once the paper was out of his pocket, however, it would be snatched from his hands.

He stood still, seemingly irresolute, really stimulated by the danger and the intense battle of wits to come. He lived for such moments. His chance was to turn the furious greed of the crowd that hemmed him in to his own ends, as a boat utilizes the force and fury of a barrier of surf to bear it over the obstacle.

Bill faced scoundrels who would knife him without hesitation for a glance at the paper he carried; honest citizens with personality and standing enough to weld the mob into a unit and insist that he read the secret aloud.

Bellow Bill began to smile—the smile of a boxer in the ring.

Let either faction try!

The individuals in the crowd were known to him. By the door Perrault, the spade-bearded buyer of pearls, stood with mouth half open, scowling in indecision. There was the leader of the honest faction—fortunately, a slow-witted man.

The rascals had already worked their way closer to the bed. Next to Bill stood "Fatty" Clarke, a hogshead of gross, sweating flesh. Hairless arms burned a light pink by the sun were crossed over the rolls of soft fat draped across the enormous chest. A head shorter than Bill's six feet and two inches of hard muscle.

Fatty's mere bulk barred his exit. Three hundred pounds of fat cannot be shoved aside. Fatty also thought slowly, but the piggish eyes were buried in the bloated cheeks, crisscrossed with the blue veins of dissipation.

Fatty's plan was already settled. The position he had chosen, near the bed and beside the open window, seemed part of it. He was waiting—and Bill waited, too, tensed for the first word or movement in the crowd.

"Twist" Keith, Fatty's partner, edged toward the open window. Twist was little and sun-dried and lame. His left foot was twisted inward, so that he swung it sidewise, but despite that, he was sinewy and active enough. In height he barely reached five feet, and his weight never exceeded a hundred pounds, but few men were more feared by the natives or granted more respect by white men.

Twist was dangerous, and quick as a hungry tomcat. Even Bill, who was expecting some movement, was caught aback by the suddenness of his actions.

A gun jabbed Bill's spine. Another flashed beneath his arm and was leveled at the face of the nearest man, who flung himself backward with an oath.

"Git back—git back, all!" Twist snarled.

The crowd knew he would shoot. A few in the rear continued to shove, but those in front fought to widen a space between themselves and the muzzle of his gun.

Fatty drew a revolver.

"Right against the wall!" he shouted.

"Gimme that paper!" Twist commanded. "Move slow, Bill!"

Bill moved very slowly. He wadded the paper into a ball between his fingers before taking it from his pocket, intending to snap it through the open window, but Twist was alert. He pocketed one gun, leaving Fatty to cover the crowd, and seized Bill's wrist. The bony fingers snatched the crumpled paper, popped it into his mouth. Twist's lame leg swung over the window sill.

THE CROWD growled. From the window to the ground was a drop of less than ten feet, but they dared not rush Fatty. A thud told that Twist had landed.

"Keep away from that door," said Fatty thickly.

Sweat was pouring in streams from his bloated face, for the strain of maintaining the drop upon so many was tremendous. He could not hold them long. His purpose was to give his partner a start.

Bill measured the distance to the window and waited for Fatty to direct all his attention to those in front. The instant the fat neck shifted, Bill caught the sides of the window and flung himself feet first through the opening. He fell heavily.

Above him burst a concerted roar, and heads thrust through the window. Evidently his diversion had cost Fatty the drop.

But before any one else could follow his example Bill was sprinting down the road toward the harbor. He led his nearest pursuer by as much as Twist led him, and he was positive the lame little man would make straight for Fatty's schooner. At worst, the race for the pearls would he confined to two boats. With luck, he might catch Twist before he reached the beach and prevent him from reading the paper at all.

Twist, however, had made too good use of his start. As Bill sprinted out onto the beach, a dugout was moving away from the shore and the flare of a match lighted the lame man's emaciated features.

Behind Bill sounded the shouts and footfalls of running men. He did not hesitate. Trusting to the darkness to conceal him, he ran straight into the surf and swam in the wake of the dugout.

Of course, he was distanced. The two Marquesan divers who worked with Twist and Fatty were plying paddles with all their strength, and they gained two hundred yards in the three that separated the schooner from the beach. Before Twist could get under way, however, he would have a cable to slip and a mainsail to hoist, and that he had perceived the swimmer behind him was altogether unlikely.

The halyard blocks were still squealing when Bill swam under the schooner's stern. He could guess that the two divers were swaying on the tackles, but Twist's location was highly problematical. Though Bill could reach up and catch the low rail of the schooner, the movement would alarm any one at the wheel, where Twist would probably be located.

Nevertheless, that was a risk Bill had to take. He came out of the water with a leap and a kick, hauling himself over the rail with all the strength of his arms, and tumbling head first onto the deck.

By the binnacle light he glimpsed Twist. The latter yelled to his divers, dropped the wheel, and pawed for his gun. Bill caught him by the ankle and jerked him to the deck.

Once down, the little man was as helpless as a child before the pearler's strength. Bill twisted the gun out of his hand and flung it overboard, punched once and felt the emaciated body go limp under the blow. Then the two divers leaped upon him.

Had they been white men wearing shoes, Bill would never have risen, but their bare heels only hurt him without crippling. He caught their legs and dragged them down upon him. The three rolled across the deck, biting, kicking and punching, while over their heads the main boom slatted to and fro and wild yells from the shore indicated that the pursuing crowd had taken renewed heart, and would soon be off in any boat they could find.

BOTH MARQUESAN divers were big and powerful men, but the native of the South Seas fights like a cat—with nails and teeth. Bill was bitten. Fingers gouged at his eyes, and the two fought so well together that for a desperate minute all he could

do was to roll over and over, keeping them all in the compara-
tively open deck and avoiding the disaster of being penned,
between the after cabin and the rail, where one diver could hold
him while the other found some sort of club.

Purposefully he fought to get one arm free. Their biting hurt
abominably. Bill flung himself on his back, glimpsed a curly
head against the whiteness of the mainsail, and swung. His fist
landed on the point of a chin, and that diver promptly ceased
from troubling.

With considerable relish Bill started after the one who had
been doing the biting. He caught his second enemy by the
throat, held him while he got up, and, still holding him, swung
for the jaw. The blow knocked the Marquesan ten feet. His head
struck against the after cabin with a thwack that made the big
pearler feel much better.

Bill stooped over Twist, found and pocketed the second gun,
and started to search for the paper. It was not in the trousers
pockets. Twist was coming to, so Bill got a bucket of water and
flung it in his face.

"Ain't you got no respect for a last will and testament? Where's
that note?" he demanded.

Twist groaned and dragged himself to a sitting posture, his
back against the binnacle.

"Hell, Bill, you damn near broke my jaw," he complained. "I
didn't mean to pick on you. I thought One Eye was going to
pass the word to some fathead like Perrault. Worked it pretty
neat, didn't I?"

"Next time muzzle your divers. Biting's uncomfortable,"
objected Bill, who was still sore. "Where's that note, I said?"

The lame little man pulled a sodden ball of paper out of the
waistband of his trousers. Bill threw it overboard.

"Twenty degrees, sixteen minutes and eighteen seconds south
latitude, one hundred thirty-six degrees, thirty-seven minutes,
and forty-two seconds west longitude," Twist quoted sarcastically. "Too bad I got a good memory for figures, ain't it, Bill? Lots

of men, just glancing at that by match light, might have forgotten it. Know of any volcanic island down that way? I don't."

"Damned if you ain't a cheerful cuss! So you're going, too, huh?" Bellow Bill renewed his chew, and spat thoughtfully over the rail, "I ought to steal your schooner and take you along—except that three men in irons ain't cheerful company," he remarked. "I suppose you'd plug me if you still had this gun and I knew so much."

"Not me. That'd be Fatty's speed. He's the lad for the rough stuff," Twist contradicted. "I do the thinking and he the dirt. Suits us both perfect. However"—he hesitated—"what are you going to do, Bill?"

"Cut up your running rigging and swim over to my schooner. I can't keep you from following; but I'll get there first."

"Correct. In that case I'll wait and pick up Fatty—which I didn't intend to do," said Twist shamelessly. "He's handy in case of trouble. There's something queer about this."

"There's a boat putting out from shore."

Twist trimmed the sheet and took the wheel. The schooner gathered way through the water.

"I'LL SAIL out to sea and then back by your schooner, Bill," he remarked. "Neither of us wants to let anybody else in on this game. You can spoil my running rigging anywhere. Bill, we might go partners."

"You'd double cross your own mother."

"Correct," Twist admitted. "I'd like to slip one over on Bellow Bill Williams, too. We little shrimps have got our pride. But even if we're going to scrap, I'd like to swap one bit of info. Have you noticed that position is worked out in *seconds?* Now, One Eye was a rotten navigator, even for an island skipper. Do you work out your sights as fine as that, Bill?"

The big pearler shook his head. Twist was right in saying he had not noticed this point; in fact, Bill had memorized the position only to the nearest minute. A minute of latitude and longitude is roughly a mile of distance, which is close enough for all practical purposes.

"You don't and neither do I," Twist went on. "Yet we're good navigators. Therefore, I don't think One Eye worked the position. He copied it."

"From whom?" Bill asked sharply.

"That's what I want to know. My guess is, from the man who made him turn those figures over to you."

"Somebody made One Eye do me a favor? That's rot!"

Twist swung the helm over and pointed the schooner back toward the beach.

"Something had scared him. I never saw a face like his, and I've tried hard," Twist muttered. "Well, I guess we'll find out. Don't cut up my running rigging too bad, Bill, or I'll follow in another schooner and you'll have twice as many callers."

As Twist steered toward Bill's vessel the pearler was busy with a knife. When he dived over the side he left a boat that would require several hours' work before it would be fit for sea.

Twist steered toward the anchorage he had left, while Bill swam toward his own schooner. Several dugouts were still paddling around the beach, and the pearler half expected to find one or more of his rivals from Fakarava waiting on board his boat. If so, it was his intention to kick them off, now that the secret of One Eye's island was no longer on record.

When Bill drew himself aboard, however, he found the deck of his ship empty except for his native diver, Kory, a Fijian, who had sailed with him all over the world.

Kory was a powerful six-footer, almost as black as a negro. His face was disfigured, according to white man's standards, by a broad band of blue tattoo marks which ran from his ears around his nose like a mask. Abnormally keen of sight and hearing, he had observed Bill's approach through the water, but not a muscle of the savage face moved when the pearler swung himself over the rail. Curiosity was not one of Kory's weaknesses.

"White fella wait along you," he announced.

"All right. Get under way. Move seven bells, you savvy?" Bill snapped, for he was in a hurry. "What name white fella?"

"Him stranger along me. Asleep cabin belong schooner," replied Kory imperturbably, as he moved forward to break out the anchor and hoist sail.

BILL SMELLED a rat. If a white stranger was aboard, where was his boat? Kory, after all, did not know all the white men in Fakarava by sight. Bill took Twist's revolver out of his pocket—even though the cartridges were wet it would make a good club—and went down the companionway stairs in one leap.

Under a lighted hurricane lamp a tall, lean man of thirty, with jet black eyes and hair, well dressed in white ducks, had stretched out in Bill's chair with a solar topee on his knee. The dark eyes widened at the sight of the pearler's dripping garments and the drawn revolver, but the stranger made no move to rise.

"Say, is every one crazy to-night?" he inquired in a soft drawl. "Ah'm Allan Montross, of San Francisco and Birmingham, Alabama, captain. If yo're Captain Williams, yo' can put up that gun."

"What do you want? I'm sailing at once," rumbled Bellow Bill, yet in spite of his annoyance he could not help grinning. He liked this stranger who was so unflustered and so sure of himself.

"My wish exactly, suh," nodded Montross, "Ah've found this town a madhouse. Ah came to find a certain Captain Kerrigan, and was info'med he had just died. Since he seemed to have turned over some papers to you, Ah came down to yo' boat. Yo' black there kept us off with a Winchester rifle."

"Didn't seem to succeed very well," Bill grinned.

"No, suh. Ah believed he wouldn't shoot, and the othahs allowed that he would. Ah was ready to take certain chances, suh, as you will understand, since you were in Captain Kerrigan's confidence."

Bellow Bill uttered a noncommittal grunt.

"What do you want me to do?" he demanded.

"Take me to Montross Island, suh."

"Never heard of it!"

"My father's island, suh!" insisted the young man with obvious surprise. "Perhaps the name he gave it hasn't been put on the charts, captain, but it's a small volcanic peak in latitude twenty degrees, sixteen minutes and eighteen seconds south and longitude one hundred thirty-six, thirty-seven, forty-two west."

Bill could only stare. In the cabin the quiet was so profound he was conscious of the loud ticking of the clock against the wall.

"Did you mention that position ashore?" Bill asked evenly.

"No, suh. Merely asked fo' Montross Island."

"That happens to be our port." Grim amusement flitted across Bill's face. "Does your father happen to be a devil, Mr. Montross?"

CHAPTER III

SUSPICION

MONTROSS ISLAND PROVED to be a precipitous and wave-carved crag of black volcanic rock rising out of a maze of coral reefs which made approach by schooner hazardous. At first sight there appeared to be no harbor. The surf boiled over the coral and hurled itself into the caves with which the soft black rock was honeycombed.

From seaward the sound of the waves, instead of being the normal boom of surf, was a hollow, coughing roar, and Bellow Bill would have hesitated to thrust his ship into the grip of the currents that boiled along the base of the cliffs if the horizon behind had not been notched by another sail.

Though Bill had won the race from Fakarava, the schooner owned by Twist and Fatty was scarcely an hour behind him, and therefore he sailed boldly through the passage among the reefs which looked most promising.

Close inshore a break in the cliffs was revealed; through it Bellow Bill steered into a landlocked harbor which had been at one time the crater of a volcano. Almost perfectly circular, and about a quarter of a mile in diameter, cliffs of the same soft, honeycombed black rock from fifty to seventy-five feet in height ringed it around. Almost directly opposite the entrance there had been a landslide, and on this slope cocopalms and other vegetation had taken root, but elsewhere there was deep water up to the very face of the cliffs.

The water of the harbor was as still as a sheet of black glass. The cliff kept off the trade wind, and although Bill's topsails occasionally caught a puff of breeze sufficient to give the schooner steerage way, the mainsail flapped. The noise filled the harbor with echoes tossed from cliff to cliff. Otherwise there was not a sound. The dark shore and the dark water were awesome. The place seemed to hold its breath and brood evil.

"No sign of your father," said Bill, speaking softly for once. "No house even."

Montross had been sent to the bow to keep a lookout for sunken rocks. He looked aft, his face anxious.

"Ah saw a patch of pearl shell, lyin' close to that steep cliff just to the right of the entrance," he reported. "It's an odd place fo' oysters to be, unless they were dropped there. They're in a thick patch within thirty feet of the cliff, just as One Eye told yo'. Since my father seems to have—succeeded, Kerrigan may have murdered him."

"We'll see," Bill rumbled, and pointed the schooner toward the slope of green where, if anywhere in this eerie place, human beings might be expected to live.

From what the son had told him of the elder Montross's purpose and character, Bill was inclined to believe that One Eye had committed murder, yet that fact did not explain the disappearance of Kerrigan's crew, nor his death-bed reference to a devil which would give him posthumous vengeance on Bellow Bill.

ALLAN'S FATHER, George Montross, B.S., M.A., Ph.D., formerly a professor at the University of California, far from being a devil, was a distinguished ichthyologist. From the son's accounts Bellow Bill had come to understand the affection which all who came in contact with the bald, black-eyed little scientist, bore toward him, and also their amused appreciation of the professor's eccentricities.

Ichthyology is the science of fishes. Not an exciting subject, yet Professor Montross had studied and taught it with the fanatic intensity of a zealot preaching a new religion. In the classroom the deep-set eyes under the heavy black eyebrows that were the only hair on head and face, would glow as he explained why the trout *(genus Salmo)* has an embryo fin near its tail, whereas, the bass *(genus Roccus)* also inhabiting fresh water, has none.

In the laboratory where he spent every free hour studying his particular specialty—the diseases of crustaceans—working among books and microscopes and tall steel filing-cases in which the professor kept a lifetime of researches under lock and key, his enthusiasm was even more marked.

At the age of sixty-five the university had retired him as professor emeritus, but instead of returning to his native Alabama for a leisurely and pleasant old age Montross had converted his property into cash, packed his scientific instruments, and left for a destination he refused to reveal even to his son.

He held the clew, he said, to a mystery which baffled science. The experiment would require three years, and could not be conducted in the United States. His researches must be in secret, lest he be robbed both of their fruits and of the scientific credit of his discovery.

If there should be any one with him intelligent enough to guess what he was doing.... The black eyes gleamed, and the bald head wagged proudly. Of course, Allan would think he

was an old fool, but would he give his father his fling? Make no
attempt to follow him and bring him back?

And Allan, knowing the lust for discovery that burned in his
father, and secretly amused at the old man's eccentric belief that
all other scientists were seeking to steal his papers and rob him
of the academic credit due him, had consented.

For three years, at six-month intervals, he had received a letter
postmarked in Fakarava. The early ones were almost lyric in
praise of an ideal spot, ideal assistants, experiments that promised success. In the later letters appeared a growing dread of
robbery—a fear that had amused the son, knowing how barren
pure science is of value to any save the scientist himself.

And then—the letters had ceased. When nine months
passed without news, Allan had come to Fakarava, knowing
only the latitude and longitude of the island where his father
had worked, and the fact that a Captain Kerrigan had trans-
ported his supplies.

But Bellow Bill, during the voyage to Montross Island, had
supplied facts that sharpened Allan's fears. A pearl is a deposit
of nacre around a microscopic nucleus, which scientists think
is a parasite. If the old professor had discovered the nature of
the parasite, and found some means of intensifying its action,
he had indeed every reason in the world to fear robbery, and,
old man that he was, no means of protecting himself save his
scientific knowledge.

Book learning is poor defense against a Winchester in the
hands of a man who knows how to shoot, and in Bill's opinion
One Eye Kerrigan had guessed the old scientist's object, served
him faithfully while the pearls were growing, and then struck.

THE THREE great pearls proved that the old professor had
succeeded. That Kerrigan had returned with only three, and
with horror stamped on his vicious face, gave Bill little grounds
for the hope that the old man was alive. Kerrigan was the type
whose first act would have been to shoot his victim in the back.

Even if the two had been armed equally, a gentle, lovable,

and impractical old ichthyologist was no match for a hard-case pearler. Yet out of his thorough knowledge of marine organisms, George Montross must have provided a defense for his treasure which had been effective, and which had impressed the ignorant Kerrigan as supernatural.

Both Allan Montross and Bellow Bill were more concerned with this riddle than with the potentialities of the bed of pearl oysters they had discovered. Bill armed his diver, Kory, with a Winchester and ordered him to protect the schooner, Montross and he took a rifle and a revolver apiece, and hastened to row ashore to search the island in the short time that was at their disposal before the arrival of Twist Keith and his fat partner.

Even before setting foot on land they found traces of the professor's work. In the shoal water near the beach were parallel lines of pearl oysters placed a foot apart as plants would be set in a garden, and divided into beds of twenty-four oysters each.

The laboratory or "garden" extended along the beach for a hundred yards, and must have comprised nearly a thousand shells—the collection of which must have been no mean task. The shells were small for the most part, and curiously misshapen and distorted as by disease or the work of marine borers. In the garden was a significant gap. From eight beds the oysters had been removed.

"Do yo' reckon these were dumped into the deep water by the cliff?" Montross suggested.

Bellow Bill reached over the side of the boat and brought up three oysters from the adjacent bed. Opening the shells, he kneaded the meat between his fingers.

"Probably. No pearls in this lot, anyway," he rumbled.

A stroke of the oars sent the boat to the beach, and with his rifle ready for instant use he led the way into the thicket of coconut palms and jungle.

Underfoot there was a dim path. Some time in the past the overhanging vegetation had been cut back, but since this path had been used slender vine tendrils had grown across it, so that

Bill had to break his way through with impatient sweeps of a hairy, tattooed arm.

Within a hundred yards the path led in a clearing. Once a house had been here; none of it remained except a square patch of black ashes.

Montross poked in the ruins with the muzzle of his gun, and picked up a microscope blackened by the flames.

"My father would have saved this or picked it from the ashes if he'd been alive at the time of the fire." Montross's eyes were narrow and hard, his face white. "A microscope to him's what a sextant would be to yo', Bill. The damn' murderers! Father wouldn't have harmed a fly! He'd have given them the pearls if they'd left him his papers and the proof of his discovery."

"Steady!" Bill reproved in his deep voice. "Maybe your father was thinking of you, buddy. You've told me you weren't rich."

With a frown the big pearler let his eyes wander around the clearing, and suddenly strode to a large garden, mostly over-grown with weeds. His rifle barrel pointed toward a patch of earth recently upturned.

"**THE HOUSE** was burned a week ago at least, but there's been yams dug there within the week!" Bill rumbled.

"Well, Kerrigan didn't have such a long sail!"

"Fact," Bill admitted, and moved toward the edge of the clear-ing, only to stop, so surprised that he spat out the quid of fine-cut in his cheek with an explosive *pagh!*

Shielded behind a mass of bushes in full bloom, the flowers of which were like a dome of gold, was a grave, well made, well tended, and—wonder of wonders!—with a headstone roughly shaped from a slab of the soft, slaglike volcanic rock of the island.

"Murder be—blowed!" Bill cried out, refilling his cheek with tobacco as Montross ran beside him pointing to the inscription:

Here lies
GEORGE MONTROSS

Scientist
Who Found the Secret of the Pearl
Born May 6, 1859
Died   1930

The inscription was neatly lettered and deeply cut.

"Your father made that himself. Kerrigan could hardly spell his own name," rumbled Bill.

"Obviously," Montross snapped. "But did my father make that stone to be used here, or is he buried under it? Granted he was sick and expected to die, does that prove he died naturally? If I had a spade I'd open that grave and—"

"Kerrigan was tough," Bill contradicted. "He'd have tossed body and gravestone out into the coral where the devil himself couldn't have found it. No, your father was sick and expecting to die. You'll note he left the day of his death blank, and it hasn't been filled in. Why?"

Montross shrugged.

"Making that stone took weeks," Bill insisted. "It gives me the shivers, a bit. A man old and sick chiseling his own headstone on this damn, black silent island. He knew he'd done something all other scientists were going to brag about him for, and yet he knew he couldn't last long enough to get back to his friends. It's a morbid notion, ain't it? Maybe he knew that Kerrigan would murder him sooner than let him get away with his pearls. Schooners don't touch at this island. Kerrigan could wait. The pearls were getting bigger and bigger. To know my life was in another man's hands, particularly a damn ignorant hard-case devil like One Eye Kerrigan, would give me the willies.... Your father had time to cut that stone. What else did he have time to do?"

"What do yo' mean?" Montross demanded.

"Why, he took his good oysters and dumped them in the deep water under the cliff; and in some way he found or trained him a devil," Bill boomed. "I've wondered some whether One Eye wasn't plain out of his head when he died, but I think now he told the strict literal truth out of hate to me. Get a spade and open this grave if you want to, Montross, but I'm going to that honeycombed black cliff and see what happens when Twist and Fatty spot that shell!"

Faintly through the trees came the echo of rattling blocks as the other schooner sailed through the passage. Bellow Bill loosened his revolver in the holster, felt to see that he had plenty of rifle ammunition, and started off through the underbrush at a run. Montross hesitated only a moment, then followed.

THEY HAD less than a quarter of a mile to go, but once out on the black rocks the footing was terrible. They climbed over cracked and broken slabs of volcanic slag that cut their light shoes. They circled chasms and blow-holes left as the molten stuff had cooled, looked down into dark, jagged caves, ran across narrow bridges of slag with no time to test their security.

Scratched and panting, they came to the edge of the bay and crawled through a jumble of broken rock to the edge of the cliff.

Below them Twist had brought his schooner to anchor as close to the rock as he dared. He and Fatty stood in the stern. Both had rifles. They were watching Bill's schooner, while amidships one of their two Polynesian divers was preparing to descend. The native had put diver's spectacles over his eyes, hung a bag of netting around his neck to hold the shell, and was drawing a glove on his right hand.

"Ahoy!" Bellow Bill hailed. All around the bay cliffs sent the echo back. "Ahoy—Ahoy—Ahoy!"

Like a flash Twist Keith dropped behind the cabin and poked his rifle upward. Fatty Clarke, too big and too slow-moving to find shelter, looked up like a sweating, angry hog.

"Save your lead, Twist," Bill boomed. "These rocks will stop a bullet a lot better than that cabin roof. Before you let that native dive I'll make you a proposition: I've been over the island, and that shell down there is the stuff we're both after. Furthermore, One Eye Kerrigan was kind enough to tell me there was a devil guarding it, and I'm passing the tip along. One Eye was right."

"You're offering a partnership? Suits us!" barked Twist.

"Like hell! I'm making you a sporting offer!" Bill boomed so loudly that the echoes rolled all around the bay. "One Eye put this job up to me, and I don't want any help at all. So you can hoist your anchor and go back through the reef. When I've got the pearls, you can try to get 'em away from me when my schooner comes out through the passage. Or—send that native over the side, and I'll try to keep you from getting away with whatever, you bring up!"

With an awkward leap that would never have saved him if Bill had cared to shoot, Fatty Clarke tumbled down the companionway.

"Dive!" he shouted to the native.

Twist's answer was a shot that flattened against the rock near Bill's head. The second diver leaped for the fo'c's'le scuttle and disappeared; the first plunged into the water.

Despite Bill's advantage of position, the raiders' chances of getting away with the shell were excellent. The diver could rise on the opposite side of the schooner, perfectly safe from Bill's bullets. The anchor could be unshackled under water, and the schooner would then drift with the tide through the passage, while Twist, partially sheltered by the cabin, could sling enough lead to keep Bill from taking careful aim.

Bellow Bill, however, did not answer the shot. From the shelter of a slab of lava he could look straight down and follow the movements of the diver, which the others could not. The native was swimming toward the bottom and had almost reached the shell when from the base of the cliff spurted a black discharge which covered the bottom for ten yards in every direction with a cloud as impenetrable as ink.

THE STUFF was like the ink discharged by a cuttlefish, but, if a cuttlefish produced it, the size of the monster was enormous. The deep sea animals upon which sperm whales feed might have produced such a cloud. Their tentacles are thick as a man's leg, and their parrot-like beaks rip deeply into the flesh of a whale.

Even the sperm whale, despite its enormous jaws and teeth,

finds this monstrous squid no mean adversary. They live in the warm depths of the tropic seas, but— This water was warm enough, and through the narrow pass between the cliffs the tide would bear all manner of food.

Bill shuddered. There was no way to verify his suspicion— nothing but a black cloud spreading in an ever-widening circle from the base of the cliff. Two minutes, three passed, but of the diver there was no sign.

"Twist! I won't shoot! Look over the side, quick!" Bill shouted.

The lame little man obeyed instantly. From a porthole Clarke stuck his head, while Bellow Bill, and Montross leaned far over the cliff edge. They stared while the dark cloud drifted slowly away with the tide, revealing first the scattered pearl shells, and in the midst of them, the body of the diver, lying limply on the dark sand.

The sun was just touching the cliffs, and as they stared a shadow seemed to fall across the bay, but in the last clear light Bill saw the red stain of blood in the water around the body.

"Get him up, Twist—but use a grapnel!" called the pearler.

Without a word Twist obeyed. After a little fishing, the three-pronged hook caught in the bag the diver had worn around his neck. Twist hoisted the body over the rail. In the stomach Bill could see a horrible wound.

"Something's cut him half in two."

Fatty Clarke, however, was fumbling with the diver's neck bag. The diver had caught one shell. Glaring defiance at Bill, Clarke opened it—and heaved himself erect, holding a pearl as large as the end of his thumb.

Twist's emaciated features turned to stone. "*All* the shells must hold them," he snarled under his breath, and added, still sharply, "You were watching, Bill. What was it?"

"One Eye named it," rumbled the pearler. "Are you ready to go outside the reef and wait for me?"

Twist looked up.

"Think you got a monopoly on nerve? No!" he sneered. He

picked up his rifle and laid it in plain sight on the cabin top. "I'm going to work right out on this deck, where you can plug me if you want," he challenged, and the lean face blazed. "Go outside? *Why, that one pearl is worth a hundred pounds!*"

CHAPTER IV

TWO KINDS OF CHANCE

"**FOR A LITTLE** guy, Twist Keith's quite a fellow!" Bill rumbled aside to Montross, and stretched himself out more comfortably behind his slab of lava, his chin in one tattooed fist, his jaws moving comfortably.

That his bluff had been called did not disturb the big pearler in the least. Less than half an hour of daylight was left, and he was content to postpone his own activities, while his rivals took the offensive against—whatever it was.

Twist moved his schooner nearer the cliff and anchored by a cable that could easily be slipped. He then prepared a bomb of six sticks of dynamite wrapped in canvas and twine and attached to a weight. Cutting a long fuse, he tossed the contraption at the cliff, so that it sank near the point from which the dark clouds had been ejected.

The cliff trembled to the heavy explosion, and a column of water deluged the schooner's decks. Bellow Bill, however, could see little signs of damage. A few pieces of rock had been torn from the cliff, but the shock of the explosion, which must have been terrific beneath the water, had not caused the creature to hurl out its inky cloud.

Twist, however, was satisfied.

"That'll kill whatever it was!" he exclaimed loudly, and came limping aft, while Clarke squeezed his fat body into the fo'c's'le hatch. As Twist reached the cabin he whipped up his rifle and covered the Polynesian diver.

"Down you go, Mapiao!" he grated.

"Pearl belong one fella devil! He *kai-kai* belly belong me!" the diver wailed.

"Gun *kai-kai* heart belong you," barked Twist inflexibly.

"He won't—he can't do that!" Montross gasped.

"The hell he won't! One Eye did!" growled Bill, taking swift aim.

His bullet knocked a long splinter from the cabin close to Twist's head. The little man only dodged behind the mainmast.

"Down, Mapiao!" he grated.

The diver gave a sob, and leaped from the rail. He did not dive, however. Once under water where the bullet could not reach him he turned and swam five feet below the surface, parallel to the cliff and in the direction of Bellow Bill's schooner. Twist cursed aloud.

"The 'devil' took no notice of that!" reported Bill excitedly. "The diver has got to get down where the pearls are. One Eye, y' see, could follow his divers in a boat and keep them from swimming away. A man to a pearl!"

Bill spat out his squid in savage disgust

"Ahoy, Twist!" he called. "Come out from behind that mast and take a dive yourself—or send down Fatty. I won't hinder!"

The answer was a rattle of chain as the schooner slipped her cable.

"Can't you swim?" Bill shouted with grim sarcasm.

The schooner drifted slowly away from the cliff with the tide. Beyond rifle shot Twist hobbled forward and threw overboard another anchor. Already the twilight was dark in the bay. The sun had dipped below the horizon, and in the western sky stars leaped into being, serene and distant and peaceful. Over the bay silence rested.

"OUR TURN now," Bellow Bill whispered. "We got to get Twist's schooner. That pearl set him crazy. I've got to count on you for a hell of a lot—"

"Going to row out and board?" Montross interrupted coolly.

"Be shot before we laid hands on the rail. Kory'd do as much for Twist, Neither of them will be asleep. No, we got to improvise. Can you find your way back to our schooner without breaking your neck?"

"In time."

"Then bring me a coil of thin rope, the life preserver, and a diver's knife. I'm going fishing for that devil. If we could just find out what it is—"

Bill began to chuckle deep in his chest, and in the dark the sound was like the deep bass purr of a giant cat.

"I see why One Eye picked on me," he rumbled. "The mean old hellion sized me up pretty well. And there's Twist, trying to horn in and make me out a false alarm. Don't hurry, buddy. We got the whole night for this job."

While Montross made the slow trip to the schooner and back Bill lay on the cliff in perfect silence. His vigilance was unrewarded. There was no sound but the faint, hollow roar of the surf in the caves on the seaward shore of the island, and no suspicious movement in the harbor or the water below the cliff.

Like most lagoons in the South Seas, the harbor water was faintly phosphorescent. Fish that broke water left a circle of pale blue light on the glassy surface. When Montross pulled from the beach, Bill could follow his progress by the fiery drops shaken from the oar blades, and hear him hail Kory. By the same means he was positive that no boat had left Twist's schooner.

Montross returned at last. Bill tied the life preserver to the end of the rope and stuck the diver's knife into his belt.

"Give me half an hour to climb down the cliff, then drop that life preserver overboard and keep bouncing it up and down in the water," he instructed. "Something may come investigating to see what all the splashing is about."

Before Montross could protest he swung himself over the face of the cliff.

Though the rock was nearly as steep as the side of a house,

the lava was so seamed with cracks and pitted with blow holes that Bill reached a narrow shelf just above the waters of the bay in half the time he had allowed. The splash of the lifebuoy as it fell drenched him. At his feet a flaming commotion began in the water.

He crouched, gripping his knife, and though long experience and many tight corners had schooled his nerves, his jaws moved faster than their custom. The tentacle of a devil fish, grasping for the decoy, might touch him. Other tentacles might pluck him from the rock. His knife would be useless against a monster, the beak of which could rip a man's body in half.

Thus whispered nerves strained by silence and suspense. Stubbornly Bill's mind told him that the octopus and cuttlefish both use tentacles first, and their beaks last.

In the depths below nothing stirred, but as ripples thrown by the movement of the buoy sent phosphorescent ripples in ever-widening circles a boat left Twist's schooner and sculled toward the cliff.

Bill slipped off trousers and shoes. Powerful swimmer though he was, he hated to trust himself to that black water, but as the boat approached within a hundred feet he lowered himself from his perch.

He made no splash, and the movement of the buoy concealed any ripples of his making. Once under water he swam with all his strength below the surface, guided by the phosphorescence ahead.

IN THE boat Fatty Clarke was preparing to touch a match to the fuse of a second bomb. On the cliff top Montross screamed a warning to Bill and dropping the rope, seized a rifle.

Bill was almost to the boat. He rose beneath it, seized the gunwale, and capsized Fatty and his unlighted bomb into the bay. The huge man shouted as the boat went over, rose thrashing and kicking, and then screamed a shrill cry cut with pain and terror in sharp contrast to his bellow of rage.

From the cliff top a bullet cut into the water within a yard of Bill, who was blocked by the boat in his efforts to reach Fatty.

Flinging himself across the keel, Bill struck Fatty with the hilt of his knife. As the blow fell he realized to his surprise that the huge man was already insensible, and seized him by the hair. Another bullet plopped into the water.

"It's me!" Bill bellowed.

"Then that devil followed right at yo' heels!" shouted Montross. "Yo' were all three together; something came back—under water both ways! It went under the cliff again."

Bill drew Fatty across the boat.

"Ahoy, Twist!" he hailed. "Your pardner's hurt, and I didn't do it! I'm swimming to your schooner."

What sort of reception the lame little man prepared for him Bill did not care much at that moment. The boat was far too small to keep two heavy men out of the water, and Bill's toes tingled out of dread of something rising from below.

Taking Fatty's head in the crook of his arm he swam toward the schooner at the best speed he could make. Every yard away from the cliff eased his mind, however, and when he touched the low side of the schooner he was alert. Twist would use this opportunity to the utmost.

The little man leaned over the rail, and even in the starlight Bill saw a revolver in his hand. The pearler sank low in the water, sheltering his own head behind that of Fatty.

"Lift him up!" Twist barked.

"Think I'm a derrick?" Bill snorted. "He's fainted. Lean down and hold his head above water while I climb aboard. You're too much of a shrimp to lift him."

The revolver barrel poised in the starlight. Bill sank till only his mouth and nose were above water.

"Go on!" he growled. "Grab him, or I'll let him sink and I'll swim away like Mapiao."

"I'll give you a rope," said Twist smoothly.

"You will like Billy-be-damned! Think I'm going to give you a decent shot at me?" Bill taunted. "Grab his hair! He's hurt bad, but I don't think enough of him to let you get a shot at me!"

The contest was of wits and speed, the hand against the eye, and both knew it. Like a flash Twist stopped, covering with his revolver the hand that reached for Fatty's head.

Bill went completely under water. His hand swung over Fatty's head, caught Twist's wrist. With feet braced against the schooner's hull Bill flung himself backward, pulling Twist over the rail and into the phosphorescent water.

A revolver shot burned Bill's wrist, the bullet seared like hot iron across his arm, but once under the surface he twisted the weapon away from the weaker man and rose, holding Twist by the throat, and supporting Fatty with his other hand.

"**NOW BE** good!" he gasped. Giving Twist a final shake, he released both, and pulled himself aboard the schooner. To catch a rope and toss it to the struggling pair in the water took only an instant.

"Come on aboard, Twist," Bill chuckled. "Mapiao's waiting ashore, if you're thinking of swimming. He might like to see you!"

With an oath the little man surrendered. He swam to the rail and climbed aboard, silent, but radiating an anger that Bill could feel.

Despite the pearler's watchfulness the fight between them might not have been at an end except that the sight of Clarke, when they lifted him aboard, drove personal enmity from the minds of both. On the huge, hairless leg between thigh and knee was a gaping wound that pumped blood in a stream which must be stanched at once.

Bill picked Clarke up and carried him toward the cabin. Twist hobbled ahead. He had the medicine chest open, bandages out, and a surgeon's needle threaded with catgut in his hand before Bill staggered in with his burden.

Both were expert in the treatment of wounds. They drew the

flesh together, put in stitches, applied compresses and bandages, then faced each other beside the blood-stained bunk.

"Well?" purred Bill.

Twist's lean features hardened. "I'd fight any man living, but not this thing! That bomb this afternoon killed every fish in the water within a hundred yards. Did you notice that?"

Bill nodded.

"I'll sail out of here, to-night, and I won't wait outside the reef, either," Twist continued violently. "I've thought I was a hell of a guy! I was the bird that got the dope from One Eye, away from everybody, and I was going to show you where to head in at." A grimace, bitter and self-contemptuous, crossed the lean face. "I wouldn't go into that water myself for a hundred pearls, and now I'm cooled off, I wouldn't send Mapiao in either. That was Fatty's idea. I done the work because he was too big to take shelter on deck."

Again Bill nodded.

"Well, help me hoist anchor," Twist snapped. "Bring Mapiao with you—if you come. It *is* a devil, Bill. I've seen the marks. Even a shark can't make wounds like those. If you've got any brains—as you'll admit I have—you'll sail right along with me!"

"I don't mind being called a fool. Maybe I am." Bill's great voice filled the tiny cabin like the drone of a deep organ note. His eyes shone, grim, and still eager. "If it was just the pearls, the way it is with you, Twist, I'd go. Only One Eye Kerrigan put it up to me, you see." Bill smiled almost apologetically, went on:

"I don't take backwater from any man, alive or dead. What's more, there was a nice old duffer that was smart enough to make those pearls, and a pretty decent kid that owns them. Are they going to get nothing because I've got a yellow streak?"

"Damned if I'm yellow!" Twist snarled.

"You sent a brown boy; you wouldn't follow yourself," Bill accused. "This thing ain't like anything I know in the sea or out of it, but I don't put much stock in devils. This 'devil' ain't a fish, or your dynamite would have killed it. It might be some kind of octopus, which could have crawled out of water in some cave behind the face of that cliff, but I can't be sure. So—neither of us will sail, Twist. Instead of raising your anchor, I'm going to lock some handcuffs on you."

Twist stared.

"No hard feelings," Bill rumbled. "Just want to have you off my mind for twelve hours. You can look after Fatty in irons, and later he or somebody can file the irons off."

"But what's the idea?"

"Why, I mean to make sure about this business, that's all. I got a guess, and in case I should be wrong I want some one around that can navigate young Montross back to Fakarava."

CHAPTER V

BILL MAKES SURE

TO MONTROSS HIMSELF, however, the big pearler was less frank. Throughout the remainder of the night and the following afternoon Bellow Bill spoke and acted as though he were carrying out his previous plans instead of improvising a new and more daring one.

Bill liked to play a lone hand. He preferred risks, provided he could take them himself, to argument.

With Allan Montross the object of the expedition was to discover the fate that had overtaken his father, and to bring back the proof of the professor's scientific attainments.

Bill's desire was to solve the mystery of a "devil" which had already taken four lives, and which would, unless solved, take a larger and larger toll among the more daring and unscrupulous pearlers, who would go to any lengths while the pearls remained at the foot of the cliff.

That he was unusually daring or reckless did not enter Bill's head. What success he had had in the past arose from the promptness with which he took the risks that his rivals avoided, confronting the difficulties that balked them.

Audacity—always audacity—was his creed: he merely took care that his own acts did not involve his companions if he chanced to fail.

Therefore, after ironing Twist Keith, Bill swam back to the island. He gave the cliff a wide berth, shouting across the water for Montross to return to the schooner, and, after much more shouting, persuading Mapiao to come aboard also. All three ate and dropped into their bunks, exhausted.

Bill slept until noon, and then sailed his schooner close to the dark cliff, anchoring in the same spot which Twist had occupied the previous day, and preparing the same kind of dynamite bomb, though its fuse was considerably shorter.

With this in his hand and a cigar glowing between his teeth, Bill came on deck. He was barefoot, dressed in a cotton singlet, and duck trousers cut off at the knee, into the waistband of which he had thrust a diver's knife. Montross, Mapiao, and his own diver, Kory, crowded around him.

"Kory, you fright devil belong pearls?" he demanded.

"Belly belong me walk about—fright big bit too much," answered the Fijian emphatically, squirming in expressive pantomime, while Mapiao's tobacco-colored countenance grew ashen at the prospect that he might be ordered to dive again.

Bellow Bill had expected exactly this.

"Guess it's your job, then, Montross," he announced cheerfully. "I want you to dive down toward that shell as if you were going to pick them up, savvy? But halfway down, you turn and swim straight away from shore like the devil was after you—which it will be, see? The ink that 'devil' squirts out blinds it, and I'll drop this little firecracker right on top of it."

"Ah reckon that will work," said the Alabaman coolly. "The devil don't swim very fast. Last night I saw a glow in the water moving out from the cliff which was you, though Ah didn't know it then. Right behind yo' was another glow, just the same

kind, only moving a little faster than yo' were. Ah'll be frank,
Bill: Ah ain't goin' too close to the bottom."

A SMILE of excitement twitched Bill's lips as the dark-haired
young man poised on the rail in the sunlight. The pearler's broad
chest rose and fell with deep, quiet inhalations.

As Montross dived Bill laid the bomb on the deck; it had
served its purpose in fooling Montross. Snapping the glowing
cigar into the water, he poised on the schooner's rail, knees bent
and arms outstretched.

The inky cloud shot from the cliff face, rolling toward
Montross like a billow of black smoke. Montross instantly
checked his descent, whirled, and swam desperately to keep in
advance of it. Above, Bellow Bill whipped out his knife—and
dived straight for the face of the cliff.

The dive took Bill into the heart of the cloud. When he
opened his eyes under water a bandage seemed pressed upon
them, but he swam straight ahead and not far below the surface.
He wanted to pass above the "devil."

When his fingers scraped the cliff he swam downward, feeling for the rock at every stroke. Down he went for twenty, thirty,
forty feet before the hand that groped for the rock touched
nothing.

Bill twisted toward the cliff, swinging the knife before him
in wide arcs as though he were cutting his way through the
darkness.

As he had suspected, near the bottom of the cliff an underwater cave led backward. How far, or to what, he could not
guess, but he was in the lair of the "devil," while the devil itself
was outside, groping for the escaping Montross in the center
of the inky cloud.

Again Bill's fingers scraped stone. This time he swam upward.
Already he had been under water for a minute. His lungs hurt.
The cave might be entirely filled with water. Bill swam upward,
ten, twenty, thirty feet.

Suddenly the darkness before his eyes turned to greenish

gray. Through unstained water his head rose into air. He was in a cave. The wall of rock he had used to guide himself ended in a shelf ten feet wide and a foot above the water level.

Bill sprang out and crouched, knife in hand.

Overhead, the roof of the cave was lost in darkness. How far it extended to the sides he did not observe at the moment. The light came through a narrow blow-hole extending through the cliff. He caught a glimpse of his own schooner; then bent over the dark surface of the pool.

He was in the "devil's" lair. Cuttlefish, devilfish, or as he suspected, man, Bill was prepared for a fight in which he now held the advantage.

The surface of the pool stirred. On the water appeared a green and brown mass a yard in area, resembling seaweed to Bill's horrified eyes. In the midst of it was a bright red object, like a human head in size, but featureless—a round dome of rough red hide resembling the snout of a shark.

The thing drifted across the pool till it touched the lip of rock where Bill crouched, fascinated. He leaped backward, with his shin cut.

Too late to dodge entirely, he had seen brown fingers grip the rock for purchase, a brown hand and arm wielding a cleaver slash at his legs. Yet the certainty that the mask of red shark-skin and seaweed concealed a native dispelled the superstitious horror that had paralyzed him and caused him to drop his knife as he dodged.

Feet first, Bill jumped for the featureless red head. His feet, falling upon the "devil's" shoulders, drove the thing beneath the water. Bill twisted and lunged blindly. His hand closed on a human neck.

Instantly he caught the throat in the crook of his arm, ripped the mask aside, and dug his fingers into the windpipe. He had fallen behind his enemy; had had time to fill his lungs with air after the long dive, while the other had not.

He expected to choke the "devil" into submission—but never had Bill struggled hand to hand with a man so powerful.

THE NATIVE lashed right and left with the cleaver. Bill felt the movements, and drew his legs out of the way. The other could not strike at his arms, wrapped as they were around head and throat. The native knew that. Like a flash his tactics changed. The naked body writhed in Bellow Bill's grip. Fingers tore at his, loosening his grip, but failing to dislodge it.

A leg found his own, and wrapped around it. Both unable to swim, they sank slowly, writhing and twisting downward. The native was holding Bill fast, confident that the white man's lungs would be the first to fail.

Beneath the water neither could strike a crimping blow with heel or fist. They wrestled, the native to hold, Bill to punish. Equaled in strength, the pearler had the greater skill. He caught an arm in a hammer lock, bent it backward and snapped the bone.

The agony made the native faint. His struggles ceased, and Bill bore him upward and pulled him out on the floor of the cave.

For several minutes Bill panted heavily, and before he had completely recovered the native opened his eyes. He was a Marquesan, to judge from his tattooing, of middle age, and heavily muscled, with a fierce and brooding countenance that bespoke little intelligence, but vast courage and determination. Yet as he caught Bill's eye he cringed on the black stone floor, as an ox, had it the intelligence, might cringe before a butcher.

"What name belong you?" Bill demanded.

Except that the native's fear and pain became more intense, he gave no answer.

"You bad fella," Bill charged. *"Kai-kai* marster belong you."

In the brown face of the native anger—or was it devotion?—conquered fear.

"No bad fella. No *kai-kai* marster belong me," he protested in a voice nearly as deep as Bellow Bill's. "Good marster, belong me, die. You savvy One Eye Kell'gan. Him bad fella! Try steal pearls belong marster. Marster say, 'Teli, you keep pearls belong me. Bad fella Kell'gan try *kai-kai* you.'"

Bellow Bill laid aside the diver's knife he had picked up, and removed his singlet. With the cloth he made a sling for the broken arm, then wrapped a bandage around his own leg.

"All right. You good fella," he said. "Tell the yarn in your own way, but be quick about it."

In the limited vocabulary of *bêche-de-mer* English, with its endless circumlocutions, the native complied. His name was Teli. He had come to the island with the professor as diver and servant. The professor had been a good master, very gentle, very wise. At first Teli had thought him crazy, but when the pearls began to grow, he had decided that Montross was a great magician, or a god, and served him in awe as well as affection.

But as the pearls grew, the too observant One Eye Kerrigan, who brought them their supplies twice a year, and who was a "bad fella too much," had begun to make open threats, and the old professor, weakened by constant wading in water to examine his oysters, had fallen sick.

"Face belong him burn; blood belong him capsize," Teli explained, coughing and spitting in crude pantomime.

"Consumption," Bellow Bill thought to himself.

AS SOON as Kerrigan had sailed on his next-to-last visit, more than nine moons ago, the professor had Teli dump all the pearl-bearing oysters in front of the cave, which the diver had discovered while exploring the island.

Teli had wanted to put the oysters inside the cave, too, but no. Light and movement of water were necessary to the growth of the pearls, Instead, the professor had made a pump, and boiled great pots of herbs until he had produced a barrel of thick black ink. These Teli had brought into the cave.

The native pointed into the darkness, and Bill, rising to investigate, found a crude wooden pump with a ten-foot handle by which fully five gallons of ink could be shot through a pipe that curved down into the water. The professor had also made the strange headdress and armed Teli with the cleaver.

"Marster say, 'Kill fella belong schooner,'" Teli explained excitedly. " 'Them bad fella. They kill you, kill me—'"

Bill nodded. The professor had been feverish, dying, probably a little out of his head when those instructions had been given. Also, he had been right. Any defense less terrible would have failed to drive Kerrigan off.

After Kerrigan left, Teli explained, he had been told to wait— until men with brass buttons came in a police boat. On no account was he to attack the men with brass buttons, but only schooner men. To the police he was to explain everything, as he was explaining it to Bill.

"Why, the scientific son of a sea-cook!" Bill exclaimed in admiration. Of course, the professor could not be sure that any letter intrusted to Kerrigan would be mailed. On the other hand, how could he summon help, when Kerrigan's schooner afforded his only means of communication? Trouble at the island would be certain to bring the police sooner or later—would have brought them instantly if Kerrigan had not been dying when he returned to Fakarava. They had had no opportunity to cross-examine either Kerrigan or Bill. Events had moved too quickly.

"The old boy sure guessed right!" Bill muttered.

"Why, even when the police came there'd be so many of them that he wouldn't have been double crossed—as he might have been if he had had Teli make a dugout and go off with a letter."

The pearler leaned forward.

"What name papers belong marster?" he demanded sternly. "You keep papers along you?"

Teli looked uncomfortable. Yes, there had been papers, he admitted, but whereas all men knew the value of pearls, papers were of little account. Not until he had erected the headstone for his master, and the master lay dying, had he been given a packet so large—he measured it with his hands—wrapped and sealed with wax.

He had had to bury the master, and make sacrifices at the grave, keep a lookout for schooners lest he be caught napping. He had hidden the papers in the thatch of the house, since he feared water would spoil them in the cave. One Eye Kerrigan, in fury after the death of his divers, had set the house afire—

"You come schooner along me," interrupted Bill grimly, and dived first into the pool. He had been gone so long Montross would think him dead.

An hour later he sat in his cabin facing Montross across a table in the center of which was a double handful of pearls, none smaller than half an inch in diameter. After his return Kory and Mapiao had made short work of lifting the shell.

"THE LARGEST, finest pearls the world will ever see," he boomed. "Don't look so glum because your father's papers were burned, Montross! He's made you a rich man, and— Hell! I'm a roughneck, but I'm glad we don't know what bug gets into an oyster and starts pearls growing. If those papers hadn't been destroyed, the secret would get out, and every money-hungry beach comber in the South Seas would have a pearl farm! Real pearls would have been on sale pretty soon at the five and ten all over the world.

"There's no denying your father found the secret of the pearl. These gems here will prove that! But the world's better off with a few things in it that can't be manufactured cheap. A pearl ought to stand for danger and skill—the risk the diver takes, and the years the jeweler spends in matching up a string—"

"Half of these are yours, of cou'se," said Montross.

"Sell them for me and put the jack to my credit in the First National of 'Frisco," Bill said heartily. "I don't hate money. I just dislike the guys that insist on seeing their profit in advance."

Bill threw back his coppery gold head triumphantly.

"I did just what One Eye Kerrigan figured I'd do—and won out!" he exulted. "What's the fun of having money, compared to beating out a double crossin' scoundrel by playing fair? A dying old man won the loyalty of a native and was smart enough to imitate the discharge of a cuttlefish, and everybody but you and me was sure it was a devil!"

A blow of Bill's tattooed fist made the pearls bounce.

"I'm sort of glad those papers burned, because I want to keep on in the pearling game forever! It—leads to things!"

THE HIGH PLACE

*The South Seas guard their secrets well, and
Bellow Bill thought the cannibal rites of long
pig were extinct in the Marquesas Islands—
until the fateful day he came to Hua-vana*

CHAPTER I

DAWN

WITH THE SLOW splendor of a tropic dawn tingeing the sea crimson in the wake of the oars, Bellow Bill Williams rowed to the beach of Hua-vana to learn the recipe of the cocktail which only Michel Poulain, out of all the planters in the South Seas, could mix to its supreme perfection.

All the varying mixtures of fresh coconut juice, white wine, and gin are excellent, but the flavor of Poulain's concoction had lingered on the pearling skipper's palate for many months. Since his schooner was becalmed off the Marquesas Islands, Bill was sure he would pass the day more pleasantly on Poulain's veranda, with an opalescent drink in one huge, tattooed fist, than on his own sun-broiled deck.

Thus casually he injected himself into the death throes of an expiring race, bore the brunt of the final clash between the white man and the Polynesian, held for a day the balance of power between greed and ambition, treachery and honor; and, in the darkness, amid terrible rites that he had believed were only a memory in the South Seas, came to face the greatest test and temptation of his adventurous life.

For though the sun had barely risen, Poulain was up. At Bill's hail he ran out of his house, a short, fat, swarthy little man of fifty with jet black mustaches wide and spiky as the whiskers of a cat. He was fully dressed in white ducks, with a big revolver belted around his fat belly. In fat cheeks coal black eyes swam moistly with excitement.

*The natives
hurled a barrage
of bowlders*

Behind him, more slowly, advanced his son, Henri Poulain; tall and slender, equally swarthy and dark of eye, but with only thin silky hair like a smudge of soot on his upper lip. Henri was about twenty. Because of his youth he should have shared Poulain's excitement, yet although he also was armed, he was as cool as his father was impassioned.

He stood silent and preoccupied, his eyes avoiding Bill's, while his father burst into incoherent speech.

"Ha! Welcome, *mon ami!* Nevair 'ave you been so welcome! You will come wiz us, *hein?* We march to avenge a crime the most terrible, the most unnatural! Me and my son alone, against every one—every one in ze valley, *m'sieu'!* You are a strong man," jabbered Poulain, little black eyes moist with greed to enlist so formidable an ally in his cause. "You will come wiz us, and gain ze victory, *hein?*"

BILL ABANDONED his dream of a pleasant day packed with many delicious drinks.

"I will if I've got to. But since when have you turned *gendarme*, Poulain?" he rumbled in a voice that had the low, reverberating tone of the bass note of a big organ. Bellow Bill could not whisper. At its softest his voice would carry like the growl of distant thunder, at its loudest it could drown out the roar of a gale.

Six feet and three inches in height, fifty inches around the chest, scaling two hundred and twenty-five pounds, he was ever welcome to men with trouble on their hands, not only for bull strength, but for quick wit. Broad of forehead and jaw, with dark blue eyes and curly, coppery hair, he was renowned as the keenest and most daring pearling skipper in the South Seas, He loved excitement more than profit, more even than fine cut chewing tobacco, which was his besetting vice.

His only vanity was the tattooing that covered his skin from neck to waist—from the bracelets of rope drawn in pale blue ink, through stars, daggers, and geometrical designs to the full, rigged ship that covered his broad back, the dragon in green, yellow, and blue on his chest, and the snake coiled like a belt around his hips.

"I a *gendarme?* But no!" Poulain jabbered passionately. "I am

a white man—only zat! Ze *gendarmes* and ze governor 'imself are ze blind fools. I 'ave tol' zem what I know, and zey say, 'It is nozzing!'

"Listen, *m'sieu'!* One of my laborers is gone—vanish'—*pouf! comme ça!* Moloku is here las' night at sunset. He is miss' in ze dark, and he is not yet return. Three, four time in ze las' year my laborers 'ave vanish', and ze governor say 'It is nozzing! Zose men fall over a cliff; zey swim in ze dark, and ze shark get zem!'"

"Well, that's the explanation usually given," Bill remonstrated, "Natives always have been missed from time to time here in the Marquesas, and cliffs and sharks are plenty enough."

"Ah! But now I know zat explanation is ze lie of blind, lazy fools! Look, and you shall judge!"

Poulain darted into his bungalow and returned carrying a *pareu*—a strip of figured cotton cloth such as is used as kilt and loincloth throughout the South Seas.

"Moloku, who is dead, and Mitu, his friend who 'ave found zis, are Paumotan boys," he explained. "Ze Marquesans do not wear *parens* of zis pattern. Mitu found it caught in a thorn bush by ze trail. Farther on, by ze top of a cliff, ze bushes are disarrange'. He search at ze bottom, for it is his friend, and more, because ze friend wear a ring of silver zat Mitu wants. Ze body is gone, *m'sieu'*. Why?"

Bill shot a stream of tobacco juice neatly over the veranda rail before he spoke.

"The Marquesans haven't lost their taste for long pig—when they get a chance."

"Ah! Yet ze blind fool talk of ze shark, ze fall!" Poulain nodded. "When Mitu brought me ze *pareu*, I could be no longer blind. Nor is zat ze t'ing most serious." The excited voice dropped. "Sixty years ago two t'ousand Marquesans live in zis valley. Now zere are but twenty-five. A few more, maybe, high in ze hills where white men never go. Yet zere are as many breadfruit trees as when zere were two t'ousand, and as many fish in ze sea. Zen why, *m'sieu'?*"

"The whalers brought a new disease with them sixty years ago," Bill rumbled. "That took a lot of the two thousand. Then the missionaries stopped them from bathing without clothes, and they got consumption from sleeping in wet cotton *pareus*. That took a lot more. As for the rest—they don't care whether they live or die, so they die. Same thing is going on all over the South Seas."

"And why? Because zey do *not* care!" snarled Poulain, answering his own question. "Ze old dances are forbid'! To drink *kava* is forbid'! Ze war between ze tribes are stop', to put down ze cannibals. All zat ze native wish to do is forbid'. Even opium, for which zey would work, is stop' by law."

"And a damn good thing!" rumbled Bill heartily.

"*Hein!*" contradicted Poulain. "If you had a plantation like mine, you would not say so! *Régardez!* Ten acres of coconut palms, as much as my son and I can tend, when I could plant fifty acres, a hundred, if I could get labor! Yet why should ze native work? His food grow in ze trees; so do his clothes. Sixty years ago he beat ze bark of ze mulberry into tapa cloth. Rum and drugs ze government forbids! Ze dancing, ze fighting that he love, are forbid'. He has sat down and wait' to die, until of two t'ousand zere are left twenty-five! But if ze clock could be turned back, *m'sieu'*, and ze natives live in the old way, soon zat twenty-five would be two t'ousand!"

"Well?"

"It is being done," said Poulain. "Ze old dance, ze old feast— on men, on my laborer Moloku, *m'sieu'!*"

THE JET black eyes swam moistly. The swarthy cheeks were flushed purple-red.

"Prove it!" grunted Bill, watching the son.

Henri stood silent and grim, opposition in every line of his slender figure.

Dramatically Poulain shook out the *pareu* and pointed to a wide reddish-brown stain along the upper hem.

"Moloku and Mitu are Paumotans—strangers," he whis-

pered. "Among ze Marquesans zere are no *pareus* of zis pattern.
Look, Bill! Blood has run down Moloku's back, and soak' into
ze *pareu*. He was stab' in ze back by a spear and ran for his life
along ze dark trail. He swerve, and a thorn bush tear ze *pareu*
from his body. Ze pursuers did not notice in ze darkness. He
was wounded; zey were gaining. He jump' over ze cliff as other
hunted men have done. He hope he would live after ze fall; he
know zose who chase would not jump after him. But—he died.
Zey carried him to ze High Place, *m'sieu'*, where ze old feasts
were held. Las' night I hear ze sound of drums."

Bill glanced at the son.

"It is true," said Henri. The son spoke better English than
the father, grammatical, unaccented. Yet though he substanti-
ated Poulain's fact, his attitude of opposition did not waver, nor
did his features relax.

"So! Now we march to punish!" exclaimed Poulain explo-
sively. "You will go wiz us, Bill, *hein!*"

"No excitement equals man-hunting. Sure I'll go, and willing," Bill grinned. "I've heard tales of sixty years ago. A man-
eating hell in a paradise, these islands were. Now there aren't any
villages a gunboat could shell, nor are there so many natives that
they can't avoid a landing party in all this mess of jungle and hills
with food growing everywhere. Just because there's only twenty-
five now where there used to be two thousand. Sure I'll go; but
what do you need me for, Poulain? You're armed. The job is finding the natives that *kai-kai'd* your laborer, not licking them!"

Poulain's eyes rolled.

"Not at all," he announced. "Ze natives are nozzing wizzout
ze leader! Ze leader is as well arm' as we—and white!"

Bellow Bill stared in amazement, bull the contradiction that
was on his lips burst from the son.

"*Non, non, non!*" said Henri. "*Mon père,* I will not permit it!
Mynheer Van Tromp is only a tool! The leader is the *moke,* the
magician Hanu! When we kill him the drums will speak no
more from the High Place!"

"I know what I know!" Poulain insisted. "And thou, my son, would also accuse Van Tromp had he no daughter named Frieda!"

"And you would not accuse him had he no—" The youngster's jaw snapped shut. From his forehead he wiped beads of cold sweat. *"Mon père!* I beg you, change your mind," he pleaded desperately. "Hanu, the *moke,* loves the old days! He leads his people! Without him Van Tromp could only be a planter like ourselves."

"And wizzout him, Hanu is but a black-faced savage!" Poulain snarled. "Come, Henri! I am older, wiser, and your father. M'sieu' Bill agrees wiz me, *hein?"*

The two Poulains glared at each other, one hot, one cold, both passionately determined. Between them was deadlock. Each left the decision to Bellow Bill.

CHAPTER II

FORENOON

"WHERE ARE THESE two guys?" Bill boomed. "Van Tromp and his daughter I've heard of. He's got the big plantation next to yours. Where's Hanu? In the bush?"

"He is Van Tromp's overseer. At this hour he also will be at the plantation," replied Henri gravely.

"Then what's bothering you two?" Bill paused in the hope that either the father or the son would explain. Neither said a word. The pearler shrugged. Convinced that a crime had been committed, he did not care whether he was to capture a white man or a brown. He accepted a revolver from Poulain, and the three set out in single file, the chubby little planter in the lead.

While they were on Poulain's land they moved through a typical South Sea plantation—rows of coco palms, each protected against the rats by a band of tin around the trunk, and with the undergrowth partially cleared away. As soon as they crossed Van Tromp's line, however, the cultivation changed markedly, and for the better.

Not a weed grew under Van Tromp's palms, and in addition to these there were mangos, limes, and breadfruit; oranges and pawpaws, candle-nuts, bananas, and alligator pears. Van Tromp grew on his own land everything he needed to live like a tropic prince, and his plantation, which Bill knew was fully four times the size of his neighbor's, exported copra, honey, vanilla and fruit in an amount that made the Dutchman's income almost princely.

The explanation was that he alone was able to make the Marquesan natives cultivate his fields day in and day out. The startlingly well-kept land offered silent corroboration of Poulain's accusation. All the planters offered money, and failed to obtain a month's work out of the natives in a year. Van Tromp evidently held out other inducements.

That the Dutchman himself was a cannibal was unthinkable, but that ambition and greed drove him to pander to the dearest and most secret vice of the natives was quite possible.

If he were doing so, the aid of a Marquesan *moke,* or magician-priest, would be essential. Which of the two was the more guilty of corrupting the natives seemed to Bellow Bill a matter of splitting hairs. He wondered that the Poulains should quarrel over the point—and what thing it was that the father wanted, which had led him to accuse Van Tromp to the exclusion of the *moke,* and which Henri, even in anger, had refused to mention.

Poulain began to walk more cautiously. He entered a thicket of young coffee shrubs whose foliage, higher than Bill's head, formed a dense screen. Dropping on his hands and knees, he wormed his way forward. At the edge of the thicket he stopped and motioned Bill to crawl alongside him. Peering through the foliage, the pearler found himself within ten yards of Van Tromp's veranda. The Dutchman himself was in plain view, talking to a native.

Both were remarkable men. At a glance Bill understood why

his help had been enlisted. Van Tromp sat like a bowlder poised at the edge of a cliff. He was perfectly bald—a smooth white scalp and a broad white face relieved by a scanty mustache and eyebrows of the palest yellow. He was enormously broad and thick of shoulder, chest, and neck, but no more fat than some bulging, squat, pale-colored stone. Even seated he was menacing.

Facing him across a light wicker breakfast table stood a brown giant. Subconsciously Bill noted a height scarcely less than six and a half feet and a superbly muscled torso and arms, for his eyes returned again and again to the face. The entire countenance was tattooed a sooty black. Only the eyes seemed alive.

"Hanu!" Poulain whispered.

BILL NODDED. The two were talking, but too low for him to catch a word. He nudged Poulain, and burst through the screen of foliage, hand on gun, crossing the open space too rapidly for Hanu to escape or Van Tromp to arm himself.

Both started. Van Tromp leaned forward and spoke quickly to the native, his body covering the table top. As he resumed his seat he moved to one side a sun helmet that was on the table, and then waited, with folded arms. Hanu followed his example.

Bill walked to the table, grinned when he noticed that the sun helmet now hid a revolver, and waited for Poulain to speak. The spike-mustached little Frenchman was no coward; he pushed by Bill.

"One of my men is gone. You 'ave kill' 'im!" he snarled into Van Tromp's face.

The Dutchman ignored him. "Who are you?" he demanded of Bill.

"Bill Williams. Pearling skipper."

"Of Bellow Bill every one has heard. You are a fair man," said Van Tromp. Slowly, with a thick arm and a huge white hand steady as marble, he pointed at Poulain.

"That one drools with jealousy. See?" There was indeed a trickle of saliva from the corner of Poulain's mouth. "He and I took land together fifteen years ago. I have prospered; he has not."

Van Tromp's voice was leisurely, thick, and insulting. "Therefore, he accuses me of crimes to the governor, to everybody. I am tired of it. Of a laborer that is missing I know nothing. Hanu, my foreman, knows nothing. That is all. I will not be shouted at or threatened. If Monsieur Poulain cannot keep his labor I am— No!" Van Tromp interrupted himself, "I am *not* sorry."

"The man was murdered. There is proof," Bill rumbled.

"Ach, so?" There was surprise in the voice. The pale blue eyes flickered. "Then we must talk. It is early, sir," Van Tromp went on more graciously; "perhaps you have not eaten?

"Frieda!" he shouted. "Clear the table and bring three more plates for my guests!" He heaved himself out of his chair and gestured toward some long cane chairs at the opposite end of the veranda. "Come, gentlemen! Coffee before pistols, if you please!" he commanded.

A girl appeared in the doorway. She was tall, about seventeen, with pale golden hair coiled around her head in two braids, and white with an anxiety or terror that Bill could readily understand. Though the Poulains were behind his back he could sense their hot anger and cold purpose, and that Van Tromp should inject his daughter into such a scene annoyed him. The Dutchman's subterfuge, moreover, was too obvious. Bill lifted the sun helmet aside.

Under it, beside the revolver, was a silver ring.

"Moloku's!" snapped Henri, brief and sharp.

Like lightning Hanu snatched up the ring. Bill caught the brown wrist, held it despite a lunge to escape that flung him off balance. Hanu was as strong or stronger than he. Bill clinched. The two staggered down the veranda, Bill unable to set himself for a blow, Hanu unable to pull away.

A gun roared in Bill's ear, searing the back of his neck with powder. The bullet fanned his cheek. To protect himself he let Hanu go, whirled, and dived at the knees of the man who had fired. Too late he saw that the man was Henri! Bill's tackle brought the young Frenchman down with stunning force. Before either could recover, Hanu had vaulted the veranda rail and dodged nimbly around the corner of the house.

To follow a native into the bush was hopeless. Bill did not attempt it. Instead he held Henri firmly, wondering whether the bullet had been intended for him, or had been fired in ungovernable excitement at two interlocked, struggling men.

BEFORE HIM was another puzzle. Poulain, with revolver half drawn, glared at Van Tromp, whose hand was closed about the revolver on the table. The Frenchman's lips were drawing back from his teeth. The Dutchman was paler than before, and of the two the more dangerous. Both were on the point of murder.

"None o' that!" Bill growled. Though they paid no attention, he decided they would not shoot, since they had not, and turned to Henri, who blinked at him from the veranda floor and ignored the two behind him.

"Trying to kill me?" Bill growled.

"You should have let me shoot again, *m'sieu'*, I would not have hit you." Henri was icy cool.

"You took a long chance!"

"Could I have shot Hanu through your body I would have done it!"

"Yeah!" Bill rumbled, rubbing his powder-burned neck. "Come clean now, youngster! What are you trying to stop by killing Hanu? Something more than the eating of long pig!"

"I cannot say." Under the silky mustache that was like a smear of soot his mouth set hard. "I cannot, you understand?" he pleaded. "I—you need not fear I will shoot you in the back!"

"Unless you gain by it. You don't seem to care much whether your father gets plugged," said Bill roughly, and added in a booming voice:

"Well, Mynheer Van Tromp! So your foreman Hanu knew nothing about it, hey? How'd that ring get under your hat?"

The Dutchman let go of his revolver and folded his arms.

"I lied," he said without apology. "For a foreman like Hanu, who can make a plantation like mine, I would do more than lie. But I have been accused before, by him." The bald head nodded at Poulain.

"Hanu came to me this morning," he went on, "and said that he had found a body at the foot of a cliff, from which he took the ring. What he had done with the body I did not ask, or care. It is not my business. But when I saw you armed, I knew what would be said. I acted to protect my foreman from accusations that are false. If they are not false, I apologize, even to Monsieur Poulain. What is more, to prove that I am not false, as I am accused, I will lead you to Hanu's hiding place, shoot him myself. But only if you have proof."

Briefly Bill explained about the bloodstained *pareu*. Van Tromp listened in silence, shrugged, and walked without a word into his bungalow.

"Where are you going?" Bill called suspiciously.

The bald head reappeared. "The march will be long, we will need food. I fear the shot alarmed my daughter, and go to explain. It will take less than a minute," Van Tromp explained with a sarcastic smile that seemed to jeer at Bill for his suspicions.

"Shall I follow him? I don't like this," Bill muttered.

Both the Poulains shook their heads.

"If he will go into ze bush wiz us, it is all I ask," said the father.

"He can lead us to Hanu's *paepae*—if he will," added the son.

NEVERTHELESS BILL did not like the absence. Van Tromp's confession and his proposed vengeance showed a callous indifference to the lives of others that marked him as a dangerous man. Bill knew the type that begins by not caring whether men are killed or not, and ends by preferring them dead. That Van Tromp was ignorant of the lengths to which Hanu had gone was possible. That he was fully cognizant of them was equally likely. To follow, however, would merely send the planter straight to his daughter. Nothing would be accomplished.

Had Bill been able to follow unseen his worst suspicions would have been confirmed. Van Tromp gave his daughter a curt order to bring food, and walked to the rear door of his house. His shoulders blocked the doorway. To any one spying on him from the front of the house he would have seemed to do no more than stare across the thicket of blooming plants that grew waist-deep to the steps, yet he had scarcely appeared when Hanu squirmed through the tangled mass of white spider lilies to the feet of his employer.

"The white men know all," Van Tromp whispered in Marquesan. "Gather your warriors and give them coconut brandy to increase their courage. I will guide the white men into the gorge on the trail to Tetio."

"That is near Pekia, the High Place," Hanu whispered.

"The less distance to carry them. They must not come back," growled Van Tromp, and walked back to his guests.

Hanu squirmed through the spider lilies into a thicket of young pandanus, where two natives joined him. The *moke's* eyes gleamed in the black, tattooed face.

"Fekei, are you brave?" he challenged the larger of the two, whose chest and face were tattooed in patterns of red and green. "The Bald Pig tells me to give you brandy, but there will be more brandy when the Bald Pig also is borne to the High Place and drops into the pit."

"I am brave," said Fekei stolidly.

The *moke* rocked to and fro on his heels, and though he whispered, his voice had the rise and fall of a chant:

"Brandy and death are the white gifts; before them we vanish like the mist before the sun. Once our people was great, but now the rain beats on the bare stones of the *paepaes* where the roofs have fallen in rot. The breadfruit will not grow on the coconut palm, nor will the white men and we live on the same land. Better to live in the hills where the big ships cannot throw the bullets that bang and the feet of the grunting soldiers make more noise than the rain. Once more we shall kindle the fires of the High Place and dance the dances my fathers have danced for eight and nine generations that I can name! You are brave, Fekei?"

"I am brave."

"Then tell the warriors to gather at the gorge on the trail to Tetio. Tell them to bring slings, and stones made smooth by rubbing!"

CHAPTER III

MIDDAY

VAN TROMP ALLOWED only a hasty breakfast, stuck his revolver in his pocket, and led the way into the brush. Bellow Bill, Henri, and Poulain followed in order. From the start the path climbed steadily toward the jagged lava ramparts of the hills, and within an hour the four were threading their way through vegetation that had reverted to wilderness.

Scents weighted the air. Hundreds of flowers of every color from crimson to violet were all around, and through the tangle of palm and fern great creepers coiled like serpents. Yet save for birds and insects the jungle seemed lifeless. The four white men had plunged into an abandoned world.

Occasionally they passed a native *paepae*—the broad platform of flat and heavy stones upon which all Marquesan houses are built—but the last vestige of the houses had rotted into dust decades ago. The hum of insects was oppressive, worse than silence.

Bill, who was familiar with the sounds of a tropical jungle, and who had been walking with the softness of a big cat, curly head cocked to one side, touched Van Tromp's shoulder abruptly.

"We're being followed. By some one that's careless. Twice I've heard a stone roll."

"Who would follow, and what of it?" growled the Dutchman. "At my house is only Frieda. She would carry warning to no one. My hands are scattered over the plantation. If one of them should have heard the shot and sought to warn Hanu he could not pass us on the trail."

"Your plantation hands could easily be in the hills already, after last night's—pastime," Bill rumbled. "We're followed, I tell you. I'm going to step aside into the bush while you go on, and find out by whom, and why."

"Mais non! Ze haste is mos' *necessaire!"* Poulain objected.

Van Tromp agreed. He explained that he wanted to reach Hanu's *paepae,* which was high in the hills, so quickly that the *moke* would believe his master had come to warn him. When they reached the spot the other three would hide in the brush where they could cover Van Tromp as he went forward. Hanu, seeing his master alone, would not try to escape. Van Tromp would shoot him down at sight. By a look Bill questioned Henri.

"I do not wish to be alone with these two, *m'sieu',"* was the answer.

Bill shrugged, and the four men went on. Two hours passed. The heat and the steady climb made them all pant with exertion.

The sun was vertical when the path emerged on the lip of a chasm of black lava that held the heat like an oven. To right and left stretched a barrier of cliffs, which seemed to have been wrenched apart by an earthquake. The chasm cut through the cliffs and the slope leading up to them as though the lava had been gashed by a gigantic ax while still pasty.

"The Marquesans had a fort at both ends of this gorge in the old days," Van Tromp grunted, scrambling down a declivity so steep he was compelled to use his hands. "In 1812 they stopped your American Captain Porter and thirty-five sailors armed with muskets here for a day and a night—stopped them with nothing but spears and stones."

"Yeah?" Bill grunted. The rumble of a rolling stone made him look back up the slope. "Hi! Lookout!" he roared—too late.

A bowlder as big as his head hurtled down the slope like a spent cannon ball. Poulain leaped aside. Henri, waiting for his father to be safe before he dodged himself, was struck. He cried out. His falling body swept Bill's legs from beneath him, and brought down Van Tromp. They rolled to the foot of the slope in a shower of small stones. Down upon them hurtled a second bowlder.

Bill could only flatten himself to the lava. By luck the bowlder rushed over his head. A third followed instantly—missing him by a yard. He jerked out his revolver, and fired at random.

Van Tromp gave a strangled cry of rage and terror and ran down the valley, Bill leaped up. Henri struggled onto his knees, turned dead white; and toppled over in a faint as he attempted to stand. Bill gathered him up in one arm and ran. Poulain, running beside him, gasped and swore.

A fourth bowlder sped after them with the rumble of an oncoming freight train, passed to one side, and knocked splinters of stone from the black wall of the chasm. In that broadest part of the gorge Van Tromp stopped, so pale of face that Bill absolved him from any collusion in the attack. He also had been in the path of the stones. That only one of the four had been hurt was sheer chance.

"**ONE NATIVE** could have done that," Bill snapped. "How's the other end of this damned trap you've put us in?"

"Worse," Van Tromp grunted, and wiped the sweat from his bald head. "I do not understand—*ach*, no! I do not understand," he added, so obviously bewildered that Bill shook him violently by the shoulder.

From the edge of the chasm a round stone as big as Bill's fist hummed through the air, missing him by a yard, and smashed against the rocks with a force that showered him with lava chips. Half a dozen more, thrown from different points, banished the hope that the attack had been the work of Hanu alone.

Bill caught a glimpse of a brown arm whirling a sling. He fired, uselessly. The aim of the stones was deadly, shelter in that bare lava chasm almost non-existent. Pursued by stones he carried Henri to a shallow cave that offered some protection, shoved his revolver with its four remaining cartridges into his belt, and stuffed a handful of fine cut into his mouth.

The slung stones could be dodged, though they traveled with double the speed of a rock thrown by hand.

"Hit the nigger and you get a good cigar!" Bill rumbled. From the angles at which the stones were thrown, he judged the number of assailants. There were only seven. Not heavy odds if the white men could get on level ground.

"Look after your kid. His ankle's broken," Bill ordered Poulain. "As to you, Van Tromp—you got us into this, so you'll get us out. If we stay here they'll bean us sure."

"I t'ink we shoot him! 'E 'as betray' us! We should kill him," Poulain snarled, pawing for his revolver.

"Like hell! Waste as big a target for rocks as he is?" Bill snorted. "Rush that hill, Dutchie! I'm right at your heels with a gat."

Van Tromp charged the slope willingly. Stones hummed around the two. They could glimpse the head and shoulders of the native whirling the sling as the missile was thrown, but so briefly that a shot would have been a waste of cartridges. The Marquesans, in turn, dared not expose themselves long enough to take effective aim. Bill kept his head down and climbed. A yard in advance Van Tromp used the same tactics.

They were halfway to the crest, where the path narrowed, when the first bowlder descended upon them. Both sprang aside, but Bill, forced to stand erect, was struck in the chest by a sling-stone that tumbled him to the bottom. Van Tromp, with stones flying all around him, scrambled to the lip of the chasm and disappeared.

Bill's chest felt as though it had stopped the kick of a mule, but he scrambled upward again to lend the Dutchman a hand.

He expected revolver shots, shouts, a cessation of the stones as Van Tromp's revolver cleared the crest of enemies. Instead there was nothing. Not one shot, even. It was as though Van Tromp had been clubbed over the head the instant he reached level ground: and though Bill could not believe that, there was no slackening in the stone barrage. A hurtling bowlder swept him from the path. He rolled down the slope, starting a small avalanche. In the fall his head struck against the stone base of the gorge, and darkness engulfed him.

He came to with Poulain tugging him by the shoulder. Stones caromed around both; the fat little Frenchman, puffing and panting, had managed to drag Bill halfway up the cave. The pearler made the rest of the distance on his own feet and dropped against the cave wall. Poulain squatted opposite.

" 'E 'as trick' us, Bill," he said bitterly. "I should 'ave shot him—long ago, at ze bungalow."

"And we'd be a lot better off!" jeered the pearler. "Bullets would be easier to face than them damn rocks. The bowlders get you if you stick in the path, and if you leave it they pop you off with slings," Bill winced as a well-aimed missile flung bits of stone in his face, and packed his mouth with fine cut.

"**WHY ARE** you so hell-fired anxious to bump off Van Tromp, anyway?" Bill demanded.

The moist black eyes narrowed.

"I 'ate him!" Poulain snarled—which gave Bill no enlightenment whatever. He spat.

"Well, I guess the natives got him, so forget it," he advised. "What now? We'll fry on these rocks in another hour. There isn't a canteen of water in the gang."

"*Oui,*" agreed Poulain.

"Yes, hell! I was thirsty when I came ashore! If we do sit here, safe and suffering, are any white men apt to come along and drive these natives off?"

"Impossible. Zere are not a dozen whites on ze whole islan'.

From here to my plantation is four hours' march, from zere to ze governor, three hours more, by lan' or boat."

"Then I won't fry like a pancake on these hot rocks," Bill decided, and raising his voice to the utmost, bellowed:

"Ahoy, Hanu! Damn you, what do you want?"

No more stones were slung, but for fully five minutes there was no other sign that Bill's stentorian shout had been heard. Then a black head and a jet black tattooed face peered over the rim of the chasm.

"Capsize gun belong you!" Hanu shouted.

Bill promptly tossed his pistol away.

"*Nom d'un nom!* You would not surrender?" Poulain remonstrated.

The pearler shook his head, but took the two other revolvers and tossed them after his own.

"If we can't get up, we got to get them to come down," he explained in his softest tone. "Buck up, man! I've been captured by natives before. They're in no hurry to kill prisoners—though I guess they scragged Van Tromp at sight."

"Non! 'E is zere leader!" spat Poulain.

Both Bill and he were partly wrong, and partly right. Van Tromp lay in the brush at the head of the gorge, surrounded by natives, bruised, raging but unharmed, and, in his own opinion, in command.

The rock that had been rolled upon him as well as the others had appalled him. Knowing Hanu to be determined and quick-witted, he had expected the natives to hold both ends of the gorge until he could persuade the trapped white men to surrender. The premature attack which risked his own life infuriated him, and it was in good earnest that he had stormed the slope ahead of Bellow Bill.

As he stepped onto the level ground a native rushed at him, swinging a *u'u*, or war club of ironwood. Van Tromp leveled his gun, hesitating to shoot one of his own laborers, thinking that liquor and excitement had sent the native into a frenzy. The

Marquesan charged on straight at the revolver, and Van Tromp was about to fire when Hanu dashed from the bushes and gathered the native into his huge arms.

"Hold the fool still," Van Tromp snarled. "Hanu—you dog! You damn near killed *me!*"

"Men no belong me," said Hanu grimly, meaning that he could not control them.

"Well, I can! Now I'm here, we'll do what you should have done in the first place. Tell them to throw away their guns. Send down one man to tie them up. Send him!" Van Tromp growled malevolently, pointing at the man who had threatened him with the *u'u.*

Bellow Bill had hardly tossed away his revolver, therefore, when a Marquesan picked his way down the steep trail and edged cautiously toward the weapons. He carried a war club, and was evidently afraid of the three whites. Bill, however, stood with hands in pockets. He allowed the native to pick up the revolvers. More confidently the man advanced. Not until he was within arm's length did the pearler act. One sudden swing from his hip stretched the native senseless. Bill knelt on his back and bound him hand and foot with his own cord, picked up Henri's revolver, which had not been discharged, and holding the bound man before him for a shield, advanced toward the slope down which he had twice been tumbled.

"Carry Henri up when I'm over the top," he roared cheerfully at Poulain.

BY USING his captive as a shield against the sling-stones, Bill could avoid the depressed path down which the bowlders trundled like balls down an alley. Though he found it hard to climb with a man in his arms, his strength made the feat possible, and the fear of injuring their own fellow seemed to paralyze Hanu and his men. Not a stone was hurled as Bill picked his way to the crest. He emerged on a bare shelf of rock, facing the jungle. Not a man was in sight. Bill was about to shout to Poulain in triumph when a revolver spat from the midst of a thorn bush directly in front. The native he held gave a convulsive quiver as the bullet struck, and went limp.

"The next is yours, sailor," snarled Van Tromp's voice. The thin powder smoke drifted away from the bush.

To rush was futile. Bill could see nothing to shoot at. He let the dead native fall and tossed his revolver down. Poulain, who came panting upward with Henri over his shoulder, was in no shape to fight. He dropped his weapon at Van Tromp's order.

"Guess you were right, Poulain," Bill rumbled. "We should have killed him while we had the chance, but I was believing Henri more than you, d'you see?"

A native squirmed through the bushes and bound the arms of the three with strips of coconut fiber. Not until they were secure did Van Tromp appear. His eyes glittered foolishly, and on the dead white face was a ghastly, mad expression of triumph. As he walked toward his captive, Hanu, in bare feet slipped noiselessly behind him.

A war club rose and fell on the bald head. Van Tromp pitched forward. Hanu squatted beside the unconscious body and bound his arms like those of the others.

"One, two, three, four, five," the *moke* counted with satisfaction.

Bellow Bill shifted his quid. The fifth was the native shot by Van Tromp.

CHAPTER IV

AFTERNOON

THE SOOT-BLACK FACE of the *moke* concealed his emotions, but the other natives, of whom there were five, were awed and uneasy because of their own success. They strutted and waved their war clubs of polished ironwood, boasted to each other of their part in the victory; and yet Bellow Bill was amused to observe that boasts and threats alike were spoken at a little distance from the prisoners, instead of being snarled into their faces. Like hunters who have captured a lion, the Marquesans feared their prisoners even in bonds.

Bill figured that he had been in worse situations, notably when he had been in the power of the Borneo bushmen. Those fuzzy-headed blacks had been utterly savage, whereas, the Marquesans were theoretically Christianized and partly civilized. He lay quiet and alert, waiting for the least opportunity.

The behavior of his companions was otherwise. Poulain, after writhing in his bonds, called to Hanu again and again. Though the *moke* paid no attention, the Frenchman persisted in his effort to talk or negotiate. Van Tromp, after recovering consciousness, lay with his pale face frozen in a snarl. Unreasonable rage glittered in the little blue eyes; he spoke neither to the white men nor the natives.

Henri's face was drawn with the pain of the broken leg, but his coolness and air of detachment from his father and his father's enterprises was intensified.

"What's wrong with you and your old man?" Bill rumbled.

"That does not matter now. It is ended, we are finished," Henri answered precisely.

"Don't be dumb!" Bill boomed. Every one looked in his direction, and he grinned at them all. Like many sailors, he wore his jackknife on a lanyard around his waist instead of in his pocket, and the native who had searched him had missed it. Knowing the carrying quality of his own voice, he dared not whisper the information to Henri, but turned his back in the hope that the other would notice the bulge under the waistband of his trousers.

"Ah! Bien!" Henri whispered, and squirmed back to back with the big pearler.

Hanu, however, unknowingly forestalled the use of the steel. He grunted an order. Fekei lifted Henri on his back, two others slung the dead native over a pole, while the other four guarded the white men able to walk. For a half mile the party took the back trail, and then branched off to the left and began to climb another shoulder of the lava cliffs. They halted at last in an open space surrounded by dense undergrowth at the foot of the steep slope.

The natives laid the prisoners in a row like cordwood, and then sprawled at their ease. Hanu put his fingers in his mouth and whistled piercingly. He listened—and suddenly cocked his ear in the direction from which the party had come. He scowled and muttered to his men—who shook their heads. They had heard nothing. Neither had Bill. On the contrary, Fekei pointed up the hillside, and in a moment the sound of rustling under-growth was unmistakable.

An old man whose tattooing had turned from blue to a pale greenish yellow with the years stepped into the open space accompanied by a handsome Marquesan girl. The man bore food—*poi poi*, bananas, a little roast pork. The girl carried a bowl and a dish of grated root which resembled shredded cabbage. Squatting, she commenced to prepare *kava*—chewing the grated root that the ferment in the saliva might liberate the narcotic element.

Bellow Bill nudged Henri gleefully. Opportunity was coming. *Kava* combines the effects of alcohol and opium. It intoxicates and induces visions. Since its drinking is prohibited by law, the Marquesans are no longer accustomed to its effect.

THE PREPARATION of the draft was slow. The sun was declining when the root was prepared. Hanu poured milk of green coconuts on the mass of masticated root, kneaded it between his powerful hands, and poured the juice into another bowl.

"*U haanoho ia te kai; a tapapa is te kai!*" he intoned. "Come to the food; the food is prepared."

A drinking bowl made of a coconut shell circulated swiftly from hand to hand. Each native tossed off two drafts of the decoction, and fell upon the *poi poi* and the meat, cramming down the food in handfuls. In a deep voice Hanu began to chant, a long tale of his forefathers and the great victory of the Typees over the tribe of Haana, while the five warriors, the old man, and the girl, who had drunk and eaten after the rest, sprawled with chin on chest and eyes dull. Henri commenced to fumble at Bill's waist.

"Hanu's head is of iron," he whispered apprehensively. "The rest are drunk."

Whether the *moke* would have noticed the stirring among his prisoners was never learned. In the undergrowth leaves rustled. The ink black face jerked upward. Over the circle of sprawling natives leaped—to Bill's consternation—Frieda.

In her hand was an open knife. She flung herself at her father, and slashed through the fibers binding ankles and wrists. Hanu lunged at her. She screamed aloud, but instead of dodging aside, she jumped straight at his face, scratching and kicking. He held her, but her frantic struggles occupied him for a moment—long enough for Van Tromp to heave himself to knees, to his feet, and then to plunge into the bushes. Hanu plucked Frieda away from him as a man might throw aside a scratching cat, tossed her to Fekei, caught up an ironwood *u'u* and gave chase. Two of the natives followed; the remainder could rise, but were not yet able to run.

Bill swore at the top of his voice, and recklessly thrust out his hands for Henri to cut. A native staggered toward him. Drawing back both bound feet, Bill landed a kick that tumbled the man end over end. The ropes around his wrists parted. He caught the knife and slashed his ankles free. A single blow knocked Fekei down. Bill caught Frieda, threw her at the bushes.

"Run!" he shouted. Fekei had found a war club, and so had the other natives; as they staggered toward him Bill plunged after the girl. He crashed through the tangle of brush and vines like a bull, unable to see six feet before him, trying by ear and by the trail to overtake the girl. He failed. A thorn bush barred his path. He passed it on the right and knew, too late, that he should have taken the opposite side. A native was close behind.

Bill could not go back, and at that moment a scream told him that Frieda had been overtaken.

The pearler crouched in his tracks. The native behind almost tripped over him, swung a wild blow with the *u'u*. Bill rose inside its sweep and seized the brown throat. He shook the man till his head wabbled, threw him down, and finished him with his own war club.

Hanu was whistling shrilly, blast after blast. The Marquesan girl was screaming. From Frieda, not another sound. The jungle itself was silent, save for the distant rustle of men starting toward Hanu, who was collecting his forces—a bit of generalship that made Bill swear. One by one he could overpower them. All five together—he left the old man and girl out—were formidable. They had clubs, and the revolvers, in case they were able to shoot. Henri could not run.

Retreat came hard to Bill, but he forced himself to circle in the direction that Van Tromp had taken. He despised the man for abandoning a daughter clever enough to follow them since the moment they had left the plantation—for the noise both he and Hanu had heard must have been made by Frieda. She was brave to sacrifice her own liberty for his. Van Tromp might be hog, skunk, and poltroon, but he was a man of tremendous strength, and he and Bill together might attack Hanu on something like even terms.

Bill swung the *u'u*. He liked its balance. Three feet long, paddle-shaped, sharp-edged, of wood heavy as ebony and so hard he could not dent it with his thumbnail, it was a combination of ax and sword. One blow had killed the Marquesan.

Van Tromp could have the jackknife that Bill had carried away in his excitement. One to five was long odds. Two to five was—fair. He and the Dutchman would attack the natives before the fumes of the *kava* wore off. If the stuff was like alcohol, the natives would already be shocked almost to sobriety.

THOUGH HE was seeking Van Tromp, it was soon evident that the latter was making no effort to join him. Bill could hear

Hanu snarling at his men, but not another sound. As rapidly as possible the pearler wormed his way through the jungle until he intercepted Van Tromp's trail, which he followed for nearly a quarter of a mile.

Far beyond the spot where Hanu had turned back. Bill found the Dutchman, glowering and at bay, his back against a vertical wall of lava, a jagged stone in his hand.

"Chuck away that rock, Van," Bill grinned cheerfully. "I'll cut you a club. That's some daughter you got. Ought to be a boy. Let's go get her!"

The Dutchman's bald head sank into huge shoulders. More than ever he stood like a bowlder tottering for a mad rush. Beneath the pale yellow eyebrows the pale blue eyes glittered.

"And afterward?" he growled.

Bill stared. The violence and unexpectedness of the question, the glitter of the pale blue eyes warned him he had to deal with a man beside himself with rage, disappointment, or an emotion less allied to reason than these.

"You tell me what to do, you that brought the Poulains and found the ring," pursued Van Tromp hoarsely. "Afterward, you go to sea, but I sit on my veranda and watch the vines swallow my orchards. Fifteen years I have built, you meddler! Only I can make this island blossom like a garden, only I can ship copra by the schooner load—and you would make me like all the others! Poulain and I bought land together! Look at him, now, and at me! He says the natives will not work, but I"—still gripping the jagged stone, Van Tromp pounded himself on the chest—"I found the secret. I am a great man, a rich man! I can control the natives. A little later—by dawn tomorrow—they will obey me!"

"D'ye know what you're saying?"

"That some will not see the dawn? Enemies!" Van Tromp snarled. "Yes, I know, meddler! More bodies than you believe will hang from the banyan tree at the High Place! That is the price. Before now I have paid it. What if these are white? The Poulains? They envy me! Frieda? She followed to warn you, knowing what I whispered to Hanu, helping you whose pistol was against my back! Though Hanu will not harm her! He dare not."

"You're mad," Bill muttered.

Horribly the planter glared at him. "They watched me. They reported me to the governor—come to me, the yellow hair hanging to the waist, to pray that I stop, that I let the ground be choked with weeds," he mouthed. In the grip of his mono-mania he confused acts performed by Frieda and the Poulains.

Bill's face hardened. He had lived among rough men who did not let a life stand between them and their goal, but the thought of Frieda pleading with her father and being abandoned by him was proof of an insanity awful in its purposefulness and cunning.

"They will hinder me no more," said Van Tromp. "By to-morrow there will only be you!"

Bill read the purpose in the insane eyes. He ducked. The stone that Van Tromp hurled at his head missed. With a yell that rang through the jungle the Dutchman rushed forward, caught Bill's war club, and flung himself backward to wrench it from the pearler's grip.

Muscles loose, Bill let himself be jerked from his feet, thereby keeping both hands on the weapon. He was on the defensive. He wanted to knock sense back into Van Tromp's skull, but though he was on top as they fell, the latter changed the wrestle into a death grapple.

THE DUTCHMAN'S knee jabbed Bill in the groin. Nausea all but mastered Bill. His fingers slipped on the polished iron wood. His palms seemed to run sweat. He clung while Van Tromp's boots battered his shoulders and face. As the effects of the disabling blow passed he hauled himself forward along the club until he lay upon it and upon Van Tromp.

The latter rolled over, carrying Bill underneath. With the pearler flat on his back, Van Tromp twisted the club crosswise, tugging to push it up over Bill's chest and press it into his throat. Bill heaved to dislodge him, and failed. The club, however, did not move. In Van Tromp's throat the sinews stood out like oak roots; his eyes bulged, but in strength of arm and fingers Bill matched him. With a snarl he bent to bite Bill's fingers.

Though the pearler had never wrestled for a cane, he had watched Japanese divers wrestle on his schooner, had seen what a fall a man who yields suddenly in a test of strength can give his adversary.

As teeth gnawed his knuckles he relaxed. The club shot over his head and Van Tromp's whole body followed it. With an upward thrust of legs and back Bill turned them both in a somersault, shifting both hands to the handle of the club as they whirled, and throwing all his strength into a jerk as they crashed against the ground.

The sharp club edge cut through Van Tromp's fingers. Bill snatched the club from beneath the Dutchman's body and jabbed the paddle-shaped blade at the base of the bald skull— a six-inch blow backed by the weight of chest and shoulders.

The Dutchman's thick body jerked, and then lay still. Bill rose. The other remained in the circle of broken bushes like a bundle of clothes, flattened, and formless, with a thin red wound where the thick neck joined the bald skull. He was dead.

"Gone native," Bill panted. "God—how he had! He had this coming."

He sucked the blood from his bitten finger and stepped into the jungle. Since he must fight alone, he hoped that Hanu would come to investigate the maddened yell with which Van Tromp had launched the attack.

CHAPTER V

TWILIGHT

FOR THE PREDICAMENT in which he was involved, Bill blamed himself. Van Tromp had spoken the truth in one particular: Bill had meddled when he should have led. Because he had relished the idea of a chase into the jungle, he had not taken Poulain's accusations at their face value, and thereby compelled Frieda, who knew the facts in all their horror, to follow—though to rescue, not betray, her father. In that respect Van Tromp had been deceived by his monomania.

Well—so be it. Bill's shoulders were broad enough to bear plenty of responsibility. Though he was involved in a game more sinister that he had believed, he was neither worried nor disturbed. Long .contact with Polynesians had convinced him that the brown men could not exhibit steadfastness of purpose unless a white man was leading or secretly supporting them. Without Van Tromp, Hanu was only a native. He—and even more likely, the men with him—would release their prisoners and take to the hills when they discovered their patron was dead.

Bill, however, had never encountered a native of Hanu's fiber, and because Henri's broken leg made rescue border on the impossible, he overlooked the fact that Hanu had already knocked his boss over the head. Bill discovered his error promptly.

Step by step he retraced the trail to the scene of the *kava* drinking. The sun was setting. Under the jungle foliage the light had changed from green to gray, and from the silence ahead Bill feared that his enemies had moved on. Of the noise he made himself he was careless, though as he came close he abandoned the trail and pushed through the dense brush in order to flank any possible ambush. When he was able to see the clearing, however, he found all five of the natives bunched in the center. Hanu held a revolver. He sighted and fired.

The bullet ripped a yard over Bill's head. The pearler froze in his tracks, grinning at this evidence of bad marksmanship. The war clubs of the five were more threatening than revolvers in the hands of a man who had probably never discharged a short gun before, for the Marquesans were drawn up in line, and stood like soldiers, waiting for orders. It was marvelous discipline for primitive warriors. Poulain, Henri, and Frieda lay on the grass beside them, bound. The old man and the girl had vanished. They were harmless in any event.

With a frown at the revolver, Hanu tried a second shot, aiming this time almost at the roots of the bushes. Again he missed badly, but Bill instantly changed his own tactics to meet the defensive attitude of the natives.

He cried out—a roaring, echoing yell of mingled pain and fear, simulating a mortal wound. Throwing himself backward, he kicked and thrashed until the bushes swayed violently, then began to crawl away—slowly, as though he were creeping off to die, yet taking care that he made commotion enough to be followed easily. It was the old trick of the bird that thrashes on the ground just beyond the hunter's reach and leads him away from the nest.

The device succeeded in that the Marquesans followed— but not with the reckless triumph for which Bill hoped. Step by step and shoulder to shoulder, all five plowed through the brush, never faster than a walk, and never breaking rank, though Bill groaned with the utmost realism not five yards in advance. When he had retreated less than twenty feet the natives stopped and muttered in undertones. Bill overheard Hanu's order:

"Go back!"

ABANDONING THE hope of separating his enemies, Bill changed his tactics again. On hands and knees, with his utmost speed and bushcraft, he crawled toward the little open space. Hanu's retreat was as deliberate as his advance had been. The pearler was able to get back first. Swiftly, in silence, he crawled into the open, finger on lips to prevent the prisoners from greeting him with a shout. In Henri's hands he pressed his jackknife, dragged Poulain and Frieda where their bonds could be reached, and then charged into the brush to meet the returning natives.

Like a bull he broke through the line. Hanu dodged the blow Bill swung at his head. With a second swing of his club the pearler stretched a native on the ground, and turned, striking right and left. Hanu, teeth and eyes gleaming in a dead black face, shouted an order.

The natives jumped left and right as the *moke* rushed straight at Bill with upraised club. The ironwood rang as Bill parried the first blow. Hanu shouted, held his club straight before him, on the defensive.

Out of the corner of his eye Bill could see Fekei working to get behind him. Knowing he was outgeneraled, he struck with all his strength at the soot-black face. Expertly Hanu squirmed aside. Bill leaped backward, barely sidestepping Fekei's rush, then turned and ran.

Now they would follow; now surely he could separate them and fight them one by one. Despite the *moke's* equal strength and greater skill in the use of the *u'u,* Bill felt himself a match. He hoped that Henri had made good use of the diversion he had created. He could not have fought the five together for ten more seconds.

The natives did pursue—for as long as it took Hanu to gather his breath.

"Stop!" he shouted. "To me! Let the live pig go!"

Fekei, who was close to Bill's heels, stopped instantly. The brush crackled as he rejoined his companions.

With an oath Bill pulled up short. Though outgeneraled again, he saw: the third possibility. If the prisoners had freed themselves, such slow and disciplined pursuit would never overtake them. Though he had failed to scatter the natives, their fear of him made their number of little use.

"Ahoy! Frieda, Henri! Poulain!" he bellowed. "Sing out! I'll reach you first!"

"Bien! They have gone!" Henri answered, but to Bill's horror, the reply came from the clearing. The young Frenchman had sacrificed himself—was still a prisoner.

Worse followed. Much too close at hand, Frieda screamed one cry of consternation and terror that rang shrilly, that seemed to hang in the air, that brought the sweat to Bill's forehead. This was no response to his shout—and from Poulain not a sound.

Careless of what noise he made, Bill forced his way toward the girl. The denseness of the tropical foliage mocked him. The vines that laced the tree trunks together tripped him, tightened across his chest like ropes. He halted at last, snatched a mouthful of fine cut, worked it into a quid, and spat. Haste had best be made slowly. There was no pursuit.

"Frieda!" he called again in his deep voice. "For God's sake, sing out, girl!"

A low cry answered. In a moment he had approached near enough to be guided by muffled, half hysterical sobs. He found Frieda alone, crouched like a hare in the thick brush, her face buried in her arms, her shoulders shaking.

"STEADY, NOW!" Bill rumbled. "You're all right now, kid. Where's Poulain?"

She lifted her head. Blood was flowing from her mouth.

"Gone!" she said. "He knocked me down and ran—that way."

She pointed toward the plantations.

"Gone!" Bill ejaculated.

"Why not? I am the daughter of Van Tromp," said the girl dully. "He hates me, too. He hates his son because Henri loved me. When you dropped the knife Henri cut my bonds first, and then his father's. Poulain seized me. I begged him to carry Henri in his arms, but he would not. He dragged me here, knocked me down, and ran. He knows Hanu will kill us all."

"Yeah?" grunted Bill, who had recovered himself.

The girl smiled at his cheerful aggressiveness. Hopelessness and too much knowledge made the twist of her lips awful to see.

"He is right," she said. "The old man and the girl have gone to kindle the fires on the High Place. Soon Hanu will start the drums beating to summon all the natives to the feast. The drums can talk. Few natives dare to fight the white men face to face, but many are brave enough to club an unarmed man from behind. You have been over the trail. Can you run that gantlet in the dark?"

"Me? Yeah, or hide till morning."

"Or be hunted down like a pig in the morning," said the girl. "Where is my father?"

"He—uh—he fell over a cliff!"

"I heard him shout. You killed him. We all knew you killed him when it was you that returned, and not he. I do not blame you. He was mad. Poulain and Henri guessed my father was insane. I—knew it. I know—all my father knew, and that is why I tell you we will all die. Even Poulain, even you."

"Shut up! I can get you home!" said Bill.

He was curt, for he saw the grim choice that he must make. To take her home meant to abandon Henri to a horrible fate.

"You are a stranger. You were blind this morning. You could not guess what Henri and I knew," Frieda went on. "Living in the same house, I overheard a word here and a word there. I saw things my father could not keep me from seeing. *M'sieu'*, I watched my father sell his soul to the devil!"

"Meaning Hanu?"

"If there had not been Hanu, there would have been another *moke!* No—first my father closed his eyes to what his workmen did, and soon more workmen came to his plantation. Then he helped. He let Hanu preach of the old gods and the old ways, and shielded him when men disappeared. I knew, but I could not send my own father to the guillotine. Poulain knew, though he had no proof, as I had, and the governor would not listen to him. Poulain wanted to kill my father and take his place; then *he* would let Hanu preach, and shield him. His plantation would stretch back to the hills."

"Why didn't he shoot your father? I don't mean in the open, but by accident—out hunting?"

"Because Henri swore that if my father were shot he would tell the governor why. His father was not guilty yet, like mine. He could threaten. Poulain did not dare. He had to wait—"

"Till a copper-headed, tattooed fool named Bellow Bill came in and did his dirty work for him, huh?" rumbled the pearler. "Meanwhile Henri figured I might bump off Hanu for him, and clear up the mess? Kid—" Bill paused. Twilight was merging into night. In the gloom of the jungle he could no longer distinguish the girl's features. From the heights a drum began to beat, a dull long throbbing with an irregular cadence. "Are you sure the trails are blocked?"

"You hear," the girl muttered. "Faint strokes, and heavy ones. We hear a mutter like the surf, but to the natives it speaks like a telegraph."

"Men have tried to stop me before. I'm still here," Bill rumbled. "Hanu and his gang had me licked in the brush to-day. On the High Place there'd be firelight, and open ground to make it easy for one of them to get behind me. Women first, that's the rule. I could get you home, and fix Poulain. Why, hell, on the trail I'd meet the cowards!"

The girl was silent. For Bill the temptation to take her silence for consent was strong. Death he did not fear particularly. What shook him was the knowledge that his death would mean the girl's. All the afternoon he had schemed to separate his enemies, and failed. He must face one against five, and with all his self-confidence he was far too level-headed to count on victory. Women came first. No one would blame Bill—excepting himself.

"And another coward on that trail would be me," he boomed. "I'm sorry, kid, but I can't leave a buddy helpless. You'll have to take the chance—I'm going to give Hanu a busted head or a bigger dinner."

"I am glad! I love Henri, and am glad you will try, even though you must fail!" she called after him with a courage that was heartening.

CHAPTER VI

DARKNESS

HE DECIDED TO settle the issue quickly. Guided first by the sound of the drum and later by the glimmer of fire, he climbed to the rim of the High Place to strike before his adversaries numbered more than the five able-bodied men.

Before him was a level plateau set with grim black rocks chipped and polished into gigantic chairs. Trees shrouded the place, making the darkness impenetrable. The flickering red light of a bonfire beat upward from a deep pit, over which a huge banyan tree with gnarled and distorted limbs writhed like a thing in torment. This was the High Place, sacred to devilish rites, fit to be the abode of demons.

The rumble of the drum beat at Bellow Bill's ears. At first he could distinguish no human figures. Then the fire blazed up, and against the darkness his enemies were silhouetted. They were clustered amid the twisted roots of the banyan tree. The old man pounded the drum, the men knelt at some task he could not distinguish. Hanu sat in the wizard's seat.

Bill failed to locate Henri. For a moment he was in despair— which changed swiftly to horror. He had looked on the ground, whereas the Frenchman hung from the tree by a rope looped under his shoulders, dangling above the deep pit and the fire. He still lived, for his head was erect.

One slash of a knife and his body would fall into the pit, to be crushed on the stones beside the fire. The rope must lead down among the banyan's roots which dropped from the limbs to the ground, like props. Among them, therefore, Bill decided to make his stand, lest during the combat the cord be severed. He gripped his club and sprinted across the *paepae*. He was among the natives while they reached for weapons.

"Hi!" he roared. The swing of his *u'u* split a Marquesan skull. "Hi!" Back among the banyan roots he leaped as the natives scattered. He found the cord by which Henri hung, and tensed to meet the onslaught of Hanu. As his men scattered, the *moke* leaped from his chair. He was stripped for the rites he had to perform, his *pareu* twisted into a roll of cloth around his loins. He carried only a club.

Bill leaped from the shelter of the banyan roots and swung a two-handed blow at the black face, a blow that would have knocked Hanu's war club aside, and crushed the skull had it landed. The *moke* stepped back, like a boxer who side-steps a roundhouse swing. Bill swung half around with the force of his own blow. The *moke* chopped at his neck.

By a leap sidewise Bill escaped, but Hanu had maneuvered him away from the tree. The swish of the *moke's* club by his cheek taught Bill that in this duel footwork was everything. Unless he were incessantly active his guard could be beaten down. Hanu was as strong as he, as able to snap the shaft of the war club with a fair blow. Bill jabbed the point of his club at the soot-black face and sprang clear into the open. From the side Fekei struck at him. He saw the dull gleam of a revolver in the native's *pareu*, dodged, parried a blow from a third. Hanu ran up, club upraised with both hands.

Back and back Bill was driven, dodging, hitting when he could, but never striking these foemen more agile than he. He was pushed into the brightest of the firelight. Behind was the edge of the pit. In a rapid flurry of blows the four natives forced him to give ground until further retreat was impossible; yet at least the precipitous drop at his heels now prevented them from attacking him on either side. Fekei dropped his club and dragged out his revolver, screaming to the others to let him shoot; but Hanu pressed the fight, his body shielding Bill.

No fencing, no dodging now. Face to face, both with war clubs raised, they feinted. The issue hung on a single blow.

The *moke* saw an opening and struck. As his club poised, Bill smashed home his own blow, beating Hanu as a boxer beats his opponent to the punch. The clubs met with a resounding crash of splintered wood. Hanu's weapon snapped at the handle, but before Bill could strike again the *moke* lunged forward, crowding under the swing of Bill's club. His shoulders drove against the pearler's hip to hurl him into the pit.

For an instant they were locked, straining. Bill did not yield. He dropped his club, struck once with his fist at the back of Hanu's neck. Staggering, the *moke* grabbed behind with both hands at Bill's throat.

Fekei, dancing behind the wrestlers with the revolver, unable to shoot because the two bodies were as one, yelled with horror— for Bill caught the *moke's* right wrist with both hands, whirled on the verge of the pit, bringing his back to Hanu's breast, and the brown arm rigid over his shoulder.

Hanu's feet shot from the ground. He was catapulted over Bill's shoulder, arms and legs flying. In mid-air he uttered one scream and fell—straight into the heart of the fire. Behind Bill sparks shot up. There was no second cry. The fall stunned Hanu; the flames ended him.

The suddenness of the throw was too much for Fekei. Before the native realized he had a target, Bill grappled him, wrenched the revolver away and sent him sprawling. The two other natives rushed with their clubs. Bill fired twice. Both went down. One lay still. The other uttered a whimpering cry and pressed both hands upon a chest wound that poured blood.

FEKEI LIFTED his head and blinked at the revolver pointing at his forehead. Tense muscles relaxed. Slowly, very slowly, he rolled upon his stomach and dragged himself inch by inch toward the white man's feet.

"It is finished. I am brave no more," he groaned. "O master, I am *paopao*—sick of life. May I eat the fruit of the *eva*, O master? Our sun is set. Soon only the white man and the sea will be left. The white man does not care, and the sea—the sea does not remember."

The reddish-purple fruit of the *eva* is deadly poison. Marquesan warriors wounded or utterly ashamed use it to escape from pain or contempt. Bill, flushed with victory, knew from the request how utterly he had destroyed the work of Hanu and Van Tromp. He shook his head.

"You must ask your new chief," he rumbled. "No, not him of the black face who burns in the fire. Your chief is there!" Bill pointed to Henri, swinging gently in the boughs of the banyan tree.

"Roll the drum into the fire, and wait to tell your brothers that it summoned that fires in the High Place are taboo, that long pig is taboo, now and forever."

As the drum fell on the flames Bill himself lowered Henri to the ground. The Frenchman was barely conscious. Reaction from the certainty of horrible death had left him limp.

"*Magnifique*—magnificent!" he murmured. "But Frieda? My father?"

"Frieda's right as rain," Bill rumbled with significant emphasis, and carried Henri to the wizard's chair.

The Frenchman shrank at the touch of the stone.

"No!" he muttered. "I dangled and watched Hanu sit here. I cannot stand it—lay me somewhere else!"

"Hell, you got nerve enough to stay here," Bill insisted. "Chuck a front to-night, and you'll damn near own these islands. There's natives coming."

For though the drum had beaten but a short time, voices were audible and torches of candle-nuts glimmered at the edge of the High Place. Henri slumped in the black stone seat, and Bill squatted at his feet, revolver in hand.

In the darkness beneath the trees only Fekei, who stood

brooding at the rim of the pit in the glow of firelight, was visible to the newcomers. They advanced confidently—a party of four natives, supporting a fifth man whose feet dragged—a short, corpulent little man, whose clothes had been torn from a body that glimmered white when the firelight struck it. The message of the drums had closed the trails to Poulain. No bullock was ever dragged more abjectly to slaughter.

"Bring him here," Bill growled in Marquesan, and in his deepest voice. The natives obeyed, unsuspecting. Poulain groaned, for Bill's counterfeit of Hanu's voice had been lifelike. Not until the party was within twenty feet did they recognize Henri's head against the glow of the fire and observe that Bill wore clothes.

With a howl of consternation and with one accord, they dropped their burden and fled.

"STOP!" BILL roared, still in Marquesan. He might as well have spoken to the wind. Screaming with terror, the four natives sprinted down the trail.

"They'll carry the news," the pearler rumbled. "The trails will be open now. Well, Henri—speak up!"

"What can I say? After all, it is my father," Henri muttered.

"Why, I can think of plenty," Bill murmured, he raised his voice. "Poulain, what do you think of natives that eat long pig?"

Still flat on the ground, the planter shuddered and groaned. *"M'sieu',* I am overwhelm'," he gasped. "Zis is no time to mock.'

"You double crossing worm, what have you got to say?" Bill boomed. "Hanu was a man, according to his lights, and Van Tromp was crazy, but *you!* If it wasn't for your son I'd march you to the governor! As it is, day after to-morrow you're going to sail away with me in my schooner, and you're never going to come back again. Savvy?"

Poulain groveled in the dirt.

"To-morrow," Bill went on, "Henri's going to marry Frieda. You've got to be at the wedding, and deed your plantation to your son as a wedding gift. That will take care of them, and you too, in case Van Tromp's goes to weeds. Which I doubt. I think,"

Bill chuckled to Henri, "that Fekei will persuade the natives return to work for you."

"That does not matter,", Henri whispered. "But for saving Frieda and me—how can I thank you? How repay—"

Bill stuffed a handful of fine cut into his mouth.

"I got my pay when Hanu's feet left the ground and Fekei forgot to shoot," he grinned. "Still, after the wedding you can mix me a quart of those coconut juice, gin, and wine cocktails of yours. Let me see how you mix them. That's what I came ashore for."

"Gladly, *m'sieu',*" Henri answered with wide eyes. "Though— for me—if I had come ashore for that, I would see Hanu's face, tattooed black as soot, when I lifted that cocktail. The liquor would choke me!"

"It'll only make it taste better for me, being a roughneck like I am," Bill boomed. "Only, next time some one starts crying because the poor Marquesans are dying, I'm going to say, 'It's a damn good thing they are, for they were hellions to live among before white men broke them.'"

Bill lifted his voice.

"Frieda!" he bellowed until the black rocks of the High Place rang. "Frieda! Henri wants to see you! Sing out, girl!"

MAN'S WAY

*Pearls were the smallest of the prizes at stake on
a South Seas isle of hatred and heroism, where
Bellow Bill Williams battled for a doomed girl*

CHAPTER I

THE LONE ATOLL

IN AN IMMENSITY of sky and sea, colored blue and gold by the setting sun, lay one small atoll. Less than a mile in circumference, nowhere rising higher than ten feet above the surf which begirt it, the ring of white sand fringed with wind-bent coco palms seemed lost in the vastness of the ocean.

In the truest sense the atoll had been lost. The best chart of the South Pacific showed no land there. Far away, at a spot where the water actually rolled deep, the chart did show a tiny dot, marked "existence doubtful." For many, many years no white navigator had considered the task of exploring that lonely, empty sea worth while.

Potentially, the atoll represented the greatest ambition of every pearler in the South Seas—a lagoon where oysters had grown for decades, and no diver had been to snatch the fattening pearls. As a practical matter, however—did any one know that there was an atoll at all, or whether the lagoon contained shell? Men could employ their time to better advantage elsewhere. And did, until the hint came that in the lost lagoon lay a fortune. Then those who guessed what that fortune was crowded on sail.

One schooner first. Three days later, two more; and now, an hour behind the pair, a fourth schooner charged across the sun-gilded sea toward the same anchorage.

"Bellow Bill" Williams swung his boat into the wind and motioned Kory, his Fijian deck hand, to drop the anchor.

"I win, Kory!" the big tattooed pearler exulted, in a voice that

boomed like the surf and was audible through the rattle of the anchor chain. "Here's where that schooner was bound, and it must be pearls that Tivi is after! Trust that smart old Polynesian to be wise to the native secrets and know more than the government charts! He's had three days to dive, but we'll get our share of the shell that's left, eh, Mop-head?"

The Fijian, however, gave the bristling mop of hair to which Bill had alluded a doleful shake.

"Three fella schooner, massa," he grunted. "One fella schooner belong 'Motopu Mike.' Him bad fella!"

"Motopu Mike's a one-eared, red-bearded old pirate. Cut black fella's throat. Wreck white fella's ship—and there's no law here to cramp his style," rumbled Bill cheerfully. "But—say! What's bothering you, Shag Head? You afraid you can't get our share of the pearls, or I can't keep them?"

The blue and gold sunset was darkening with the swift oncoming of night in the tropics. On the atoll the light of a fire sprang into being. Bellow Bill spat out the last of his quid of fine cut chewing tobacco and placed another in his cheek. He was grinning. From his heels to his thatch of coppery yellow hair he stood six feet three inches. He was broad and deep of chest in proportion.

Everything about him was large—the rumbling, sonorous

*A fourth schooner
was heading toward
that same anchorage*

bass voice; his personality, untrammelled and restless as the sea he loved; the amount of tattooing that covered his torso from wrists to waist in a tracery of blue, green and crimson. Even in the South Seas, where the art of tattooing is taken seriously, the dragon on Bill's chest, the full-rigged ship inked on his back and the green snake that coiled around his hips, made natives stare.

"You think me weak fella?" he chuckled. "You stay along boat. Watch out like seven bells for Motopu Mike. I go ashore alone, savvy?" He moved toward the boat, his big face becoming grave. The presence of as thorough-going a reprobate as the South Seas could boast worried him not at all, but finding three schooners where he expected one complicated a situation already puzzling enough.

NO NATIVE with the wisdom and the excellent reputation which Tivi enjoyed would have deliberately allowed Motopu Mike to get wind of an unfished pearl bed. The second schoo-

ner was Japanese, by her rig. That was almost as bad; Japs come
to the South Seas to make money quickly, and are fighting men.

Tivi of Raratonga was not. He was strong as a killer whale.
No one ever faced the dangers on or below the surface of the
sea more bravely. But he was a Polynesian—a race that has not
been allowed to fight nor possess modern weapons for generations. Bill admired and respected Tivi. Though nearing sixty,
with hair that had begun to turn gray, the Polynesian could still
pick a pearl oyster from the bottom in twenty fathoms.

Wise in the old lore of the South Seas, he was also the equal
of any white skipper in navigation and seamanship. Among his
own people he was a chief; among the whites, the missionaries
admired him for his honesty and genuine Christianity, while the
traders were forced to respect one who could out-sail, out-trade,
and out-venture them. He was a remarkable man. That he would
keep this atoll and its pearl bed a secret for years was character-
istic. That he should divulge it at the last moment, unthinkable.

Bellow Bill had been able to follow Tivi through luck and
his own quick wit. A week before he had met the Polynesian
at sea, and noted that Tivi was tacking into the wind, though
the breeze was fair for all the ports Bill knew of. The pearler's
curiosity was whetted. He looked at the chart, and found the
tiny dot marked "existence doubtful." It lay in the direction that
Tivi was steering.

Bill could not follow at once. He had passengers aboard
whom he had to land, but as soon as he reached port he made
inquiries to learn what Tivi was up to. He found that the Polynesian had loaded a cargo of trade goods and cleared for the
Solomon Islands—a logical voyage for a trader at that time of
year. But Bill had sighted him steering in the opposite direction!
Obviously, then, Tivi meant to keep his real destination a secret.

TIVI HAD also carried, ostensibly as passengers for the Solo-
mons, a drunken old beach comber who went by the name of
"Squareface George" because of his fondness for trade gin, and
a girl called Emily, whom gossip declared to be the half-caste

daughter of Squareface. On the night of sailing, the father had got very drunk and boasted that he was going to make a fortune for himself and his girl.

The drunkenness and the boasting were both habitual; and if Bill had not been ferreting out secret motives he would have laughed at the statement. Under the circumstances, however, he had sailed as quickly as possible to find the lost atoll. Motopu Mike and the Japanese pearlers must also have taken the drunken babbling of Squareface seriously. Perhaps the beach comber had given them an explicit clew. That was immaterial. The important point was that since they were here, Bill was exceedingly glad he had followed also.

Tivi was a good guy, and more than that, Squareface George had been Bill's friend. Though the beach comber had plumbed the lowest depths to which a man can sink, Bill still owed him a debt of gratitude. That Squareface had been too weak to withstand the temptations of the South Seas was in Bill's eye merely his misfortune. The big pearler remembered the George Masterson who had been a trader years before, and in islands far from those in which Squareface had cadged for drinks.

That George Masterson had had a wife and a daughter named Emily. When Bill had been overturned in the surf near the trading station and badly injured by cuts from poisonous coral, Mrs. Masterson had nursed him through an illness which might otherwise have been fatal. Bill had never forgotten her, nor the little girl who had played with him on the beach.

Later Mrs. Masterson had been caught by a shark while bathing. Grief, as well as a character naturally weak, had sent Masterson to drink and degraded him into Squareface George. In his worst sprees he cared for his daughter as well as he could. He refused to let any one separate them, though he could not help drinking up any money Bill was able to give the girl.

Though the gossip was that Emily was a half-caste, Bill knew the truth. The girl was a brunette, with an oval face and an olive complexion, tanned as dark as a Polynesian. She had lived

among natives since she was a child, but she was as white as
Bill himself.

If Squareface were making one last effort to give his daughter the position she deserved, Bill was resolved that she should
not be robbed of it because her drunken father had blabbed the
secret of the atoll to a one-eared pirate and Japanese strangers. Why Squareface had been selected by Tivi to share in the
venture Bill could not guess, but whatever the reason, the beach
comber was in luck. Any arrangement between them would be
fulfilled to the letter by the Polynesian, in case Motopu and the
Japs left them anything to divide.

BELLOW BILL rowed ashore with a gun in his coat pocket,
and strode determinedly toward the blazing fire. From a distance
he could see that seven persons were seated around it. Squareface,
Tivi and Emily were together. Near them were the two Japanese;
opposite, Motopu, with a red beard trimmed square just below
the chin and a white, nobby scar where the left ear should have
been. Beside the pirate was a small, dark, undersized man, Spanish in appearance, presumably Motopu's deck hand.

None of the seven spoke nor moved as Bill approached. He
felt unwelcome. With Kory, his arrival increased the popula-
tion of the atoll to nine—nine who must settle any difficulties
among themselves. On this uncharted ring of sand they were
in a world of their own.

"Hello, Emily!" Bellow Bill hailed in his deep voice. "Glad to
see you. Aye there, Motopu! Ain't seen you since you moved the
channel lights and put the Montparnasse on the reef. Neither
have the police, and they've been looking harder than me. Is the
wrecking business good?"

"Go to the devil!" muttered the pirate in his beard. Bill crossed
the fire and shook hands with Tivi.

"You have eaten? I will bring more fish," the Polynesian said
hospitably.

"Didn't stop to eat. I could do with a snack," Bill boomed. He
pressed the strong brown fingers firmly. "Quite a mob you've got.

But you rate choice of the diving ground—as discovered, eh?" he demanded, staring at Motopu and the two Japanese.

"The damn' brown psalm-singer had already stripped the bed to the last shell," growled Motopu. "He's got the gall to tell us he won't divide the pearls! The heck he won't! There's a pile of shell on the beach as high as your waist. Twisted, sick-looking shell like pearls are found in."

Motopu's red beard bristled.

"Tivi's got them hid!" he declared. "Me and Carlos ain't going to sail back with nothing but some stinking shell, we ain't! Divvy up, I say!"

The two Japanese nodded like flat-nosed yellow dolls, and gave a hiss of assent. Tivi had left the fire and was already at the beach, casting a line into the surf. Squareface lifted his bloated countenance.

"You're too late, so you can all get out of here!" he blustered. "We don't want you, none of you!"

"Including me—Masterson?" Bill rumbled, deliberately using the name the beach comber had not heard in years. The man darted him a venomous look.

"Yes, including you!"

"Emily?" the pearler questioned.

"I—I guess you might as well, Bill," the girl answered slowly. "That is, if you'll *all* go."

Bill nodded. For a young woman to live among the kindest of savages was one thing, he reflected: to be left on an atoll in such company quite another. "The shell really has all been lifted, and the pearls well hidden," Emily went on. "When we saw two strange schooners heading for us Tivi thought it best. He hasn't any weapons, you know, and—and—" Her voice faded.

"Yeah, I savvy. The pearls will go to the best scrapper, and nothing's barred," Bill answered cheerfully. The situation was clear enough, and the sooner it was settled, the better.

HE FACED Motopu across the fire, the hand over his coat pocket sagging with the weight of a gun.

"Here's what!" he declared in his great voice. "I don't like to sail back with nothing, either, but if there ain't any more pearls, there ain't. That's my hard luck, and yours, too. You ain't going to pull rough stuff on two unarmed men and a kid. Fight now, or pull your hook. We'll send Tivi after the pearls, and all sail out of here as quick as we can raise anchor. I'll stick with Tivi till I see him safe in port, so you won't pull anything at sea, either."

The red-bearded pirate looked ugly, but Bill was on his feet, ready for trouble. His decision had been immediate, and his intention of settling with the pirate first, however the fight with the other three came out, was evident. Motopu hesitated. In a moment he would have permitted himself to be disarmed, but Squareface broke the tension.

"I won't sail nowhere in your company, Bill!" he snarled.

"Yeah?" boomed the huge pearler, his eyes never leaving his three enemies "You'll do like I tell you!"

From seaward came the rattle of an anchor chain suddenly slipped. Seaman's instinct brought all four sailors to their feet. Bill jerked out his revolver and leaped back, covering the others, but daring a look seaward.

Tivi's figure was no longer visible against the white background of the surf. To Bill's amazement, his own schooner began to swing broadside before the wind and drift out to sea.

"Stay in the firelight, you!" he shouted at Motopu, and backed slowly toward the beach. He could guess what had happened, what must have happened. Tivi had swum out, and been welcomed as a friend by Kory. Once aboard, the Polynesian had overpowered Bill's deck hand, and set the schooner adrift.

But why, with three vessels to choose from, should Tivi have selected his—knowing him to be both honest and friendly and the others the reverse? For some good reason; some overpowering reason.

The body of a swimmer showed for an instant in the surf. Bill turned and ran toward the beach. The riddle must be answered, and since Tivi was also the one who had hidden the pearls, Squareface and the girl were in no immediate danger from the open war he had initiated with the other three.

CHAPTER II

GOOD TRICKS WORK TWICE

BILL'S DASH TOWARD the surf was quick enough to enable him to recognize the swimmer as Tivi, not Kory. At his approach the Polynesian dived back through the surf. Bill, who was almost as good a swimmer, followed suit. He discarded his coat, and when his revolver slipped out of the waistband of his trousers, he kicked out of the trousers also in order to keep Tivi in sight. The native was swimming away from the schooners and parallel to the beach; and sprinting his best, Bill slowly lost distance for the first quarter mile of the chase.

Tivi, however, was unable to shake the pearler off. Though he could swim for hours, so could Bill, and halfway around the atoll the superior stamina of the younger man asserted itself. Foot by foot the gap between the two heads and flailing arms began to shorten. At last Tivi seemed to realize that he would finally be caught, for he took advantage of a big sea to ride in to the beach. On the seventh big wave that followed Bill plunged through the combers, and tumbled out on the sand at Tivi's feet.

The Polynesian made no attempt to run. He even reached down and helped Bill to stand, facing him with squared shoulders but hanging head, like a thoroughbred that has turned back to receive a well-deserved licking.

"Get off this beach. We show up like a pair of black cats against a whitewashed wall," said Bill sharply. There was not much cover anywhere on the island, and though the fire was only a dim speck of yellow at the opposite side of the circle of sand, he had no way of knowing where Motopu had gone in the meantime.

"Are you crazy, Tivi?" he growled when he had pushed the native into the partial concealment of a clump of pandanus. "If you've hurt Kory I'll break your neck!"

"He is not hurt. I tied him. He will untie my knots before the schooner drifts far. There are no reefs to wreck it," answered the Polynesian sulkily, in the vernacular.

"But, you fool! I can't leave a schooner knocking around the South Pacific!" Bill grunted. "Blue blazing damnation, what was the idea?"

"You had a boat. You could have caught the schooner if you had rowed after it."

"Maybe I could, though I'd have had to row all night, on account of the breeze. I'd have been out of the picture here for quite some time. Long enough for the pearls to be recovered, and for every one to skip!" Bill boomed indignantly. "So you wanted to be rid of me! Do you think *I'd* steal your pearls?"

Tivi shook a grizzled, curly head.

"But Motopu would?"

"Can't find pearls," grumbled Tivi.

"YOU UNDERESTIMATE that guy. He's a hold-over from the days of Bully Hayes. He'd use torture as quick as he'd cut your throat—and that's practically instantaneous."

"I am not afraid."

"Who cares? It's pearls we're talking about! I want you to keep what's rightfully yours, but by blue blazing damnation, you might help yourself a little, too!" Bill was exasperated. "Kory can squirm out of ropes like an eel. I'll let what you did to him pass," he went on. "You've gummed the deal, but I'm trying to be your friend, and Squareface's friend, not that he's worth it. Emily is worth the lot of you.

"You savvy?" Bellow Bill demanded, when Tivi did not respond. "I'm going to help you whether you like it or not. I'll hold off Motopu till you get the pearls, and then the four of us will sail in your schooner back to Thursday Island. We'll pick up Kory at sea and you can sail my boat back. We'll start right now, too. I got a living to make and can't fool around."

Tivi shook his head. His shoulders squared in dogged refusal.

"I don't want to act rough, but what I'll do to you ain't a circumstance to what you'd get from the others," Bill threatened. "That plan is the only one that will get you out, and if you didn't have some crazy notion in your head you'd see it. What's your objection?"

"Squareface is not honest. He would cheat me. I would lose the pearls rather than be cheated." The Polynesian sighed. "They are big pearls. You could not hold them all in one hand."

"Squareface isn't anything that's decent these days, and you knew that when you brought him along," snapped Bill, brushing the excuse to one side. "You leave him to me, too. Now, where are those pearls?"

Tivi shook his head.

"I'm going to find out if I have to kill you. We've got to get them before Motopu and those Japs get organized. Right now they are between us and your boats. Where—are—those—pearls?"

The grizzled head gave a stubborn shake.

ONCE A Polynesian has made up his mind, the best arguments are futile. Bellow Bill shrugged and struck a short, clean blow to the point of the brown jaw, that stretched Tivi on the sand, dazed and momentarily helpless. Bill knelt on the broad brown chest. He hated what he was doing, was able to do it only because he was certain that it was for the good of every one involved. Slowly his fingers closed on Tivi's throat.

"The pearls, Tivi!" Bill rambled. "Give in, man—I don't want to hurt you!"

There was no answer but a desperate struggle. As a surgeon holds a refractory patient quiet beneath the knife, Bill pinned Tivi to the sand and tightened his grip. The brown face turned

purple, and then black. The body under Bill's knees went limp.
He rose, lest he should kill the native, waited till consciousness
returned, and then gripped Tivi's throat again.

Too weak to struggle now, the Polynesian still shook his head.
He would not speak, though he died.

Bill gave up. He felt half sick and thoroughly ashamed of
himself. The native had too much passive courage. Had he
yielded, a quick end to the situation might have been possible;
as he had not, Bill was puzzled both as to the native's motive
and his own best course of action.

He rose and went to the beach, bringing back salt water which
he flipped in Tivi's face until the broad brown chest began to rise
and fall normally. At the camp on the opposite side of the atoll a
lantern was moving away from the fire. Evidently Motopu bad
decided to make a search for Tivi and Bill.

That the forces against him were divided was the first lucky
break the big pearler had obtained since landing on the atoll. He
much regretted the loss of his revolver in the surf, however, for
even with his enemies separated he could expect to encounter
two well-armed men in either party. But with a club he could
at least attack in silence. Bellow Bill grinned; he enjoyed odds.

Tivi he dragged deeper into the pandanus thicket. The native
would be found if the search were conducted with any care, but
the partial concealment would gain Bill time and increase the
distance between his enemies, which was what he wanted.

ARMING HIMSELF with a billet of driftwood found on the
beach, he hastened toward the camp fire, choosing the side of
the atoll opposite to that on which the lantern moved, in order
to avoid the oncoming party. In ten minutes, for the distance
was less than half a mile, he was close to the original camp. A
big fire was blazing in front of a shelter built of palm leaves and
sail cloth. The hut threw a dark band of shadow across the sand,
and along this Bill squirmed, belly down on the warm sand, until
he could part the leaves that formed the rear of the hut and look
out through the low doorway.

The two Japanese—men, like all their race, of some military service—were on guard. Both sat cross-legged. They had placed themselves at opposite sides of the fire and well back from its light, so that they were separated by fully thirty feet. The butt of a revolver and the hilt of a heavy diver's knife was visible in each waistband.

Between them, close to the fire, sat Emily, whom they were guarding as their hostage. Motopu and his man Carlos were gone, and had taken Squareface with them. Naturally, the Japs supposed that Bill was still armed. The tactics they had adopted were evidence of their fatalism and courage, since both were exposed to a shot from long range. On the other hand, even if Bill had been an expert marksman he could not have disabled more than one of the two before the other leaped out of the firelight; and since, unarmed, he must come hand to hand, their position gave him a hard nut to crack.

Attack he must. There would never be a better opportunity to get Emily into a place of comparative safety, and when a chance had to be taken Bill's question was "Why wait?" Accurate shooting by firelight isn't so simple. And he would have about forty feet to charge; he could be within club swing in something less than two seconds.

Like a sprinter Bill crouched, and filled his big left hand with gritty sand. Then he rushed—so suddenly, so swiftly that Emily uttered a shrill, piercing scream of surprise and terror. Instinctively the nearest Jap jumped to his feet before drawing the revolver.

No error could have been worse. As he jerked the weapon clear Bill was on him. The handful of sand lashed against the Jap's eyes, confusing his aim. Though he fired, the bullet missed. Bill's club came down with a hollow *clump* on the cropped black head. The Jap dropped in a heap, and Bill sprang upon the unconscious figure, throwing his club aside and rolling over and over on the sand with the little brown man gripped tight in his huge arms.

Gun poised, the second Japanese waited for a fair shot. At that moment a bullet would have been as likely to kill his friend as Bill. Again Emily screamed. Bill was up. He held a limp body before his chest. Behind that shield he charged toward the second revolver. There was a shot. Too high, however. The Jap meant it to go high, to intimidate rather than wound, for he flung his revolver down and jerked out his knife as Bill reached him.

The pearler hurled the limp body at the smaller man's head. Agilely the Jap dodged, but he could not avoid Bill's flying tackle in the wake of his human missile. One tattooed arm closed around the Jap's knee, bringing him to the ground. The knife flew into the air. For a second the two wrestled. Jiu-jitsu was no match for greater weight and long experience in rough-and-tumble. A tattooed fist rose and fell—once. The fight ended. Bellow Bill rose, breathing heavily, and grinned at the girl.

"Shouldn't have screamed, Emily," he reproved. "Look alive, now, and bring me an ax. I want to smash up all the boats but mine."

"There's another boat Tivi used to dive from, way up the lagoon!"

"Well, we'll have to let that one go," the pearler grinned. He was picking up the two revolvers. With one of the captured knives he cut long strips of canvas from the sailcloth shelter, and bound the two unconscious Japanese hand and foot. Dragging a man under each arm he ran to the beach, Emily following with a hatchet that had been brought ashore to open coconuts.

Faintly Bill heard Motopu shout. Far down the island the lantern was being swung in wide circles, as though signalling.

"Well, your screaming didn't tell him any more than the shoots," Bill rumbled to Emily. "Don't blame yourself, kid. Only you damn near made me jump out of my skin. A woman's scream will paralyze most anything for a second or two…. Get the oars out of the boats; no use wasting good gear."

A dozen blows with the hatchet left gaping holes in the

Japs' boat, and Motopu's. Bill shoved his own into the surf with Emily and his two prisoners aboard, caught the back wash of a big sea, and was at the oars before the next wave could swamp him. Once outside the double line of surf he rested, chuckling. "If Motopu had fought in the war, instead of spending 1918 robbing poor brown pearl divers while most of the gunboats was away, he'd know the importance of guarding a way of retreat," he commented cheerfully. "He won't want to be marooned on a lost atoll. Not much. He'll turn honest.... So now that we're top dog, Emily, tell me—why would Tivi rather let me kill him than tell where he hid the pearls? He knows I'm no thief."

The girl hung her dark head. "I—mustn't. I don't dare," she refused flatly.

CHAPTER III

THE BARGAIN

BILL ROWED BEYOND revolver range. Close to the Japanese schooner he shipped his oars and faced the girl. The boat rolled heavily. The two men rolled back and forth across the bottom boards. Darkness was around them. In the stern Emily seemed to have withdrawn.

"Scared?" said Bill gently, in his deep voice, "We built sand forts ten years ago, Emily, when you were eight. And I got starfish out of the lagoon to man them, do you remember?—while you skedaddled up and down the beach for seaweed and bits of shells to make them pretty. I mean no more harm now than I did then, kid. How can you be scared of me?"

The girl was silent. The lack of confidence hurt Bill. He shrugged in his discomfiture.

"I'm beginning to put two and two together, kid," he warned. "Don't be stubborn like Tivi. Where are the pearls?"

"I don't know."

"That's a lie, Emily. You saw them hid. You must have, on this bare atoll. But let that pass. Who knew of this atoll? Your father, or Tivi?"

"Tivi."

"Naturally, he would. I'm glad you told the truth there," said Bill gravely. "Look here, Emily. Two and two make four, though I'm sorry to add the sum. Why did you promise to marry Tivi?"

The dark head, previously bent low, lifted bravely.

"My father gets worse every year. Decent white men won't speak to him any more. Except you. You're our only old friend, and you see us seldom. Father is getting worse than a native. But with money held in trust he could go back to the States. I'm not a fool, Bill, but I know he would live decently among his own kind."

"Yeah. And you'd live as Tivi's wife. Emily, it's all right to love your father, but—" Bill paused.

"Tivi's a good man! A kind man, and he loves me. More than any man I've ever met loves me!" the girl cried vehemently.

"No one denies that, but—"

"I knew you wouldn't like it. That's why we were afraid of you—all of us, more than we feared Motopu. But, Bill! I've got to take care of my father, and what else can I do? You know I'm thought to be a half-caste, How can I help my father unless I marry, and who can I marry but a white man that's no account— or a native? Tivi can trace his ancestry back sixty generations, all chiefs. He's a man, Bill. I'm—rather fond of him. I could do worse!"

"Squareface couldn't," rumbled the big pearler. "You're thinking of him. He agreed to the marriage on condition that Tivi turned the pearls over to him, eh?"

"The atoll has been a secret passed from father to son in Tivi's family for generations. The bed was small, but it was very rich, Bill." The girl's chin set stubbornly. "I'm going to save my father, Bill, and you needn't think you can stop it. I'm of age, and my mind's made up."

"Back on Thursday Island I could not stop you," Bill admitted. "Don't argue, Emily. I've nothing against Tivi, but you shan't throw yourself away. I've played with you when you were a kid, and you're not going to make any bargain for the sake of a drunken…." Bill's fists were clenched in impotent rage.

"Squareface is your father. I won't call him his proper names. However, this changes my plans. I could wait Motopu out if the pearls just meant so much money, but since they're part of a bargain…." Bill shook his curly head. "Where are they? Don't lie, now."

"Tivi wrapped them in cloth and sank them in the lagoon in deep water. He said nobody but he could get them."

"What's deep water to a man in a diving suit or a good diver?" Bill grumbled.

"There's something more than the depth," the girl insisted. "Of course, the cloth could be seen by using a water-glass."

BILL PICKED up the oars and drove the boat against the Jap schooner. He tossed the two prisoners on deck, and went below. He reappeared in a minute, walked forward, and slipped the anchor chain. The schooner began to drift before the wind that blew over the atoll, as his own schooner had. Bill swung himself back in the boat and rowed toward Tivi's schooner.

"The Japs will free themselves in time, just as Kory will," he remarked to the girl. "For the time being they're out of the picture. Now, I'm going to put you aboard your boat, and lead the main halyards to the windlass so that you can hoist sail. You can slip the cable and get under way alone, can't you?"

The girl nodded.

"I'll leave you the skiff, so you'll have plenty of time before Motopu can swim out or get the other boat back from the lagoon," Bill instructed. "If you see him coming, get out of the way. Sail before the wind till you sight some ship or island, and then make distress signals. Whatever happens, you've got to be safe, Emily. You'll promise to do that?"

"If necessary," said the girl stiffly. Bill helped her to the deck of her own schooner, and tied the painter.

Ashore, the lantern had returned to the main camp; he could see two figures moving about and two more lying near the blaze. Motopu had evidently caught Tivi. The one-eared pirate had not come to the beach. The rattling of the anchor had evidently informed him, if the shots had not, that Bill had become the master at sea.

One of the small black figures outlined against the firelight picked a blazing stick from the flames. A second later the two on the schooner heard a yell of terror.

Emily caught Bellow Bill's arm. "Father—" she began.

"Squareface is frightened—not hurt," said Bill. "Motopu's finding out where the pearls are hid. That father of yours will tell all he knows before he'll let a hair be singed. Don't worry, kid. He ain't like you or Tivi. Number One is his only thought. Remember now, you've promised to slip the cable if you see me getting the worst of things."

BEFORE THE girl could protest Bill dived overboard and swam to Motopu's schooner. As he climbed the rail he noted that the group by the fire had broken up. Evidently the mere threat of torture had been sufficient, and Motopu had learned of the pearls. Bill crammed a handful of water-soaked fine-cut into his cheek and spat vigorously till he had got rid of the taste of salt.

Already, aboard the Japanese schooner, he had cut the diving suit into ribbons and broken the air pumps. Now, at his leisure, he destroyed Motopu's diving equipment also. When he finished nothing remained intact but the heavy copper helmet.

Bill turned his quid ruefully. By destroying the equipment he had practically made Tivi's boast good. To hide the pearls in deep water, where they could be seen and recovered by divers, seemed to him an aberration on the part of a man usually astute. It was the native blood in Tivi coming out. No white man would have been so childish.

Yet, without gear, neither Motopu nor Carlos had the strength and skill to swim into the depths for the loot, and Bill doubted if they could force Tivi to be their cat's-paw. Any torture extreme enough to break Tivi's will would incapacitate him for the descent.

Bill doubted whether he could make such a dive himself. He had the strength and the skill in the water, yet the pressure on a diver at twenty fathoms amounts to more than seven thousand pounds to the square foot, and he lacked the practice in holding his breath and handling himself at great depths which native pearl divers receive from boyhood.

However, between diving alone, and diving in a suit with Squareface, Tivi or even Emily handling the air pump, Bill preferred the former. Emily loved her father with an intensity that even welcomed the prospect of a lifetime of sneers for herself, in order that his last years might be passed in such respect as civilization gives the drunkard who has sufficient income to support his vice.

She was against Bill no less than was Tivi or Motopu; and though she was actuated by the highest motives, the big tattooed pearler was determined to save her from the consequences of her own courageous folly.

On shore the red-bearded pirate and his lean Spanish associate were getting the boat across from the lagoon to the seaward side. Bill dried off the revolvers he had taken from the Japs and waited the attack. The irony of the situation amused him. Motopu Mike was going to fight, at a disadvantage, for broken gear which would be useless to him if he won.

CHAPTER IV

MANHOOD—
POLYNESIAN STYLE

MOTOPU PLACED SQUAREFACE and Tivi in the bow of the boat. Once through the breakers he propped up the two bound men like a breastwork and lay down behind them. Carlos also lay down, sculling the boat with one oar.

As the boat drew near, Bill had no target but his friends; and the red-bearded pirate did not make the mistake of trying to board. The boat sculled round and round the schooner, tempting Bill to open fire, which Bill refused to do. He was no more than an average marksman with a revolver. In the dark he would be likely to hit the wrong man, and Motopu, firing at his flash, far more likely to center an effective bullet. Even in the act of boarding, Motopu would still be one of a group; while Bill would be silhouetted against the night sky if he attempted to defend the schooner's rail.

Cheerfully Bill gave the one-eared old roughneck credit for a level head; equally cheerfully he crawled across the deck, bent low to prevent his withdrawal from being observed, and returned to the cabin in which the diving gear had been stowed. Bill's idea was to stand in ambush behind the door, but he found he was far too deep-chested for such a narrow hiding place. Instead, he hooked the door open and set his back against the bulkhead opposite. Though he stood in absolute darkness, he could follow Motopu's movements by the sound.

First there was the thump of the boat's bow against the schooner side. There followed the rapid slither of bare feet across the planking above Bill's head as Motopu and Carlos searched the deck, and then a whisper:

"Did he stay on the other boat?"

"*Quién sabe?*"

"Hoist them two on deck and then stand by the companion-way while I have a look below," Motopu growled. "I don't fancy looking for Bill."

Nevertheless, the one-eared man did not hesitate. The light of a flash danced down the companionway steps and was extinguished. In the dark Motopu leaped from the deck above. For a moment he stood still—Bill could hear the panting intake of his breath—then Motopu fired two quick shots. The flashlight snapped on and off, quick as a flash of summer lightning. Motopu was in the room opposite to the one in which Bill waited. Before entering he had searched the room with bullets fired around the door jamb.

Bill leaped away from the bulkhead against which he leaned as though the planking had suddenly turned red-hot. In the center of the room he crouched, a-tingle with the keen thrill of excitement and danger. A barrage of revolver bullets was something he hadn't counted on. He guessed that Carlos was at the top of the companionway Stairs, with another flash and a gun. The passageway commanded from the stairs would be no place for a hand-to-hand struggle.

He waited for Motopu to sweep the second room with lead. If he were hit—well, he doubted whether one bullet could stop him.

Streaks of flame stabbed from the doorway. Headlong, Bill dived below the gun flashes. His shoulders struck Motopu's legs, bringing him to the floor. Blindly the big pearler pummelled a wrestling body with fist and gun butt. A gun exploded near his face. There was a shot from the companionway and a bullet ripped into the planks beyond his head. Then Bill's gun butt thudded on bone. Motopu's struggles ceased, and the pearler dragged him back into the room, then struck a match.

"Mike!" yelled Carlos from the deck above.

"Mike ain't got nothing to say!" Bill bellowed recklessly. There was a gash in the red-bearded pirate's forehead, and he was completely out. Bill tied him with strips of the diving suit, and bound up the injured head. Motopu would live. There remained Carlos, who had dodged back from the companionway at the sound of the pearler's voice, and who now lighted a lantern and set it on the deck where it flooded the hatchway with light.

BILL DIDN'T like the idea of lifting his head into the open, but he was afraid that if he delayed Carlos might row over to Tivi's schooner, and force Emily to set sail. He grabbed up the copper diving helmet, put it on his curly head, and promptly took it off. He couldn't see anything through the thick eyeglasses, and the copper plate would offer little resistance.

Nevertheless, the thing might draw a shot, and luckily the lantern was set close to the companionway. Standing beneath the opening, Bill lifted the helmet slowly on the end of a boat hook.

The copper dome was scarcely raised above the deck level when a revolver crashed, up forward, and a bullet ripped through it, knocking it from Bill's hands. At the shot Bill straightened up. His own bullet smashed the lantern to bits, and as the light winked out he flung himself up the steps and onto the deck, rolling behind the wheel.

A bullet zipped over his head, knocking a spoke to splinters. Bill fired at the flash that leaped from behind the mainmast. Dimly he could see Carlos against the lighter sky, crouching, his revolver spitting fire. Bill shot at the orange streaks that stabbed at him; kept on shooting till his gun clicked on an empty shell, though the mast spat flame no more. With his gun empty, the big pearler charged before Carlos should be able to reload. The whole exchange of shots had not lasted two seconds. Unhit himself, he was sure that Carlos was also uninjured.

Yet as he leaped forward the dark body crouched at the foot of the mast did not move. Bill caught a lean shoulder and jerked the little Spaniard up, raising his revolver barrel to strike.

Black eyes, wide open, stared back at him unseeingly. The lean face wobbled and dropped against the scrawny chest. Only then Bill noticed the stain spreading through the singlet from a wound halfway between the base of the throat and the left armpit. The severed artery pumped blood in a stream. A rattle sounded in the Spaniard's throat. He was dead before Bill could lower him to the deck.

To the suddenness of gunplay Bill could never get accustomed. He felt dazed. His ears still rang to the booming of the shots; his right hand stung from the backspit of his revolver, and yet here was Carlos dead, and the fight over. Mechanically he stuffed fine-cut into his cheek, laid the Spaniard down and closed his eyes, and then walked heavily to the rail.

SQUAREFACE AND Tivi were tumbled in a heap on the deck where Motopu had dropped them after lifting them over the rail to act as a shield. Bill dragged the Polynesian clear, and somewhat more roughly propped Squareface against the rail.

"You're a complete skunk, Masterson," he boomed, stripping away the gags that kept both men silent. "A father that'll take advantage of a daughter's love for him is— But what is the use of talking? I respected you once because you kept her with you when I'd have brought her up as she deserved. Did you have this planned all the time?"

"No. It was Tivi's idea," whined the beach comber. "Come, Bill, untie me!"

"Untie, nothing! Not until morning, when I've got the pearls."

"My brother is angry. I do not understand," said Tivi gently in the liquid speech of the South Seas. "Why should I not marry? I am not poor, and that is what the white men fear. I am a widower; I built the church for the minister who will marry us. Many white men have married the girls of my family."

"We needn't discuss it," Bill rumbled. He was sorry for the big brown man, for the bewilderment on Tivi's face was like that of a puzzled child.

"But why? Our Lord Jesus held all men alike. He made fishermen and publicans His disciples," Tivi went on with simple dignity. "Does my brother think I am not enough of a man?

That I am weak, or a coward? I am trying to do all things as a white man."

"Nothing against you personally. When I've got the pearls and we're back in civilization you can ask Emily again." Bill knew he was taking the right stand, and yet Tivi was putting him in the wrong. There was nothing against the Polynesian personally. If the Polynesian's name had only been Smith, if he had only been born north of the Equator!

"Only I can get the pearls," said Tivi decisively. "Am I a child, Bellow Bill, to drop a fortune under a diver's nose if any man could recover it? Only a chief can bring them to the air again. Aye, in the old days we of Raratonga chose our chiefs by that test, among others. You will not dive, Bill."

"I think I can make bottom in twenty fathoms."

Awkwardly because of his bound arms the Polynesian shrugged that feat aside as a simple matter, which it was to him or any good diver of his race.

"But I dropped the pearls beside the hole of a conger eel," Tivi warned. "Not even I could get the pearls without being bitten, and to win free takes a man. Almost I was caught while gathering the shell. When I saw the schooners come, I swam down, dropped the pearls near its hole. *I* am not afraid of the teeth."

"Eels don't scare me, either," Bill rumbled nonchalantly. That was true. Yet of the three great dangers which the diver for pearls must face—the shark, which is not hard to fight off; the huge *tonu,* which has head and jaws large enough to take a diver's whole body, but which is sluggish and easy to avoid; and the conger eel, which strikes more quickly and surely than the shark, and from which the one method of escape is an acid test of muscle and nerve—the eel is most greatly dreaded by divers.

"Then you are a man, too, brother," said Tivi gravely. "This is not a small eel, but a grandfather. I will go down, to-morrow, with you to watch. When I rise you can take the pearls from me, for I will be weak."

"You go, after hinting I'm afraid? Not much!" Bill boomed.

"Rest easy, you two, while I put Motopu in irons and get some sleep."

THERE WAS, however, very little sleep that night for the tattooed pearler. He had, first, to swim to the other schooner and reassure Emily as to the outcome of the fight. He returned with the skiff, for he wanted to keep the girl away from her father. Of course, she could swim the distance between the schooners while he was absent at the lagoon; on that account he searched Mike's craft carefully for handcuffs.

He found almost everything else—a stand of half a dozen Winchesters, which he threw overboard, a box of dynamite and detonating caps, forty per cent stuff used for fishing or defense against natives, several half barrels of contraband liquor and other appliances of a schooner captain who continued to make a living in the old illegal ways.

Of handcuffs there were but two pairs. With one of these he ironed Motopu to a stanchion; the other he passed through a ringbolt on the deck, snapping one cuff on Tivi and one on Squareface. With the keys in Bill's pocket, Emily would be unable to free either, unless she found another key, which was always possible.

Bill had then the task of hauling the rowboat back into the lagoon. That was not hard, for his strength. He had learned the location of the cache from the Polynesian, and as he waited for dawn he recalled all he had ever learned of the habits of conger eels.

With the first light he must dive. The wind was steadily strengthening. Clouds had blotted out the starlight, and spits of rain were falling—level rain, blown with a velocity that made the drops beat against his body like hailstones. Even in the lee of the atoll the schooners were tugging heavily at their anchors, and the signs indicated that by morning the wind would increase to gale force.

WITH THE first streak of gray in the sky Emily joined him at the lagoon, walking across the sand, bent forward to make progress against the wind. Evidently before swimming ashore she had been to see her father.

"Bill, I'm ashamed of you!" was her first word. "With everybody handcuffed what could I do if the anchors dragged? Are you going to dive with the keys in your pocket?"

The pearler flushed and handed the keys to her. "I mean to come up again, but—you're right, at that," he growled. "You'll give me your word you won't set Tivi free while I'm under water?"

At the girl's nod Bill grinned, more at his ease.

"I can't take my revolver down with me either, you see," he explained. "Say, Emily, how about calling it off? I hate to feel you're against me, too!"

"Call it off? Doing that means father must comb the beach forever," snapped the girl. "I promise to do just what you asked, while you're below. Still, I'm against you." Emily smiled rather tremulously. "I'd rather not be. Why don't you let Tivi go down for you?"

"Nice guy I'd be—objecting to him because of his race, and letting him take on a job I flunked," Bill grunted. "You going back?"

"I'd rather stay here. You may need help coming out of the water," Emily pleaded. "Tivi told me to. He knows what you're up against better than you do, Bill."

"Trying to scare me over a twenty-foot sea-snake? Well, watch, then!" Bill grunted.

Day had dawned gray through the clouds. He shoved the boat into the water and let Emily scull, while he examined the bottom through a water-glass. On the bearing Tivi had given him he saw a patch of oyster shells some ten feet square, among them a red and white object which was the strip of cloth Tivi had torn from his *pareu* to wrap around the pearls.

Bill made the ordinary preparations for a dive. He dropped an anchor stone to the bottom, the rope of which would guide him in his ascent, put diver's spectacles over his eyes, and crouched in the bow, breathing in swift, short gasps that filled every corner of his lungs with free air. To save time in the descent he was using a diving stone. When he was ready he grinned at Emily, rolled the heavy block of coral over the bow, and let it carry him down.

AT FORTY feet the pressure was tremendous. He thought that his eardrums would burst inward and his chest collapse. Grimly he held on, going deep into water that was darker and darker gray. The pressure, though all he could endure, seemingly got no worse. The bottom marked by the oyster shells seemed to float upward to meet him. His lungs were bursting.

In good diver fashion he blew out a bit of air, though he had been under less than ten seconds. The diving stone grounded, and he reached out for the bit of red and white rag, only a yard from his hand.

Further he could not see in the gray murk of the water. Though his nerves were steeled and the thing expected, the flash of a dark body toward him swift as a striking snake, the grip of viselike teeth upon his forearm, made him exhale precious air.

Almost he dropped the pearls, for the grip of the eel was like a trap, nearly paralyzing his arm. The jaws were closed between wrist and elbow. He felt the prick of needle-sharp teeth. The black body, thick as his own arm, trailed away into the gray.

Bill pulled with all his strength. The thing that held him did not yield an inch. He twisted, but the hold of those tiny, pointed teeth could not be shaken. He had heard as much in many divers' tales. No man is strong enough to pull a big conger eel from its hole; as well might the diver that is caught attempt to pull himself from the grip of a bulldog.

Bill slashed and stabbed at the snaky body. The knife edge slid over the black skin. That he had heard too, but he could no more refrain from the vain fight than from the vain efforts to escape.

He wished that he might see the eyes of the thing. The black rod of cold flesh clamped to his arm did not seem alive. It was tireless, inexorable. For the man it caught there was but one escape. A bull lowers its head to charge; a devilfish advances its head when its tentacles hold its victim fast; a conger eel will shift its grip. Against each enemy there is one instant that must be seized for victory.

Bill dropped his knife and set his feet in the sand. He waited. His head rang. Slowly the pressure of the depths was squeezing the strength from him. The eel held on. Bill was weakening, but excitement was gone, and fear he had never had. The change of grip would be quick. Specks of black floated across his eyes. The desire for air was overwhelming. He locked his lips to keep from gulping water. Waited—waited.

INSTANTANEOUS WITH the release of the eel's jaws Bill gave a jerk that freed his arm and leaped upward from the sand, swimming desperately. He had escaped. The great danger—that the eel might fasten again on his ankle—passed. The anchor rope brushed against his face. With bursting lungs he swam up and up until his head rose into the air.

He barely had strength to reach up to catch the gunwale of the boat. He was thankful for the arm Emily slipped under his shoulder, supporting him, for the pain of breathing and the release of pressure on his body was torture. He tossed the pearls into the boat, and grinned. In his weakness the girl's dark head and dark eyes swam before him mistily.

"Tivi's—a man—all right," he gasped. "That—takes—a chief—"

Emily was trying to lift him. Summoning the last reserve of his strength he scrambled over the gunwale and tumbled head first into the bottom of the boat, where he lay face downward, too weak to raise his head.

The girl bent over him. She held his revolver by the barrel, but Bellow Bill did not see that; indeed, if he had seen he could hardly have made any resistance. He barely felt the impact of the revolver butt behind his ear. Darkness blotted out the pain that racked him. With a long sigh he collapsed.

The revolver slipped from Emily's trembling fingers, but as she had forced herself to strike, she now summoned the resolution to lash Bill's wrists and ankles. She drew the cords no tighter than she had to. She gave a gasp of relief when Bill stirred, but nevertheless the knots she tied were strong. No sailor could have bound a prisoner more firmly.

Pulling up the anchor, she rowed to the shore of the lagoon, and with an anxious look at the flying storm clouds overhead, took the pearls and the handcuff keys and ran back toward the schooners, her skirts and her dark hair flying before the rush of the wind.

CHAPTER V

STORM WRACK

BILL WAS CONSCIOUS before Squareface and Tivi were released. By the time the Polynesian returned to the atoll for him, the pearler had recovered both from the effects of the dive and of the double cross. Against Emily he felt no resentment. She had warned him she would fight for the sake of her father, and Bill could only admire her for fighting to the finish, even though it was his finish.

When he saw Tivi he grinned.

"You picked a good seagoing watchdog for those pearls, fella!" he rumbled in the deep voice. "To plan to swim down into the mouth of that eel deliberately—well, you're there, that's all!"

"I am used to the deep water. My brother is not," replied the native gravely, and bending over he swung Bill onto his back, no mean feat of strength. The boat Tivi abandoned. Carrying Bill, he ran across the atoll, and swam to his own schooner.

He took care to hold Bill's head above the water, and once aboard the ship he did not join in either the threats or the jeers which Squareface heaped upon the prisoners.

The beach comber's bloated face was savagely triumphant. To hear him talk one would have thought that he alone had overcome both Motopu Mike and Bill, and that nothing remained but a safe and uneventful cruise to some missionary. In imagination, Squareface was already tasting the delights of a debauch in New York, and the last vestige of friendship Bill had for the man as the father of Emily died there on the heaving deck.

Tivi, on the contrary, was grave; as well he might be. The wind was rising into one of the short, fierce storms that lash the South Pacific at the beginning of the hurricane season. Even without the encumbrance of prisoners the task was one to try all the resources of a sailor.

The native, however, shrank from none of it. He carried Bill into the fo'c's'le, by which the pearler inferred that Motopu Mike was still ironed in the cabin, and commenced to get under way. By the sounds Bill could follow the progress made almost as clearly as though he had been on deck.

He wondered first what would be done with Motopu's schooner. A timid or unscrupulous sailor would have abandoned her at the anchorage, where she would certainly have been wrecked. Tivi did not. In the distance Bill heard the sound of an anchor being raised, and nodded his coppery yellow hair in grim approval.

Tivi was going to take the schooner in tow, dealing with Motopu in honest seagoing fashion. A ship is more than the crew: kill a skipper if you must, but don't wreck his boat. So Bellow Bill himself would have done.

Tivi swam back to his own schooner, loosened canvas which slatted with the cracking roar of a battery of 75s, and raised the anchor. Once under way the schooner careened till the rail was flat to the sea. Bill rolled down the deck, slanted like a house roof, till he was stopped short by the bunks on the lee side.

Owing to the schooner in tow, Tivi could not heave to. Sailing as he was, a little free, the schooner caught heavy weather. At the more violent gusts she went all but on her beam ends. Green seas swept the decks, and when the slide of the fo'c's'le hatch was pulled back spray drenched Bill as though the contents of a bucket had been tossed over him.

EMILY CAME to visit him. She tried to roll the big pearler into a bunk, which was a task much too great for her strength.

"I'd like to make you comfortable," she said, after having failed. "I—don't just lie there, Bill!" she broke out vehemently. "Say it! Tell me I'm no good, that I betrayed you. I deserve it!"

"Quit adding hysteria to sentiment, kid," Bill rumbled. "You might get me a mug of water, though. I got rid of the others, and you got rid of me. O.K. Fair enough. I ain't worrying."

Emily went to the scuttle butt, and Bill raised the thick China mug awkwardly with bound hands. There was a calculating, almost exultant light in the dark blue eyes that the girl failed to observe.

"I never waste energy worrying over the past, or the future. Take a leaf from an old roughneck's book," he rumbled. "You shouldn't apologize for fighting. Lot of people would say you was noble for doing what you did. In my opinion you're just wrong, and that's that."

The schooner lay far over in the sea and a big wave tumbled on the deck overhead. The sound was like the dumping of a truckload of rock. Bill shook his head.

"Yes, Tivi had begun to shorten sail when I left," said Emily in reply to his unasked question. "Well—that's all, Bill. I was anxious for you to be sure that I didn't want to strike you." She held out her hand for the drinking mug.

As Bill extended it he appeared to lose his balance as the schooner pitched down the crest of a big sea. The cup struck against the deck and broke into pieces. The pearler shrugged.

"Little loss," he grunted. "So long then, kid."

But when the girl was gone Bellow Bill took a sharp-edged fragment of the cup which he had hidden under his body and commenced to scrape at the lashings on his wrists. He had said that he never worried. He might have added that he never gave up. In a few hours at most he could free himself, and the storm would keep Tivi and Squareface on deck for that length of time.

Bellow Bill had not more than raised a little lint on his bonds, however, before any prospect of freeing himself vanished with the suddenness of all disasters at sea. The schooner was beaten flat by the most violent squall yet, and in the worst of it her speed was checked. Squareface, terrified, had luffed. The drag of the vessel astern twisted the schooner onto the opposite tack and the boom jibed, swinging like a flail from port to starboard.

THE SHOCK snapped the fifty-foot spar like a match stick. Half dropped into the sea, where it battered against the schooner's side. The first blow started the butts of three planks. Bill saw water spurt into the fo'c's'le as the schooner fell into the trough, swept by every wave, helpless because of the drag of spar and sail. The only hope was to cut her free, quickly, and Bill ground his teeth in helplessness.

In a literal sense the mishap put Tivi between the deep sea and a pair of devils named Motopu and Bellow Bill. One man might cut the wreckage clear before the schooner was stove in; though Bill, in a perfect position to judge, doubted it. Three trained seamen, or two, could save her. Though he doubted Squareface's courage and Emily's strength, Bill supposed the native would try to use them.

He was surprised when the fo'c's'le slide was thrown back and Emily leaped down, knife in hand, and began to saw at his wrists.

"Tivi's unlocking Motopu," she planted. "Dad said not to."

"Your father would!" snapped Bill. He caught the knife from her, severed his ankle bindings in one sweep, and ran for the deck.

Squareface was hacking at the main sheet with a pocket knife—futilely, for the sail would hold the broken boom alongside even after the sheet was severed. Bill leaped for the hatchet kept near the wheel. One blow, struck in passing, severed the sheet; half a dozen more as he ran forward parted backstays and shrouds. The mast snapped five feet above the deck and went overside, where it battered at the side planking; but the schooner, freed from the pressure of the wind on the canvas, rolled back on a level keel.

Green water was sweeping the decks knee deep, and Tivi was still nowhere to be seen. Bill chopped through the remaining shrouds and stays. The wreckage floated clear, and for the moment the drag of the schooner towed astern, which still offered bare spars to the gale, kept the battered craft head to the sea.

The operation took less than ninety seconds, but without help one man could do no more. Both vessels would be in the trough of the seas unless emergency sail aft could be rigged. Louder than the gale Bill bellowed for Tivi. The big pearler's voice was made for such emergencies. It galvanized the panic-stricken beach comber, who came running aft and stood by the wheel ready to steer. Yet though Tivi must have heard he made no response. Bill went down the companionway in one leap, hatchet in hand.

He was not too quick. Tivi and Motopu were locked in a desperate wrestle. Careless of danger to the ship and to himself, the pirate was fighting to obtain the pearls, which, torn from Tivi's *pareu,* lay on the deck across which the two rolled.

Each had the other by the throat. Each was swinging short-arm blows, making no attempt to guard, but while Tivi had no weapon Motopu had snatched up the handcuffs, which he held like a pair of brass knuckles. Already he had laid the Polynesian's forehead open by a glancing blow, and he was trying to steady himself against the violent rolling of the schooner for a finishing punch at his dazed, half-unconscious adversary.

Bellow Bill wrenched the two apart, lifted Motopu to his knees, and knocked him clear to the companionway stairs with a right hand swing. For an instant the red-bearded pirate crouched, panting and glaring, full of fight. But Bill was nearest the pearls, and stooped swiftly to snatch up the hatchet he had dropped to separate the combatants.

The pearler was anxious only to get back to the deck. Without stopping to pick up the pearls he lunged far the ladder. What Motopu saw was a huge tattooed man with teeth bared and a hatchet half upraised leaping toward him. The pirate expected to feel the steel crash into his skull. He uttered a scream of terror and went up the stairs at one leap, Bill at his heels.

ON DECK Motopu collided with Squareface. He struck one blow. His steel-wrapped fist crashed against the beach comber's temple, dropping him like a log. Without pausing, Motopu plunged straight over the stern into the sea.

He caught the towrope as he rose, which alternately raised him into the air and plunged him into waves foam-white and beaten flat by the force of the wind. He kicked and spat like a wet cat clutching a string, yet managed at the risk of his life to shake a fist at Bill. Motopu must have expected the towline to be cut, which would certainly have drowned him. He was game and vicious to the end.

Bill, however, only waved his hatchet; and the pirate, understanding that his life was to be spared, set about working his way along the rope toward his own schooner. The distance was not over a hundred and fifty feet. A strong man could make it, and Bill, who cared little whether Motopu lived or died, knelt beside Squareface.

He was still on his knees when Tivi reeled up the companionway with a diver's knife clutched in a brown fist. The native was on the point of hurling himself at Bill when the pearler held up his hand—empty, palm forward.

"Steady!" his ringing voice boomed out. "Dead men don't make bridegrooms, brother! Get a storm trysail on what's left of that mast, if you can, while I look after George here. We can settle when the sea's calm—if we're afloat."

In mid stride Tivi stopped, the fury dying from his black eyes.

"Thy pardon, brother," he responded in Polynesian. "I seized the knife thinking all white men were alike, but thou—almost thou art fit to be a chief of Raratonga!"

Though the moment was not one for laughter—green water swept ankle deep across the decks, and Squareface lay very still—Bellow Bill could not restrain himself. His laugh went roaring over the sea. He—fit to be chief of a few hundred brown divers! He should hope so! And yet, Raratonga was Tivi's world. The brown man could have paid no higher compliment.

Suddenly grave, the pearler felt for Squareface's pulse. Emily was making her way aft, her face whiter than her father's.

"He's living!" Bill called. The pulse was strong, though ominously slow. The only visible injury was a bruise on the temple, yet Bill dared not feel the spot. He had seen the work of brass knuckles before, and feared to discover the skull had been fractured.

Emily dropped to the deck beside him and took her father's head in her lap. She kissed the dead-white forehead.

"I don't like the way he breathes," she gasped. "So slow—"

"Why, he's been knocked for a loop, that's all!" Bill almost shouted, for he was trying to drown the girl's fears by the loudness of his voice. He doubted whether Squareface would ever be conscious again. A slight flow of blood from the ears was an ominous symptom. "Just hold him quietly while Tivi and I rig a trysail. Then we'll get him into a bunk."

The pearler rose, picked up the hatchet. Astern, Motopu had reached his own schooner and was climbing up the bobstay. Bill severed his towline, which permitted his boat to drift more easily before the seas. Forward, Tivi was struggling with the sail. Bill ran to help. Fifteen minutes of hard work saw the canvas rigged. The schooner came head to the seas. Less water swept down her decks. If the gale got no worse she would live through it. If the wind rose, all that seamanship could do had been done.

Bill filled his cheek with fine-cut, chewed and spat.

"Damned if I wouldn't like some tobacco that wasn't water-soaked," he rumbled, gazing aft. Half a mile away Motopu had hove to under triple-reefed spanker and storm jib. "Is he standing by to help us if we need it, or is he still pearl hunting?" Bill rumbled to Tivi.

The native stared gloomily at the other schooner, which was

keeping as close to them as possible. Out of the corners of his eyes he studied the big tattooed man at his side. Bill understood.

"Tough to have the game slip out of your hands because you played fair, ain't it?" he asked. "Still, you had your chance. Don't hurry to get rid of me. I think Motopu's pearl hunting, and I may be useful yet. Meanwhile, we can make Squareface comfortable—poor devil!"

CHAPTER VI

THE CRIPPLED SCHOONER

UNTIL THE MIDDLE of the afternoon, when the gale blew itself out, the situation did not change. The crippled schooner drifted, with Motopu never more than a mile away. Squareface lay in the cabin, nursed by his daughter, but not recovering consciousness. Pulse and respiration continued at the same rate.

Though Bill was now sure that the skull had been fractured, there was nothing that he could do. A surgeon could not have operated aboard the schooner. He said as much to Emily.

"Father'll need me more than ever when we get him ashore," she answered resolutely. "The cost of an operation—"

"You mean you're set on going through with this?"

"Of course. The more I can do for father, the more I want to do. You won't agree with that, because you're a man. Men think of themselves. They think they've got a right to make a girl do just what they please." She stared at Bill defiantly. He shrugged. "And they don't like helpless things, like sick men and babies, that a woman will do anything in the world for!"

"Well, I got to follow a man's way, ain't I, being a man?" Bill grinned. "We needn't argue, kid. You look after your dad, while I see to the schooner."

Back on deck Bill discovered that the gale had dropped to a fresh sailing breeze. The schooner, of course, continued to wallow in the big waves kicked up by the storm, and he was able only to set a jib in addition to the trysail. The crippled schooner crawled along at a scant mile an hour, yawing widely, and almost unmanageable.

In marked contrast Motopu Mike shook out mainsail and jib and drove down upon Tivi's craft with the swoop of a hawk diving upon a crippled pigeon. Obviously he was making an attack, but of what kind Bill could only guess. He turned the wheel over to Tivi and stood ready with his revolver.

The best of marksman could not have done accurate shooting in that sea, but Bill hoped his bullets would keep the pirate from ramming or boarding. He was positive that Motopu had no firearms, and these were the only tactics he could anticipate.

As the two schooners neared, Bill could not see his enemy. Motopu must be lying flat on the deck, beneath the wheel. Foam creamed under the cutwater of his schooner as he drove in with a speed and on a course that made collision seem inevitable. At the last second, however, Motopu swung out and passed in front of the bow. As he crossed, Bill saw a yellow-colored stick, trailing a wisp of smoke, arch over the rail of the pirate's schooner and fall into the water, directly in the path of his own.

"Dynamite!" boomed Bill. "Hold hard, all!"

The explosion wrenched the schooner as though she had struck a rock. At the bow a column of water leaped into the air and fell in heavy drops. Bill pocketed his useless revolver and ran forward, to return with blazing eyes and a face of stone.

Emily was on deck.

"Needn't move your father just yet," snapped the pearler. "The explosion stove a two-foot hole in us. Mostly above the water line, but we'll sink if he keeps on bombing. He won't hesitate to drown us, either... Here he comes again—to palaver, I guess."

Motopu had gone about and was maneuvering to pass again at slightly greater distance. He remained invisible, but his voice was clearly audible.

"Throw over the pearls on a life preserver, and I'll let you go!"

"Will you, though?" Bill muttered deep in his chest, but instead of answering he looked inquiringly at Tivi. The pearls belonged to the Polynesian.

The grizzled head was bowed; and the sad resignation of a race that has seen death reduce its ranks from thousands to dozens since the coming of the white man, that has had its customs, its religion, and its pleasures swept away, and has been impotent to resist, made the native's huge shoulders droop. His people had become used to failure, and the knowledge of failure was on his face; yet the dark eyes glowed with a fire Bill had never seen in them before. Instead of reaching for a life preserver he motioned Emily to take the pearls.

"Keep them, Flower of the Sea, at least for a little while," he said. "They are my gift. I cannot give them away, and lose you. Later, if need be, they will bring you safety. Love is never wrong. Mine is not wrong nor weak."

THE BIG, brown man turned to face Bellow Bill.

"Motopu cannot steer and guard the forepart of his boat!" he suggested.

"Right!" snapped the pearler, who had the same thought. Since the one-eared pirate must pass close in order to place the dynamite charges, there was a chance for a good swimmer, who chose the right course, to swim between the two ships and board by the bobstay as the other schooner passed.

"But, here! Wait!" Bill shouted, for Tivi had given the wheel to Emily and was poised on the taffrail.

"Once, you swam in my place. That is enough!" said Tivi, and went over the side.

Bill cursed aloud. The dive was premature. Motopu was still a hundred yards away, able to see that counter attack, able to heave to and fight the man in the water, or avoid him altogether.

"More brave foolishness!" Bill commented, aware even in this crisis that Tivi's recklessness was most advantageous to him. Emily had the pearls, and whether the native succeeded or failed in his fight with Motopu, he could not board his own schooner again against Bill's will.

That Tivi would use dynamite was unthinkable. Bill had only to wait, now. The value of the pearls was unimportant; still, he had to give them away.

Fists clenched, Bill watched the other schooner rush down upon Tivi's head. Before the Polynesian could catch the bobstay the schooner swung about, and from the stern a spluttering stick of dynamite was flung toward the swimmer. Tivi kept on, taking the chance that there had been no time to shorten the fuse. The schooner was coming about, and though he must swim directly over the spot where the dynamite was sinking, if he lived he would be able to overtake the schooner while she circled.

"Damn' foolishness!" Bill muttered. He was looking at Emily now. The blue eyes were full of dancing flames, and there was an ironic twist to his lips. Prudence and common sense counseled him to stay where he was, for Tivi, however gallant he might be, was an adversary. Bill was not actuated by an impulse. The ironical smile was at himself. He could not stand idle and let a weakling's victory drop into his hands.

"And here's more foolishness!" he added, and dived overboard to give the Polynesian what help he could.

THOUGH THE distance between the two schooners was short, Bill swung himself aboard Motopu's vessel none too quickly. The bearded pirate had armed himself with a capstan bar, and with that unwieldy club was battering Tivi. The native had managed to come to grips with his enemy, but the grizzled head was streaming blood.

As Bill ran aft, Tivi's grip shifted from Motopu's waist to his knees. The pirate shortened his grip on the six-foot bar of oak for a finishing blow, but the charge of the pearler hurried him. The stroke that should have cracked Tivi's skull landed on his back and shoulder. Nevertheless, Motopu was able to kick his legs free and aim a two-handed sweep at Bill's head.

Bill caught the blow on an upraised forearm. He felt the bone snap, but at the cost of a useless left arm he was inside the swing of the club. He caught Motopu around the waist, jerked him off his feet, and fell upon him with all his weight.

For a second or two Bill could do no more than hold the pirate. The pain of the broken arm, aggravated by the fall, benumbed him. Motopu bit and kicked for a time, then squirmed, forcing an arm under Bill's body toward his own waist. He was clawing for a knife. Bill knew he could never prevent the pirate from drawing it.

Bill's good hand shifted from Motopu's waist to throat. As the steel flashed, Bill threw himself back, holding Motopu above him at the full length of a long tattooed arm. The knife nicked the pearler's ribs as he flung Motopu against the deck, and set his knees on the pirate's arms close to the elbows. Motopu's heels beat a tattoo on the deck. He tried to twist the knife against Bill's side, but the pearler was too heavy. His knee kept Motopu's arms pinned fast, and again Bill's good hand found the bearded throat.

Bill did not mean to kill. He had forgotten Tivi until a shadow fell upon him. Instantly there was the swish of a club before his eyes, and Motopu's features were horribly blotted out. Bill sprang back, believing the blow had been aimed at his own head, but Tivi only rested the end of the capstan bar upon the deck and leaned upon it, without attacking.

"He would have drowned her," he said. "He was a bad man. I am glad I killed him."

"Thought you were going to kill *me!*"

Tivi shook his head with the utmost simplicity. "No. Not yet," he replied. "I would not kill you as I would stamp on a centipede, brother. I wish to do right—as a white man would. When white men cannot agree, they fight. The English and Americans with their fists, in a ring, with many looking on. The French, with pistols, with two to watch, besides a doctor. How they fight makes no difference. They are only careful the fight shall be fair."

"You'll fight a duel for Emily?" Bill rumbled. "It's the man's way."

"We need no one to make us fight fair," declared the Polynesian, with grave pride. "Yet your arm is broken, brother, and there are no pistols."

"You're considerably bunged up yourself," grunted Bellow Bill cheerfully. "I'd fight you with one hand if you knew anything about boxing. Tell you what! Let's take a belaying pin apiece. All the same war-club, eh, brother?"

The Polynesian's eyes lighted. The *u'u* was his racial weapon. The war-club of the South Seas is a paddle-shaped, sharp-edged, three-foot club of hardwood; and though a belaying pin is only a foot long, the club play is the same with both. There is little chance for parry or riposte, as with sword. One blow decides the fight, and the odds are on the more active man.

TIVI FELT that he had an advantage, but Bellow Bill had used the war-club in the Marquesas, and in reality the duel was fair. They armed themselves from the nearest pin rail and advanced, swaying easily to the roll of the schooner. Emily's scream reached them faintly. Both smiled. They shifted and sidestepped like two boxers, each waiting for the other to lead.

Every movement sent a jab of pain from Bill's arm to the shoulder. His footwork was slow. He shrugged. There are no rules in a fight with the *u'u*. Flashingly Tivi swung out a bare foot, all but tripping him. The native's club slipped from his right hand to his left, snapped up and back. His upraised right arm guarded against a counter blow.

Like lightning Bill seized the only opening left—Tivi's body. Underhand he threw his belaying pin, before the upraised club could fall. Butt first, the missile struck Tivi. The native doubled up, and Bill snapped an upper-cut to the exposed jaw with all his two hundred and twenty pounds of hard muscle behind the fist. Tivi was lifted into the air and dropped in a heap. He did not move, and Bill stepped back grimly.

He could not have knocked the Polynesian out more thoroughly with a club. As far as the duel between them went, that was that. Tivi was licked. And yet, Bill's struggle was far from ended. Fists would not help him against Emily.

He had left his revolver on the other schooner. Emily was resolute enough to use it.

Bellow Bill was tired. His arm hurt. He was tempted to bind Tivi hand and foot, to keep the schooners apart, and command Emily to swim to him, so that he could disarm her as she climbed aboard. Certainly he could do no more fighting with a broken arm.

But to his surprise Emily was not on the deck of the other schooner. She might not have seen his fight with Tivi, and might never know of it, for though Bill had gone so far as to pick up a rope, he could not quite force himself to bind Tivi's wrists. The Polynesian deserved to be treated like the honorable foeman he had proved himself. After all, the schooners were a long way from Thursday Island, and even if Bill were able to keep the party under his thumb while they remained at sea, Emily could do what she pleased once she arrived in civilization. The men were done with their fighting, but the girl would have the last word.

CHAPTER VII

THE MEASURE OF A MAN

TIVI OPENED HIS eyes slowly and lay staring at the sky for a long time. He must have decided upon every detail of what he meant to do before he rose, for without a word to Bellow Bill he walked to the wheel and steered Motopu's schooner along-side his own. As the two craft bumped together Emily emerged from the companionway. Her dark head was bowed, and what Bill could see of the girl's face was white as chalk.

Tivi did not seem to notice the girl at all. He jumped aboard his own boat and walked to the wheel, leaning over it with his great shoulders bowed and his eyes far off on the horizon.

"Did you—kill Motopu?" asked Emily. There were harsh lines around her mouth and her voice was a dull monotone, as though to speak were an effort.

"Aye," said Tivi. With a brown arm, streaked with blood that had flowed from his injured head, he pointed toward the west. Far away the sky line was notched by two sails, white and sharply defined against the crimson of the sunset. "There are Kory and the Japanese. They live, and Motopu is dead. It is finished, Bellow Bill. *They* have no dynamite. After the storm comes the calm."

"Finished? What do you mean?" said Emily stiffly. "Don't you want to marry me, Tivi? Forget Bill! I'm willing to carry out our bargain."

"There are no bargains in love. Only gifts, Flower of the Sea." The big brown man refused to look at the girl. His eyes remained fixed on the far-away schooners.

"Want?" he went on resignedly. "The child cries for the moon, and the man for a woman. But I am no child, not to know what is beyond my reach. With me you would not be happy, Flower of the Sea. Your people would laugh at you, and I am not strong enough to still their tongues."

"I don't care what people say; I am willing to marry you. But—if you don't want me"—the hard lines around Emily's mouth disappeared, and she drew a deep breath—"of course, I'll give back the pearls."

"A chief takes back no gifts," said Tivi proudly. "Freely I gave them, and I do not fear to be poor. Not when I am alone. I am not a white man. Use the pearls for your father, Flower of the Sea. Use them to go to the islands where all people are white, and where there are schools." And now Tivi looked Emily in the eyes. "That is my gift," he declared. "Let Bill show you how to use it. He is the better and the wiser man."

"The stronger and the trickier, you mean," Bill rumbled in

contradiction, reaching out to grip the big brown hand that rested on the spokes of the wheel. From a scratch on his own hand blood was mingling with the blood on the reddening fingers in his grip.

He recalled the primitive ceremony of blood brothership, a rite more solemn and as highly regarded as marriage throughout the South Seas.

"*Ka-ohoa,* brother in the blood!" Bill greeted him.

Tivi's dark eyes glowed with pride. The brown fingers gripped tensely, then relaxed.

"Aye, brother! That is well!" he whispered. "With such a brother, I am rich. Take the Flower of the Sea and her father on the other schooner now. I would like to be alone."

"Doubt if we ought to move Squareface—"

"We can move him," said Emily. "He is dead, Bill. The shock of the explosion—"

"Dead!" cried the pearler. "Then why were you willing to marry—"

Emily flung up her head. "I couldn't welch, even if I have nothing to gain. It was only fair to Tivi."

Bill was speechless, but Tivi nodded gravely.

"Dead? That is best. He was not a good man," he muttered. "It is finished. Farewell, my brother. Farewell…" He stopped. The farewell to Emily stuck in his throat.

Bill went below quickly, and returned soon, carrying the body. He stepped aboard the other schooner, Emily following, and trimmed the sail. Rapidly a space of heaving sea opened between the two vessels. Under the cutwater the water gurgled as Bill set a course to join Kory.

ASTERN, TIVI'S schooner wallowed heavily. The Polynesian remained with arms folded over the wheel, watching Emily sail away. The great shoulders had the droop that comes to a powerful man who has found himself not strong enough to contend with forces which are overwhelming, and which he does not quite understand. Yet the battered head was erect.

Emily touched Bill's shoulder. "I ought to thank you," she whispered, very low, as though the distant figure on the crippled schooner could hear. "I do, too. And yet I'm glad you weren't strong enough to beat me. He was a man, Bill!"

"And takes a licking like a man," Bellow Bill agreed. "I hope I can do as well when my turn comes."

"You—licked?"

"Even a roughneck like me!"

Bill glanced at the fresh, vivid beauty of the dark face that stared at him with eyes widened in bewilderment, and instantly looked upward at the sail. "It's my luck to be hard-boiled and enjoy risking my neck. You take those pearls and go to 'Frisco. Get an education, and *stay* there."

"Half the pearls are yours."

"The devil they are! Not even one of 'em," said Bill, still more gruffly.

The coppery yellow head shook determinedly, the blue eyes glanced fleetingly at the girl as Bellow Bill boomed:

"No man's going to keep you in the South Seas to waste yourself on some lonely atoll and raise kids that might go native. Liquor and fighting and love—they're all good, but they don't go together. Which is a damn' shame!"

THE BLACK TIDE

One man better than a gunboat? That was
what the commissioner of a South Seas island
thought of pearling skipper Bellow Bill
Williams, when a cannibal wave threatened
to sweep the whites into the ocean

CHAPTER I

DEATH MUTTERINGS

The Residency, Mataila,
Oct. 10, 1930.

DEAR BILL:
Come and help me. The cannibals from the hills are crowding us all into the sea.

RANDALL.

THE LETTER HAD not been penned in haste or panic. The script was neat and firm; the sheet of official note paper which Randall had used was large enough to have set forth all the details of his predicament. Yet he had chosen to confess his defeat, to appeal for assistance, and write nothing more—which, considering that the letter was addressed to Bellow Bill Williams, was a most extraordinary thing.

For Sommers Randall, ex-lieutenant in the Royal Navy, was the Commissioner of Mataila and the sole representative of the British government on that large, savage, and unexplored island. If he was in trouble, a letter from him to his government would have summoned a cruiser or landed a company of marines. His authority was backed by all the power of the British Empire—and yet he was appealing for help to an American, to an individual who had no resources except a pearling schooner and his own big hands.

Yet the very brevity of the appeal made Bellow Bill respond more promptly, Upon receipt of the letter he hoisted anchor from a pearl lagoon that was not half fished out, and cracked

*"We'd like you to
marry us," he told the
amazed Bellow Bill*

on sail across the blue Pacific until the dark, mountainous mass
of Mataila Island rose on the horizon ahead. Because the letter
gave no details he was forced to judge the nature of the emergency from what he remembered of Randall, and those memo-
ries were emphatically to the Englishman's credit.

During the war Bellow Bill had fought beside the lieutenant. By the acid tests of submarines and shellfire he knew that
Randall was daring to the point of recklessness, and of dogged
determination. If he were being beaten, then the enemy was
formidable. If he had chosen to call in Bill instead of a cruiser,
it was because one man who knew the South Seas and their
savages would be more effective than all the guns of a British
ship of war.

There had been a day back in 1918 when Bellow Bill had
faced a trial by court-martial for disobedience of orders during
the pursuit of a submarine. By disobeying, Bill had been able,
much later, to destroy the raider, but at the time his act looked
like gross insubordination, and the court-martial would probably have sentenced him to military prison if not the firing squad.

Randall, however, had quashed the case out of sheer friendship and liking for the American, and Bill had never forgotten the fact. Though twelve years had passed, he was eager to serve if Randall needed him—though he would have liked to know what had changed the black, fuzzy-headed cannibals of Mataila into a black tide that was sweeping the whites into the sea. They had always been a threat but they had never attacked before.

MATAILA HAS a dark enough reputation throughout the South Seas. It is a large island of volcanic formation, a hundred miles long and thirty wide, rising from the sea to a jagged, precipitous mountain range of black basaltic rock between six and eight thousand feet high. Potentially the hills are rich in mineral and the lowlands are suitable for copra plantations, but although the island has been on the charts for more than a century no part of the world is less known.

No white man has ever crossed the hills from sea to sea. The whites, and the salt water natives over whom they rule, have clung to the beach for generations, seldom daring to penetrate more than a few miles inland. For the interior is occupied by

savage and aggressive tribes of black, fuzzy-headed Melanesian
cannibals who resent strangers.

Though the cannibals keep to themselves except for an occa-
sional raid on the coast villages for long pig, they rule the island.
White dominion hardly extends beyond the sound of the surf.
Beyond are jungles dripping under the tropical rain. Beyond
these—no one knows what. Explorers have headed into the
jungle, and vanished. A British commissioner with a dozen well-
armed men who started across the mountains disappeared—
swallowed by the dense vegetation within a mile of his own
Residency, and presumably swallowed by Melanesians later.

Later commissioners had been content to maintain the *status
quo*—a narrow fringe of half-civilized villages hugging the sea,
living in daily terror of savages, who in turn had kept to their
hills. Yet if, as Randall's letter suggested, that balance had been
disturbed, there were enough of the Melanesians to sweep the
salt water villagers and their white associates into the ocean.

There were few white men on Mataila. For years in the prin-
cipal "town" there had been one Resident whose duty it was to
keep the flag flying to prevent any other nation that wanted a
coaling station in the South Seas from taking possession of the
island, and one white trader and his daughter, who monopolized
what little business there was along a hundred miles of coast.

"CHINK" VERNON, however, would have made Mataila
notorious even if the cannibals had not. He was a lank and swarthy Yankee with a yellow complexion and the close-set, blazing black eyes of a fanatic. He had established himself in such a
place out of sheer inexperience, and been too stubborn to admit
later that he was wrong.

Similarly out of sheer ignorance he had begun twenty years
before to match a pearl necklace, and had persisted even after
he must have learned that a century would have been too short
a time to complete the task he had set himself. All through the
South Seas pearlers knew that Vernon would pay as much for
gems he wanted as the jewelers at Papeete; all through the South

Seas the saying "when Chink Vernon finishes his necklace" was a synonym for "when hell freezes."

For pearls differ from all other gems in this respect: that when one is exactly matched in size and color with another, the value of each is immediately doubled. Pearls cannot be cut nor polished, and it is only rarely that the pearl oyster is so accommodating as to produce a perfect sphere. Therefore, to collect a necklace that may contain only a hundred pearls the jeweler must handle many thousands. Even a firm which receives pearls from all over the world may require decades to form a fine necklace.

All South Sea traders handle a few pearls. In the beginning, probably, the doubling in value appealed to Vernon. That he would be able to get his necklace together in the course of a lifetime may have seemed probable. At any rate, when his daughter was born he announced that his legacy to her would be a necklace fit for a millionaire's daughter, and in the twenty years that had followed his offer to buy pearls that matched any of his had always held good.

Pearlers laughed at him when he announced his purpose, and lately, as Bellow Bill Williams knew, the laugh had become a snicker. For a rival trader had established himself on Mataila. J. Malcolm Kennedy was another Yankee, as inexperienced as Vernon had been twenty years before, and so handsome and pleasant that his native name was "Smiling Mouth."

Almost immediately the salt-water natives gave him the bulk of their trade, but throughout the islands the gossip was that Kennedy had not gone to a cannibal hole like Mataila for the sake of a few measly tons of poorly cured copra. Carol Vernon was a girl any red-blooded man would have liked to marry for herself, and—well—Chink had been matching pearls for twenty years, hadn't he? The necklace wasn't finished, but it might be worth having, eh, when you got a pretty wife to boot?

Such was the rumor, but in Bellow Bill's opinion the gossip of the islands was invariably foul-mouthed and usually mistaken.

As he dropped anchor off Mataila in the late afternoon any connection between Chink Vernon's private affairs and Randall's letter was the last thing that occurred to him.

CHAPTER II

A TWO-FACED TRADER

THE ARRIVAL OF the pearling schooner was the signal for two dugouts to paddle out from the beach, but to Bill's surprise neither of these contained Randall. The foremost, in fact, was propelled by a single native who wore an old pith helmet and a strip of gayly flowered calico, and who climbed on board the schooner with a mixture of white man's assurance and *kanaka* timidity almost equally incongruous. That he did not wait to be asked aboard was a flagrant breach of etiquette.

"What name belong you?" Bellow Bill sung out angrily—and loudly. Bill's voice was a rumbling bass. His whisper was audible at a hundred yards, and the effect of his shout was to make the native jump as though one bare foot had trod on a fish hook.

"Not be cross along Taupo," he quavered.

For Bill stood six feet three inches in his socks, and weighed two hundred and twenty-live pounds without an ounce of fat. From wrists to waist he was tattooed in a fashion that was enough to awe a native—stars, daggers, and blue circles of rope on the huge bronzed arms that thrust out of his tattered singlet, the tip of the dragon's head which covered the broad chest visible at the neck of the cotton garment, hinting that his seafaring had embraced the China Seas. His hair was thick and curly, of a bright coppery yellow, and his eyes were light blue and piercing. With a scowl he strode toward the trembling Taupo, spitting a large quid of fine-cut chewing tobacco over the rail as he advanced.

"You one fella chief?" he rumbled with thundering sarcasm.

"Me fella belong Randall!" squealed Taupo. "Him leg belong him swell up! Him sick fella! Send me ask you fella come along tiffin. No be cross—"

Bill stopped the flood of *bêche-de-mer* English by lifting his hand. So Randall was sick? That explained much.

"Tell him I'm coming," he answered the staring native, and pointed peremptorily toward the beach. Taupo fairly tumbled over the rail in haste to obey, moving so quickly that he jostled a white man who was climbing aboard. With a squeak the native disappeared.

AT ONCE the white man, who Bill decided must be Kennedy, since he was young, blond and handsome, reached over the rail and helped a white girl to board the schooner.

"You've got a ship master's license?" the visitor demanded coolly.

Bellow Bill gave a nod of surprise.

"Then we'd like you to marry us, captain," Kennedy went on. "Wouldn't we, Carol?"

"Yes, captain," the girl concurred. They were both amazingly self-possessed, and if Kennedy was handsome Carol Vernon was beautiful—tall and slender, and with level, straightforward gray eyes that went to Bill's heart. At once the big pearler was conscious that he was roughly and scantily clad, and that his cheek still bulged with tobacco.

"Do I look like a missionary?" he answered, half embarrassed. "I hold a master's ticket, yes; but this schooner isn't a passenger vessel, and we're not on the high seas. I doubt if any ceremony I performed would be legal, and besides—"

Bellow Bill stopped. He had been about to add that he would not help any fortune hunter to marry any girl for the sake of her father's pearls, particularly such a girl as Carol Vernon looked to be, but he stopped because there was not the slightest sign of weakness or avarice in Kennedy's face.

If this stranger was a fortune hunter, as gossip insisted, then Bill could no longer trust his own judgment of men. Kennedy was hard-muscled, cool, and determined. He was the kind of man Bill would have been glad to have at his back in a tight corner, which is the highest compliment one man can give another.

"And besides what?" Kennedy challenged. "If you're think-ing about a certain pearl necklace, captain, I don't want it and won't let any wife of mine take it—as I've told Chink Vernon plenty of times, whether he believes me or not. As to any other 'besides,' when the cannibals are bold enough to show them-selves in Vernon's compound in broad daylight, I maintain that Carol needs protection. She prefers mine. Now what were you going to say?"

"Why, only that the commissioner on the island has got the right to perform marriages, buddy," Bellow Bill rumbled good-naturedly. "It's still an hour till sunset, and if you'll let me go below and get a coat and a gun I'd be glad to go to him with you and act as a witness."

"Randall's too sick to bother," Kennedy refused curtly. "He started to lead an expedition into the interior and was struck by a poisoned arrow before he had gone a mile from the settlement. He nearly died, and he's barely over delirium and fever yet."

"When was he hit?"

"Two weeks ago."

At this information Bill grunted. Randall had written his appeal before he had been wounded. Speculatively the pearler eyed Kennedy.

"Well then, you can't get married on Mataila," he continued. "But since I'm going to visit Randall for a few weeks you're welcome to borrow my schooner. Sail to another island and find a missionary—"

"No, thanks. I'm not quitting under fire," said Kennedy instantly. "That would be to leave you and Vernon alone, and even when Randall gets well the four of us will be faced by more than we can handle. There is something new going on here, sir. There's a chief arisen among the cannibals who goes by the name of Boraki, though he has a second that means 'mighty warrior who can make enemies die at will.'"

The trader uttered the title so gravely that Bill could not repress a grin. Kennedy, however, was serious.

"**YOU MAY** laugh," the young trader said. "So did I—once. Of course that would be magic, yet the fact remains that the cannibals are pressing down on us, and that Boraki—whom we haven't seen, of course—is their leader. He's managed to organize all the scattered tribes into a unit. The raiding parties are fifty or sixty strong.

"Our natives have abandoned their plantations and are camped behind the Residency in a stockade. They'll starve, of course, if they don't go into the jungle to gather breadfruit, but they'd rather starve than take the chance. The cannibals show themselves just beyond the stockade constantly. We've shot a few, but of course they manage to carry off the bodies, so we're pretty much in the dark. In my opinion Boraki's title must state the literal truth. At least, his blacks must be more afraid of him than of our guns."

"They raid even after they can't get long pig?" Bill rumbled.

"Yes!"

"Do they bother you whites? Are you inside the stockade?"

Kennedy shook his head. "We have to show the natives we're not afraid, even when we are. That's the white man's duty in a black country."

Bill nodded.

"So we stay in our old houses, which are very close to the jungle. They haven't bothered us yet." The young trader's eyes wandered to the girl and away again. "I'm afraid they might," he continued half under his breath. "Vernon says he's sure Boraki wants us to leave the island Maybe he's right. But Randall can't, and I won't. You understand, sir?"

Again Kennedy's eyes wandered protectingly toward the girl. "Mr. Randall has told us all he'd written to you. Said you'd been into New Guinea and knew more about untamed cannibals than any other man in the South Seas. Thought you might dope out what was up."

"Humph! Vernon leaving?" Bill grunted.

"Says he's lived here all his life and won't go until his necklace is matched," Kennedy snapped. "That's why I say, damn the necklace!"

"If any," Bill rumbled. "How much of a string has your father matched, Miss Vernon?"

"I don't know," the girl answered frankly. "He hasn't shown it to me for years. He does say, though, that he is positive there's no danger to me."

"He seems damned well informed. Excusing me, miss," Bill purred in his deep voice. "I think I'll talk to your father. Just wait till I get my gear together."

Bill went below decks thoughtfully. He had far too much experience among savages to laugh at magic. In New Guinea, which is peopled by cannibals of the same race as those of Mataila, he had encountered sorcerers who "willed" their enemies to die, and had seen the victims perish on the day prescribed in the curse. This Boraki might easily be a powerful medicine man who owed his ascendency to the magic which Kennedy had implied. Yet even so why the persistent raiding?

Savages are lazy, bound by superstition, hampered by ritual which must be gone through before undertaking any important act. For any chief to keep fifty warriors in the field was unprecedented, and Bill could not believe Vernon's explanation. The savages had no reason to care whether whites lived on the island or not. In Bill's opinion Vernon was making use of the emergency to get rid of a trade rival and a possible son-in-law whom he detested.

A coat, a revolver, and a pocketful of ammunition were all the gear Bill required for an extended visit ashore, since he would be Randall's guest. He was soon back on deck, and asked Kennedy to help him give the sails a harbor furl and secure the hatches so that the boat might ride at anchor safely during a long absence.

When the task was done the pearler stepped into the dugout and paddled his guests ashore. The sun was close to the mountains, and there remained not more than a half hour of daylight.

CHAPTER III

VERNON'S NECKLACE

BILL'S INTENTION WAS to see Randall immediately, but as he stepped ashore Chink Vernon came slouching across the beach to meet him, tall and hollow-cheeked, yellow-faced and imperturbable. The older trader favored his young competitor with a glare and ordered his daughter roughly to go home. For an instant Carol looked rebellious. Then she obeyed, and Kennedy also moved away, his face set in anger. Vernon planted himself in Bellow Bill's path with hands on hips and jaw outthrust.

"Did that slimy, lying blackguard try to get you to take my daughter and him to another island?" he demanded.

"No. And that'll be enough bilge out of you, Vernon," Bill rumbled. "I made him the offer and he turned it down. The kid's A No. 1 with me, savvy?"

Vernon stared unblinkingly at the bigger man.

"As you say," he temporized. "Kennedy's cheated me out of the trade I nursed for twenty years. He's come like a snake in the grass to take my daughter, that I raised for something better than the likes of him. He's going to rob me of her and of her necklace, but of course, he's A No. 1!" The sarcasm of the trader bit like acid.

"I've heard it said that Bellow Bill would go places other skippers didn't dare and never asked to see his profit in advance," he went on in the same tone. "Oh, yeah! What bribe did Randall offer you this time for coming here? His excellency the commissioner—" Vernon's lip curled—"is against me too. Trying to make me pack up and go, he is, and now that he's hurt he's sent for you to get me out. Well, try it! I've told him till my necklace is finished I stick! This is my island—"

"I've heard the cannibals were taking it back," Bill remarked.

"Cowards!" snapped Vernon. "Kennedy and Randall are scared of their shadows! They'll run from a footprint like a salt-water boy. The cannibals are hunting on this side of the island, that's all, and those two yap about a king that can kill his enemies with a look. Boraki, they call him! Bosh! They're trying to scare me into sending Carol to Sydney, where that snake in the grass can snatch her up. Me—that's lived in Mataila twenty years! I hate their dirty innards—savvy?"

"Sure. You've set yourself against every other white man on the island, including me," Bellow Bill acknowledged coolly. "That's frank and satisfactory. But now, you and I are experienced, which Randall and Kennedy ain't. I've picked up a bit of the Melanesian lingo in New Guinea, and I guess you know as much after trading here twenty years. You ought to understand savages as well as I. I'll assume you do, and I'll be damned if I'll be treated like a green new-chum!"

The pearler's voice deepened angrily. "That all blacks are hunting on this side of the island or that they want to drive the whites out is bilge!" he boomed. "This Boraki sounds to me like the real goods. What does he want and why does he send his raiding parties this way?"

"I don't know," Vernon snapped.

Bill dismissed the answer with a derisive shrug of his huge shoulders.

"I'VE GOT a couple of pearls I'd like to sell you," Bill went on, changing the subject completely. "Small ones, of course, but perfect."

"Small ones?" snapped Vernon. The yellow face flushed with greed and the glittering black eyes snapped. "Small ones are what I want! I've nearly got the string matched! I'm not looking for big pearls any more. The two-grain size is what I want, but they've got to be perfect! The lustre has got to be right! Come on to my store and let me see what you've got!"

The excitement of the trader was so intense, and the speech so amazing and unexpected that Bellow Bill almost swallowed what was left of his quid.

A big necklace will require from thirty to forty two-grain pearls, but this size is the easiest to obtain and to match. Vernon should have got that part of his necklace together long, long before he had amassed the larger gems.

Yet he hadn't. He caught Bill's arm with almost frantic eagerness. "Let's trade while the light lasts. I've got no cash, but I'll swap a forty-grain baroque against a two-grain sphere. Better than in Papeete, eh?"

The bargain was twice as good. Bill yielded to the pull on his arm, and followed the trader to a store the thatched roof of which had been weathered to ribbons, and which was almost bare of goods and foul with neglect. The building gave mute testimony that Vernon had paid little attention to business recently, and Bill did not wonder that Kennedy had been able to get all the trade. But that, he was convinced, was a trifle compared to this matter of pearls. For them any trader would neglect the trifling profits from the sale of cloth, gewgaws, and copra.

Briskly Vernon walked to a safe and removed a cardboard box stuffed with kapok cotton, from which he picked about a dozen pearls of the two grain size. Over his shoulder Bill saw that the safe was full of other boxes. He wondered if Vernon had taken this means of matching his pearls. The yellow-faced man slammed the safe abruptly, and thrust the pearls toward Bill.

"No trade unless you can match one of those," he challenged, and leaned forward to examine the two gems that Bill took out of a bottle which he had in his pocket. One Vernon thrust back. It was slightly egg-shaped; but the second was round and of superb pink-white lustre, like the pearls in the box. Vernon weighed it and measured it with calipers, and unhesitatingly reached for one of his own.

"The same weight and size," he breathed. The yellowish face was purple with excitement. "I ain't matched a pearl since— since—"

"Since when?" Bill boomed.

"Since I found two alike and four hundred grains each!" Vernon snarled malevolently. "You'd like to know, wouldn't you—you and the others that claimed I'd never get my necklace finished." He whirled to the safe and placed a second cardboard box before Bill.

"Take any of these in exchange. They're all baroques," he offered.

THE BOX contained half a dozen pearls of large size but irregular shape. The smallest there would have been a good trade, but Bellow Bill, whose senses were sharpened by the strangeness of the whole proceeding, picked up one of the gems and walked to the window to give it a close inspection. Though he did not anticipate fraud, he sensed that he was on the edge of a mystery—possibly part of the mystery which had led to his presence in Mataila.

Though sunset was almost at hand, the light was still strong. The baroque in his fingers was tinged with yellow, and there was no iridescent play of light on the surface. It looked dirty, and the feel was strange. Bill held the pearl to his nose and smelled an oily, unpleasant odor. Rubbing the pearl on his coat sleeve failed to improve the luster or remove the smell.

"This pearl of yours is sick, Vernon," he rumbled. "I've fished the whole South Seas and never seen one like it. Let me have another."

"Sick?" Vernon scoffed. "Perhaps it has been shut in the box too long, but there's nothing wrong with it that won't be cured when it's worn. You know that some women have to send their pearls out to be worn by others in order to maintain the luster—"

"Yeah. Don't talk so fast. That's mostly superstition," Bill rumbled. "There's a kind of oil on these that—"

A gasp from Vernon made the pearler turn. The baroque

slipped out of his hand. In the open door of the store stood a fuzzy-headed black, tall and enormously wide of shoulder, with a chest ridged and puckered with tribal scars and smeared with wood ashes. He had entered confidently, but at Bill's movement he slipped out of the door like a shadow. The noiseless, animal quickness of the retreat and the wood ashes on the body were the mark of the cannibal.

The visitor would have escaped, but Bill, instead of following through the door, vaulted out of the window, tumbling almost on the cannibal's back as the latter ran alongside the store toward the underbrush which approached the building closely in the rear.

A flying tackle brought the cannibal down. He writhed, struck at Bill with a sharp-edged wooden club, but the pearler's revolver was out. The barrel cracked down on the fuzzy head, and the black went limp. Kneeling on the unconscious body, it seemed to Bill that the underbrush stirred. On chance, he fired, head-high. The bullet ripped through the leaves, and other motion—if there had been motion—ceased.

There was no other sound, and Bill leaned down to examine his captive in the dim light. The man was a cannibal, no doubt of that, for his loin cloth was of pounded bark instead of the usual trade calico. Otherwise he was naked except for a wide belt, pouched like a money belt, of thin leather, crudely tanned but barbarously decorated with a multitude of small symbols drawn in red and black. The man's skin was greasy with some oil or tree gum, and a half-rotten odor rose from his body which Bill found vaguely familiar.

VERNON DASHED around the corner of his store and dropped on his knees beside Bill. The yellow face was tense and the black eyes snapped dangerously.

"Let him go!" he gasped. "These cannibals don't raid alone! You'll bring half the tribe down on us!"

"Attack a white man's bungalow? Bilge! Kennedy said they

hadn't done that yet," Bellow Bill scoffed. "Let's cross-examine this fella."

"We could if you hadn't bashed in his skull," rasped the trader. "His head is bleeding enough to kill him!" Vernon pulled out a handkerchief and started to bandage the scalp wound, while Bill, who had started to reply and then changed his mind, commenced to examine the belt, which though clearly of savage make, was a most unusual thing for a cannibal to wear.

The pouch had two pockets, of which one was half full of a dirty, coarse-grained substance that looked like dried sea salt; while the other, almost empty, contained a few grains of a whiter, more finely divided substance. Cautiously Bill touched a few grains of each to his tongue.

The dirty stuff was salt; the other seemed to be a kind of salt, too, though the taste was not so sharp. He spat it out quickly. Although savages from the interior made periodic trips to the ocean for salt, which is needed both as seasoning and as a protection from the attacks of the tiny leeches that abound in the jungle, this captive had enough of the stuff to last him for months. Moreover, the smell of the oil on the naked body was—was the same queer odor Bill had detected on the pearl!

The pearler's eyes narrowed. Vernon, he noticed, was making slow work of the bandage, seemed to be having difficulty in pushing the cannibal's fuzzy hair away from the wound. Bill watched like a cat. Suddenly his hand went forward, caught the trader's wrist and twisted it, despite Vernon's resistance.

From the limp fingers a baroque pearl as big as the end of a man's thumb dropped into the trampled bushes. Still holding Vernon with one hand, Bill put his revolver back in his pocket, reached forward and picked up the gem. Though the sun was dropping behind the horizon with tropic swiftness, he was sure the pearl had a yellowish tint. He smelled it.

"Lots of your pearls seem to be sick, Vernon," he commented evenly. "Damn' sick. Not to say rotten. So you don't need big pearls for your necklace any more, eh?"

"What do you mean? I found that pearl in my hand when I got here. I jumped after you too quick to put it down—"

"Don't lie! You found that in this fellow's hair," Bill purred. "You saw he had nothing worse than a scalp wound. Come clean, Vernon! What are you doing, and how? Pearl oysters don't grow on trees, but pearls that come out of salt water don't get smeared with oil! I can swear to that, too!"

In the minute that had passed the bush had become dark. Bill could no longer see the trader's face, but his body was still as stone and his wrist tensed in Bill's grip.

"Pearls are where you find them," came the answer in a whisper. "A trader makes any bargain he can."

"Even when the blacks that come to trade kill a couple of salt-water boys on their way back?" Bellow Bill rumbled. "What do they trade for? Not calico and mirrors, or this fellow would not be wearing tapa cloth. Who's that chief they've got whose enemies die? You?"

"No!" Vernon snapped with a passionate vehemence that carried conviction. "I've traded with them, that's all! Now you know it, make the most of it and be damned to you! You claim to go where no other traders dare. So have I! I went into the bush, risking my life every step and every minute, and traded for the pearls they'd took in generations of raiding. I'm going to finish my necklace and make my daughter rich. Well, you tattooed roughneck! What are you going to do about that?"

Bellow Bill released the trader's wrist.

"Nothing yet," he rumbled. "Randall's the commissioner. I'm just a roughneck doing a friend a favor. What he wants to do is his business, but from now on he'll know what he's fighting, and who."

CHAPTER IV

SENTENCED

BILL CAUGHT BOTH wrists of the cannibal in his left hand, and with a twist and a heave, swung the unconscious captive over his back. Though the feat required prodigious strength he performed it with ease, and with equal casualness pulled his gun from his pocket.

"You'd better come along," he grinned. "I don't think you've told all the truth about Boraki yet."

Vernon made no reply beyond a sharp intake of breath that was almost a hiss. The sun had set, and the quick darkness of the tropics had filled the interior of the neglected, empty store with a gloom which made his features indistinguishable. His figure, as he strode out of the door with Bill at his heels, was stiffly erect and defiant. He walked along the beach toward the commissioner's bungalow, which was some two hundred yards away, like a soldier on parade, and without hesitation mounted the steps that led to the broad veranda of the Residency.

Within the bungalow a single kerosene lamp burned, but the veranda was dark and at first Bill could see no sign of the commissioner himself.

"Randall!" he boomed softly.

"Ah, my word!" answered a voice, faint and friendly. "That you, Bill, old thing? Taupo, you lazy devil! Bring the whisky and soda! And my word. Bill, who have you got on your back? He smells!"

"One of the cannibals," the pearler responded gravely. "He came into Vernon's store with a funny kind of pearl in his hair. Vernon has been trading with them. For what I don't know. Not calico and mirrors or any of the usual trade goods. This fellow is still wearing tapa cloth."

"He smells!" repeated the sick man fretfully. Raising his voice,

he called to Taupo to bring the light and then to take the prisoner to an outhouse behind the bungalow and tie him hand
and foot.

When the servant obeyed Randall lifted his head and grinned
weakly at his old shipmate. The Englishman was a shocking
sight. Always tall and slender, sickness and fever had reduced
him to a skeleton. His eyes were enormous in his wasted cheeks.
Bill recognized him by his eyebrows, which turned upward at the
corners like a pair of wings and gave his face a quizzical expression despite emaciation.

"Jolly good work, Bill old thing," he whispered. "I tried to
get a cannibal, too, but they got me first." The whisper became
authoritative. "Well, Vernon, what *were* you trading for?"
Randall demanded.

"The usual trade goods. Is that a crime?" Vernon snapped
crisply.

"Er—ah—no." The hammock-swayed. "So that's your tune,
what? Innocent trader, eh? Your—ah—customers spice your
goods with long pig and kill natives under my protection on
their way to trade, but that's no fault of yours, what? You don't
sell firearms or gin?"

"No!"

"That won't do, Vernon. We're four whites here. Five coun-
tin' Bill. We're the Twentieth Century sittin' on the nastiness of
the Stone Age. Our job is to help savages cross a chasm of five
thousand years of darkness. Our ancestors were like these—ah—
customers of yours thousands of years ago. Never ate men, but
sacrificed them to Woden. He was a Teutonic god. You don't
know that, or care, what? White man's burden is for the government to carry. Trading is for profits, what?"

"Yes!" snapped Vernon defiantly.

"Then earn your profits where the white man's battle has
already been won!" Randall whispered. "I won't ask you to stop
trading. You're too old a clog to learn new tricks. My sentence

is this: to-morrow you and Miss Vernon leave Mataila for good. Bill will carry you away in his schooner, eh?"

"O.K.," rumbled the pearler.

A flush darkened the trader's yellow face. "I ain't arguing either," he said. "You're right I'd trade! As long as I was half starving to death, as long as I was getting about one pearl a year for my necklace, as long as you could laugh at me, you were satisfied. Now that I'm beating the game and have got something you and Kennedy want, you chuck the 'white man's burden' in my teeth! I ain't an Englishman. To heck with your government and your duties! You rule to rob!"

"Better go to your store and pack up," Randall whispered, coldly indifferent to the tirade. "You leave at sunrise to-morrow. Peaceably, I—ah—assume?"

"Correct," Vernon sneered. "You rule the island, don't you? The two white men that will be left, and a few hundred scared salt-water boys—the subjects of 'is majesty, God bless 'im!' What else can I do, but let myself be kicked out? I'm undesirable. I am!" The trader rose and strode down the veranda steps into the dark. His back was erect, rigid, and masterful as though, in his own opinion he had got the better of the interview.

"FIGHTING MAN, that," Bellow Bill rumbled. "Wonder how close he has got to the savages?"

"He's a fanatic. Make the best fighters. Only got one idea," muttered Randall wearily. "Oliver Cromwell's Ironsides were like that. Religion is deadly when it's behind a gun. His god is that necklace. Nothing else for me to do, but deport him. Deuced unpleasant. Seems unjust, what? Er—had dinner, old thing? Been years since I've seen you. Charmed, I've champagne. No ice, of course. Can't drink myself, but glad to watch you."

"I'm not thirsty," Bill answered thoughtfully. "See here, shipmate: how does a cannibal's body oil come to get on pearls? The stuff is the same, and it has an unusual smell. Nothing I've ever known natives to use."

Randall twisted irritably in his hammock. Out of the darkness beyond the veranda two white figures materialized, walking swiftly toward the Residency, and revealed themselves as Kennedy and Carol Vernon as they approached the circle of lamplight. The girl was excited, her *fiancé* anxious.

"Mr. Randall, what crime has father committed?" the girl burst out indignantly. "He came home and told me to leave the island at sunrise with him, and then he plunged out into the bush. I don't understand it!"

"He has entered into relations with the cannibals," Randall whispered.

Kennedy uttered an exclamation of denial under his breath, but Carol, though less surprised, was more outspoken.

"Not wrongfully, sir!" she cried. "I know he learned a few words of their language long ago—long before you came here!" She appealed to Kennedy. "But he has never been in the interior lately. Never more than a few miles! I am sure of it!"

The disbelief of Bellow Bill and Randall checked the girl's vehement protest. Desperately she turned to the pearler. "You know how men get—so they think nothing but pearls!" she pleaded. "Father's like that! He's hard—except to me—but I'm sure he'd never do anything really wrong. If he's sent away it will kill him! He's been almost happy lately! Planning things for me, even though I didn't want them. I know he's a good man."

"He hates me," Kennedy cut in, "but I believe he's sound at the core. Much as I'd like to get Carol away from here, I hate to see it done this way. I'd rather take the responsibility for his trading. You could force him to deal from my store, sir—"

HE STOPPED abruptly, and the same sound that he had heard brought Bellow Bill to his feet like a huge cat. Carol's hand flew to her lips, and she listened like the rest. From the rear of the bungalow had come a thud and a gasp, perfectly audible, but so sudden, so instantly hushed, that all three waited for the noise to be repeated.

It was not. Bill heard the rustle of palm fonds and the lisp of the surf, but the previous sound had been so obviously of human origin that he drew his revolver and started on tiptoe toward the rear of the bungalow. Kennedy followed, also with a gun. The two passed through the house and out into the clear space behind it, in the center of which stood a thatched shed without side walls used as a cook shack. In the darkness under the low roof a man was squirming along the ground on his belly. Bill leaped upon the figure. His fingers caught a fuzzy head, and an odor he had come to know well filled his nostrils.

"Our cannibal is crawlin' off," he grunted. "Still tied hand and foot, too!"

"Tied?" Kennedy had also stopped in the dark. "Here's Taupo, knocked cold," he whispered. "His head is bleeding like the devil. That cannibal can't be tied!"

"That cannibal's got buddies," growled Bill, peering into the dark. His gun was ready, but, veteran of many fights though he was, he had forgotten that Kennedy and he were wearing white and that their figures were dimly visible in the dark. There was a stir at the edge of the clearing. A volley of clubs whirled out of the shadows, followed by a rush of naked men. Bill was struck a violent blow in the forehead.

Dazed, he fired once before three men hurled themselves upon him. He was thrown away from the bound cannibal and buried under a mass of oily, stinking bodies. Hands clawed at his throat. A man had caught each arm. His gun was twisted away, a fourth enemy gripped both legs. None used a weapon, but by sheer weight and numbers they held Bill motionless. He heard Kennedy cry out, once, as though badly hurt.

Grimly Bill gripped the native who lay upon him, squeezing the breath from the body and shielding his own head and face in the hollow of the black's shoulder and throat. Otherwise Bill did not struggle. Four to one are too many for the most powerful man.

His chance came when, with a simultaneous heave, his enemies tried to lift him off the ground. Savagely he struck out with both feet, tearing loose from the grip of the black who held his knees and kicking the latter backward.

With a wrench he freed his right arm, jabbed the elbow into the belly of the black who had held it. He was dropped, twisted over and over, and came erect, swinging the man he held in his arms around him like a flail to clear a space. The whirling body knocked one enemy headlong—and, sudden as the volley of club and the charge, the fight was over! There was a crash of twigs from the edge of the clearing as the savages retreated as fast as they had come. Bill had the clearing to himself.

Too much to himself. The white-clad figure of Kennedy was gone. Taupo was gone. The cannibal who had been bound hand and foot had disappeared. So quickly had it all happened that Carol, running through the bungalow with a light, had just reached the rear veranda.

"Jim!" she cried shrilly. "Are you all right—what is it?" The lamplight revealed what Bellow Bill's nose had already told him: the enemy he held was a cannibal, like the man he had captured earlier, except that he was smaller, less muscular, and stark naked.

"Kennedy has been carried into the bush," said Bill. "Steady, Miss Vernon!" For the girl had moved, and the lamp shook in her hands.

"Into the interior, where no white man has come back?" she gasped.

"Steady!" Bill repeated. He saw his revolver and stooped to recover it. "Tell Randall I'm going to follow at once," he commanded. "Look after him awhile. He's too sick to leave alone."

The girl stared blankly, struck speechless by the catastrophe. Bill grinned at her with a cheerfulness he did not feel. "Prisoners can't be carried through the brush fast, or without leaving a trail," he lied. "They haven't hurt him—at least they didn't try to club me. I'll have Kennedy back for you, Miss Vernon."

Bill swung the naked cannibal over his shoulder and strode into the bush, but not in the direction which the raiders had taken. Once out of the girl's sight he walked rapidly toward Vernon's store. The raid had been made by a dozen men. In the darkness it would have been folly to attempt to overtake them. To wait for sunrise and try to reach their stronghold without a guide would have been equally vain.

CHAPTER V

A HANGMAN'S KNOT

AS HE RECALLED the circumstances of the attack the big pearler began to seethe with anger. Taupo had been terrified of the cannibals, and no sentry is more vigilant than one whose senses are sharpened by fear. That the native had been struck down, without outcry, by a war club flung from the bush was most unlikely. No—rather he had let some one he had thought a friend get close to him; and who could that friend be save Vernon?

Bill was positive that the trader had attempted a double murder of the most dastardly kind. Vernon's weapons had been a tribe of savages. He had given them their orders, prepared the ground for their assault, and then run back to his store that he might have an alibi when Bill and Kennedy were overcome. The pearler's great strength had balked complete success, but, even so, Kennedy had been borne away to a revolting death.

Vernon might know where his daughter's suitor had been taken. He might have influence enough with the cannibals to release the captive, but Bill knew that Vernon did not have the slightest desire to do either. He would say that Kennedy was already as good as dead. He would argue that it was madness to attempt a rescue in a jungle from which no white man had returned. If he were compelled to make the attempt he would be an unfaithful guide and a treacherous companion.

The pearler strode ahead in a rage against the trader. Ahead he caught the glimmer of a lamp burning in Vernon's store. A shadow came and went across the chinks in the thatched walls. The front door was open, and a broad pathway of light streamed outward on the loose sand before the threshold. Vernon was inside, packing his pearls and trade goods—prepared, no doubt, to deny that he had heard the shot or the shouting.

Unhesitantly Bellow Bill strode forward, shifting the limp body of the black to his left shoulder, and drawing his revolver. The soft sand rendered his footsteps noiseless. He crossed the threshold, levelled his gun at Vernon, and paused—huge, menacing, utterly silent.

THE TRADER was kneeling before the safe, packing the contents in a wooden box. He looked up, and the blood drained out of his yellow face.

"Wha—what—?" he stammered.

"Never mind what," Bellow Bill rumbled in his great voice. "Surprised to see me? You've only murdered one of us, Vernon. Yes; I said murdered!"

"I—"

"Shut up! Take that gun out of your belt, by the tips of your fingers, and kick it across the floor toward me."

The trader obeyed. Keeping his own weapon ready, Bellow Bill eased the black onto the floor, picked up Vernon's gun, and hurled it out through the open door. He glanced around the store, and walked to a coil of thin, hard twisted rope, the kind that is .used for catching sharks. From this he cut a ten-foot length, and slowly and ostentatiously began to tie a noose with a complicated knot in one end. Seven times he wrapped the rope around itself, twisted in the end, and held it up.

"Ever see a hangman's knot, Vernon?" he boomed. "Funny knot. It'll tighten—see?" With a gentle tug on the rope Bill contracted the noose. "But it won't loosen." He tried to pull the knot back along the rope, and failing, tossed the noose over Vernon's head and tightened it until the rope was close about the yellow throat. "Yeah," Bill purred, "if that should tighten

any more it would just be too bad. For you." Coolly the pearler
tied the other end of the rope around his waist, which tethered
Vernon to him like a dog, then cut more line and bound and
gagged his black captive.

Some color returned to the trader's yellow face. Once sure
that Bill did not plan to shoot or hang him out of hand, he
recovered his self-possession rapidly. A sarcastic gleam came
into the dark eyes, and he found courage to smile insultingly.

"What do you mean to do?" he demanded. "I've been here
at my store, so how do you get this murderer stuff? I heard a
shot and some shouting, but I guessed that Boraki was trying
to escape. Did his tribe come after him?"

"Who escaped?" Bill thundered.

"Boraki," retorted the trader with maddening coolness. "It's
no use at all trying to bring him back from the bush. Yes, that
was Boraki you caught. Did you think I could trade for pearls
with any savage but the chief? His men believe he can kill them
by a wish, so of course they were bound to raid. Even the Residency of his excellency the commissioner himself."

"You knew that and you kept your trap shut?" Bill growled
dangerously.

"Of course. You and Randall judged and sentenced me
quickly enough," Vernon spat. "I didn't care. I assumed that
Taupo would run."

"Bilge! You walked up to Taupo and slugged him yourself
with the butt of your gun. You ordered those raiders to carry
away any white men they could—"

The trader's eyes glittered triumphantly.

"—and they got Kennedy," Bill rumbled.

"NO!" SNAPPED Vernon ironically. "Did they? And he's
such an A No. 1 guy, too! But perhaps I could persuade them to
bring him back. Of course I'm not sure. They have a feast back
in the bush. But if I had a free hand, and the freedom of the
island, I'd be willing to start—"

"You start, all right," purred Bill, shaking the rope gently. "You and I both, tied together just like this so that you won't leave me on the trail. You'll carry this cannibal here back to his friends, since you seem to know where they are. Maybe we can exchange prisoner for prisoner."

"And you sure got nerve!" Bill thundered, the anger he could no longer control sweeping aside his reserve. "Do you think I'm an ignorant new-chum? Do you think I believe you'd bring Kennedy back, bad as you hate him? You're the brains behind Boraki, and probably you're the source of his magic, too! That's what he's been trading for! The kingdom for himself, and the pearls for you, eh? Why, if I let you go into the bush alone, you'd be king of this island. You'd rule the savages, and they'd rule Randall! Bilge!"

"There will be fifty of them, at least," Vernon snarled. "What can you do against them? An enemy?"

"Have I asked you for advice?" retorted the pearler coolly. "I know something about savages myself. The fight will be between us, out there in the bush—you and your Boraki against me and my gun."

Grimly Bill shook the cord that bound him to the trader. "Remember, before you try your trick, that if you stumble you'll choke before I could loosen that knot even if I wanted to. This island is going to belong either to white men or black by sunup, according as you or I win out; but remember! If we both fail, your daughter is left with nothing but a sick man to protect her, and Boraki will figure he's king of the whole damn world! He's raided a bungalow once, and got away with it."

"You got no right to risk her," growled Vernon sullenly.

"Oh, we won't both fail," Bellow Bill grinned. "You're a fighting man. Randall said so."

"Suppose I won't go?"

"Then I'll throttle you right here."

For a second or two the trader glared at Bill in the hope

of finding a sign that the pearler was bluffing. The blue eyes, however, were stony, and at last Vernon shrugged.

"You're mad," he grunted, with complete realization of how enormous his advantage would be once the two were in the bush, and bending downward, lifted the cannibal onto his back and walked out of the door into the bush like one who knew his way perfectly, even in the dark.

FOR SOME distance indeed, there was a fairly plain trail. For about a mile the copra groves of the salt-water natives dotted the brush. They passed two of these, recently abandoned. Then the track underfoot narrowed. Leaves brushed Bill's face, and Vernon walked more and more slowly, feeling his way with hands and feet. He stopped so often to put down the prisoner and rest that at last Bill swung the black onto his own shoulders.

After that they went faster, though more than an hour must have elapsed before they had covered two miles. The ground began to rise and a faint sound that heartened Bill immeasurably grew audible.

Boom, boom, boom. Boom, boom, boom.

Drums.

In thick woods a native drum beaten a long distance away, giving little clew as to its direction. The sound seems to come now from one point of the compass, now from another. Vernon, however, halted.

"I found Boraki's village last year, by accident," he whispered. "I was scouting for the explorer that had disappeared. I only got away by luck. I did Boraki a favor, and he gave me a pearl off an idol they have. But the village is halfway to the mountain top. That drum's within a mile of us."

Bill grunted indifferently.

"They've never had a feast so close to the sea before," Vernon replied nervously. "If they've begun I can't do anything with them! You're just getting both of us *kai-kai'd!*"

"We've got to make a play and we can't show them we're

afraid even if we are," Bellow Bill grunted. "That's the white man's medicine. To go in on bluff and get out by nerve."

"I did plan that attack on you," Vernon whispered back. "Take me to Randall and I'll confess. I'll leave the island. He can have me hanged if he wants. I'd rather risk that than face a tribe of blood-mad blacks. There's something filthy about cannibals. They're worse than beasts!"

"You gave Kennedy to them," Bill reminded. "If we get him back I'll say nothing about what you done. You can leave the island like a decent trader. That's the break you get."

Vernon moved forward a hundred yards and stopped again. "If we don't get Kennedy and escape ourselves, I'm hanged, eh?" he demanded.

"Are you trying to decide whether to play square or not?" Bill grunted impatiently. "That depends on how we escape and what you do. How'd the savages get so many pearls, anyway?"

"Got an idol on some raid. Saltwater idol, decorated with all the divers had brought up for a long time. Must have been made before the whites came here and started to fish the waters. Pearls are big and lots of them perfect. I'll go halves with you, Bill—"

For answer the pearler jerked the neck cord. The offer ended in a gasp and a curse. Vernon moved on, feeling his way. Little by little the sound of the drum grew louder. First, Bill no longer doubted that it was ahead. Later he could hear faint shouts; another half mile and the yells had become words—though words he could not understand.

The trader was pressing on grimly, but at last, when a gleam of firelight showed through the jungle, Bill ordered him back and commanded him to carry the prisoner. Bill now took the lead and advanced yard by yard. The drum was beating frenziedly; and the yells of the cannibals were a snarling undercurrent which rose moment by moment in pitch and tempo.

CHAPTER VI

THE DEATH RITUAL

BEFORE BILL'S EYES the jungle gave place to a small clearing, in the midst of which a huge fire blazed, sending leaping tongues of flame and sparks twenty feet into the air, and filling the clearing with down-rushing swirls of smoke as the wind veered. Around the blaze in an open semicircle a file of dancers, fifty or more in number, and all men, swayed with interlocked hands like a serpent trying to coil, steadily drawing inward upon the fire.

Back to the blaze and facing the dancers stood Boraki, swaying to the drum beat, his arms waving slowly, and chanting at the top of his lungs. Bill could see the teeth in the wide-opened mouth, note the throat strain as the chieftain howled, but the chant itself was drowned in the snarling of the dancers. Close behind Boraki cavorted a medicine man, squat, wizened, and bedecked in the long fur of monkeys until he resembled a monkey himself. This individual danced, too, but stayed within a triangle formed by three posts.

Two of these, closest to the fire, were set in the ground. To one Kennedy was bound by a cord passed around his waist which left legs and arms free. Taupo was similarly bound, but while the Polynesian's head was sunk on his breast from a terror that had rendered him unconscious, the white man's chin was up. He shook his head as the smoke swirled by him, flinched involuntarily at the touch of falling sparks, and strained vainly at his bonds.

The third post, placed in advance of the others, was a dark log of wood a foot in diameter and three feet high, set on a rude altar and roughly carved into the semblance of a human figure with a wide-open and enormously distended mouth. The mouth was set with white, realistic teeth, and the blackened wood of the idol was begirt with long strings of pearls.

As Bill watched, the medicine man danced forward and anointed the idol with oil poured from a gourd at his belt, which he also smeared upon the faces of Kennedy and Taupo. The dancers howled, and Vernon, at Bill's back, groaned and touched the pearler's belt.

"That's the sign they're devoted to the service of their fetish," he groaned. "For God's sake, Williams, come away! You can't fight fifty of them! It's a kind of religious ceremony. They will rush you in a second if you interfere."

"Kind of devil's ritual, you mean," Bill rumbled. "Everything has a ritual with savages." He ripped off his shirt, baring his tattooed body to the waist, and twirled the cylinder of his revolver to make sure it was ready for action. "They're worshiping their boss devil—which looks powerful like a log of wood and a pearl mine to me. There's worse devils, Vernon. We'll show them one. Follow close now, or I'll strangle you in the center of them."

Straight from the underbrush Bill strode, leading Vernon, who was bowed again under the weight of the black, like a dog. A howl greeted the pearler, Boraki's arms dropped to his sides, and the semicircle of dancers writhed, uncertain whether or not to attack.

Yet Bill did not advance like an enemy. His feet fell in time to the throbs of the drum. In the leaping firelight the dragon tattooed on the chest seemed to twist like a living serpent. He looked neither right nor left. He did not hurry. He was a new, strange, and formidable worshiper of the idol coming to bring sacrifice. On each side clubs were brandished, but for all the attention he paid he might not have seen them.

STRAIGHT AHEAD into the ring of dancers he advanced until he was breast to breast with Boraki. The chieftain recoiled a step, waiting to see what Bellow Bill would do, but the pearler only turned indifferently in time to the drum throb, and picked the bound cannibal from Vernon's shoulders. Bill's knife flashed, severing the bonds. He dropped the black at Boraki's feet, spat, and rubbed his hands as though he freed them of dirt.

The yelling of the dancers was hushed. Their eyeballs rolled in the firelight. The circle crowded closer.

"Now for it!" Bellow Bill instructed Vernon in a rumbling whisper. "They don't know what to do. We've got to keep things moving too fast for them to think."

With a slash of his jackknife Bill severed the rope that bound Vernon to him. With a quicker movement he jerked the gun from his belt and tossed the weapon into Kennedy's hands.

"Don't shoot unless you must," he snapped, and leaped toward the idol. With one hand in the wide-open mouth of the idol he picked up the heavy figure of wood and swung it high over his head. The medicine man sprang forward, only to pause as Bill made a feint of hurling the idol into the fire. Step by step Bill moved backward, swinging the idol round and round his head like a gigantic club. The blazing fire was at his back; before him, Boraki.

Suddenly Bill's long tattooed arm shot out, pointing straight at the staring chief.

"Man-who-wills-his-enemies-to-die," Bill thundered at Boraki in the Melanesian dialect, "try now to kill me!"

The heavy idol was circling over the chief's head. Bill's words were only partly understood, but the defiance and challenge to the chief were unmistakable. Dumfounded, the cannibals stared, waiting for their leader to give them a sign.

Instinctively Boraki sprang backward to be beyond the reach of Bill's enormous club. The brutish face of the savage was a pattern of irresolution where anger struggled with fear. Kennedy covered him with the revolver, and if the bullet failed Bill was in a position to brain him before the nearest tribesman could reach Bill with a spear.

Yet the chief was no coward. With his prestige threatened and his idol desecrated he might have sacrificed himself to destroy his enemies had not Vernon taken the initiative. The trader was afraid. In the firelight the whites of his eyes showed like those of a terrified Negro, and before the moment of suspense could pass he stepped to Boraki and whispered in the chieftain's ear.

Boraki's head came up. Evidently he accepted the trader's suggestion, for he raised both arms like one pronouncing a curse and glared at Bill.

"You die!" he shouted, dropped his arms and turned suddenly upon his tribe, which had uttered a moan of superstitious awe as he accepted Bill's challenge.

"Wait!" the cannibal leader shouted, beckoned to the medicine man, and moved slowly and confidently away from the fire, followed by the wizard and by Vernon.

For an instant Bellow Bill expected that the chief would shout to his tribe to charge now that he had extricated himself, but though the savages moved forward a pace or two man after man among them dropped to a squatting posture until the entire semicircle was seated, like spectators. The throb of the drum slowed to a dull *boom, boom, boom,* eerie and mournful as the boom of a muffled bell.

Half amazed, the pearler realized that Boraki had chosen to work his magic, and that the tribe had the utmost faith in the powers of their chief. What that magic would prove to be, Bellow Bill did not bother to wonder.

HE SET the idol down and stepped to the posts to which Kennedy and Taupo were tied. Coolly he cut the bark cords that bound them and helped them close to the fire, for their legs were cramped and both were scarcely able to stand.

"Rub the kinks out of yourself and keep hold of Taupo," Bill ordered Kennedy under his breath. "We're likely to have to run for it. If you have to shoot, don't miss. Any kind of failure will do for us!"

Kennedy nodded. Out of the shadows Boraki was advancing, with the medicine man and Vernon close behind. The chief was carrying a coconut. An ordinary coconut as far as Bill could see, yet the circle of savages swayed and moaned. With a knife handed him by the medicine man Boraki split the nut and divided the soft pulp into halves. From his leather belt he took a large pinch of dirty salt, sprinkled the coconut and began to eat—slowly, pausing to mutter charms between his mouthfuls.

"What's up, you double-crossing blackguard?" snapped Bill at Vernon.

The trader stood with folded arms. He would not answer.

"Shall I shoot him?" Kennedy whispered.

"Not yet," Bill growled. "They'd get us, buddy. They'd get us on the trail in the dark even if we got away, unless we can scare them out of following. Wait."

Boraki finished his meal. He reached into his belt and sprinkled the second portion of coconut with white powder.

"Eat!" he shouted, pointing to Bill. "You die!" He patted his own stomach to indicate that he had enjoyed his own meal, and grinned venomously at the white men.

Very clear in Bill's memory was the fact that there had been two pockets and two kinds of powder in Boraki's belt, yet he know that to the superstitious savages who watched, the two portions were exactly the same. Obviously one powder was salt, the other poison furnished by Vernon.

Savages are well acquainted with vegetable poisons, but common and harmless salt is the only mineral they know. In their eyes the test was fair enough. Boraki had eaten without harm. If Bill ate and died it would be Boraki's magic that killed him. The pearler had no desire to eat, but for an instant he could see no way to avoid it. A protest would be fatal.

"I die?" Bill roared, stepped forward and scooping up the coconut in his right hand. "I only? Your charm is against me?"

The pearler was towering over Boraki. The latter nodded.

"You hear?" Bill thundered at the staring tribe, and suddenly threw back his head and laughed at the top of his lungs. "Then I change the magic."

BILL'S LEFT arm shot out and caught the medicine man's skinny neck. As the latter opened his mouth to scream Bill crammed in the poisoned coconut. The palm of his hand prevented the wizard from spitting it out. Holding the squirming, monkeylike figure under one arm, Bill held the nose until the need of air made the throat contract. Certain that some of the stuff was down Bill flung the skinny figure onto the ground before the fire and snatched up the idol.

"I change the magic against you all!" Bill thundered.

Mineral poisons work quickly and painfully. The wizard screamed and doubled up, writhing; then staggered to his feet and tried to run. With a swinging blow of the ponderous idol Bill knocked him down.

"See!" the pearler thundered. For a second the savages stared, and then with yells of consternation they commenced to scramble to their feet. Instantly Bill leaped for Boraki, swinging up the idol for a crushing blow. The chief dodged aside, and with a squeal of animal terror ran for the safety afforded by his tribe.

With a curse at the unwieldy weapon Bill tossed the idol into the flames. He would have liked to flatten the chief, but the shrill cry of terror that resounded as the fire caught the oil-soaked wood was some recompense.

"Now!" Bill snapped. He caught Kennedy and Taupo by the arms and charged with them for the point of the semicircle where the savages were fewest. Vernon was directly in the path of the rush. The trader's mouth was open, and his yellow face stiff with fear. He stepped aside, gasping out, "Wait! Wait!"

Before Bill's rush the savages scattered right and left. He crossed the clearing and plunged into the brush, feeling for the path with his feet. Moans and yells of terror were sounding behind him, but not the fierce shouts that would have indicated pursuit.

In the dark, on the overgrown path, speed was impossible. Bill groped his way, even when some one crashed into the bushes directly behind him. He heard Kennedy curse, and the thud of a blow.

"Don't!" groaned a voice in English—Vernon's voice. "For God's sake let me come! They'll tear me to pieces now they know my magic is no good! Kennedy—if you're a white man—"

"Shall I shoot?" panted the young man.

"No, let him come," growled Bill without ceasing to feel his way forward. "He won't double-cross us again, and we need a guide. Damn it, why did I have to miss Boraki? He slipped from under that log like a rabbit. If we'd gotten him we'd be jake. The rest are sure scared of white man's magic."

"He'll get them to follow us, I think," Vernon muttered. "Bill! I only turned against you because I was sure they'd rush in another second. Somebody had to be left to control them for the sake of Carol—"

"Shut up, Benedict Arnold!" Bill grunted. "Hear that? Boraki has started alibi-ing himself!"

CHAPTER VII

FLOOD TIDE

IN THE CLEARING one voice had begun to dominate the babel of fifty frightened savages. Louder and louder Boraki's tones rose above the others until he was shouting alone. His harangue gained in fierceness and confidence as he proceeded.

Bill could not catch the words the chief used, yet these were easy to imagine—the claim that his powers had not had a fair test, that although the white man had turned his course aside it was as effective as ever, that the enemies who had spoiled the feast were few and still close at hand.

Stumbling along the pitch-dark path, Bellow Bill heard the tribe begin to shout approval. These were the guttural, angry yells he dreaded, and as he went Bill sought for a place where

the three white men could make a stand. Distance the pursuit
they could not. The savages were familiar with the trail and
the ground, and would make three feet to their one. Nor could
Taupo, whose teeth were chattering with fright, be counted as
any aid to defense.

Among the bulkwark-like roots of a silk-cotton tree which
grew beside the trail, Bill turned at bay, The trunk buttresses were
higher than his head and formed triangular stalls nearly five feet
across at the widest point so that once among them an attack
could be made from in front. Bill wedged Taupo in the narrow
space next the trunk, and placed Vernon, whom he did not trust,
next to the native. The revolver he left in Kennedy's hand. Bill
was a poor shot, and knew it. He contented himself with stuff-
ing a fresh quid into his cheek and hoping that by strength and
agility he could overawe the savages even yet.

The yelling drew nearer. A savage passed down the trail. He
either heard the white men move, or smelled their unfamiliar
odor. A shrill yell informed the others of his discovery. The brush
rustled as man after man came down the trail.

Five minutes passed, and ten. By the faint sounds of breathing,
the stir of bodies, Bill guessed that the savages were clustered
before him, yet the attack was delayed. At his orders Vernon and
Kennedy had stripped off their white clothing, and he himself
was naked to the waist.

The cannibals could not see them, and hesitated to rush in
the dark. The white men might be magicians; in any case, the big
white man with the pictures on his skin was a mighty warrior.

AT LAST a gleam of light shone through the trees. From the
clearing came two savages, each with a torch. In front of the pair
walked Boraki, and as he drew near Bellow Bill swore under his
breath. The chief was carrying a war club, and from the thicket in
front of the root buttress half a dozen spears projected. Bellow
Bill rose, lest the savages think he was afraid, and hiding. As he
moved Vernon squirmed past Kennedy.

"Sit down," growled the pearler without looking around.

"Give me a chance to fight," Vernon whispered. "I want to go out like a man. We're all done for."

"Sit down," Bill repeated. "I'm going to jump Boraki when he starts to palaver. If I can kill him quick enough the rest will run away."

The pearler opened and shut his big hands and eyed the advancing chief. Vernon grunted skeptically. Fifteen feet from the root buttress the torch bearers paused. Boraki strode on, club upraised. He was opening his mouth to speak when Bill leaped out of his refuge like a charging grizzly.

Side-stepping the blow of the club, he struck Boraki in the body. With a grunt the chief doubled forward over the pearler's fist. Bill stepped hip to hip whirling the shorter man around, and twining one leg around Boraki's ankles. Holding the squirming savage fast, he thrust one knee into the small of the naked back, and slipped his left arm under Boraki's chin. With a quick jerk he bent the cannibal backward.

To break that deadly hold Boraki flung both arms upward. Like a flash Bill snatched at the war club. He was quick, but not quick enough. For a second or two the two bodies strained together in the torchlight while Bill twisted the club away, and in that moment four spearmen rose from the thicket, their weapons poised for a cast, but unwilling to thrust or throw at the pair of interlocked bodies.

Straining every muscle, Bill wrenched the war club from Boraki's fingers and brought it down upon the fuzzy head under his arm. The sound was like that of a mallet on a block. The blow shattered the chief's skull. One instant every muscle stood out on legs and chest; the next, Bill was holding a form limp as a sack to shield himself from the threatening spears. The pearler was about to charge the thicket, but from behind a hand gripped his belt.

"Step back and get down," snapped Vernon; "let me charge!" Before Bill could move or answer he slipped around the pearler into the open.

Four spears were hurled instantly. Two struck Vernon, one transfixing his left arm, one plunging deep in his chest. Vernon staggered, but in the firelight his yellow face revealed only one spasm of pain. Quickly he jerked the spear from his chest, reversed it, and flung it into the thicket. Blood flowed down his chest. He swayed and yet like one only slightly hurt he drew the spear from his arm and lunged forward. With a terrified scream the spearmen fled, but Vernon stumbled onward into the thicket, the spear leveled.

"Shoot, Kennedy!" Bill roared. From the buttressed roots he snatched a spear and charged down the path where the torches still smoldered. He paused to stamp them into the ground. The savages were running in every direction, terrified by these men whom spears could not stop. The sudden change from light to dark completed their terror. Roaring at the top of his great voice Bill ran back to the tree and caught up Boraki's body.

"Get Vernon! Get him back—he's dead on his feet!" he snapped at Kennedy, whose revolver was spitting into the darkness, and with new and louder shouts, ran down the trail toward the clearing, spear in hand. The boldest of the savages had paused there, but they turned and ran as Bill burst among them. He did not pursue, but ran to the fire and hurled Boraki's body in the blaze upon the flaming mass of the idol.

From the brush where the savages lurked arose a howl. Bill snapped the spear over his knee as though he did not need it, tossed it into the blaze, and swaggered back the way he had come, pushing confidently into the brush and down a trail from which even the most daring savage, confounded by the destruction of his magic, his chief, and his faith in his own weapons, was running as fast as feet winged by the utter fear of superstition could carry him.

"Vernon's dead," whispered Kennedy as Bill returned.

"Shut up, buddy," the pearler retorted. "No cannibal is going to know that, or salt-water boy either if I can help it. We'd have been dead without him. He's paid his debt."

"He was afraid that Carol—"

"Yeah. Get him on my back and let's pull out of here," Bill rumbled. "He was fighting for her all along, buddy. A white man can send savages against men, but not against women. He turned white in the end—and that ought to be his epitaph."

OVER THE beach of Mataila dawn was breaking. On the veranda of the Residency, Randall awoke from a fitful sleep and felt for the revolver that lay beside him. The abrupt movement made the hammock sway. Carol Vernon rose from the chair where she sat awake all night and crossed to the sick man.

"Lie still," she said soothingly. "Nothing has happened."

"Nothing? I—I thought I heard shouts. I was dreaming, what?" the commissioner gasped. "It was very vivid. The savages were charging out of the bush. Dozens of them. But"—he grinned with deprecation of a strong man who is ill—"of course it was a dream, for what I saw was the brush behind the Residency. I couldn't have seen that from here, what?"

"Nothing happened," Carol repeated. "Not a sound. Not the stirring of a leaf." Her face quivered. "Could anything be worse than that?" she whispered. "I suppose we'll never know. They've gone into the interior and vanished like the others. My father and my sweetheart—"

"Hush. Carry on! Must keep a stiff upper lip," said Randall hopelessly. "Hard to think of Bellow Bill Williams dead. Too much life in him. Shouldn't talk of a friend to you who have lost more, but a friend that will come at a word and risk his life…" Randall's mouth shut firmly. "I'd give the island to hear that booming voice of his again," he muttered, struggling up in the hammock and staring out to sea.

His eyes widened. Excitedly he pointed with a long arm that was wasted to skin and bone.

"Look! Don't tell me that's delirium!" he exclaimed.

Carol jumped up.

"No!" she cried, and at the top of her lungs called out, "Jim! Jim!"

Along the beach Kennedy and Bellow Bill were walking. The pearler was naked to the waist. His trousers dripped water, and the rising sun gleamed on his wet, tattooed skin. Kennedy's clothing was in rags, but he was dry. Carol ran off the veranda and threw herself into the arms of her *fiancé*, babbling in her relief. Bellow Bill walked on gravely and mounted the veranda.

"It's all right," he grinned in answer to Randall's anxious glance. "It's us, buddy. Don't stare so. Boraki is dead, and I think that from now on the savages are going to stay in their own hills. A white man will be able to walk from end to end of this island unarmed. You can send the salt-water natives back to their plantations."

"But where is Vernon? And Taupo?" Randall cried.

"What happened to Daddy?" Carol echoed, running forward. "Jim won't tell me!"

Bellow Bill's face was a mask. He noticed that even as Carol asked after her father her arm remained tightly clasped around Kennedy's waist as though she were determined that he would never leave her again. Love was more potent than grief, and that fact made Bill's task easier.

"You can be proud of your father," he answered. "He did the bravest act I ever saw. When the savages were about to spear Kennedy and me, he threw himself in front of us and charged them. He was wounded, but he gave no sign of that. He rushed the savages as though the spears had not hurt him. I'm sure the savages believed they had not hurt him."

"And he—?" Carol demanded.

"He sacrificed himself for us. His wounds were mortal," said Bill. "He was white, Carol. White to the backbone. I've brought him back and put him on my schooner. You can see him."

"I SEE Taupo."

"You can see your father's head by the taffrail as though he were sitting on the deck," said Bill. "Taupo decided he wanted to go home. He's from the Marquesas, a good two thousand miles away, and I've promised he should get back. He saw too much last night."

Randall uttered an exclamation under his breath, and looked hard at Bill. The pearler stared back, his face impassive, and after a moment the commissioner gave a brief nod of understanding. He guessed what Taupo had seen and must not be allowed to tell about Vernon.

"But why can't we bury father here? And why did you say twice that he was white?" Carol cried. "I've always known he was brave."

"Why, he asked to be buried at sea," said Bill impassively. "I call him white because that's the finest compliment I can pay. I've lived among savages all my life myself, Carol, and I know mighty few men aren't affected by it. We pull the natives up, but most times, they drag us down, too. Not your father. He had only to sit still to let Kennedy be speared, but he went into the bush with me, and took the great risk himself. You know, I didn't think he liked Kennedy, but he must have."

"I didn't think he did, either," the girl whispered. Bill caught Kennedy's eye, and the latter drew the girl away. They moved down the veranda and out upon the beach, arm in arm. Carol had begun to sob, and Kennedy was talking to her softly.

Randall's hammock stirred. "That's not the truth, Bill!" he whispered.

"Why, it is, partly," rumbled the pearler under his breath. "Why tell Carol he was willing to go black, when he was doing it for her? As far as I'm concerned, he made up for living badly by dying well. Maybe those pearls of his can be cleaned. Carol is going to be rich, so why not let her be happy?"

Randall nodded. "You're leaving?" he questioned.

"With the morning breeze. I'll be back, though. I want to be best man at the wedding, and to be one of the party that crosses Mataila from sea to sea for the first time." Bellow Bill grinned. "Maybe," he boomed, "having me along might make the trip easier."

ABOUT THE AUTHOR

THE TROUBLE WITH writing an autobiography is that you begin to ask yourself, "Why?"—and no reason is discernible. I was born in Medford, Massachusetts, on the 23rd of March, 1895, and so qualify as a Yankee even among Yankees. When I was a kid I was captain of a baseball team and played third base, instead of pitching, which shows unusual restraint. The trouble was I could throw an in, but not an out, and what's a pitcher without an out? Exactly. A third baseman.

Nothing else happened until I graduated from Columbia in 1916. I was a Fellow in English (maybe that was prophetic) but, as the event turned out, no scholar. I wanted to write a history of Sunday newspaper sections, all about the "Yellow Kid" and "Why Girls Leave Home," but the professors chose a newspaper that had been out of print for two hundred years. To disturb a literary corpse so remarkably quiescent seemed a shame, so I got a job with a trade exposition, which is a combination of circus and business convention, and when that was over, with the New York *Globe*. I was and am the worst salesman in the world, and was trying to sell advertising.

Then the war, which landed me eventually in command of a sub chaser. Getting there I wore every uniform in the navy, missed getting to France on the *Noma* in May, '17, because a bosun's mate thought my name was Sperry—I've never felt so low before or since—just had brains enough to get off the ship before they coaled her, and ran down the dock with my

gear wrapped up in a blanket, and
that bosun's mate bawling at me to
come back and work.

Stayed at sea during the war,
and for a year afterward. Saw fog
and ice and France, finally; got
shot at in mistake for a sub, and
learned something of seagoing
from Captain Hugo Osterhaus,
who finally decided I could be
trusted with a deck watch while we
ferried the A.E.F. across the Western Ocean.

Ralph R. Perry

Late in 1919 the navy, in peace time, became dull. There were
more merchant seamen with ten years' experience against my
three than there were berths, so I came ashore. If I'd saved my
pay everything would have been swell, but I never could make
more than two successive passes in craps. Jobs weren't to be had
in 1920, so I began to write. Didn't quite starve, but was pretty
glad just the same to land an editorial job in the summer of
'21. Four years later I quit to write fiction, and here I am, with
a hundred stories back of me, and more interested in writing
than ever. Some people think any grandmother could go to sea
these days, and five hundred yarns wouldn't demonstrate the
contrary too strongly.

Avocation? Building up a run-down Connecticut homestead.
There's stone walls to lay, wood to cut, and painting and carpen-
tering *ad lib*. Pleasures—going somewhere far off. Loading the
Underwood and my wife into the car or onto a boat, and seeing
how people do things two thousand or ten thousand miles away.

THE ARGOSY LIBRARY ™

SERIES 5 INCLUDES:

* WORTS * SHEEHAN * SERVISS *

* BRAND * PERRY * ROSCOE *

* BEECHAM *

* WIRT * FORSYTH *

* ROUSSEAU *

THE BEST FICTION
FROM THE FRANK
A. MUNSEY LINE

Made in the USA
Middletown, DE
15 July 2020